T0105875

# MEMORIES . . .

Jake stepped closer, drawing in a lingering breath and expelling it slowly. "Your scent reached me before I was even certain it was you. Lilac, isn't it?"

Lexy nodded, but she wanted to tell him to stop talking about scents and smells. One of the memories hardest for her to shake was the smell of his skin. She had especially enjoyed standing near him when he'd returned from riding his mare, for he smelled of wind and woods and earth.

"What do you want?" she asked.

A mirthless laugh. A step closer. "To turn back the clock."

Her breath came quickly. "Step away, Jake."

He moved closer still and drew her hands away from her breasts.

"Do you ever wonder what would have happened to us if I hadn't . . . broken the spell that night?" he asked.

# THE REVIEWERS RAVE ABOUT JANE BONANDER

## *WARRIOR HEART*

"This fine final volume in Ms. Bonander's trilogy combines the aura of an Americana with the rough and ready grit of the Old West. It's the kind of story that makes you cry with happiness for those good people who get the happiness they deserve. Filled with the magic of love and the inherent goodness of man, this is a special read. SENSUAL."

—Kathe Robin, *Romantic Times*

## *WINTER HEART*

"*Winter Heart* blends romance and mystery to perfection, drawing readers into a well-plotted tale filled with memorable characters. Jane Bonander reaches out to her readers' hearts with this powerfully emotional and very moving romance."

—Kathe Robin, *Romantic Times*

"*Winter Heart* is a fast-paced, exciting, and sentimental Western relationship romance."

—Harriet Klausner, *Affaire de Coeur*

# BOOKSTORES COAST TO COAST GREET *WARRIOR HEART* WITH GLOWING PRAISE

"Once you start reading *Warrior Heart,* you don't want to put it down until you've read the last page."

—Margaret Stilson, Paperback Exchange

"This book tells it all! Jackson is every woman's fantasy."

—Ruth Curtin, The Paperback Place

"Jane Bonander's *Warrior Heart* was full of warmth, grit, and humor."

—Yvonne Zalinski, Paperback Outlet

"The best one of the trilogy. Are you sure you can't make this last longer?"

—Marilyn Elrod, The Book Bag

*"Warrior Heart* is a terrific story that belongs on the keeper shelf. I look forward to Jane's next book—each one just gets better!"

—Nancy Michael, Book Exchange

"An absolutely stunning tale of love and the triumph of good. A must-read!"

—Donna Harsell, Voyager Books

"A warm-hearted, honest, straightforward, and wonderful story."

—Joan Adis, Paperbacks and Things

**Books by Jane Bonander**

Dancing on Snowflakes
Wild Heart
Winter Heart
Warrior Heart
Scent of Lilacs

Published by POCKET BOOKS

For orders other than by individual consumers, Pocket Books grants a discount on the purchase of **10 or more** copies of single titles for special markets or premium use. For further details, please write to the Vice-President of Special Markets, Pocket Books, 1633 Broadway, New York, NY 10019-6785, 8th Floor.

For information on how individual consumers can place orders, please write to Mail Order Department, Simon & Schuster Inc., 200 Old Tappan Road, Old Tappan, NJ 07675.

# JANE BONANDER

# Scent of Lilacs

**POCKET STAR** BOOKS
New York   London   Toronto   Sydney   Tokyo   Singapore

The sale of this book without its cover is unauthorized. If you purchased this book without a cover, you should be aware that it was reported to the publisher as "unsold and destroyed." Neither the author nor the publisher has received payment for the sale of this "stripped book."

This book is a work of fiction. Names, characters, places and incidents are products of the author's imagination or are used fictitiously. Any resemblance to actual events or locales or persons, living or dead, is entirely coincidental.

An *Original* Publication of POCKET BOOKS

 A Pocket Star Book published by
POCKET BOOKS, a division of Simon & Schuster Inc.
1230 Avenue of the Americas, New York, NY 10020

Copyright © 1998 by Jane Bonander

All rights reserved, including the right to reproduce this book or portions thereof in any form whatsoever. For information address Pocket Books, 1230 Avenue of the Americas, New York, NY 10020

ISBN: 978-1-4767-9852-3

First Pocket Books printing April 1998

10  9  8  7  6  5  4  3  2  1

POCKET STAR BOOKS and colophon are registered trademarks of Simon & Schuster Inc.

Cover art by Lina Levy

Printed in the U.S.A.

For Alan, "the son of a preacher man,"
Who never lost his sense of humor through the most
Difficult time in his life.
For his strength to fight a relentless disease,
For his dignity as it ravaged his body,
For his missionary's heart,
For his hunger to learn and help find the cure.
May you run and leap and cavort with the angels, love.

Alan L. Bonander
May 14, 1940–August 2, 1996

# Scent of Lilacs

# Prologue

RHODE ISLAND WEATHER, LEXY TATE'S FATHER USED TO say, was as unpleasant and changeable as her sister's disposition. One day could be sunny and warm, the next so violent and stormy it was best to avoid it.

This was a day to avoid. Street trash sailed haphazardly in the air on a damp, cold wind that threatened rain. Gray clouds tumbled from a slate sky like dingy bed sheets, obscuring the hills. Men and women hurried along the sidewalk, huddled in their macintoshes as they pressed against the wind, anxious to get indoors.

Lexy shivered as she stood beside Ben Stillwater on the stoop of her apartment building, the damp wind snaking through her clothing to chill her skin. Ben drew her close, to warm her. Her gaze drifted to a couple scurrying into a coffee shop across the street. Couples. The world was made up of couples.

"Lexy?"

She knew what he wanted from her. His proposal over dinner hadn't come as a surprise. "Oh, Ben, I—"

Ben pressed one long finger over her lips, then

*1*

tweaked her chin, leaving his fingers against her cheek. "You know I'll hound you every day of your life until I wear you down."

Lexy gazed into his handsome face and kind hazel eyes. In many ways, he was probably the best friend she'd ever had.

She removed one hand from the warmth of her military cape and briefly pressed his fingers to her skin. "Marrying you would probably be the most sensible and intelligent thing I could ever do."

His eyes twinkled. "That sounds promising."

"But you know I wouldn't do that to you."

Gruffing a sigh, he stepped off her stoop and shoved his hands into his pockets. The wind continued to howl, tossing dirt and dried leaves into the air. "Love is highly overrated."

*Not to me,* she wanted to say. Love was the one emotion that had cracked her sound, pragmatic facade. In the stalwart profession she'd chosen for herself, a little bit of love, blind or unrequited though it might be, kept her from becoming too hard.

"I know what you're thinking," he scolded. "He's never going to love you or marry you, Lexy. If you wait for that, you'll wait forever."

In her head she knew that; her heart felt different. She had loved Jake Westfield most of her life. He had loved her sister, Megan, most of his.

She forced a laugh. "Who says I want to get married? In a year, I'll be a physician. How can I possibly do both?"

He caught her reluctant gaze and returned to the stoop. "You could if you married me. There would be a place for you in my father's practice; I'd make sure of it. We could work together."

A wave of wistfulness rolled over her. How ideal that would be, to practice medicine without having to fight for the opportunity. But she wouldn't do that to Ben. He was too fine a man to be taken advantage of.

The campus clock tower struck seven, and Lexy was grateful for the interruption. Further conversation was pointless anyway. She gave him a quick kiss on the cheek. "I have anatomy to study. Thank you for dinner, Ben. I'm a hopeless cause.

"I don't deserve you!" she shouted over her shoulder as she lifted her skirt and scurried into her building.

She ran up the stairs to her tiny apartment, grateful to be in out of the wind. She hung her cape on a hook by the door and rubbed her hands together to warm them. With a wistful sigh, she eyed the fireplace, wishing she had enough wood to splurge on a night like this. But she had to be frugal; winter was only beginning.

She lit one lamp on the table where she studied, and another by her bed. Rain spattered the window, drawing her to it. Her breath fogged the glass as she looked out over the city, her gaze drawn to the eastern hills where her sister lived with her new husband.

They hadn't spoken in months, not since Lexy had scolded her for flirting so outrageously with Jake the evening before Megan married Max York. Lexy felt bad about the rift, because Megan was her only living relative, but her efforts to mend their quarrel had been met with silence.

Her older sister appeared to have no sense. She was pretty and vivacious and, to be perfectly honest, very spoiled and self-centered. And, Lexy thought, smiling wryly, she could be as unpleasant as the weather.

Lexy knew that Megan loved Max, but it was as if she couldn't let go of her other admirers. And Jake Westfield was certainly one of her sister's biggest admirers. Lexy wondered how he would fare now that he was out of the running for Megan's affections.

But Lexy had to let it go. Her love for Jake had nothing to do with anything. They had drawn closer because of medical school, and she knew he valued her opinion, which pleased her, but in her foolish little heart of hearts, she wanted more. Much more.

She wanted that studied look he gave her to mean something. She wanted that little wink he would pass her to be his secret way of telling her he loved her, not just his way of showing the sort of affection one would show a pet or a child.

Shifting her gaze toward the Brown campus, she mulled over Ben's blunt words. "He's never going to love you . . ." Had any other man said them, she would have gotten her back up. But Ben was different. His only concern was for Lexy's often fanciful heart. One he knew could be easily broken.

There was no love lost between Ben and Jake, but in an odd way, they respected each other's differences. Ben, whose family had so much money they could have bought him a medical degree without him having to earn it, was a serious, conscientious student. He didn't know how to relax and simply have a good time.

Jake, on the other hand, had no money and had to work for every cent. Yet he was flippant in his studies only because he was so brilliant. And he'd pulled more pranks on professors at Brown than all the other students put together.

With a resigned sigh, she moved away from the window and prepared for bed. She was removing the last of the pins from her hair when there was a knock on her door. Buttoning the last few buttons on her nightgown, she called, "Who is it?"

"It's me, Lex."

"Jake?" She hurried to open the door.

He looked exhausted. His big, gypsylike eyes were filled with a sadness that frightened her. His mouth, frequently quirked into a cocky smile, was pinched with pain. His dark, glossy hair fell in a tangle of wet curls over his forehead and around his ears. His shirt was plastered to his skin.

"You're soaking wet." She pulled him into her

4

apartment and closed the door behind him. "I'll start a fire."

She quickly crossed to her dry sink and grabbed a towel, tossed it to him, then went to the fireplace. When the fire was burning, she turned. He sat on her sofa, his face in his hands, the towel draped over his shoulders. Never had she seen him so dejected.

Warmth curled around her heart, and it had nothing to do with the fire burning in her fireplace. She loved this man with an intensity that frightened her. She couldn't bear to see him in such pain. "What's wrong?"

"I lost them."

He began to shiver. Lexy took the towel and tenderly rubbed it over his wet hair. "Both of them?"

At his nod, she closed her eyes. "Oh, Jake, I'm so sorry." It was hard enough to lose a patient, any patient, but it was devastating to lose a mother and her child. "What happened?"

He straightened, moving about uncomfortably beneath his wet shirt. Lexy began unbuttoning it, wanting to scold him for never wearing a coat but knowing this wasn't the time. He sat forward and pulled his shirttails from his trousers. She peeled the wet fabric from his skin, went to the fireplace, and draped it over a chair so it would dry. When she turned toward him again, his face was in his hands.

"The mother went into convulsions and expelled the fetus. The cord was wrapped around its neck."

Lexy returned to the couch and sat beside him. She took the towel and rubbed the wide expanse of his back. Her fingertips touched his taut skin; it was damp and cold. "And the mother?"

"Kidney failure. She never regained consciousness."

Death had taken on a new meaning in medical school. Though they both had experienced the deaths of their parents, which had left gaping holes in their lives, death in medical school was so frequent it was dangerously close to becoming mundane. Lexy had promised herself she would never let that happen to her. For Jake, death was always a personal insult.

She pressed her head to the towel across his shoulder and said nothing more. When he turned to her, she went into his arms, dragging the warm, healthy scent of him into her lungs.

"She convulsed right on the table. Right there, in front of me, and I couldn't do a damned thing." His voice was raw with emotion, and he clung to her.

"You did everything possible, Jake, and more. No one would have spent as much time with her as you did."

"And for what?" He expelled a ragged sigh. "Her husband . . . God, I had to tell him. It was the worst thing I've ever had to do. He cried, Lexy. He *cried*. He's left with no one."

She rested her cheek against his shoulder. The depth of his feelings for his patients frightened her. He would be a magnificent physician, but he couldn't save the world.

"You can't save them all, Jake."

"Then what's the point, damn it?"

"You're not God. Don't be so hard on yourself." Medicine was a personal thing to him, not merely a career. It was a vendetta against death, against diseases that killed people in their prime, like his own father, his grandfather, and his uncles. She was afraid his failure to attain his goal would defeat him.

"I can't change the way I am." He absently threaded his fingers through her hair.

"If you don't," she warned, purposely softening her tone, "you won't survive."

After a poignant pause, he answered, "I won't anyway."

She cringed, knowing she shouldn't have said what she had. Every male in his family had died before the age of forty, and Jake's fate, in his mind, was sealed. He was doomed.

They sat in comfortable silence, neither feeling the need to speak. Slowly, by degrees, something changed. Jake's fingers moved through her unbound hair, and his hand stroked her side. His thumb touched the round edge of her breast, and her nipple pebbled against her nightgown.

A delicious weakness filled her, and she didn't dare move for fear he might realize what he was doing and stop. His fingers found the fullness of her breast, testing her size. His free hand gripped her hair and moved her head so that he could kiss her.

His mouth was hard on hers as his tongue forced its way in, the rasp of his whiskers burning the skin around her lips. With shaky fingers, she tested the mat of hair on his chest, feeling the softness of it tickle her palms.

He'd never kissed her before. She responded as though he had, for she'd dreamed of it so often it had become as natural as breathing.

With ease, he lifted her onto his lap. She put her arms around his neck and pressed her cheek to his, enjoying the roughness of his beard, the smell of his skin, the sounds of arousal in his breathing.

His fingers moved to her throat; he unbuttoned her nightgown, dragging it over one shoulder. He lavished her with wet kisses, pressing his tongue into the hollow at the base of her throat. Shuddering spasms of hunger beat a path to the swelling secret part of her, and she nearly wept from the pleasure of it.

Once again, he found her breasts, loose beneath her cotton gown, and cupped them, squeezed them, drew them together so he could press his face against them.

His need for her, whatever it was, thrilled her. Perhaps finally . . . finally they would have something . . .

He was hard beneath her, sending a rush of heaviness and desire into her pelvis, making her feel hot and wet and weak. His fingers deftly finished undoing the tiny buttons of her gown, and when he slipped his hand inside to scrub his thumb across her bare nipple, she swallowed a moan. Beneath her rump, he grew harder, and she squirmed against him, loving the ache that undermined every good, sensible thought.

"Take off your gown," he whispered, his voice husky with desire.

With swift fingers, she slid her arms from the sleeves, exposing herself to him, for him. Her breasts tingled, the tightness sweet agony.

His gaze wandered over her, hungry, intense. He drew the backs of his fingers over the indentation between her neck and shoulders, then he bent to lick the pulsing at the base of her throat once again. His mouth dipped to her breast, and when he drew her nipple into his mouth, she gasped her pleasure, need making her weak. Oh, how she'd wanted this, dreamed of it. Ached for it.

"You smell so good. Flowers . . ." His mouth claimed hers again, and she clung to him while his hand moved to the hem of her gown, snaking beneath it to her calf. "Smooth. Soft," he replied, his fingers moving higher.

Like a wanton, she spread her legs. How could she not? His fingers grazed her fluff of hair, and her bones melted. One finger nudged through the hair to the aching part of her, and she closed her eyes, feeling energy from between her legs rush into her breasts and on into her throat. She bucked and straightened as the intense pleasure of his touch set her blood afire.

She climaxed again and again, and suddenly he was there, hot, hard, and long, drawing her legs on either side of his lap. She sank onto him, gasping in pleasure at the brief bite of pain. Catching the magical rhythm, she wrapped her arms around his neck and rode him, loving everything about him—his power, his desire, his hands on her hips, guiding her on their ride.

The rhythm changed, became disjointed, stronger, until she felt the explosion of his seed inside her. He filled her with devastating energy, as if his own orgasm became hers. Never had she felt such bounding, delicious satisfaction, such beauty and hope and all-consuming love for him.

"Megan!" The name came out on a groan of pleasure.

Lexy went still, unwilling nausea welling up inside her. She swallowed hard and moved away so she could look into his eyes.

He knew what he'd done. "Lexy, I'm—"

"Get out." She shoved at his chest and quickly left his lap. Without ceremony, she turned away and shrugged into her nightgown, buttoning it to the tip of her chin with fingers that shook with humiliation and anger. Behind her, she could hear him dressing, crossing to the fire to retrieve his shirt.

"I'm sorry. I don't know why it was her name I spoke," he said, his voice a husky whisper behind her.

She swallowed repeatedly. "I do," she whispered, not loud enough for him to hear. It seemed to take him an eternity. She was in agony, wishing he hadn't come to her, wanting him gone.

"Lexy, you have to know I didn't mean—"

"I said, get *out!*" She marched to the door, flung it open, and waited, arms folded across her chest, for him to leave, unable to say more for fear she'd cry.

"Lexy, don't do this—"

"Damn you, Jake Westfield, get out of my sight." Her lips trembled, and she bit down on them hard.

The door closed behind her. She turned and stared at it, waiting for the dam to break. The floodgates to open. It didn't happen. She had thought she would cry. Sob. Wail. But the threat of it passed. Instead, her insides went cold, and a part of her died. What he had done was unforgivable. She couldn't believe how in one instant, the time it took to take in a breath, or with the single beat of her heart, one word could turn love to hate.

She gripped her stomach, stumbled to the bed, and threw herself onto it. What a fool she was.

Jake paced in his room, his fingers raking through his hair. How could it have happened? What in the name of God had made him say it? To lose Lexy's friendship was like losing his soul, as pathetic as the state of his soul was.

He had folded her into his arms, knowing it was Lexy and not Megan as he did so. Long before this night, he had realized she had become far more than a good friend. When was the first time he had known it? He couldn't remember. But often at night, his dreams were filled with the fresh, flowery scent of her. Sometimes, after she had innocently brushed against him, she would leave the lingering lilac smell on his clothes.

Yes, he had most definitely wanted *her,* not Megan.

Everything was coming apart. He felt as though he were drowning, and it wasn't natural. Not for him. He personally demanded progress for himself, and he was failing. Failing in his personal life, his friendship with Lexy in ruins. Failing in his professional life, his patients dying before his eyes. Failure. Defeat.

He studied the street below, the light from the street lamps flickering in the wind. A gust snatched a hat from a pedestrian's head and carried it into the storm. Jake felt like an extension of the tempest, his insides tumbling about haphazardly, threatening to erupt.

He couldn't do this anymore. It was getting harder and harder to separate himself from his work. And what was the point, anyway? These two patients weren't the first he'd lost, and they wouldn't be the last.

Maybe if he stepped away from it for a while, things would look different. And maybe he'd just say to hell with it. One thing was certain. He had to try to see Lexy and explain.

Suddenly, everything was clear. He dropped to the

chair at his desk, pulled out a sheet of paper, and uncapped his pen.

*28 November 1889*

*Ben,*
   *We haven't always agreed, nor have we truly been friends. But I have admired your integrity, so it is to you that I now turn. It isn't easy to admit failure. I hate quitters, yet I have become one. For me, the ideals of medicine have been shattered. To continue my studies would make me a fraud. I'm leaving Providence the end of the week.*
   *You may wonder what it is I ask of you. Only two things: one, that you persuade Lexy to meet with me before I leave, and two, that you care for her after I'm gone. It's no secret that you are fond of her, as am I. I can't leave and not know that she'll be all right. I can't promise to write often, but I do want to hear about her, to know she's doing well. Please, if you will, keep me posted. If there's ever anything I can do for her, or you, let me know.*
   *Don't kick up your heels too enthusiastically at my departure. You might hurt something.*
                                          *Jake*

He folded the letter, wondering if Lexy would even agree to see him.

*3 December 1889*

*Jake,*
   *Sorry to bring you bad news, but Lexy refuses to see you. I don't know what transpired between the two of you, but she is adamant. Perhaps in*

*time she will mellow, but for now, I think I would let it go. Sorry. Best to you, and you know I'll watch out for her.*

*Ben*

"Just like that, you're leaving?"

Jake studied Max and gave him a quick nod. As painful as it was, he had told his friend everything. It had never been a secret that they had vied for Megan's affections. But when Jake lost, he had made it known that there were no hard feelings. As it was, Jake felt relief over Megan's choice.

"I have to get away from everything for a while."

Max muttered a curse. "But to leave Lexy's welfare in Ben Stillwater's hands . . . it's like leaving the fox to guard the hen house." He swore again. "If Megan and I weren't scheduled to leave for California next week, I'd watch out for Lexy myself."

"I know that," Jake murmured.

"Have you tried to see her? Talk to her?"

"Yes, I've tried." But only through Ben. Perhaps that hadn't been a good idea. Some might say he hadn't been insistent enough, but how many times did he have to apologize before he realized she wasn't going to forgive him? And what else could he say?

"Are you in love with her?"

The question stunned him, and he spun away and strode to the window, his heart thudding hard. "Of course not. I care for her, of course. But love?" He could feel Max's gaze. "Hell, Max, what do I have to offer any woman?"

"We could all die tomorrow, Jake, not just you."

But his early death was a certainty. He couldn't avoid it. It hung over him like a shadow, blocking out warmth and sun and his future.

Jake turned from the window as Max rose to leave. "Good luck at your post, Max. I know you'll do a fine job."

They shook hands. "If you get out our way, you'd better damned well let us know."

California? Not a bad thought. He couldn't get much farther away from Lexy Tate without falling into the ocean.

*July 4 1891*

*Jake,*

*Sorry I've been slow in responding. I hope this missive finds you. I'm sending it general delivery to your last address.*

*To ease your mind, I pass on greetings from Lexy. She graduated at the top of her medical class, which I'm sure will not surprise you. I have asked her to marry me. You know I will take care of her. She will join me in my father's practice. Wish us happiness.*

*Benjamin Stillwater*

Jake crumpled the letter in his fist. So. She was married. A hollow ache attacked his gut. What had he expected, and why in hell should he have expected anything at all? As much as he hated to admit it, her marriage to Ben Stillwater was a good move. She would have everything she deserved: a lucrative practice, wealth, and a husband who adored her.

Why, then, was Jake's gut on fire with envy and regret?

# Chapter 1

*Northern California — August 1893*

LEXY WATCHED THE TRAIN DISAPPEAR, THE SMOKE STILL pungent as it lingered in the hot afternoon air, the sound of the engine waning in the distance. She gazed at the empty platform; the only luggage heaped on the planking was her own.

She removed the hat with the straw crown and straw braid trim that Ivy Stillwater had bought her and tossed it onto the bench. It seemed to languish there, wilting in the heat. She also unbuttoned the top two buttons of her dark blue Eton suit jacket, hoping to cool off.

Her gaze lifted to the wild, hilly landscape. Gnarled, stunted oaks clustered in threes and fours over the yellow grass, their leaves a dry, brittle green. Other trees, thicker and more lush, hugged the hillside, leaning toward the sun. A few hardy, bristly wildflowers clung to roots that were buried beneath craggy gray rocks, but there was no colorful wash of flowers swimming in the breeze on this prairie. There was only a hot wind. August appeared to be a harsh month for greenery.

Impatient for someone to pick her up, she took her brother-in-law's letter from her purse and read it again. She'd been pleased but surprised to hear from him. She and Megan hadn't spoken in four years, and she was anxious to renew their relationship.

Max had been worried, he'd written, because Megan was going to have their first child, and as often as his job had required that he leave her, he hadn't wanted her to be alone. He begged Lexy to come. Assured her she would be welcome.

Lexy eyed the unmerciful landscape, wondering how Megan had adapted to such a land. Megan, who could not survive without being catered to. Megan, who wanted to control the weather to suit her. Megan, to whom inconvenience meant no tea kettle of warmed water to wash with each morning.

Lexy wondered how she would be greeted after all these years. So much had happened to her; there was so much to share.

As automatic as breathing, her thoughts turned to Krista. Sweet, cinnamon-haired, black-eyed Krista. Her three-year-old daughter was the real reason Lexy had decided to come west. Born with a weakness in her lungs, she suffered from constant colds in the Rhode Island weather, and Lexy was always concerned about pneumonia.

She took a deep breath and removed her jacket, the air so hot it nearly blistered her lungs. Perspiration had wrinkled her new Persian percale shirtwaist. How could women wear so many clothes and not faint dead away? Maybe they didn't. Maybe the rules of proper clothing etiquette were done away with out here, so far from the rest of the civilized world. She hoped so.

As uncomfortable as the heat was, she felt as if every hot beat of the sun was a gift; it was exactly the kind of weather Krista needed.

Closing her eyes, she leaned against the rough boards of the station house and thought about how much she missed her child. It hadn't been easy to make this trip alone, but Lexy was determined to open a practice here and raise Krista. When she was settled, she would send for her.

Lexy pushed back an anxiety that threatened to break through her pragmatic facade. Ever since she had made her decision to come west, she had worried about the sanity of it. To take Krista away from everything familiar to a place as foreign as this was a bit mad.

Ben and his sister, Ivy, would accompany Krista. Lexy knew they would not stay, although she knew Ivy would miss Krista terribly. She had cared for Krista since her birth, allowing Lexy to finish school and work.

And Ben had a lucrative practice with his father in Providence. One, Lexy thought with a sad smile, that could have been hers, as well. If she had given in. If she could have.

But Ben deserved so much more than she could give him. Ben, whose patience with her daughter bordered on saintly. Ben, who always had a lollipop in his pocket for a fidgety child. Ben, who had been "Poppy" to Krista from the day she was old enough to speak.

She felt a fluttering of hot air and opened her eyes to find the station master fanning her with his battered hat.

"It's the heat, ain't it?"

"I beg your pardon?"

"Heat always makes a lady swoon. You all right?"

She cleared her throat and tried to press the wrinkles from her skirt with her palms. "I'm fine, sir, and I never swoon."

He studied her through ageless eyes. "You the lady sawbones Cap'n York's been expectin'?"

Lexy tried not to cringe. Lady sawbones. Now, wasn't that just what she'd been hoping to be called? Years of grueling class work, autopsies where she'd nearly tossed up her breakfast, and constant condescension from male colleagues, plus countless other indignities she'd experienced over the last few years, and now, praise the Lord, she was a lady sawbones.

"Yes, I am." The station master was a study in extremes. While his eyes were bright and almost youthful, his face was wizened. His lips disappeared into his toothless mouth as he gummed a wad of tobacco. His head reminded Lexy of a long-forgotten apple in the dark corner of a cellar. Juiceless.

"Goin' to the fort, are ya?"

She gave him the briefest of nods. "Yes, I am."

He studied her, his expression serious as he removed his faded, threadbare conductor's cap and scrubbed his arthritic fingers over his whisker-spattled skull. "They already got a doc there, ya know."

"I know that." She was hoping he could help her find a place to practice. In exchange, she would assist him in any way she could. She'd even written to him, a Dr. Monroe, but he hadn't answered her letter. She wondered if it had been an oversight on his part. But years in the company of men in a "man's" profession had made her realize how unwelcome she was when she tried to "overstep" her bounds and become an equal.

"Just got a new one, 'bout a month ago."

Surprised, Lexy asked, "A new doctor? Dr. Monroe is no longer there?" Well, maybe there was hope.

"Nope. Died."

"Oh. I'm sorry to hear that."

"Drowned, I heard."

She nodded. "I see." A new doctor might give her the opportunity to help while she set up a practice of her own. She would have to be especially cordial. Maybe, she thought with a wry twist of her mouth, even beg. A little. However, that was not something she did well.

Graduating at the top of her medical class from Pembroke had yet to become an asset in her attempt to practice medicine. As far as the Providence medical community was concerned, she might as well have been a leper. Had she been one, she might have gotten a bit of sympathy. As a female physician, she'd gotten nothing but condescending smiles and little pats on the back. Oh, how she detested that treatment. But if there were pros and cons, that treatment was certainly on the positive side compared to the treatment she received when someone learned she had a child and had never had a husband.

She'd thought she was ready for a public shunning but discovered one can never be totally prepared for blatant humiliation and downright nastiness. But she'd bitten the bullet and had withstood all the slings and arrows, working as an operating-room nurse for a year to save money for this, her future. And Krista's. She had developed a "to hell with them" attitude, which wasn't easy, especially for a woman who was basically a dreamer at heart.

Impatient now, she scanned the horizon. Straw-colored hills rolled into the distance, sparsely dappled with the same scruffy, monotonous, dry green trees. Purple mountains, thick with firs, created boundaries on either side of the valley. The sky was as clear and blue as a painting. No birds flew near, no hawks or eagles. It was simply too hot. And there was not a sign of another soul. Not even a distant cloud of dust to indicate someone was on the way.

She expelled an impatient sigh as a boot scuffed the planking behind her and a tall shadow blocked out the sun.

"Ma'am?"

She sat forward and looked up. A well-muscled soldier in casual cavalry uniform stood before her, gazing down at her from beneath the sharp ledge of his brow. Most of his face was covered with a fuzzy, gray-speckled beard. He looked more like a mountain man than a soldier. "Yes?"

"You Captain York's sister-in-law?"

"I am."

He extended a hand the size of a leg of mutton. She took it, and the thickly callused palm swallowed hers. "Sergeant Parnell Byron. Little Pete, for short."

Lexy raised an eyebrow. Little? He stood well over six feet if she was any judge, and from the looks of him, he could have hoisted a wagon onto his shoulders and sprinted up a hill. He wasn't a young man; his face had a weathered, leathery quality to it.

"I'm here to take you to the fort, ma'am. That your luggage over there?"

Nodding, Lexy watched as he strode to the huge mound and began loading it into the wagon. He lifted her new crystallized-metal-covered trunk, a gift from Ben, groaning under the weight of it.

"Ma'am, pardon me for sayin' so, but I never thought a lady's frippery could weigh so much."

She smiled and picked up her languishing hat and limp jacket. "I should have warned you. That's got medical supplies and books in it."

He gave her a steady gaze through pale gray eyes. "I heard you was a lady sawbones. You plannin' to go into practice out here?"

"I certainly hope so. Tell me," she began, "how is the new doctor working out?"

His face softened; his wide smile was warm, sporting a gold tooth among his own. His eyes crinkled at the corners. "We got lucky. He's not only a great doc, he's a helluv—"

A blush spread over the parts of his face she could see, and he apologized. "He's a good man. He'll be able to give you a lot of help." He finished loading her luggage, then helped her into the wagon seat. "Sure is an improvement over ol' Doc Monroe."

Lexy breathed a sigh of relief. It all sounded so very positive, she was more than anxious to get to the fort. Her only concern was how Megan would receive her, for although she knew Lexy was coming, she hadn't extended the invitation. But Lexy had a feeling everything would fall into place.

Lexy's nervous excitement mounted as the fort came into view.

The moment they rode into the huge yard, she felt a surge of relief, for Megan waddled from a tiny cabin, waving frantically. She wore a handsome, colorful foulard wrapper that billowed out in front over her huge abdomen. Oh, Lexy had missed her sister so very much. She leaped from the wagon almost before it came to a stop and ran to her.

They clung to each other. Through their clothing, Lexy felt the baby kick against her stomach. She gasped, delighted.

"Oh, Meggie." They rocked together. "How I've missed you."

"And I you," Megan answered against her cheek.

"You're absolutely beautiful."

Megan sniffed and laughed. "For a heifer, you mean."

Lexy pulled away, holding her sister's shoulders. "Your condition has only enhanced your beauty, Meggie."

"Oh, I suppose you're right," Megan agreed, causing Lexy to swallow a smile. As always, Megan was the first to agree that she was, indeed, beautiful.

She wiped her eyes with a dainty linen handkerchief that was edged in fine lace crocheting. Lexy knew her sister had done the work herself. It was a talent Lexy never had time to nurture, much to their mother's dismay.

"And look at you," Megan answered, her blue eyes shining. "Heavens, I can't believe how you've changed."

*If you only knew.* Lexy was eager to tell her sister about Krista, but there would be plenty of time for that. Right now, she just wanted to be with Megan, talk with her, find out everything that had happened over the past four years. She could only hope that all the old hurts and hard feelings were behind them.

Clasping her hands over her huge stomach, Megan studied her. "You look . . . different somehow." She frowned, then shook her head. "I suppose it's because you're a full-fledged doctor now, and when I left you were simply my little sister."

She fussed with Lexy's hair, clucking like a hen. "You really should wear your hat at all times, dear. Those freckles over your nose are unsightly. And that hair." She expelled an exaggerated sigh. "Perhaps you should try ironing the curl out. It would be much easier to manage and make you at least slightly more attractive."

Lexy nearly laughed out loud. Leave it to her sister to mention the negative aspects of Lexy's features. Meggie hadn't changed. For better or worse, Lexy was glad. She felt she'd come home.

She patted her sister's stomach, returning the "compliment." "You're awfully big, aren't you?"

Megan frowned. "Well, I am having a baby, you know. And Dr. Monroe died suspecting I'd have twins."

They strolled toward the tiny house.

"Twins?" Lexy touched her sister's stomach again. She knew from personal experience that one baby was more than a handful. Two would surely overwhelm her flighty sister.

Megan turned and waved at Little Pete. "Thank you for bringing her to me safely," she called.

"My pleasure, Miz York." He'd begun lugging Lexy's baggage off the wagon. "Do you want all this stuff in the house?"

"Of course. We'll make room for it."

With wary eyes, Lexy studied the tiny cottage. When they stepped inside, she inhaled sharply. "Why, there's hardly room in here for the two of you."

"There's plenty of room. There are two bedrooms,

and one of them is yours. Don't you dare fret, Alexis Tate, or I'll be angry with you, and you know very well it isn't a good idea to get a pregnant woman angry."

Lexy quietly gave in, but she knew she would have to find other accommodations soon. She couldn't bring Krista here, especially after the baby, or babies, came.

"My," she exclaimed, "it's sure cozy."

Megan rolled her eyes and shook her head. "It is, isn't it? *Cozy* is a nice word for it, actually. When I first saw the place, I let out a howl that could have been heard clear to the border. But it won't be forever. Max has promised he'll take me back to Providence one day soon, or at least Boston or Washington, D.C. This fort is one of the last to stay open in California. They all say it will close soon, then we can leave this godforsaken place. Anyway, Max knows I can't survive out here for the rest of my life and be happy."

"What about him? Would he be happy back east?"

Megan looked shocked. "Why, of course. Who wouldn't be?"

"Well," Lexy demurred, "I hope you get your wish."

"I hope so, too." She expelled a sigh. "It's been four years since I've seen civilization. I try not to complain around Max, because he's been such a dear, and I do love him and don't want to hurt him. But truth to tell, I don't like it here."

Megan's wistful words surprised her. Gone was the petulance she'd come to expect when Megan didn't get her way. "Where is Max, anyway?"

"Oh, he had to go to Sacramento. He'll be gone for a few weeks, I guess." She gave Lexy a warm smile. "I suppose that's why he sent for you, so I wouldn't have to be alone, especially now." Her eyes misted. "He knows how much I hate to be here by myself."

Lexy felt a twinge of envy at the relationship that had grown between her sister and Max York. At the time of their marriage, Lexy wouldn't have given them four happy months, much less four happy years.

Megan winced and arched her back. "I do wish he didn't have to leave, though. What if I have the baby and he's not here? I just don't think I can stand going through this alone."

"I'm sure he'd be here if he could," Lexy responded.

"I know he would. It just won't be the same without him here to share—" She covered her mouth and giggled. "To share both the pleasure and the pain," she finished, still smiling. "Before he left, I teased him about leaving me on purpose, just so he wouldn't have to go through my labor with me." Again, her smile turned wistful. "But truly, Lex, I think he'd have the baby for me if he could."

Lexy's envy returned, but she was happy for her sister as well. Turning her gaze away, she studied the tiny cabin. Despite the fact that Megan had done little in the way of homemaking while they were growing up, her tiny cottage was clean and homey. For the Megan of yore, it would never have been enough. Marriage had indeed mellowed her sister.

Megan crossed to a marble-topped dry sink and straightened a vase of flowers on top of it. Lexy recognized the piece as the one that had been in her own bedroom when she was a child. And one, she realized, that had been promised to her by their mother. Odd that Megan should have it.

"You know, I learned something about myself, Lexy. I learned that, unlike you, I'm not the least bit independent. I enjoy having a husband. I'm sure I'd feel like half a person without one."

Lexy blinked and studied the scrolled pulls on the dry sink drawers. "I don't mean to change the subject, but . . . isn't that my dry sink?"

"No. It's mine." A familiar look of stubbornness crossed Megan's face.

Lexy ran her finger over the gouge in the drawer

that had happened when she'd tried to remove the pulls more than twelve years before. "No," she argued. "See here? This happened when—"

"It's mine, Lexy. Mother gave it to me."

Lexy recognized the defiant tone. The stiffened spine. The pursed lips. They were Megan's trademarks when she lied; they always had been. The dry sink was Lexy's, but it was pointless to argue. Obviously, some things about Megan's old personality had not changed.

Megan would always take what she wanted, the same way she would always need someone else to make her happy, someone who would cater to her and admire her, as Max did. She would never be happy being by herself. She'd never learned to; she'd never had to.

"About our argument, Megan," Lexy began.

"Oh, Lexy, that was years ago. I realize you meant well, but at the time, all I could think about was myself. It *was* my wedding day, you know."

She was right, of course. All brides deserved to be selfish on their wedding day. Trouble was, four years ago, Megan was that way all the time. "Point taken. I probably shouldn't have been quite so vocal about my concerns. I knew you loved Max."

"I know, and Jake still loved me. You were being your usual cautious self. I just didn't want anything to spoil things."

"And did I spoil it, Meggie?"

Megan gave her a quick smile. "Not for long." She went to the stove and tested the outside of the teapot.

"I can't wait for Jake to see you."

"Jake?" Suddenly, without warning, four years of repressed anger and pain hit Lexy in the chest with such force she couldn't breathe.

Megan nodded. "He's been so busy, I haven't seen much of him today, but—"

"Jake is here?" Lexy interrupted, hoping to hide her panic, amazed she could breathe, much less speak.

25

Megan turned, the tea kettle handle in her fist. "Why, yes. He's our new fort doctor. Didn't you know?"

Lexy grabbed the back of a kitchen chair and stumbled into it, her knees shaking. "No. I . . . I didn't."

Before she had to ask, Megan continued, "He finished medical school out here, in California. Can you believe it?"

Lexy could do nothing but shake her head. Jake was here. *Here.* Where she was bringing Krista. The knowledge was like an anvil weighing on her chest.

"It'll be like old times, won't it? I mean, the four of us again, just like back in Providence."

There was a buzzing in Lexy's head, and she was dangerously close to fainting—something she had thought she would never do.

He couldn't be here. She didn't want him here. She had made a life for herself without him, and she had convinced herself years ago that she was happy.

"He keeps me company sometimes when Max is gone. I don't know what we'd do without him. Why," she continued innocently, "Max insisted that Jake sleep in the spare bedroom the nights that he is away."

Lexy attempted to rein in her alarm. "He sleeps in the house when Max is gone?"

Megan took down two cups and saucers and poured them each a cup of tea. "Of course. He slept there last night. Isn't it lucky that he was able to get this post?"

Lexy wondered if luck had anything to do with it. Knowing what she knew about Jake and how he felt about Megan, Lexy was certain he'd been able to pull some strings. He'd always had the gift of getting what he wanted. In that respect, he and Megan were very much alike.

"I'm here now, so I'll keep you company."

Megan put their tea on the table, then gave Lexy a quick squeeze. "I'm so happy you came."

Absently, Lexy returned the embrace. "I am, too." At least, she had been. She pulled in a breath, releasing it slowly.

They sipped their tea quietly.

"I worry about Jake, though."

She studied her older sister, noting the subtle violet shades of weariness under her eyes. "Why?"

Megan shrugged. "He seems to take foolish chances. Like he did back in Providence." She winced and rubbed her abdomen. "You know, I could have as easily been married to him as to Max, but he would never do as a husband. Not mine, anyway."

Lexy felt a headache coming on. "And why is that?"

"Well, for one thing, he didn't cater to me like Max did, although I know he was crazy about me. And for another, he hadn't seemed interested in settling down."

"He didn't think he was going to live long enough to see a family grow up, Megan." Lexy tried to keep the sarcasm from her voice.

"Oh, all that foolish stuff about him dying young just because his father did," she said with disgust.

"You didn't believe it?"

"No. I thought it was merely an excuse for not asking me to marry him."

Lexy pressed two fingers between her eyes, hoping to ward off the migraine. "Why are you worried about him now?"

"Shortly after Jake arrived, I overheard heard him arguing with Max. They were shouting, but every now and then, Jake would laugh. Only it wasn't a happy sound, if you know what I mean."

Lexy massaged the tension in the back of her neck. Yes, she remembered Jake's laugh. And his smile. And his kiss. And his hunger. And the name he called out at the height of his passion. "So, what happened?"

"Well, I crept closer to the door to listen. Max thought I was asleep. I think Jake worked as some kind of scout before he finished medicine. He seems

*27*

to have good rapport with the Indians, anyway, and one night shortly after he arrived here, he went after a bunch of renegade braves. Bad ones. Ones who didn't want anything to do with us and refused to sit down and exchange ideas." Megan squirmed to get comfortable. "By the way, they continue to cause problems. Don't wander outside the fort without an escort."

It made Lexy ill to think Jake would purposely put himself in such danger. "Why would he put himself in such a position?"

"He's got a death wish, Max says."

Of course. Max was right. Jake himself once had told her that if he was going to die young, he wanted to live fast. She squirmed in her seat, feeling sick to her stomach. "Exactly what happened?"

Megan grimaced and rubbed her stomach. "Oh. It's doing back flips in there," she muttered. "Always kicking and carrying on, making me uncomfortable."

*Wait until the baby keeps you up all night, every night for weeks,* Lexy thought.

"Anyway, the Indians were in rare form. They'd been drinking all night, and by the time Jake got there, they were ready to hang the first white man they saw."

"They tried to hang him?" A squeezing, crushing pain in her chest added to her nausea. Her tea sat precariously on her stomach.

"They didn't merely try, Lexy, they did."

Lexy leaned into her chair and pressed her arms across her stomach, hoping to keep her tea down. "They . . . they actually put a rope around his neck and . . . and . . ." She couldn't finish. The vision was too horrible.

"Fortunately for him, the rope was rotten. The drunken Indians left him to twist in the wind. Before Jake lost consciousness, the rope broke through, and he fell to the ground. Max was so angry. He'd told Jake not to go at all, and especially not alone. Even after Jake told Max the whole story, he sounded disappointed that they hadn't succeeded. If Max would have had the nerve, I think he'd have strangled Jake himself for his cavalier attitude."

"It sounds like a rather irresponsible thing for any man to do, especially one who has just begun a new position, one he obviously wanted."

"Yes," Megan answered on a sigh. "I guess some things never change. He's so good with everyone, especially the Indians. Doc Monroe refused to treat them. Jake never turns one away." She shook her head. "I can't understand why he wants to be out here in the middle of nowhere when he could go into a city and practice *real* medicine."

Probably because Megan was here, Lexy mused. But he was still tempting fate. Living a careless life, assuming the end was inevitably near. His attitudes had not changed; he'd merely become a doctor and changed locale.

The pounding between her eyes continued. "I think I'll take a walk around the fort, Meggie. Do you mind?"

Megan stood and stretched her back. "Not at all. Stop in and see Jake. He must know you're here. I can't imagine why he hasn't popped in to see you."

Lexy could. If he was feeling only half the intensity of emotion she was, he'd avoid her forever. At the mention of one word, her love for him had turned to hate. But it had been four years, and hate had a way of dissolving into something quite different when you bore the child of a man you once loved.

# Chapter 2

FROM HIS OFFICE WINDOW, JAKE WATCHED LEXY STROLL through the camp. Alexis Tate. No, Stillwater. For some reason, that thought irked him, and it shouldn't have. He'd never had anything to offer a woman, and that hadn't changed.

As he had years before, Jake recounted the reasons Lexy married Ben. She deserved a good, solid life. Ben Stillwater was steady. Rich. Established. And he'd never made a secret of his feelings for her. Hell, if anything, Jake had pushed the two of them together.

He swore as pain gripped his chest. Yeah, it was his heart, all right, but the pain was emotional, not physical, he convinced himself. The only time he experienced it was when he thought about Lexy, and what he'd done to her.

But he often wondered if his father had had pain. Had he any warning at all through the years? He wished to hell he knew. When he'd reached thirty, he frantically began to think about what he could do to save himself. It had started simply; it had become a passion.

When he left Providence, he'd lived a fast, dangerous life, not giving a damn whether he lived or died. But determination to discover the cause of his father's death had finally driven him to finish medical school. He only hoped he would learn something useful before he met the same fate. He still had moments when he didn't give a good god damn, but this was not one of them.

He focused on Lexy again. She meandered through the yard, her skirt swinging in the dust like a flirtatious young girl's. Marriage, he realized, his heart twisting again, hadn't turned her into an overweight hausfrau. Her hair, the color of warm honey, was shot with gold in the late-afternoon sunlight. He forced a grim smile. She never had been one to care whether her skin tanned. No bonnet, no gloves.

His approving gaze wandered over her. She'd become more lush. Her curves were evident beneath her gown. She'd been a stunning young woman four years ago. Now she was breathtaking. A not-so-surprising bite of envy twisted his gut. Obviously, marriage agreed with her. The envy turned to pain. Just the thought of another man giving her pleasure ripped through him.

He swore and slammed his fist into his palm, fighting unwanted desire as the memory of their tempestuous lovemaking overwhelmed him. Maybe he could have lived with the reality of her marriage if he hadn't known the man. Maybe. But Ben Stillwater . . .

He swore again, angry, frustrated, envious . . . jealous.

He'd been surprised she would come alone, but when Max explained that it was merely to keep Megan company until the baby came, Jake thought he could understand it. He hadn't heard from Ben in two years, but he assumed that was because there was nothing more to say.

That thought made him curse and turn abruptly

from the window. He could only hope her trip would be short. He couldn't stand the thought of having her here for any length of time. How long could he keep an air of aloofness when there was so much more in his heart?

Cursing his weakness, he returned to the window. And found her gazing in. Before her expression changed, he was certain he had seen shock. Perhaps it had been fear. Or hate.

His mouth went dry, and his gut burned. He cursed again, feeling a nip of rage at how quickly everything had changed for them. As he sat on the train four years ago, Providence behind him, he'd hoped he could forget everything that had happened. It would have been the smart thing to do, but his heart and his mind wouldn't let him.

Lexy deserved happiness; he'd have been happier if she'd married someone he didn't know. Hell, who was he kidding? In his pathetic, ideal world, she would have married no one at all if she couldn't marry him.

But after all these years, he hadn't counted on the pain and shame he would feel when he saw her again.

The memory of her last words hit him like a sucker punch to the jaw. He'd hurt her. He'd humiliated her. He'd used her.

She turned and walked away.

He grabbed his coat off the back of his chair and raced out of his office after her. "Lexy!"

She stopped, turning slowly toward him, her expression remote. A fleeting smile came and quickly disappeared. "Hello, Jake."

She seemed detached. Had he been wrong? "It's good to see you."

A smile returned, pleasant this time but not personal. "It's good to see you, too. And I was so happy to hear you'd finished your degree."

She spoke to him as one would to an acquaintance,

someone she had met maybe once and had not thought of until she met him again.

Whatever she'd felt for him once was gone. He could see it in her eyes. Eyes that had never before hidden an emotion from him. He experienced an emptiness, a sense of regret. He would almost have preferred to see hatred there; at least it would have been something.

His own expression became guarded. "Yes. It gives me something to do."

There was awkward silence.

"Well, I should get back to Meggie." She gave him another cool, impersonal smile. "It was good to see you, Jake."

She walked away, and he knew she'd walked out of his life.

Lexy prayed her legs would hold her. He'd given her just enough time to compose a facade before he came after her. Oh, but it had been so hard. To look into his face, a face she'd once loved so fiercely . . .

Through all the levels of emotion that had followed their last evening together—hate, anger, shame—she'd fought her deeper feelings of love. That's what made her angry now. That what he'd done to her hadn't killed every ounce of love.

He looked harder. More seasoned. Like a sea captain standing at the window, his feet wide apart and his hands clasped behind his back, watching the world slip by. He wasn't happy; she could sense that. But then, had he ever been?

She dragged herself up the steps to the cabin and sank onto the porch swing, moving it to and fro with one foot.

She thought she would feel anger at seeing him again. But there was no anger. Not really. Through the cold numbness that surrounded her heart, she felt that other wild emotion, and *that* made her angry.

The door squeaked open, and Megan stepped onto the porch. "Well, did you see him?"

"Yes. Briefly."

Megan sat across from her with hand work. She held up the long white baby's gown and gave Lexy a questioning look. "Like it?"

"It's beautiful. If you tell me you made it, I'll faint."

Megan laughed. "I can do a lot of things, like crochet, knit, and even enjoy quilting now and then, but I still can't sew worth a darn. The commander's wife made it for the baby."

"It's beautiful," Lexy responded.

Megan rubbed her stomach absently. "Every once in a while, I feel like I'm jailed with nothing to do but fabricate my own amusement. Or maybe I'm simply going mad. Look." She dragged out a long, thin piece of crocheted hand work from the basket beside the rocker.

Lexy frowned. "What is it?"

With a shake of her head and a sigh, Megan answered, "I haven't the foggiest notion. I just got going on it one day and couldn't stop. This place is driving me crazy." She shoved it into the basket and continued working on the lacy hem she'd obviously begun earlier.

"I thought Max said you had wanted to help Dr. Monroe. He wouldn't have let you, Lexy, but I'm sure Jake would be delighted if—"

"No." Her sharp tone startled Megan. "I'm sorry. I didn't mean to snap at you, Meggie. I guess I'm just tired."

Megan studied her. "He wastes way too much time caring for the savages and the pitiful families on that farm nearby. That's something you two have in common, anyway. He could use your help, Lex."

*Not in this lifetime.* "I've . . . had a change of plans, of sorts. I plan to stay—"

34

"You're going to stay?" Megan's laugh was one of relief. "Oh, am I ever happy to hear that. Then you and Jake can work together. It will be perfect."

"You didn't let me finish, Meggie. Yes, I plan to stay, but I want to open a practice of my own." Megan's look of mixed disappointment and pleasure was almost humorous. If there was any humor in the situation, which there wasn't.

"But—"

Lexy raised her hand to quiet her. "If I'd wanted to share a practice with a man, I could have stayed in Providence. Ben has been after me to go in with him for years."

Megan shot her a bored look. "How is the dull Benjamin Stillwater?"

"He's very successful, Meggie, and he's hardly dull."

Megan wrinkled her nose. "I always thought he was. He had no dash. No élan. Expensive clothes don't always make the man, you know. Or like Cook used to say, 'You can dress up a donkey in a starched shirt and trousers, but he'll still be a donkey.'"

Lexy couldn't help laughing. "That isn't fair."

"The only good thing I can say about him is that he has enough sense to practice medicine in a place where he can be paid in something other than livestock. Of course, being born rich helps," she added, almost wistfully.

Lexy raised an eyebrow. "Livestock?"

"Oh, you know what I mean. People out here are so poor, they have trouble buying the few little things they need, much less the luxury of medical care. That's why," she added, pointing her crochet hook at Lexy, "I'm so anxious to leave here. Lord, I haven't been to a decent party since I left Providence, and it's impossible to entertain, considering I have no truly nice things. Oh," she said, tossing Lexy a quick glance, "not that I blame Max for that. I mean, we have some nice things stored in Providence, but it didn't seem wise to haul them all the way out here when we knew we'd be returning east eventually.

"And . . . and there are a few very nice women, like Mrs. Billings and some of the ladies in town, but . . ." Again, a wistful, faraway look. "Nothing is the same out here. Life is so . . . temporary. It's as if we're all simply biding our time until they close the fort and send us home."

"They will close the fort? Even if the Indians continue to cause trouble?"

"That's what Commander Billings says." She stopped, glancing down at her hand work. "Max thinks it's a mistake. With the few soldiers we have gone, the Indians will continue to cause the ranchers trouble."

Megan's words gave Lexy pause. "What is it that they do, exactly?"

With a shake of her head, Megan answered, "I'm glad I don't live outside this fort, let me tell you. I've heard tell that they enter any house they please, lounge around on the furniture, demand to be fed, and, frankly, simply scare the womenfolk to death."

Lexy frowned. All she'd wanted to do was come west, hang out her shingle, and practice medicine. She hadn't thought about the dangers to herself or to Krista.

After dinner, Lexy helped her sister with the evening dishes, then returned with her to the porch.

Megan eased into a rocking chair, sighing as she settled into it. "I'm sure Jake would have joined us for dinner if the commander hadn't called a meeting."

Lexy was grateful he hadn't. She was too tired to keep up the facade. "Do you know what it was about?"

"We have new recruits, and they have to be warned about the Indians. I imagine those same young braves are making more threats about taking back the land that has already been purchased by white ranchers."

Lexy continued to think about the hazards of living so far from the rest of the country. It wasn't that she was truly having second thoughts, but it was a worry.

Forcing herself to think about something else, she listened to the noises of the night. Crickets chirruped in the grass beside the porch steps. Something unknown rustled through the brush under the porch, and Lexy shuddered. She never had liked the dark.

Megan yawned and stretched. "I love this time of day."

Lexy shifted in the creaky porch swing. "I was just thinking about how much I dislike it. Early morning is my favorite."

Megan laughed. "I don't know about that. I don't think I've ever been up early enough to judge."

"So, you don't get up at the crack of dawn and fix Max breakfast?"

"I used to. But since I've gotten so big, the dear man lets me sleep. He reminds me that after the baby is born, I'll be awake enough."

Lexy pushed the swing with her foot. "Not many men would be that considerate, Meggie."

"I know that," she answered.

Footsteps came toward them, crunching on the gravel, and Lexy heard Jake's dry laughter. *Pull up the facade,* she warned herself, for even in the darkness her feelings could be exposed. Her heart pounded. He was coming. Nowhere to hide.

He walked out of the shadows, into the pale light from the moon, stopping at the bottom step. She could profess until her dying day that she hated him, but her body would forever refuse to listen. Thank God it was dark. Pretense was easier in the dark.

"Well, it's about time you showed up," Megan scolded.

He came up two steps and touched Megan's arm. The gesture was not lost on Lexy. Her stomach spiraled downward.

"How are we doing tonight?"

She gave him an indelicate snort. *"We* are doing very poorly, thanks to you. I expected you for dinner, Jake."

A lamp glowed inside the cabin, sending light over him as he went behind her and rubbed her shoulders. Lexy was forced to turn away.

"Sorry. The meeting took longer than I expected. I grabbed grub with the men."

Something acidic and unpleasant bubbled in Lexy's stomach, for the two of them sounded as if they were married.

Megan made a retching sound. "How can you eat that slop?"

Out of the corner of her eye, Lexy saw Jake put a shawl around Megan's shoulders. Had his fingers lingered there?

"Oh, it's not such bad food. Can I get you anything? Some warmed milk?"

Megan declined the offer but thanked him.

Lexy thought she would be sick. He was as solicitous as a new groom.

He finally turned his attention to her. "So, Lexy, I didn't ask how your trip was."

"It was long," she answered abruptly.

"And lonesome, I imagine."

For a moment, only a brief, fleeting moment, she thought he knew about Krista. But it was merely her overactive imagination. "It's always a little lonesome traveling alone."

"Is Ben coming out later?"

The question took her by surprise, and now that she had Jake's attention, she didn't want it. "Um, yes. As a matter of fact, he is. He and his sister, Ivy." *And your daughter,* she thought, her stomach tensing like a fist.

"Oh, pooh," Megan interjected. "Who wants to talk about that old bore? And that sister of his." She made a disgusted sound in her throat. "An old maid if I've ever seen one."

Lexy looked at the floor, unwilling to encourage her sister. "She's become a wonderful friend, Megan. There were many times over the years that she was like a sister to me."

Megan threw up her hands. "All right, all right. I suppose there could be more to her than meets the eye. But we're together again, and you won't need her ear anymore; you have mine."

Lexy stifled a sigh. Megan would never understand.

"How long are you staying?" Jake asked.

"Oh, Jake," Megan enthused. "That's the best part. She's going to open a practice here."

He straightened, drew his arms across his chest, and studied her anew. "Really." He sounded more amused than interested.

"Yes, really," Megan answered for her.

Nodding sagely, he asked, "And how does Ben feel about this?"

Again, the mention of Ben. It was puzzling. "Well, I—"

"No more talk about Ben Stillwater, Jake," Megan pleaded. "Come, Lexy," she ordered, pulling her cumbersome body from the rocker. "Let's go inside. The bugs are beginning to annoy me. Jake, you can only join us if you talk about things *I* want to hear."

"I've got some paperwork. Another time, perhaps."

Lexy breathed a sigh of relief and followed Megan into the house.

Megan pressed her hands into the small of her back and yawned. "Ben, Ben, Ben. Nothing makes me sleepier than listening to someone constantly talk about a bore. Unless, of course, it's listening to the bore himself."

Lexy made a noncommittal sound in her throat. What she found odd was that Jake had mentioned Ben at all. And not once, but twice.

That night, after she went to bed, she could think of nothing but Jake. He'd slept in her bed the night before, and with every breath Lexy took, she found his scent.

When she'd learned he had left medical school, she'd been disappointed. He'd been such a gifted student, although she knew he was there because he'd promised his dying mother he would discover why the men in his family died at such a young age. It was a terrible weight to carry on his shoulders. An awful promise to have to make, one he would find impossible to keep.

Part of her, a petty, petulant part, had hoped he'd become shiftless and useless. She didn't want him to have a successful life after so successfully ruining hers. But those moments didn't last long. They were fleeting moments of weakness when she was especially tired or when she'd nearly bowed under the hurtful, weighted words of those who called her names.

But after his display with Megan tonight, Lexy would have an easier time hiding her true feelings. He still cared for Megan; it was obvious. The realization still hurt, and even her anger couldn't wash that away.

She pressed her nose into the pillow again, the scent of Jake making her think of Krista. Nighttime was always the worst. Lexy worried that her daughter was ill, or missing her miserably, and it kept her from sleep. But morning would come eventually, and with it the lifting of her mood. At least, it should. Now, however, with Jake right under her nose, she wondered if she would get any rest at all.

The following evening, Megan wandered into the bedroom as Lexy undressed.

She plopped herself onto the bed. "You surprise me."

"Really? Why?" Lexy attempted to hang her skirt in the tiny wardrobe so it wouldn't get any more wrinkled than it already was.

"I thought you'd be more excited to find Jake here. You barely acknowledged him at dinner tonight. The only time you spoke to him was when he asked you a question."

Feigning nonchalance, Lexy answered, "I guess I've grown up. Anyway, a lot can happen to change things in four years."

"To who? Him?" She studied Lexy carefully as Lexy removed her chemise. "Or you?"

Megan stopped her from drawing the nightgown over her head. "I recognize stretch marks when I see them, Lexy. I have some myself. One of the curses of my present condition." She waited a cryptic moment, then added, "You didn't have them the last time I saw you."

Lexy pulled on her gown and quickly buttoned it to her chin. "Since when were you interested in my bosom?" she asked, keeping her tone light even though she felt herself blush.

"We used to compare sizes, remember? I was always envious because yours were bigger and rounder than mine."

"Don't tell me I actually had something you wanted," Lexy joked, still trying to diffuse the tension inside her.

Megan scooted herself further onto the bed. "We haven't seen each other for four years. That was my fault, I know. But I would hope that if you'd been expecting at any time during those four years, you'd have let me know."

Lexy brushed out her hair. Her stomach tightened. "I wrote you many times, Meggie. I never got an answer."

"But you never wrote to tell me you were going to have a baby, did you? I think I would have remembered that."

With nervous fingers, Lexy braided her hair. When she finished, she rearranged her things in the chest of drawers for something to do. She was torn. Part of her wanted to confide in someone, draw a mental picture of her daughter. She didn't think she could keep all of it inside. Another part of her feared that Jake would find out before she had a chance to tell him.

"You should get some sleep, Meggie."

"I never go to bed before midnight. Don't change the subject."

Lexy sighed and pulled herself into a cross-legged position on the bed. She gave Megan a thoughtful look. "I don't want you to breathe a word of what I tell you to anyone. Promise me?"

Megan pulled back, studying her through wary eyes. "I can't promise anything until I know what it is."

"This is serious, Meggie."

Megan's face crumpled. "You know I'm not good at keeping secrets."

Lexy was aware of that. It was Megan who got her into trouble when Lexy accidentally broke their mother's antique vase as she danced and spun in the parlor. Lexy would have owned up to it, but Megan was quick and ratted on her before Lexy could pick up the pieces.

"But you must. Otherwise, I won't tell you."

Megan bit her lip. "It isn't because I don't want to. It's because I don't seem to be able to."

"Then I can't tell you."

An honest expression of regret crossed Megan's face. "I'll try, Lexy. I truly will."

Lexy was bursting to tell someone. Krista's photograph was carefully wrapped in a silk scarf in Lexy's traveling bag. She left the bed, retrieved the treasure, and returned, handing it to her sister.

"Her name is Krista. She's three."

Megan stared at the likeness, her mouth open. She looked at Lexy, her expression one of shock. "She's yours?"

"Yes, she's mine."

"Why can't I tell anyone?"

Nerves quivered beneath Lexy's skin. "You simply can't, that's all."

Megan's gaze returned to the photo. "She's very pretty, Lex." She gave her a playful smile. "She looks like me."

*No,* Lexy thought, *she looks like her father.* "She was born with a weakness in her lungs. One of the reasons I wanted to come west to practice was the climate here. Rhode Island is so damp and cold. Or hot and humid. It's not good for her." A wave of longing for Krista overpowered her.

Megan sagged onto the bed and stared at the ceiling. "My God." She turned and glared at Lexy. "I should be furious with you. You shouldn't have been alone. How . . . who . . ."

Lexy cracked a smile. *"How* should be obvious, even to you. *Who* . . . isn't important."

"Not important? I beg to differ, Alexis. Any man who would do that to you, then . . . then leave, is a *worm."*

*Hmmm. A shared sentiment.* "He didn't know. He still doesn't, and I'd like to keep it that way." *At least, for as long as possible.*

Megan made a face. "It isn't Ben's, is it?"

"No." Lexy shook her head and laughed. It wasn't that Ben hadn't wanted to claim Krista. All she would have had to do was agree, and Krista would have had a trust fund she could have shared with a hundred other children and lived comfortably for the rest of her life. As it was, Ben had taken it upon himself to set up a fund for her education.

"Thank the Lord for that."

They sat in silence, Lexy wondering if she'd done the right thing by telling her blabbermouth sister.

"Well?"

"Well, what?"

"You know very well what I want to know, Alexis."

"It isn't important. I'd just . . . rather we kept this between the two of us, all right? Promise me?"

Megan struggled to sit. "I'd be more inclined to promise if I knew who he was."

"I'm afraid you'll know soon enough."

"Meaning what?"

Lexy drew in a deep breath. "Ben and Ivy are bringing her on the train. They'll be here in about a month. Maybe less. Then I'll tell you."

Megan pouted. "What if I guess it right? Will you tell me?"

"You don't even know him," she lied.

"Then what can it matter if you tell me?" She pressed a hand to her mouth. "It *is* Ben, isn't it? You're just trying to confuse me. Oh, Lexy, how could you?"

"Megan, she is *not* Ben's. I'm going to bed, and you should, too. Just promise me you'll keep this to yourself. If you don't—" She made a fist and threatened her with it.

"Ha! You wouldn't strike a pregnant woman," Megan teased.

"No," Lexy cajoled, "but you won't be pregnant forever."

They both smiled, then Megan went to the doorway, her expression turning unpleasant. "If this child is Ben Stillwater's, and I can't imagine who else could be the father, it's not the sort of news I'd like to spread around. It's not even something I can imagine."

"Promise me you won't tell anyone. Not Max, not one of the officers' wives, not Jake. No one, Meggie."

"All right, all right. I promise." She spread her hands in front of her. "See? My fingers aren't crossed."

"Thank you," Lexy answered. She turned off the lamp and stared at the door. Perhaps it hadn't been wise to confide in Megan, but she'd had to tell someone. And Megan's response was what she'd expected. But that didn't bother Lexy. She'd have been shocked if Megan had asked a meaningful question about her daughter, such as whom she really favored. She'd have been stunned if Megan had embraced her and cried happy tears.

No, Megan's response was perfect. And typical. And she would let her think it was Ben's. That was enough to keep her quiet. But Lexy didn't understand why Megan thought so little of the Stillwaters. On the other hand, maybe she did. After all, they were old Rhode Island money, had three homes, one of them in France, and Ben had never been interested in Megan's flirty ways. Any man, especially one with money, who did not swoon at her feet was pond scum.

Now, if her dear sister could hold her tongue, maybe Lexy could figure out just how she would handle Jake when Krista arrived. Then, too, perhaps there would be nothing to handle. He'd left her without looking back. Without so much as trying to find out how she was. Without a thought. Perhaps his child wouldn't mean much to him, either.

# Chapter 3

Early the following morning, Lexy awakened and listened to the quiet. So different from Providence, where street noises often kept her awake well into the night, and morning came early with the clip-clopping sounds of horses and muffled cries from eager vendors hawking their wares. Here, there was nothing but mourning doves and the bustling twitter of awakening birds. An occasional barking dog. Men's voices, inaudible within the confines of a building.

She pressed her face into the pillow, finding Jake's scent once more, then slid from bed, pillow against her chest as she crossed to the window.

Sunny again, she had thought, regarding the clear, gray dawn. Inhaling deeply, she savored the spicy pine-scented breeze that blew against her face. No dirty street smells. No brief, pungent salt air whipping in from the ocean.

Jake's scent wafted up from the pillow. Something inside her twisted like a rope, and she vividly remembered her feelings when she'd seen him again after four years.

The idyllic, magical morning spell was broken.

She clenched the pillow to her stomach, then tossed it across the room, as if to shatter the feelings inside her. Inhaling deeply, she began to dress, preparing herself for the coming day.

Later that morning, Little Pete stopped by to see if either Lexy or Megan wanted anything from town.

"Not me," Megan answered. "I'm not leaving this cabin until I look human again."

The offer delighted Lexy. When they'd driven through Burning Tree on the way to the fort, she'd noticed a doctor's shingle. Little Pete had told her the doctor was elderly. Lexy wanted to talk to the man. Maybe this was her chance.

"I can be ready in five minutes," she promised.

"Fine. The doc will be by in the wagon to pick you up."

Lexy's enthusiasm dwindled. "I thought you were going, Little Pete."

"Nope. Got me some horses to shod." He tipped his hat and was gone.

Five minutes later, Jake was out front.

Hiding her reluctance, Lexy hurried outside and stepped into the wagon before Jake could come around to help her. The horses skittered as two dogs raced by, one chasing the other. Lexy gripped the wagon seat until her fingers ached.

Horses and dogs. Two animals people seemed to adore, including her daughter. And two animals among scores that Lexy couldn't quite figure out.

Megan was petulant as she stood on the porch and looked at Jake. "I thought you were going to remove the rocks from my garden today."

"I'll get one of the other men to help you, Megan."

"But I'd counted on you, Jake."

Lexy held her tongue, but it wasn't easy. Megan's tone was simpering. Helpless.

Jake sighed and cleared his throat. "There are some things I have to take care of. Corporal Anderson is itching to do something physical, Megan. Why not let him clear the garden of rocks?"

"Will he do more than grunt at me, like you do when I ask you a question?"

"He's not much of a talker, but he's a hard worker, Megan."

"If this is going to be a problem, maybe someone else could go with me," Lexy suggested, the idea oddly appealing. Being alone with Jake wasn't something she looked forward to. And what in the name of heaven would they talk about?

She glanced at Jake; his expression was inscrutable.

"No. As long as I have business near Burning Tree, I'll go with Lexy. Corporal Anderson will be more than willing to work with you, Megan. He admires you a great deal."

"Really?" The pleasure in her tone was evident. "I had no idea. But then, isn't that sweet? Of course I can work with him."

Lexy hid a smile. Jake knew how to push her sister's buttons. Simply remind her that someone admired her, and she twittered like a happy chickadee.

Megan waved gaily from the porch.

They rode in silence for what seemed an interminable length of time. To Lexy, it felt as though each second were ticking slowly and loudly in her head. And surely Jake could hear the beating of her heart. Why would he not, when it pounded so loudly in her ears that she could barely hear anything else?

"I know the doctor in Burning Tree, and he's not about to give you any advice for opening a practice of your own." Jake sounded cocky and bored.

His blunt statement broke into her foolish, lovelorn thoughts, and she silently thanked him. "I'll find out for myself, thank you."

"You're wasting your time."

"Fine," she answered, her voice cool. "It's my time to waste." It was important that he not sense her feelings, but she couldn't hide them forever. She'd had trouble enough hiding them in the short time she had been at the fort.

An hour later, they left the old doctor's office, and Jake was quiet as he pulled himself in beside her.

Lexy settled into the wagon and stole a quick glance at his profile. "All right," she began. "Say, 'I told you so,' and get it over with."

Jake snapped the reins, and the buggy lurched forward, causing Lexy to grip the sides again. "I told you so."

With a disbelieving shake of her head, she said, "Men. They're the same everywhere. If it were up to them, women would never do anything but cook, clean, cajole, and . . . and . . ."

"Cavort before them naked?"

Despite everything, he could make her laugh, but she bit the insides of her cheeks to prevent it. "You find this very amusing, don't you?"

He gave her knee a brotherly pat, but she felt it clear to her toes.

"Doc Hasley has been around for a long time, Lexy."

"And he's so old, he should be thinking about a replacement," she retorted.

"I think he has. Word is that he has a nephew who graduates next year from a very fine Eastern school."

Lexy nearly snorted. "And I suppose this fine young man will give up a lucrative practice in the East to take over his uncle's rustic practice here."

"It's possible. You are. Or you're trying to."

*But I have no choice.*

With an exaggerated sigh, she said, "What will it take for men to realize a woman's potential?"

"Don't paint all men with the same brush, Lexy."

She turned on the seat to study him. "You're different, I suppose."

"I am. I'd rather you treated me than any doctor I know. Including myself."

*49*

His statement overwhelmed her. She continued to study him; he appeared sincere. "I'm surprised you feel that way."

"Why?"

She shrugged. "I don't know. I . . . I guess because I've had such a hard time convincing male doctors I'm an equal, I'd forgotten there might be some who believe I am."

She thought of the difficult time she'd had, boldly claiming Krista as illegitimate at a time when the word wasn't even whispered in proper society. She thought of her day-to-day abuse, both verbal and professional, when at least one person made a snide remark about her station in life loudly enough for her to hear. The words *bastard* and *whore* had become constant companions. She'd learned to toughen her skin; she didn't want Krista to grow up in the same environment.

"What about Ben?"

She shook herself, relieved to return to the present. "Oh, Ben. I know it sounds petty, but I wanted to have a job on my merit, not one that was given to me."

"Well, since you're here and not there, I assume you didn't find one."

She shook her head, memories of her failed attempts to convince anyone other than Ben that she was more than capable still vivid. "Of course not." She paused, briefly. "I've been working as an operating-room nurse."

He scraped his knuckles over his jaw and said nothing.

They rode in the kind of silence that made Lexy uncomfortable. She felt the urge to fill the quiet void. "Why did you request this fort, Jake?"

"What makes you think I requested it?" His voice held caution.

She shrugged a shoulder. "It seems quite a coincidence that you'd end up here, with Meggie. And Max, of course."

He barked a laugh. "Ah, yes. The fair Megan. Didn't you know? I've always been partial to married women." Although his words were said lightly, his voice held an edge of anger.

Well, that certainly ruled her out, didn't it? She shouldn't have been surprised that he continued to carry a torch for Megan, but she was stunned at the sinking feeling in the pit of her stomach.

When they reached the fork in the road, he guided the team down the one that didn't lead to the fort.

She tossed him a questioning glance.

"I have an errand up this way."

They rode in silence again. Lexy studied the landscape, marveling at the variety of wildflowers that grew in abundance along the side of the road. She loved the open spaces, the vast meadows and hills that stood naturally dressed in greens, golds, and browns. It was almost as if breathing was easier out here, as if there was more than enough air for everyone. Not like Providence, where she had often felt she was suffocating.

In the distance, she saw a building. As they got closer, she realized it wasn't occupied, for it was a bit ramshackle and broken-down.

"What did that used to be?"

"A whorehouse."

Lexy studied the building with growing interest. "Really? Out here in the middle of nowhere?"

"I hear it was pretty busy at one time."

"What happened?" The windows were boarded up, and there appeared to be a hole low on the roof. Scraggly brush grew in wild abundance around the building, not entirely hiding an occasional hollyhock that resisted being strangled.

"The madam ran off. To Denver, I think."

Lexy continued to study the building, turning in her

seat as they passed it. She wasn't much good at detecting the finer points of a well-crocheted doily, but she knew structures. She was a better carpenter than she was a doily maker or a knitter or a quilter.

"Except for that hole in the roof, the building looks sound. Why doesn't someone else use it?"

He chuckled. "Would you want to set up a business in an abandoned house of ill repute?"

"I wouldn't mind." She felt his gaze, but when she looked at him, it was quickly masked.

"You never were one to judge, were you?"

"I don't like to see something so useful go to waste, that's all." Lexy kept her gaze on the building until it was obscured by a thicket of trees, then turned and studied the road ahead. "Who owns the property?"

Jake slowed the team as they came to a run-down farm. "The Army," he answered, pulling the team to a stop.

The farmhouse was little more than a shack. The barn, though sturdy, needed paint.

A middle-aged man came out of the barn and greeted Jake with a wave. Jake left the rig and met him. They spoke for a few minutes, then the man rolled up his sleeve and showed Jake something on his arm. Jake examined it, said something to the man, then returned to the wagon.

She looked at him from beneath her lashes. Her reluctant heart was at risk here. Four years of vowing to hate him forever for humiliating her threatened to dissolve.

The sun glinted off his black hair, drawing out the burnished copper highlights. She gazed at the stubble on his cheek and jaw, remembering that he had a fast-growing beard. She focused on the bump on his nose, where he'd broken it running into the oak tree in her backyard.

He'd been twelve, she a mere six. She caught a smile. He'd been knocked flat, and she was glad, because he'd been chasing her, threatening her with a frog. It had been shortly after that that she'd begun to look at him differently, because even though he'd been terrorizing her, he'd paid attention to her.

She gnawed on her lower lip, her thoughts returning to the pain he'd caused her four years ago. It had run too deep to forget. Too deep to forgive entirely.

There would be no more blind trust. Without knowing or caring, he'd given her the most wonderful gift a man could give a woman. But the painful part was that in exchange, she had to accept what he'd taken from her.

Jake sat at his desk, staring at the blank tablet before him. They had been back for an hour, and he hadn't accomplished a thing. His thoughts were on Lexy, and he couldn't shake them off. Determined to take notes on his brief meeting with Jasper Hansen, he took a deep breath and forced himself to begin. Instead, he started a letter to Lexy—a letter she would never read.

Finishing with a growling curse, Jake returned his fountain pen to its holder, capped the ink, and leaned into his chair. He was restless and frustrated. Writing didn't help; it merely accentuated his agony.

Sitting beside Lexy on the wagon had been hell. All of the mannerisms he used to enjoy came back to him. Her little one-shouldered shrug. Her full, delicious lips that she bit at when she was nervous, her blush when she was angry or embarrassed. And the sweet smell of lilacs that mingled with a secret woman's scent that threatened to drive him mad.

He would never forget the softness of her skin, the plumpness of her breasts beneath his searching fingers, the quick and forceful release of her passion when he touched the moist and steamy curls between her thighs.

He had loved the sweet nature that always lurked

beneath her pragmatic exterior. How her eyes would puddle with warmth when she treated a child. How she could be childlike herself when doing something she loved. How she could rear up in defense of those unable to defend themselves.

His feelings for her had come on so gradually, he hadn't realized how deep they were until he'd started making love to her that night. But he didn't know why he'd called out Megan's name. Maybe because until that moment, he hadn't even realized that his feelings had so permanently and soundly changed and that he'd transferred them from one sister to the other. There were many things he would like to change about his life, and that night with Lexy was very high on the list.

She had an inner beauty that no woman he had met since could rival. And once a man was around her for any length of time, her sunny warmth seeped into his pores and addled him.

It had happened to him. It had happened to Ben Stillwater, too.

Jake massaged a knot of tension in his neck and wondered how many hours he'd mentally flogged himself for being the man he was, instead of the man he wanted to be. A man with a future. A man who dared dream of a wife he loved, one he could grow old with. Of children and grandchildren.

He'd spent useless hours cursing his fate. It mattered little now. Fate had taken matters out of his hands. With an angry shove, he pushed his chair back and stood, restless again. He grabbed his coat off the hook, shrugged into it, and went outside. He needed a ride to clear his head.

Lexy was trying to figure out a way to approach the post commander about the whorehouse. It would be perfect for her needs. Big enough for her and Krista to live in and still have an office for her patients.

A niggling voice reminded her that with Jake practicing medicine at the fort and Dr. Hasley in Burning Tree, she might have no patients, but she refused to listen to such logic.

There was a rapid knocking at the door. She rose to answer it and found Little Pete on the porch. Beside him was an Indian woman and a child, whose chest was wrapped in a bloody shawl.

Shocked at the amount of blood that had soaked through the shawl, she brought her hand to her throat. "What happened?" She bent over the boy, studying his condition, relieved to see the rise and fall of his chest.

"Accident, I guess," Little Pete replied.

That was obvious, she thought, but held her tongue. She looked over his head, toward Jake's office. "Why didn't you bring him to the doctor?"

Little Pete shook his head. "Couldn't. Doc isn't there. Don't know where he is."

Lexy hustled them inside. "Can you . . . do they speak any English?"

In what must have been her native tongue, Little Pete asked the woman what had happened. When she responded, he said, "The boy was in the meadow, and a bull charged him."

Lexy carefully studied the wound. "He's been gored in the chest. Come. Bring him into the bedroom."

He followed her in and laid the boy on the bed. His mission completed, he turned to leave.

"I'll need a translator, Little Pete," Lexy announced. "Please stay."

Megan lumbered into the room, wringing her hands. Her face was pinched. "What is it? What's wrong?"

Lexy peeled away the bloody shawl to get a better look at the wound. "This boy was gored by a bull."

"But . . . but . . . what is he doing *here,* in my cabin?"

"Jake isn't in his office." She shot her sister a careful look. "I don't want him moved again until I can stop the bleeding." She could see Megan's throat working. "I need you to help me, Meggie."

"I . . . I . . ."

"Please, Meggie. I need a few things. Can you get them for me?"

Megan began hyperventilating.

"Don't breathe so fast. Slow down. Megan," she said, her voice stern, "I need your help."

Megan briefly closed her eyes and took a few deep breaths. "What do you need?"

"Hot water. And an old sheet that you can rip into long strips." She watched her sister waddle from the room, then she turned to Little Pete. "There's soap and a jar of compound lead ointment in my trunk at the foot of the bed. Would you get them for me, please?"

She crossed to the dry sink, catching the soap as Little Pete tossed it to her, and began scrubbing.

"Little Pete, ask the mother if she can help Meggie with the sheet," she said, carefully wiping her hands on a towel. "It should keep both of them busy."

Little Pete translated, and the distraught woman nodded. Megan entered the room with a basin, a tea kettle filled with hot water, and a sheet draped over her arm. She put the kettle and basin on the small table beside the bed just as Lexy was wrapping her hair, turban-style, in a scarf.

Megan tore the old sheet and gave half of it to the boy's mother. They began ripping it into long, thin strips.

Little Pete stepped to her side. "Anything else I can do?"

"If you'll stay with me so I can communicate with the boy's mother, I'd appreciate it."

The child moved his gaze back and forth between Lexy and Little Pete, his dark eyes wide, his mouth quivering. His mother sat in the chair beside the bed, stealing glances at her son as she worked.

"What's his name?" Lexy gently cleaned the wound with a cloth and soapy water.

Little Pete bent close and spoke with the boy. "His name is Joseph."

Nodding, Lexy gave the boy a tender smile. "You tell Joseph that he's a very brave boy."

Before Little Pete could translate, the boy's face broke into a tentative grin. "I am brave like my father and my grandfather," he answered, trying not to cringe at Lexy's gentle probing.

"And you speak English very well, Joseph," she praised. "But what were you doing playing so close to that bull?"

"I did not see him," Joseph answered. "I was studying the tracks of a coyote."

"Hmmm," she responded, studying the wound. "I suppose it takes lots of practice to have all of your senses alert, doesn't it?"

She kept the conversation going in an attempt to distract him. Now and then, he would grunt with discomfort, but he did not cry out.

After thoroughly cleaning the area, she realized that a few well-placed stitches were in order.

"Little Pete, in my trunk you'll find a red box with needles and surgical thread. Would you get it for me, please?"

He rummaged around in her trunk, found the box, opened it, and handed it to her.

Lexy gave Joseph an encouraging smile. "We're going to have to close that wound, Joseph, and it's going to hurt. Think you can stand it?"

Joseph's large black eyes were filled with a bite of fear, but he stiffened against the oncoming pain and nodded.

"Little Pete, tell the mother what I'm going to do, and ask her to hold his hand."

"Gosh," Little Pete murmured. "Shouldn't ya at least give him a shot of whiskey?"

She raised a disbelieving eyebrow. "To a small child? I don't think so."

With a shake of his head, he translated for the boy's mother, and she quickly grasped her son's hand in her own.

When Lexy had finished, she noticed the silent tears that tracked Joseph's cheeks and felt the sting behind her own eyes. "You were very courageous, Joseph. Not many grown men would have been as brave as you."

He gave her a watery smile, which quickly faded.

She spread salve around the wound, covered it with a clean square of cloth, then bound it with the strips of sheeting. "I'd like him to stay here for a few days. Do you think his mother would mind?"

Little Pete's gaze rested on the Indian woman, who was clearly distressed. "She won't want to leave him, ma'am."

"Then she can stay." She turned and caught Megan's gaze. "Is that all right with you?"

Megan merely shrugged, her face pale. "Well, I—" A fleeting look of impatience was replaced by surrender. "Whatever you want to do, Lexy."

There was a commotion outside, and a large Indian elbowed his way into the room. Lexy's breath caught in her throat, for the man filled the doorway. Lord, he *was* the doorway. A threatening scar meandered from the corner of one eye to his chin. His hair was straight and long, giving him a savage look.

Goosebumps rose over her skin. He looked angry enough to lift a scalp.

He scowled at everyone, then strode to the bed.

"My son go home now." He spoke with authority.

Little Pete cleared his throat. "This is Dooley, ma'am. He's a tribal leader." Pete cringed. "He's not exactly happy with the army. He don't want to stay on the reservation, but he understands the consequences if he tries to leave."

Lexy stepped to him, her fists on her hips. "Well, he can't move Joseph. Not yet. I won't allow it."

Dooley gave her a bemused look, then glanced at Little Pete. He nodded his huge, shaggy head toward Lexy. "Who she?"

Lexy grabbed the man's arm and turned him toward her. His eyes filled with arrogant surprise, as if her touch was a personal affront.

"I am a doctor, and Joseph can't be moved. Not for at least two days." Lexy crossed her arms over her chest and stared up at Dooley, her stance defiant.

He looked to Little Pete, his expression questioning. "A woman healer? Where Doc Jake?"

"Gone," Little Pete answered. "Joseph was gored by a bull, Dooley. This here lady sawbones mended his wound. It wouldn't hurt to let him stay a few days."

Dooley frowned, but Lexy could tell he was thinking hard.

"I stay, too, then."

"Fine," Lexy answered. "You and your wife can keep vigil as long as you like, but I want no interference from you."

Dooley gave her a grudging nod, then took his place next to his wife. He hunkered down beside the bed and studied his son, his face lined with concern.

Lexy's gaze found her sister's. Megan's eyes were huge as they looked back at her. Odd, she thought, before she turned back to her patient. She could have sworn there was fear in them.

Although Lexy was anxious for Max's return, she wondered what he'd think if he walked in and found an Indian family camped out in his spare bedroom.

"What's going on here?"

Jake's voice startled her. She swung toward the door as he strode into the room.

"The boy was gored by a bull," Little Pete answered. "I brung him to you first, but you weren't there."

Jake stopped beside the bed. Lexy took a step back and watched him.

He lowered himself until he was at eye level with the patient, then gave him a warm smile. "Well, Joseph. Got yourself a little too close to that bull, huh?"

Around an answering smile, Joseph nodded. "I was tracking a coyote, Doc."

Their familiarity made Lexy realize they had met before. She tried to ignore the warmth she felt at Jake's bedside manner. He had always been wonderful with the patients, especially the elderly and the children, patients who too often got overlooked.

Without unwrapping the binding she had applied, he gently probed the wound. Lexy shifted with discomfort. It made her angry to think she was actually looking for his approval.

Dooley cleared his throat. "Dooley want to take him home."

Lexy bristled. She'd already told him he couldn't. Obviously, because she was a woman, her word wasn't good enough.

With those strong, capable fingers, Jake touched Joseph's brow. "What do you say, Joseph?"

Joseph shot Lexy a quick glance. "I will do what the doctor wants."

Jake raised his gaze to hers. Lexy forced herself to hold it. "And what did the doctor say?"

"That I should stay here for two days."

Jake continued to look at Lexy, who was ready to defend her decision. "And your father is aware of this?"

Dooley grunted. "Dooley aware."

Jake stood. "Then I think you should stay. Doctor's orders. But I don't think it would hurt to move him to my office." He paused, giving Lexy a careful glance. "What do you think, Doctor?"

Lexy hadn't realized she'd been holding her breath. She released it slowly. "I don't suppose it would hurt."

She knew this was merely the beginning of many such confrontations. It was too bad they all wouldn't be this easy.

Later, when the house was quiet and she knew Megan was finally in bed, Lexy went outside. The night was clear; the fort was bathed in moonlight. Crickets chirruped in the grass. A wakeful mourning dove lamented in the distance. Now and then, the sounds of the soldiers who bunked together could be heard. A laugh. A shout. Camaraderie.

Footsteps sounded on the gravel.

Lexy leaned against the porch pillar, not surprised to see Jake ambling toward her. She could feel the pulse at her throat accelerate. She quickly hid behind her facade.

He climbed the porch steps and leaned on the opposite column. "You did a good job today."

A wry smile. "It's what I was trained for."

"I don't mean the treatment. That, as usual, was impeccable. I meant with Joseph and Dooley."

Again, his compliments caught her off balance, threatening to expose her true feelings. "I didn't have much time to think about it. I'm not sure I'd have been so calm if I had."

He laughed, a soft, warm, male sound that made her think of intimacy. "Dooley can be threatening, especially if he puts his mind to it. The first time I saw him, I have to admit I was a little intimidated myself."

Jake's easy dialogue threatened her facade. "I suppose if I'd thought about it, I'd have reacted to him differently."

His answering chuckle, one that washed over her skin and caused goosebumps, reminded her how easily he could get to her.

"I don't completely trust him," Jake said. "He's amiable enough, but he's a sly one. He lets Commander Billings believe he has the Indians under control, but he doesn't. Not really."

Lexy felt a bite of alarm. "What do you mean?"

"They want their land back. They don't want to be told they have to stay on the reservation, and I can't blame them. All the prime land has been taken up by the ranchers. Land the Indians had used for centuries. Who can blame them for being disgruntled when our government, which they don't even recognize, orders them onto land that has absolutely no merit whatsoever?"

"Do you think there will really be trouble?"

"Yes. I have no doubt about it."

Lexy bit her lip and studied the shadows beyond the trees. "Megan told me a little about them. They sound brazen."

"They are. Brazen, clever, cunning, and deceitful. Of course," he added dryly, "in our dealings with them, we are, too."

They stood in silence, Jake's words echoing through Lexy's head. Suddenly, his hand gripped hers.

"Take a walk with me, Lexy."

The touch of his callused palm against hers wiped away all thoughts of cunning Indians. Her entire body was invaded by him. His presence enveloped her.

*Take a walk with me, Lexy. Undress for me, Lexy. You smell sweet, Lexy, like flowers, Lexy* . . . She shied away, attempting to remove her hand from his. "I should really go in—"

"I promise I won't bite." He sounded amused.

*Why not? I might like it.* She swatted at a mosquito, grateful for the sting.

"When we get back, we can check on Joseph together."

Like a fool, she followed him off the porch. He released her hand as they walked, but every inch of Lexy's body felt him beside her anyway.

Something ran toward them, brushing against her skirt as it passed. She yelped, instinctively grabbing Jake's arm.

"It's a dog, Lexy."

Her heart continued to race. She pried her hand from his granitelike biceps. "I know that," she lied.

He laughed. "Like hell. You're still afraid of anything with four legs."

Indignant, she answered, "It's not so much fear as . . . as an inability to understand them. They can't be reasoned with. If I can't reason with it, I can't understand it, and if I can't understand it, I . . . I tend to be a little cautious."

He brushed against her as they walked. "You dissect everything, don't you?"

She flushed, grateful it was dark. "I suppose I do."

They entered the stable. He lit a lamp, and she followed him to a stall. The horse whickered as they approached.

"Hey, Beauty, how's my girl?"

He talked to the horse as he would to a lover. She should know. "What's wrong with her?"

"Nothing. She's pregnant, that's all."

*She's pregnant. I was pregnant.*

He entered the stall and greeted the horse, rubbing the length of her nose. He drew something from his pocket, and she nuzzled his palm. "Greedy little wench, aren't you?"

His voice was a caress. "What did you feed her?"

"Sugar," he answered around a sheepish smile. "I love to spoil her."

If his tenderness hadn't touched her so, she might have found it amusing that the woman in his life was his horse. She did find it a relief. What a ninny she was.

He nodded toward the animal. "Come in here."

Lexy stepped away and shook her head. "No, I—"

"Come in here, Lexy. She won't bite, either."

Drawing in a sigh, Lexy cautiously joined him. The size of the animal astounded her. It would not have overwhelmed his daughter. She felt an ache when she realized all the things they would never share. "She's so big. What kind is she?"

Jake caressed the animal's neck. "She's a quarter horse."

"When will she—um—" She couldn't think of the proper term and was unwilling to sound ignorant, although she was.

"Drop her foal?" At her nod, he answered, "In the spring."

Lexy drew closer and tentatively touched the white stripe on the horse's nose. The animal shied away, but Jake gentled her.

Lexy studied Beauty's big brown eyes. Beauty appeared to return the scrutiny. "How will you know what it's time for her to . . . drop her foal?"

"She'll become restless, anxious. She might inspect her flank by turning her head, because she feels a tension there. Lots of little signs."

Still not comfortable being so close to the animal, Lexy stepped away. "I suppose you'll stay with her, then."

"Not likely," he answered.

Surprised, she asked, "Why not?"

He brushed Beauty with a soft-bristled brush. "Horses have an amazing way of timing their own deliveries. They can actually control their contractions. They prefer to have their foals alone. It makes them feel safer."

"What if there's a problem with the delivery?"

"Then I'll be there, because she won't be able to do things instinctively."

Lexy watched him pamper his mount. With a gentleness that made her hungry, he lifted each of Beauty's hooves and probed her shoes. He rubbed her belly. He combed her black mane. He treated his horse with more care and respect than she'd seen many husbands treat their pregnant wives.

Blinking furiously, she glanced away, her thoughts drifting into unsafe waters. She wondered if he would have been as thoughtful with her, had he known. It was a futile exercise in dreaming, for the episode was four years in the past, therefore four years too late.

Yet she found herself imagining him hovering over her as he now hovered over Megan and Beauty. She visualized him lying beside her, gently massaging her abdomen, kissing it, talking softly to their child.

But would he have felt that way about a child of his own, considering how he felt about his future? Would he have perhaps been angry that she had wanted to bring his child into the world, knowing that he would not live to see that child grow to an adult?

After she returned to the cabin, Lexy felt a quiet rage against fate building inside her. She hated her weakness for wanting what she would never have. Jake.

Like *death, survival* was a word that took on different meanings for different people. Lexy knew that for Jake, to survive meant to overcome a tragic history that deprived him of life. For Krista, it was moving to a clime that would help her overcome her physical weakness. For Lexy, it meant existing in a world where the one man she loved would never be.

# Chapter 4

The following morning, Lexy was cleaning vegetables for stew when Little Pete stepped into the kitchen, his battered hat in his hand.

"Excuse me, ma'am. You busy?"

She wiped her hands on her dress. "Not at all. Why?"

He cleared his throat and appeared to study the fancy teapot on the table. "Well, um, there's a farmer 'bout half a mile from here. Name's Frazer. He's got a problem."

Lexy felt the rush of adrenaline. "Someone's hurt?"

"Ah, you could say that," he hedged.

She frowned. "Where's Dr. Westfield?"

He cleared his throat. "Busy. Wants you to take care of it, he says."

Lexy made a face. So, he was sending her pity cases, was he? Well, fine. A patient was a patient. "Let's not waste time talking about it."

On her way out the door, she grabbed her medical bag from the sideboard. The rig was waiting in front of the cabin.

Not far down the road, she saw the farmer waving them down. He had a friendly hound dog appearance, with droopy eyes, oversized earlobes, and jowls that would one day hang loosely over his jaw bones.

"Hurry, Doc. She's in a bad way. A real bad way. I'm afraid it's coming out wrong."

Lexy allowed Little Pete to help her down. "Coming out wrong? She's delivering, Mr. Frazer?"

"Yes, ma'am. It's Millie, and she's bawling something awful."

Alarm mixed with her energy rush as Lexy followed the farmer, having to run to keep up with him. He veered away from the house and strode toward the barn.

"The barn? She's delivering in the barn?" Lexy was aghast. Of all the dirty, bacteria-infested places to have a baby!

"Pete, go to the house and get me some fresh bedding."

He cleared his throat. "I'll be in to give you a hand in a minute."

She tossed him an odd look. Give her a hand? Why would this poor woman want a grizzled old soldier staring at her naked backside? Furthermore, why would he want to? With a shake of her head, she rushed after the farmer.

She stepped inside, the smell of hay and manure mingling in the air. Particles of dust danced in the stream of light coming from a small opening high on the wall, just below the roof. Nothing could be worse. Absolutely nothing! Animals shouldn't even have to have their young in such squalor.

She shot a quick glance around the interior. "Doc?"

The farmer's voice was coming from the other side of a wall. Lexy hurried toward it, stopping short when she met the farmer's gaze. "Well? Where's your wife?"

He gave her a puzzled look. "My wife? Why, she's in the house putting up preserves."

Lexy swallowed. "Your wife isn't about to deliver?"

A slow, amused grin spread across the farmer's weathered face. "Heck, no, ma'am. Millie's my cow."

Lexy shoved back the strangled sound that climbed into her throat. She cleared it, her heart hammering dangerously. "Your . . . cow?"

"Sure," he answered. "You're a vet, ain't you?"

She cleared her throat again. "A . . . vet?"

"Yeah, veter'narian."

Lexy felt a slow burn. "Is that what you were told?"

"Yes, ma'am. Well, not exactly."

Her gaze narrowed. No doubt, Jake was laughing his butt off.

She opened her mouth to correct Farmer Frazer when the cow bawled loudly, as if trying to get their attention. Lexy's gaze wandered slowly to the stall.

Something akin to hailstones rattled around in her stomach. The cow was on her side, raising her head briefly to let out her pathetic cries. Lexy looked toward her tail and saw one tiny, feeble hoof protruding from beneath it.

"I . . . I . . ." Her jaw clattered her back teeth together.

The farmer opened the gate and urged her through. "She's been like this for too long, ma'am. Ordinarily, I can handle it, but this un's different."

She'd never even seen a cow up close. Never. "I'm not a veterinarian," she murmured, unable to take her gaze off the delicate hoof.

"Well, shouldn't matter none," the farmer urged. "Comes out pretty much the same, to my mind."

His words hit home. Yes. Yes, of course. How different could it be? She continued to think about the smug Jake. What had he expected, that she'd come running back to the fort, carrying on like some ninny, just because it was a cow and not a person? To hell with him.

She rolled up her sleeves. "What seems to be the problem?"

"Danged calf is coming out backwards," he answered. "The birth sac has already broke."

Lexy fell to her knees and tentatively touched the cow's flank. "Tell me what's happening, and tell me the right way."

The farmer knelt beside her. "Supposed to come out nose and front legs first," he explained. "This is a hind leg."

Breech, she thought. "Have you tried turning it?"

He shook his head. "My hand's too big." He left for a moment, then returned, resuming his position.

Even though it was an animal, Lexy was loath to touch it without washing her hands.

A pail was placed beside her. She glanced at the farmer, who smiled shyly. "I heard you was a fanatic for being clean."

She flushed, took the hunk of soap he gave her, then dunked her hands into the water.

"I'll hold her down," he offered.

With her hands slick and wet, Lexy said a quick prayer, then moved one hand into the birth canal, carefully forcing the spindly little leg back inside.

The poor animal bellowed and tried to rise, but the farmer was able to settle her.

Suddenly, Little Pete was beside them, lending his strength, trying to soothe the cow. Lexy shot him a quiet *thank you* but vowed to deal with him later. He'd obviously known the circumstances.

A sudden, severe contraction gripped her arm, and she bit down on her lower lip to keep from crying out. When it was over, she felt around for the calf's nose. Finding it, she grasped it carefully and began rotating the baby inside its mother, slowly turning its face toward the opening.

Lexy ignored the awkward angle she was forced to take and continued moving the calf until the nose poked into the fresh air. Within seconds, the cow had another contraction, and moments after Lexy removed her arm, the calf slid from the birth canal.

Lexy slumped to the floor and rested her back against the stall, amazed and exhausted. She watched in awe as the mother began eating away at the afterbirth and licking her calf. Lexy couldn't speak; it was such a miracle. And it was the first time she'd had respect for a dumb animal. How wonderful that Millie intuitively knew what to do. She'd met many new mothers who didn't have the sense that this cow had.

Lexy sat on the dirty stall floor for at least fifteen minutes, watching the calf transform from a lump of flesh curled in a ball to a teetering youngster, testing its ability to stand.

Lexy continued to be amazed. "It's so instinctive, isn't it? Just look at him." The youngster bawled and searched for a food source. Lexy pressed her hands to her chest. This had been a wonderful experience. She would have to thank Jake.

After she punched him in the gut and drove the pointed toe of her Dongola oxford into his instep.

Farmer Frazer grinned at her, sporting a few missing teeth. Feeling exhilarated, Lexy dunked her arms into the water again and washed, scrubbing until she'd nearly broken the skin.

"You done good, Doc."

She blinked and stared up at the farmer. "I did, didn't I?" She studied the mother and her calf. "I've witnessed a lot of births, Mr. Frazer, but I don't believe one of them has affected me like this one."

He helped her to her feet. "The wife'd like you to come in for a piece of pie."

She brushed off her skirt, noting that she was wet all the way down the front. Water or birth fluid, she couldn't be sure which. Touching her hair, she discovered the pins had come loose, and most of her mop hung down her back. She did her best to put herself back together. "Thank you. That would be lovely."

He led her outside, and they passed a shack Lexy

sensed was a pig sty, for oinking and grunting abounded inside. She wrinkled her nose. The odor was telling, too.

Mr. Frazer stopped. "Gotta check on my sow. She just had a litter."

Curious, Lexy followed him inside. If the barn smelled like manure, the sty smelled like something she couldn't even describe. She breathed as little as possible as she looked over the side of the stall. The sight made her laugh.

"Why, they're darling!" Six little pink piglets oinked and grunted and rooted around, jockeying for a place at their mother's bounteous table. How Krista would love them!

"Yep, Hermione is a good mama," the farmer explained, his voice tinged with pride.

Lexy couldn't stop grinning. Never had she seen something so funny and beautiful at the same time. "She certainly seems to be. Why, look how patient she is, lying there while they fight and squirm and squeal."

Almost reluctantly, she followed the farmer from the sty to the house, where she met his wife and children, and ate sweet potato pie heaped with whipped cream.

On the ride home, she glared at Little Pete. "You knew, didn't you?"

He had the decency to blush. "Doc told me not to tell you, 'cause you wouldn't have gone."

"And why couldn't he go himself?"

Little Pete cleared his throat. "Don't know that, ma'am."

It wasn't fair to vent her anger at him. He was obviously just taking orders.

It was Jake who deserved her wrath, and it was Jake who would get it. Sure. Send the little woman to the farm, and see if she has the guts to deliver a calf. She, who hadn't had rapport with an animal her entire life.

God, but that must have given him a good laugh. She hoped he'd ruptured something.

As Jake closed the door to the tiny back room where Joseph slept, he glanced out the window and saw Lexy storming toward his office. Her skirt billowed out behind her, and her cape was caught up in the breeze she created as she moved. Her hair was disheveled, falling from her pins, and with an angry swipe of her hand, she pushed it off her face.

He braced himself and moved from the window as she flung open the door. It cracked as it hit the wall.

She stepped into the room, grabbed the door handle, and swung it shut. Loudly. "You *ass.*"

"I did it for your own good."

Her eyes narrowed. "You sent me there simply to see if I could do it."

"And could you?"

She gave him something that resembled a grin, but it didn't reach her eyes. "I wouldn't give you the satisfaction of failing, you miserable cur. You . . . you sadist."

He hadn't seen her angry since she'd thrown him out of her apartment. "You think I did this to embarrass you?"

She marched up to him, her fists on her hips. There was a strong barn odor about her. He had a brief vision of her scooting around on the dirty hay-covered stall floor. It could have been humorous. Under other circumstances.

"I don't doubt it for a moment." Her eyes glittered like cold pieces of sky.

He hadn't counted on this reaction. Her anger, yes, but not her quickness to judge his reasons for doing it.

"You must get great gratification out of humiliating me. Once wasn't enough, was it?"

Jake nearly flinched. "Believe it or not, I have better things to do than plan embarrassing events for you," he growled. "And I did this *for* you, not *to* you. If you plan to practice out here, you'd better damn well be prepared to do a vet's job, because that's the kind of work you're going to get, whether you want it or not. If you can't deal with that, then you'd better put your sweet ass back on the train and hurry on home to your husband."

The word stunned Lexy so, she was momentarily speechless. Suddenly, her anger was gone. "My . . . what?"

"You heard me," he growled again.

"Yes. I heard you. But why would you think I was married?"

A flash of emotion lit his eyes, then was gone. "You aren't married?"

"I think I'd know if I were," she answered dryly. "What made you think—"

"It doesn't matter now," he interrupted. "My mistake. Getting back to the delivery, I suppose I should have warned you, but would you have gone?"

Still mulling over his comment, she could barely answer. "Possibly. If . . . if you had explained it to me." She stared at him. "Is that why you invited me to the stable last night, to prepare me for today?"

He laughed; it held no humor. "I hardly could have predicted that Millie would have her calf on cue. But a doctor out here is only as good as his willingness to treat cows, pigs, horses, and mules."

He went to his desk and closed a leather-bound book. "If you offer your services to their animals, you may get the family as your patients." His voice was abrupt.

She regarded him. He was intolerant. Blunt. She wondered if he was thinking how upsetting it was that she'd arrived, throwing a monkey wrench into his plans. "You don't really want me here, do you?"

He raised his gaze, snagging hers. "No. I don't."

Everything inside her wept—with anger, pain, regret. She suddenly remembered how he treated Megan. How he catered to her, made sure she was warm, comfortable. Yes, that was why he wanted her gone.

Lexy prayed nothing would ever happen to Max, for she had a sinking feeling that if something did, Jake would be there to pick up the pieces and would stay on indefinitely.

He sat at his desk and shuffled some papers. He sniffed and made a face. "If I were you, I think I'd bathe. You're beginning to take on the squalid characteristics of a mule."

Heat from the insult spread into her scalp. "At least I have an excuse. You, on the other hand, appear to come by it naturally."

She tossed her mop of hair over her shoulder, drew her cape around her, and sailed from the room.

Jake's smile was grim. His remark had probably been uncalled for, but her announcement that she wasn't married to Ben Stillwater had left him adrift, like flotsam on the sea. It had been easier to deal with her when he'd thought she was married. And his reasons to believe that she was were sound. Ben had told him so. Or had he?

He flipped to the back pocket of his journal, drew out the folded letters from Ben Stillwater, and reread them. A wry smile touched Jake's lips. What a clever son of a bitch.

*I have asked her to marry me.*

Not *she has agreed to marry me.*

He stared at his notes about Jasper Hansen, but Lexy's spirited face kept interfering. Growling a curse, he shoved his chair back. The door opened, and Pete poked his head in.

"Anything I can do for you, Doc?"

Jake crossed to where Joseph slept, opened the door, and checked him, making sure he was sleeping soundly. "Keep an eye on Joseph. I'll be back in a while."

As he crossed to the stable, his gaze found Lexy. She

marched toward Megan's cabin, her bright hair, loose from its pins, floating around her like a long gold cape.

She was right. He didn't want her here. Now more than ever, he wanted her gone. And it didn't matter what he wanted, anyway. She had successfully detached herself from her feelings for him; he'd discovered that the first time he talked with her.

But Jake knew her only too well. He knew her determination. Her drive. Her stubborn nature. As he rode toward the Hansen farm, he knew it would take more than delivering a few calves or treating a couple of semifriendly Indians to scare her off. Her interest in the whorehouse had given her away. He could almost read her mind.

Maybe the best lesson was to let her practice out here for a while. Let her try it on her own. With maybe just a little help from him. He'd have to talk to Commander Billings about the whorehouse. Soften the old man up. Assure him it wouldn't be long before Lexy Tate hightailed it back to safety.

He found Jasper waiting.

"Now," Jake began, directing his conversation to Jasper. "Let me hear about that friend of yours. That Oriental."

Jasper Hansen nodded. "Yep. Well, he weren't really no friend, but when we first came to California, them Chinamen grew rice on land not far from here. We kinda got to know each other. They was a private bunch, didn't mingle with us much. But I watched them work, watched what they planted other than rice, and got to figgerin' that maybe it was them things that helped them live so danged long."

"What other things did they eat besides rice?"

"Veg'tables. Some strange kinds we ain't seen around here, not before or since. Carrots and such, too. And they fished the river a lot, bringin' home lots of fresh fish."

"Where are they now?" Jake asked, curious.

Jasper shook his head. "Dunno. One day, they just up and left."

"Tell me about this . . . this nephew of theirs. The one who moved to San Francisco."

Jasper pulled out a snuff pouch and poked some into his mouth, hiding it in his cheek. "Yep. After a few years, his nephew returned to settle some family business. Everyone was sure surprised at how he looked."

Jake gestured. "How he looked? You mean his physical appearance?"

"He was bloated. His skin had poor texture, wasn't healthy-lookin'."

Jake massaged the back of his neck. "And they attributed that to what, exactly?"

"To the way he was livin' once he left the family."

Jake gazed at the garden. It was four times the size of anyone else's out here, and it was as well cared for as a precious woman.

"And where is this nephew now?"

"Died, I guess. Only twenty-eight, if I remember right."

"What was the cause?"

"Danged if I know. I do remember the old China-man sayin' that his nephew had started drinkin' a lot of whiskey and eatin' stuff we eat, you know, meat and potatoes and the like."

Jake tapped the pad against his chin. His studies of the Chinese while he was finishing medical school proved his theory. With their Spartan lifestyle and diets of rice and vegetables and very little meat, they outlived any people he'd ever known. But why? Was it because of what they ate, or was it simply their genetic makeup?

He muttered a curse. It all probably meant nothing. He'd known men in Providence who had smoked cigars, drunk like fish, and eaten like Henry the Eighth who had outlived their tea-drinking, bird-eating, straight-laced wives. He had no doubt that alcohol caused liver damage, but how in the hell could he prove that certain types of food caused heart damage? It couldn't be done.

He checked the rash on Jasper's forearm again. It hadn't improved. "I doubt this is from something you've eaten; it's probably something you've come in contact with outside. Either way, it's not serious."

Jake instructed Jasper to use the laurel powder he'd brought with him to prevent the itching, wishing he had access to baking soda instead. But truthfully, the herbal remedies worked extremely well, and each time he found one that did the job, he felt a surge of satisfaction. He only wished his other dilemmas were as easily remedied.

Upon his return to the fort, he drew his journal from under his mattress, settled into a chair, and began to write.

*13 June. Jasper Hansen—in excellent physical condition, currently eating a diet similar to the Chinese. No meat. Fresh vegetables and rice. Currently has a rash on torso and arms. Treated with laurel powder.*

He flipped through the journal, his gaze resting on one of his earliest entries.

*22 March. Crude autopsy performed on indigent laborer. Cause of death, massive blood clot lodged in left carotid artery. Arteries thick with yellow fatty substance, as seen in autopsies at Brown. Under microscopic inspection, substance continues to appear thick and viscous.*

He closed his journal and stared at the plain leather cover. What in the devil was that material, and why was it not always there? How many times had he wondered if it had been in his father's arteries, and his uncles'? And, he thought, his chest tightening, in his?

It was obvious that the fatty substance clogged the arteries, preventing proper blood flow. He'd dissected hearts that had dead portions where the arteries had been completely clogged, disallowing a blood supply altogether. How many had to be plugged before a major event took place, rendering a patient either near death or dead?

He opened the bottom drawer of his desk and drew out the paper he was working on. He intended to have it published, once he came upon a proper conclusion. His mentor at Stanford, with whom he corresponded regularly, had all but assured him it was a subject worthy of publication.

He skimmed through the papers, replaced them, then crossed to the window and looked out at the compound. For the moment, he had to pull his thoughts away from the work that he wasn't being paid for and concentrate on the new recruits.

With Max gone, Jake felt an obligation to keep an eye on them. Most of them were raw country boys, anxious for adventure. A couple had chips on their shoulders. One in particular. A fierce Irishman named O'Brien. He had to watch them all. They were too anxious to fight. Too anxious to *pick* fights. Jake understood them too well.

Lexy had just hung the last of her wrapping strips on the line when Dooley lumbered toward her from across the compound. At the mammoth sight of him, an involuntary shiver stole up her spine.

"Is Joseph all right?" She felt a nibble of guilt at not checking on him when she was at Jake's office. But then, poor little Joseph hadn't been foremost on her mind.

"Him fine. Dooley want you to look at neck."

Lexy drew in an anxious breath as the big Indian

casually and without hesitation strode into Megan's cabin. She hoped Megan was napping. Once inside, he headed straight for the kitchen and plopped himself onto a chair by the table.

"All right, now, what's the problem?" she asked, attempting to sound as casual as he looked.

He turned his head and lifted his hair off his shoulders, exposing the back of his neck. "Dooley hear you deliver a calf."

She gave him a dry look. "News travels fast." Bending close, she noted the formation of a large pimple that would surely become a boil.

"If you can deliver a calf, you can treat Dooley, but Twisted Nose Doctor not happy I come."

She frowned. "Twisted Nose Doctor?"

With a nod, Dooley answered, "Medicine man."

Lexy's heart beat faster than usual. "Oh. Your . . . your medicine man." She hesitated briefly. "Will he be angry?"

Dooley shrugged. "With you, not me."

Lexy forced a weak smile. "Thanks a lot," she murmured under her breath. Crossing to the dry sink to wash her hands, she asked, "How long have you had the pimple, Dooley?"

"Don't know. Dooley notice it this morning."

"You'll need a poultice to draw out the pus. I'll have to prepare one, so don't leave, all right?"

She went into the bedroom, took out a box from one of her trunks, and returned to the kitchen. Megan stood just inside the door, staring at the Indian, her hands flat against the wall.

"Oh, Meggie, we'll be out of your hair in a minute. I have to prepare a poultice for Dooley's boil."

Megan paled. "In . . . in my kitchen?"

Suddenly realizing how revolting it sounded, she hurried to apologize. "Oh. Of course not. We can do it on the porch—"

"No, really, Lexy, it's all right." Megan swallowed hard. "This once, anyway." She stepped close to her sister and whispered, "It's just that . . . I've never had a . . . a savage Indian in my kitchen before."

Lexy felt awful. "We'll hurry," she promised. She rushed through the preparation of the poultice, mixing carbolic acid, cocaine, and ergot extract together with an egg yolk and some salt. She held the poultice to Dooley's neck with a soft cloth, which she tied around his neck.

"I'll want to change that in the morning," she instructed.

Dooley stood, his head nearly touching the ceiling. "You deliver a calf, you can treat Dooley."

She watched him leave, feeling a giddy elation along with the new fear she had of her Indian counterpart, Twisted Nose Doctor.

As she returned her supplies to the trunk, she began to think more and more about the brothel. The more she thought, the more excited she became.

Poking her head into the kitchen, she found Megan sitting at the table with a cup of tea. She looked tired. Lexy knew her decision was a wise one. "I'm going to find the commander, and when I come back, I want to find you lying down, resting."

She didn't find the commander at his quarters. As she wandered toward the shed where they kept the feed for the animals, she heard angry voices. She moved closer.

"You're a cheat."

Lexy stopped and held her breath as a small table was upended, sending playing cards flying.

A number of men stepped back, their expressions anxious.

Jake stood slowly. "I don't cheat."

The new recruit balled and unballed his fists. His face was red, his eyes hot with anger. "I say you cheat, and I want my money back."

Jake crossed his arms over his chest. "The game was fair, O'Brien. Learn to play, or get used to losing."

O'Brien glanced at the others, appearing uncertain of his next move. Suddenly, he stepped close to Jake, pulled a gun, and shoved it at Jake's temple.

Lexy gasped and pressed her hands to her mouth, her heart in her throat.

"I want my money back, you cheating bastard, or so help me, I'll drop you where you stand."

Lexy's gaze was glued to Jake. She could hardly breathe.

A smile, cold and careless, spread slowly over Jake's features. His eyes were expressionless. He looked dangerous. Remote. Almost cruel. Nevertheless, Lexy felt the telltale flutterings she always did when she saw him.

"Go ahead," Jake taunted.

O'Brien began to bluster, then he laughed, a strained, harsh, nervous sound. "You're crazier than a two-headed buzzard with worms in his ass."

Jake didn't answer O'Brien's levity. "Grow up, O'Brien. Next time you threaten someone, he may not be as generous with you as I've been."

Lexy stumbled behind the shed and slumped against the wall. The scene she'd just witnessed was proof that Jake still didn't care whether he lived or died.

Perhaps she should quit trying to believe he would change. It would certainly make her life easier.

She waited until her heart rate was normal, then stepped out from behind the shed.

Lifting an eyebrow, Jake walked toward her. "Meeting someone special behind the woodshed?" His tone was light, casual.

She glared at him, her hands on her hips. "You'll never change, will you?"

The recruits had gone their separate ways, but the table was still on its side, the cards scattered over the ground. "Oh. You heard."

"I thought that maybe you'd outgrown your childish desire to tempt fate."

"You mean O'Brien? That was nothing. He was merely spreading his tail feathers."

"But he could have meant it, Jake."

He stared into the distance, his expression unreadable. "Maybe. But then, we all have to go sometime, don't we?"

Despite the flippant tone, Lexy noted a hungry edge to his words. She stared at the toes of her kid oxfords, generously coated with dust, and dug one toe into the dirt. She absently noted the powdery dust that clung to the hem of her black serge skirt.

"I thought earning your degree would have changed your attitude," she finally said.

"Yeah, maybe if I cut up enough corpses, I'll discover what killed my old man. Then, if I can prevent it from happening to me, I'll make plans to live a long and fruitful life."

His sarcasm stung. "I hope you do, Jake. I really hope you do."

"Don't hold your breath." He turned and walked away.

Lexy stared after him, chewing on her bottom lip. He looked upon his life as a tragedy. No one could convince him otherwise. She was a fool to think that anything she said to him would make the slightest bit of difference.

With a weary sigh, she remembered her purpose. Gathering her thoughts and her poise, she went in search of the commander.

She found him at his residence. An hour later, she had him reluctantly persuaded to let her use the brothel at a rent she could afford.

Lexy woke the following morning refreshed, even though she'd slept little. She hadn't even seen the inside of the building, and she had already planned out an office. Commander Billings had offered her a few men, not on a regular basis but as he could spare them, to help her get the building into shape.

His wife had been an eager champion, delighted that a woman was going to set up a practice, promising her she would seek her out when she had "female problems," and promising as well that she would champion Lexy's cause in town, to the women there. It was a positive start.

The commander had been concerned for her safety, but after he heard how she'd treated Joseph, he felt that with Dooley in her corner, she would be well protected.

Lexy released Joseph early, surprised not to find Jake in his office. Dooley had carried his son away, his expression appreciative. He wasn't much of a talker.

She wandered over the grass toward the stable. Ever since she'd delivered that sweet little calf, she'd been curious about her reaction to other animals. She wondered if it had changed.

She stopped off at the cabin, dropped a few lumps of sugar in the pocket of her wrapper, then continued toward the stable.

The smell of horse flesh and hay floated toward her, and she breathed it in as she stepped into the stable's interior. Beauty whickered from her stall, and Lexy crossed to her and tentatively rubbed the horse's nose.

"Good morning, Beauty," Lexy said, offering a lump of sugar. When Beauty nuzzled her palm, Lexy bit back a sound of surprise at the sensation of the horse's muzzle against her skin and forced herself not to jump.

She offered her the second one. "Your whiskers tickle."

With surprising grace and elegance, Beauty lifted the sugar cube from Lexy's palm.

"You're quite a lady, Beauty." And a lucky one, Lexy thought, remembering Jake's obvious affection for the mount. She touched Beauty's mane, gently smoothing her hand over it, feeling the coarse texture against her fingers.

Her gaze wandered the length and breadth of the

horse, and again she was in awe of its size. "So. You're going to have a baby." She tentatively moved her hand to Beauty's flank. "He treats you with such love, girl. Do you know that? There isn't a woman alive who wouldn't want that kind of attention."

Beauty whickered, briefly startling her. She shook her head in dismay. She might be able to feed a horse a bit of sugar, but she still couldn't ride one. She hoped she never had to. Well, one step at a time.

Beauty reared her head, causing Lexy to jump away. *Goose,* she scolded herself.

She moved farther inside, her eyes becoming accustomed to the dimness and her nose getting used to the smell. As she gazed at the tiny streams of light that poked through the rustic boards, she felt a shiver of unease.

A noise pricked her ears, and she followed it to the back of the building. She came to a dead stop. There, standing before a crude table that held a bucket of water, was Jake, stripped to the waist, washing.

Unwanted, unwilling desire burst inside her, burning hot. He was magnificent. He was perfection. An anatomist's dream. She longed to touch the places where the muscle was taut, where it pulled tight, where it narrowed into sinew, where it bulged and relaxed with movement.

The hair on his chest, black and thick, tapered to a fine line as it slipped beneath his jeans. She stared, noting with mounting alarm that they were unbuttoned and hung low on his hips. A wedge of hair, secret and dark, grew beneath his navel. She dared not look any lower.

She must have made a sound, for when she glanced at his face, she found him watching her. Her mouth moved, but nothing came out.

"Good morning." He picked up a towel and rubbed it leisurely across his chest.

Lexy's mouth went dry, and she tried not to look at

him. "Good morning." She studied the wall behind him with interest.

"Did Beauty recognize you?"

She flushed, wondering if he'd heard her entire one-sided conversation. "Oh, didn't you hear?"

He regarded her, his eyes disconcerting. Gentle.

Emotion rushed inside her, storming her heart. "She told me men are ninnies when it comes to pregnant mares. She said," Lexy hurried on, "if the stallion she mated with had been as caring and concerned as you, she wouldn't have been attracted to him at all. She likes her studs rough and wild."

She always blathered on when she was nervous, and a half-naked Jake Westfield made her very, very nervous.

He chuckled, still rubbing himself with the towel, seeming to concentrate on areas that would have drawn Lexy's gaze no matter what. "Is that the way you like yours?"

She focused on the wall, remembering how she had longed for Jake to treat her the way he'd treated Beauty. "In case you hadn't noticed, I'm not a mare."

"Oh, I've noticed, all right."

His voice held appreciation, and that enhanced her topsy-turvy feelings. Out of the corner of her eye, she could tell he was buttoning up his pants.

She cleared her throat; the sound was strangled.

"Something wrong?" he asked.

"No. I mean, of course not. I mean, I didn't know you were here, or I wouldn't have—" She let out a whoosh of air.

"You wouldn't have what?" He was toying with the top button, pushing it in and out of the buttonhole.

Her gaze was on his hairy navel, and her thaw threatened to drown her. "I wouldn't have interrupted your bath."

"Then I'm glad you didn't know I was here."

Her blush deepened. "Now, don't go thinking—"

"Thinking what, Lex? That you came looking for me? Hoping to find me naked?"

Her jaw dropped. Another time, another place, and she might have appreciated the good-natured teasing. But not now. His constant ability to send her mixed messages confused and angered her.

"You are so arrogant. Just because . . . just because you . . . just because I . . . we—"

"Made love?" he finished, grinning at her.

She tried to ignore him as he shrugged into his shirt. "I'd hardly call it that."

"And what would you call it?" he urged, his gaze causing a fluttering low in her belly.

"I'd say we had sex. Pure and simple." She had forced a hardness into her voice that she felt nowhere else in her entire body. "Making love requires two people who care about each other."

His gaze continued to taunt her. "And you didn't care for me, is that it?"

She wanted his bantering to stop there, for to allow him to continue would have merely weakened her further. "Oh, I cared for you. But then, I knew who I was with."

He had the grace to look away, but he didn't argue with her. "Touché."

When he'd completed buttoning his shirt, she felt more in control. "I don't like the way you're treating Megan."

"What?"

She swallowed, finding it difficult to continue. "You treat her like . . . like a wife rather than a friend." There. She'd said it. His eyes changed, and she couldn't read his gaze.

"Max left me in charge, Lexy. Not of the fort but of his family. *His* wife, pregnant with *his* unborn child. What would you like me to do? Ignore her?" He swore. "She's a damned hard woman to ignore, as you well know."

"You still have feelings for her," she accused.

"Feelings?" He snorted a laugh. "I have feelings, all right, but I think they'd surprise you."

His answer puzzled her. "But you hovered over her the other night, acting like . . . like a husband."

His mouth curved into a hard smile. "Do I detect a note of envy?"

"Of course not," she huffed. "It's disgusting the way you fawn over her, that's all. But then, I suppose it's hard to get over someone you've cared about for so long."

He gave her a long, lingering look, one that made her uncomfortable. "Yes. It is."

She fussed with her wrapper pocket, then turned away. She refused to analyze his answer. One way or another, it would bother her. "Well, I'd best get back to the cabin."

"Yes, you'd best," he mimicked.

She hurried from the stable, stopping briefly outside the door, hoping to calm herself. Until the day she'd given herself to Jake, she'd scoffed at women who allowed themselves to be seduced. Any sensible, intelligent woman could prevent it, she'd thought. And she'd thought it very strongly. And here she was, silly ninny-goose fool that she was, finding herself seduced all over again merely by his innocent teasing.

Lifting her skirts, she ran over gravel and weeds until she reached the cabin. She scrambled up the porch steps and flung herself into Megan's chair, hiding her face in her hands. This was not how things were supposed to be.

It didn't matter that she loved him. It didn't even matter to her that he probably still loved Megan. What mattered most of all was that Jake would never be hers.

Resting her head against the back of the chair, she wondered how she would handle Jake once he learned of Krista. If he changed because of the birth of his daughter, could Lexy forgive him for not even once trying to get in touch with her? She wasn't even sure she wanted him back in her life.

Those thoughts and questions were fantasy. She drew in a breath and released it slowly, trying to calm herself. Reality was, could they live in the same town, and if they did, could she ignore him?

Something would have to be done once Krista arrived, but heaven help her, Lexy didn't know what it was.

# Chapter 5

Lexy and Megan were having their second cup of tea when there was a commotion on the porch. Megan rose to check, but Lexy stopped her.

"I'll go."

She stepped outside, confronting Dooley. "Good morning. I'm glad you're here. We can change the poultice."

Dooley gazed at the porch floor and stepped from one foot to the other. "First Dooley have something for you."

Lexy brightened. "Really? What is it?"

He nodded over the porch railing.

Lexy stepped past him and peered over the side. There was a crate on the ground, and strange noises were coming from it. Her stomach convulsed, but she hid her uncertainty. "That . . . that's for me? But why?"

"You make Joseph better. You treat Dooley's neck. Dooley has no money to pay you."

Livestock. Lexy swallowed hard. "You . . . you don't have to pay me, Dooley."

"Dooley want to."

One look, and she knew he meant it. Now was not the time to cause bad feelings. "Well, thank you, Dooley. Thank you so much."

Dooley nodded, padded down the steps, and strode away.

With dismay, Lexy left the porch and walked to the box. Squatting, she peeked between the boards, then closed her eyes and sighed. Chickens.

Megan came outside and glanced over at her from the porch. "Sounds like chickens."

Lexy gave her a weak smile. "A gift from Dooley for treating him and Joseph." She inhaled sharply. "Oh, I forgot to change his poultice."

Megan's face filled with menacing glee. "The chickens befuddled my stalwart sister so much she forgot her duties."

"It's not that funny," Lexy scolded.

"Well, we can always have them for supper."

"Eat them? You expect me to eat them?"

"That's why he gave them to you, to eat."

Lexy's hand went to her heart. "No." She shook her head violently. "Absolutely not. I refuse to eat something I've seen alive."

Megan laughed, truly amused at Lexy's expense. "You're not serious."

Lexy returned to the porch and planted her fists on her hips. "I'm dead serious."

"What are you going to do with them?"

"I don't know. But I'll think of something."

But it wasn't easy to think about chickens when she knew that the following morning, she would get her first glimpse of the inside of her new office. Whorehouse or not, it was the beginning of Lexy's dream. And she was determined to make it come true.

From her seat on the wagon, Lexy listened to her chickens squawk in their crate behind her. "They're sure noisy little things," she groused.

Little Pete chuckled beside her. "You shoulda left them with the cook."

"No. I will not have them killed."

"So," he continued, amusement lacing his words, "you're gonna keep them as pets."

With a thoughtful nod, she answered, "Yes. I just might."

"You'll have to name them," he suggested.

Name them. Oh, this was getting entirely out of hand. She didn't want them, she refused to give them away, and she couldn't eat them. Well, she'd think of something.

"So, what do you think, Doc?"

"What?"

"How about Hazel and Hortense?"

She frowned at him, puzzled.

"For the hens. Hazel and Hortense."

She felt herself giving in, not because she was softening in her attitude toward critters but because she didn't know what else to do. "Will I get eggs?"

"I imagine ya will," Pete answered.

"Then I guess there's no hope for it. Hazel and Hortense it is."

He roared, the guffaw of a man truly amused. "I can see it now. People from miles around'll come and gawk at the eccentric lady sawbones who has set up an office in a whorehouse and who keeps chickens as pets."

She tried to send him a dangerous look, but he made her smile. "Laugh all you want. Make fun of me, if it pleases you, but I'm not changing my mind."

How could she? It wasn't that she wanted the darned things, but to get rid of them meant that someone would surely kill them and eat them. She shuddered at the thought. And at the memory of the countless chicken dinners she'd eaten in her lifetime. This was her penance.

The brothel came into view, and Lexy felt a surge of excitement.

"Excited, Doc?"

He'd started calling her that, and she preferred it over "ma'am." "You read my mind."

When they pulled into the weed-snarled yard, she jumped from the wagon and sprinted to the door, shoving it open.

It squeaked on reluctant rusted hinges. Lexy shivered but stepped inside, refusing to let go of the remainder of her excitement, even though the inside of the house was, well, almost beyond description.

Cobwebs draped the doorways. Dust sifted through the air, settling on what she presumed was a sofa beneath a worn blanket. She crossed to where it stood in the corner, lifted the blanket, and discovered the sofa was covered with what had once been a rich velvet fabric. It was a bawdy red, but it was velvet. Telltale holes sprouted in the seat, suggesting mice, and tiny round droppings scattered over the surface verified it. Except for a table with a broken leg, it was the only piece of furniture in the room.

"Seems as if everything else has been taken. I wonder why no one hauled this thing away."

Little Pete scratched his beard. "It's kind of appropriate that it was left behind. I imagine it would have quite a tale to tell if it could talk."

Lexy shot him a look of disapproval, but he merely grinned at her.

Surveying the room, she tried to envision a clean, light office with clean, light examining rooms. It wasn't easy.

They toured the house, finding most rooms empty but now and then discovering a rickety nightstand or wardrobe. All of the wallpaper was gaudy, much in reds and gold. Most of it would have to go.

Little Pete came up behind her. "Shore nice of Doc Jake to talk the commander into lettin' ya use this place, wasn't it?"

Her stomach dipped, and she bristled. "Jake talked to him?"

"He didn't tell ya?"

She reined in her anger. "No. I guess it slipped his mind."

"Well, ol' Doc Monroe wouldn'ta wanted you within fifty miles of him. Hated women. Hated 'em. Never took him a wife."

While she simmered in her stew of fury, she calmly asked, "And you, Pete?" She looked up at him, noting the crinkles in the corners of his eyes. "Are you married?"

"Oh, no, Doc. Who'd have a big lummox like me? Can't sing worth a darn, can't dance, ain't got two nickels to rub together, and I don't like bathin'. Ain't no woman gonna want to tackle a man with bad habits like that."

She smiled at his candor. "You never know, Pete. You just never know. There are plenty of women who could do a whole lot worse, believe me."

He blushed. "I can't rightly imagine one."

"They say there's someone out there for everyone."

"What about you, Doc?"

"Me?" She forced a laugh. "I'm too busy to worry about that."

He shook his head, clearly disagreeing. "That's a shame. A pretty woman like yerself oughta have a husband."

"Yes, well," she answered, nervously dusting an old lamp with the hem of her wrapper, "we're not all meant to marry, Pete."

At that moment, Jake stepped into the room. Lexy gave him a cool smile.

"Is that right, Doc Jake?"

"What's that, Pete?"

"The doc here says everyone ain't meant to marry."

Jake studied her, his expression masked. "I imagine she's right."

"But ain't it a shame? Why, she'd make some man a fine wife, don't you agree?"

Lexy flushed, wishing she could blend into the woodwork.

"Yes," Jake answered, sounding bored. "If a man could get past her prickly, independent exterior."

His words hurt, especially when he was the reason she was prickly in the first place. But she was proud of her independence. "Well, thank you both very much for analyzing my desirability as a mate. However, I don't think either of you has room to talk."

Pete chuckled. "I sure as hell don't, yer right about that."

Jake said nothing, but his dismal gaze said more than words.

Lexy refused to pity him, and he would not wish it. "Jake," she continued, her chin jutting dangerously, "did you talk the commander into letting me use this place?"

His gaze narrowed briefly, and he rubbed the back of his neck with his palm. "I did."

She gave him a cold smile. "I suppose I owe you a thank you, but for some reason, I don't think you did it as a favor."

"What other reason could there be?"

She leaned against the door and crossed her arms over her chest. "I imagine you did it to hurry me out of here."

He gave her a dry, lopsided smile. "You always were the clever one."

"I'm not leaving, Jake. You can send every unsavory derelict in California to me for treatment. You can drive cattle to my door, insisting I examine each and every one. You can force me to castrate a bull, if you like, and I'll find a way to do it." She narrowed him a frosty gaze. "In fact, I think I'd rather enjoy it, if I can use a rusty knife and make you watch."

He lifted an eyebrow. "A bit vicious, aren't we?"

"Yes. *We* are. But if you thought that by forcing me to work under less than satisfactory conditions you could make me leave, then you'll be disappointed. Sorely disappointed."

"We'll see about that." With that cryptic response, he turned and left the room.

Little Pete scratched his head and frowned. "You two sure got a bitter feelin' between ya. Sure is too bad. I'da thought you'd have been perfect for each other."

Giving him a long-suffering sigh, Lexy wandered toward the front of the brothel. Jake might want her gone, but she wasn't going anywhere. She'd make it out here. It didn't matter what he did to try to send her away.

Upon returning to the fort, Jake met Megan in her garden. "How are you feeling?"

She blushed, which she always did when Jake asked about her condition. "I'm fine. Just fine."

"You know, one of these days, I'm going to have to examine you."

"Lexy can do it," she said too quickly.

He nodded. "Yes, I suppose she can. You would prefer that, I expect?"

She gave him a curt nod, and for once, her expression was naked, void of pretense and vanity.

"Then you'd better ask her to do it soon." He turned to leave.

"Jake?" When he acknowledged her, she leaned on her hoe and put her fingers to her mouth. "I do have questions . . ."

He actually felt some sympathy. "If you're more comfortable talking with your sister, I suggest that you do so."

"I . . . yes. I will. I mean, after all, she went through—" She stopped, the color draining from her face.

Jake was instantly alert. "She went through what?"

Megan shook her head and clamped her mouth shut. Jake went to her side. "Are you all right?"

She gave him a weak smile. "Go. Please go before I say something I shouldn't."

Curious now, Jake probed. "Like what?"

She shook her head again. "Something I promised I wouldn't."

He quirked a smile. "You never were very good at keeping a secret, Meggie."

Her face crumpled, and she was nearly in tears. "I know, I know, but this time I don't want to say anything. Jake, please don't make me."

There were times when she was actually sensitive. "All right. I won't probe. Have Lexy examine you, though, or I'll come back and torture you," he teased.

But as he walked away, his curiosity was primed. Fortunately, he didn't want to dwell on it. Instead, he returned to his office and dug out his journal, turning to one of the early entries:

*17 June 1893. The material clogging a heart attack victim's arteries continues to elude me. Even studying it under a microscope hasn't given me any brilliant ideas. I have poured over the journals I have received and have found nothing useful. Perhaps my observations will be the first in print—if they elect to print something that sounds so outrageous. The material I see has the consistency of fat, the sort that one skins from a chicken. I find it hard to believe that eating too much fat is the cause; surely it can't be as simple as that.*

But he uncapped his fountain pen and began a letter to his mentor at Stanford, mentioning his new insights with enthusiasm. He also wrote of the diet differences among the Chinese, the Indians, and the whites. More often than not, the answering correspondence helped Jake sort things out in his mind.

He was also putting his research to the test by

eliminating fatty foods from his own diet. Quietly, of course, for medicine was full of doctors who felt that fat in the diet was what kept a person healthy. Jake wasn't entirely sure they were wrong, but if he didn't test out his theory on himself, how would he ever know?

He put down his pen and stared at his letter. He was running out of time. And with each day that passed, he felt a bit more urgency to stay alive. To live long. To grow old. To have children. A daughter with butter-scotch hair; a son to pass on his name. The dreams of every man. Live long enough to see his children's children.

He swore again, restraining from crumpling the letter and tossing it across the room. He was punishing himself. The worst of it was, he'd been doing it more often, ever since Lexy had reentered his misera-ble, stagnant life.

She wasn't married. It didn't matter. Actually, it just made things worse.

Reluctant to leave Megan alone, for upon examina-tion she appeared ripe, Lexy decided to bring her along to the new clinic nearly every day the following week.

Lexy was also a little concerned, for with her stethoscope she was unable to hear two heartbeats even though Megan was indeed becoming larger.

While Lexy worked on cleaning the old wood stove in the kitchen, Megan sat at the table behind her, rolling bandages.

"I want you to know," Megan began, "that I've kept your secret about Krista. I haven't told a soul."

Lexy wiped her nose with the back of her hand, hoping to avoid getting dirt on her face. "I appreciate that, Meggie."

"Tell me something," Megan continued.

"If I can."

"When I finally have this baby, will it hurt?"

Lexy couldn't give her any false hopes. "There will probably be some discomfort. I'd like to tell you there won't, but you might as well be prepared for the worst, and if it turns out to be an easy delivery, then we'll both be delighted."

Megan's hands paused around a rolled-up bandage. "I hope Max returns soon."

*Amen to that,* Lexy thought. She wasn't usually a pessimistic person, but with each passing day, she worried that something had happened to her brother-in-law to prevent his return.

Lexy swept up the charred wood chips from the stove and dumped them into a basket. The day was warm, and she was perspiring. She glanced at Megan, who sat without so much as a moist sheen to her forehead.

Lexy wiped her face with the hem of her wrapper. "Good Lord, doesn't it ever cool off out here?"

Megan smiled. "Sometime in October, we should see some cool weather, along with rain."

"October?" Lexy expelled a mouthful of air. "If I didn't need this kind of weather for Krista's sake, I'd opt for a cooler climate."

"I agree it takes some getting used to," Megan mused, "but I much prefer this to that horrid Rhode Island weather."

Lexy picked up the basket of charred wood chips and crossed to the door leading outside to the stoop. "I'll be back shortly."

She stepped out just as one of the recruits was striding up the hill toward her. He carried a string of fish.

"Oh!" she said, delighted. "Where did you catch those?"

He nodded behind him. "There's a spring-fed creek down the hill, ma'am. I thought you and Miz York might like them for supper."

"That sounds wonderful. Thank you very much."

The thought of cool water was inviting. She dropped the basket on the stoop and swung open the door. "Meggie, there's a creek nearby. Let's go dangle our feet."

Megan waved the thought away. "I'm perfectly comfortable here, Lexy, but you go ahead."

Hesitant to leave her alone, Lexy asked, "Are you sure you'll be all right?"

Megan leveled her a gaze. "I haven't had one contraction yet. I'm sure I won't be having this baby in the next hour. Now, go."

Lexy nearly skipped all the way to the water's edge. It was no wonder she hadn't noticed it before, for it was well hidden from the house and the road by thick patches of scrub oak and willow trees.

She sank to the ground, pulled off her shoes, and rolled down her stockings, carefully placing each stocking into a shoe. Scooting to the water, she dipped her feet in and uttered a sigh. This was heaven. But after a few moments of splashing her feet around, she knew it was not enough. After pulling her wrapper off over her head, she unbuttoned a few of the buttons on her gown, wantonly wishing she dared shuck everything she was wearing, down to her drawers and chemise.

She took the handkerchief from the pocket of her discarded wrapper, dipped it into the water, and brought it to her face and throat. After a moment, she hiked up her gown and stepped into the water, discovering a flat, sandy bottom just beyond the shore.

Bringing the back of her gown between her legs, she fashioned a pair of makeshift trousers and began wading downstream. The sand felt squishy between her toes, and she dug them deeper into the cool bottom as she sloshed through the water. The air didn't seem quite so hot here. A cool breeze blew gently off the small river.

She continued downstream, curious about the path the river took and why she hadn't noticed it before, for it appeared to curve and widen in the direction of the fort. The trees along the shoreline changed as well, growing out and over the water as if trying to reach each other in the middle. Some had, creating a shady canopy. And the water was noisier, had more momentum as it churned across the rocks and debris, creating a freshness in the air.

She kept toward the shore but now and then tempted fate by stepping further out into the water. She longed to be as cool all over as her legs and feet were.

All at once, the current became stronger, and she felt it pull at her legs. Trying to keep her balance, she reached for an overhanging branch, clinging to it until she could right herself. But the flow was strong, and it dragged her, pulling her feet out from under her.

With a scream and a yelp, she released the branch and found herself on her back, plunging toward the center of the river. Try as she might, she couldn't get her footing. The current turned her onto her stomach and forced her on. Lexy spat out a mouthful of water only to have another forced in. She flailed her arms, attempting to regain her balance, but it was no use.

The water was deeper here, deep enough so that she couldn't touch the bottom. Her clothing weighed her down, and her hair came loose, slapping around her face, obscuring her vision when she was able to keep her head above water.

Out of the corner of her eye, she saw someone on the shore. "Help!" she sputtered. "Please, help me!" She was pulled under again. The cold water churned around her, as if taunting her, tempting her.

In a matter of moments, she felt a strong pair of arms around her, dragging her to the surface. Closer to shore, she was able to get her footing.

She worked hard to catch her breath as she crumpled onto the grass. "Oh, dear heaven," she said,

panting. "It got deep so quickly, I lost my footing. If you hadn't been there—"

She raised her gaze to her savior, and her heart dropped. "Oh, it's you."

Jake shook the hair from his eyes. "You're welcome," he said, his voice laced with sarcasm. "Now, what in the hell did you think you were doing?"

She felt foolish. Imprudent. Especially now, when Jake had to save her. "I was merely wading in the river. It . . . it got wild and deep rather suddenly, and I wasn't prepared for it." She grabbed a length of hair and twisted the water from it before tossing it over her shoulder.

"And you don't have to snap at me. I didn't nearly drown to ruin your day, Jake. Had I known you were here, I certainly wouldn't have come this way. The less contact we have with each other, the bet—"

His mouth came down hard on hers, and she grasped his shoulders to prevent herself from falling backward. The kiss took her breath away, creating an ache in her chest that dissolved any fight she might have thought to make. Her fingers roamed his shoulders, his chest, his back, and she hugged him to her, answering every pounding facet of his kiss.

His palm cradled her head, and he bent her over his arm, drawing her gently to the ground. He threw one leg over her and deepened the kiss, exploring her with his tongue.

She felt the heat begin, the slow heat that pulsated through her, warming her, making her swell, creating a dampness that no mere river water could duplicate.

He raised his head and looked at her. His dark eyes hid much, but they did not hide his passion, which triggered her own. He bent to kiss her again, and his knee insinuated itself between her legs.

"Don't," she whispered, pressing one hand limply to his chest as she attempted to close her legs to him.

Ignoring her, he reached under her sodden gown and petticoat and ran his hand over her cold, damp

thigh. A bolt of electricity shot up between her legs, further weakening her. His touch softened her, created spasms of desire deep in her pelvis where nothing else had ever touched.

This was what she feared the most, her inability to push him away because of the kind of pleasure he could give her. And she wanted it. Oh, heaven help her, she wanted it.

His fingers moved higher, and her heartbeat increased. She spread her legs, waiting for him to touch her there, where he had awakened her all those years before. He grazed her with his thumb, and she made a sound in her throat to show her joy as she rose toward his touch.

She waited, eyes closed, for him to continue, her heart bounding and her ears ringing.

The next thing she knew, he stood over her, staring down at her. "You should get back to the house and get out of those wet clothes." His voice was abrupt.

Heat flushed her face and neck, making her scalp tingle as it inched into her hair. She was ready to curse at him when she noticed that his gaze was focused on something behind her.

Turning slightly, she noticed two Indians on horseback, watching them. Her heart stuttered in her chest, and she caught her breath, quietly making herself decent.

The Indians moved slowly toward them. They stopped, and one of them spoke to Jake.

"Why you save her?"

"Because she was drowning," was Jake's dry answer.

"She the woman who claims to heal," he observed, his mouth curling with disdain. He jammed his thumb at his chest. "Twisted Nose Doctor is the only healer."

Lexy's stomach dropped. So. This was the medicine man Dooley had spoken of. She forced herself not to

shudder, but he was a sinister-looking man. His cheekbones were high and sharp. His eyes were black, bottomless, without a shred of light. His nose was oddly twisted to one side. She could see how he got his name. He wore a dirty, torn shirt that looked as if it had been picked from a pile of rags. His hand-me-down jeans were too snug by far, and disgustingly revealing. He wore no shoes.

"I heard it was Dooley's choice to be treated by her," Jake observed, tugging his jeans on over his hips.

Twisted Nose Doctor spat onto the ground. "Dooley fooled by your medicine. He will die from your medicine."

Lexy squeezed water from the hem of her gown, attempting a nonchalance she by no means felt. She should have stood up for herself, but this one time, she let Jake do it for her. She'd been taken by surprise by Twisted Nose Doctor's arrival, and she was not at her best, having just been rescued from the middle of the river. That had been humiliating enough, thanks very much.

Jake shrugged into his shirt. "That sounds like a threat."

Twisted Nose Doctor sneered at him. "You another one. White medicine is weak." He pointed from Jake to Lexy. She swore she felt the thrust of his finger. "Two white doctors don't make as good medicine as one Twisted Nose Doctor."

Lexy shifted her gaze to his companion, a man who sat astride his mount, his burly arms crossed over his bare chest. One of his eyes was a mere slit, the other bulged, giving him a frightening look. His mouth was hard. One hand gripped his reins, and Lexy noted a large ring on his middle finger, glinting in the sun. With her stomach churning, she wondered if he'd merely stolen it or had taken it off a dead man. One he himself had killed.

Twisted Nose Doctor spat again, and with that, he and his silent companion turned and cantered off toward the trees.

Lexy's knees almost buckled, but she stood fast. "He has all the charm of a hungry snake."

Jake barked a humorless laugh. "He's unwilling to give up his power over his people. Dooley's defection to you for treatment stands as a threat."

Lexy swallowed the fear that climbed in her throat. "Is he truly dangerous or merely well practiced at intimidation?"

"Probably a little bit of both," Jake answered, his voice void of humor.

"Who was that with him?"

"Eagle Eye Jim. He's a troublemaker if there ever was one. If any of the Indians is working against Dooley's attempts at peaceful coexistence, it's Jim."

"Eagle Eye. Twisted Nose. I thought Indians had Indian names."

This time, Jake's laugh held a trace of humor. "They do. Translate them into their language, and they are Indian names."

They walked together, Lexy's thoughts scattered. "I hadn't truly thought about the dangers of living out here." Oh, how she wanted to ask him if he thought it was a good place to raise their daughter, but of course she couldn't. She thought about it, though. How safe was it for Krista?

"Jake, is it . . . safe for families out here?" There. That was general enough.

"Reasonably," he answered. "As long as the fort is here. The cavalry is a deterrent, at least. If they close the fort, well, there could be problems."

"So, it's safer to live in town than to be out on a ranch or a farm, I imagine." Her clinic stood in the middle of nowhere. How safe would it be once the fort closed?

"At least in town, they have the advantage of numbers, plus some sort of law enforcement. In the country, they have to fend for themselves, and the Indians take advantage of that."

"I hadn't thought about the Indians being wild. I guess I assumed that once the government made a decision about them, they would obey. Not that I think we're right about herding them onto land they don't want, but . . . I simply didn't think they would fight back." How naïve she was.

They hiked up the hill that led to her new clinic. Beauty, Jake's mare, followed behind them, as tame as a dog.

"When the fort closes, we'll have other problems," Jake said ominously.

"Besides the safety of the ranchers?"

With a nod, he answered, "The farmers and ranchers are determined to form a militia to defend themselves."

Lexy lifted her wet skirts to keep from tripping over them as she trudged up the hill. "But that sounds like a good idea, Jake. Why would it cause problems?"

She stumbled, and Jake caught her. His touch sent telltale tingles everywhere. She wanted to curse at the depth of her feelings for him. It wasn't fair that the nerve endings in her body couldn't be controlled. It was also unfair that she felt bereft when he released her.

"Because there are those who would just as soon kill all the Indians as look at them. Those are the men who will make trouble for everyone else. It's one thing to band together to help each other; it's another purposely to form a defense just to have the strength to eliminate your enemy."

All of this made Lexy's head ache and spin. It wasn't merely the reality of living in the wilderness, it was bringing Krista here, away from excellent medical care and a bright civilization, to eke out a living where possibly none could be made. And to expose her precious daughter to danger. Guilt began to assail her.

She glanced sideways at Jake, wondering what he

would think if he knew her plans. Forcing her gaze away, she realized that each time she looked at him, she felt the depth of her love, and it made her angry. Love was not a pleasant emotion, she decided. It exposed one to so many other agonies, like vulnerability, jealousy, even obsession. She despised the baggage that went with her love for him, for she detested feeling vulnerable to something she couldn't control. And she hated the petty jealousies she felt when he fussed over Megan. She refused to believe she was capable of obsession, but she knew that loving Jake meant anything was possible.

"You're awfully quiet," Jake observed. "Have I successfully scared you into hightailing it back to Providence?"

Grateful to him for tugging her back into reality, she answered dryly, "Was that your purpose?"

"No, but if it works, I'll claim it was."

There was no humor in his words. His lack of emotion for her only made her angry with herself for feeling so deeply. She took a deep breath and hurried on ahead of him. "Don't hold your breath," she called over her shoulder as she headed for the clinic's back door.

He was beside her immediately. "How's Megan?"

She cursed the agony in her heart. "Go in and see for yourself. She's inside, rolling bandages."

"Have you checked her lately?"

Lexy stopped at the stairs. "Of course, I've checked her," she snapped. "I hear only one heartbeat. I don't think she'll have twins. She has not had a single contraction yet, and I'm sure she's safe where she is, because there are soldiers here to protect her from marauding Indians and highwaymen."

What a fool she was to open herself to ridicule and hurt. But she always showed such strength that no one would ever have thought that she, as well as Megan, needed comfort. Love.

"Sarcasm has never become you, Lexy." He pushed

past her, took the steps in a single leap, and disappeared into the clinic.

Knowing her eyes were filled with longing, she let her shoulders slump and went around to the front door so she could avoid them both. Damn him for making her feel this way. Damn him, anyway.

# Chapter 6

COMMANDER BILLINGS SETTLED HIS CORPULENT FRAME into his chair, then lit his cigar, his plump cheeks tightening as he pulled on the stogie. "I think we ought to get the upper hand immediately and let them Indians know we mean business."

Jake, filling in for the still-absent Max York, disagreed. "Any aggressive behavior on our part will make matters worse, Commander."

Billings moved his cigar to the corner of his mouth. "Nonsense. If we sit here on our asses, we'll look weak. And they aren't even willing to talk. Every time we've set up a meeting between them and us, that Eagle Eye Jim comes up with an excuse not to go through with it. And he's not even the worst one. Those other two tribes don't even pretend they want some kind of peaceable settlement."

It was true. Of the three tribes the army had to deal with, the Klamaths, which included Dooley, Eagle Eye Jim, and Twisted Nose Doctor, at least pretended to want peace. After all, part of the treaty of 1864 had indicated that some Klamath land was reservation land. The other two tribes, the Modocs and the Paiutes, were not allowed one piece of their ancestral land. But even if the Klamaths were the most reasonable, they were also sly and clever. Any man who underestimated them was making a big mistake.

But even with the fragile truce with the Klamaths, it was well known that Twisted Nose Doctor wanted to break away and join the other tribes against the Army. Eagle Eye Jim was eager as well. Of the leaders, Dooley stood alone in his support of the government in Washington.

The other two tribes hid themselves up in the lava beds, a forbidding place to strangers but a place in which the Indians felt safe. They refused to talk at all, probably plotting exactly how to regain the land that was now in the hands of the settlers. They were not many in number, but they knew the land, and they had been defending it for centuries. The Army had the manpower, as weak as it was, but they were arrogant. Jake sensed that any confrontation would be costly against the Army.

"We can't just sit here, Westfield. The higher-ups in Washington want some action on this project."

"With all due respect, sir, I think we should at least wait to hear from Dooley."

Billings cursed and set his cigar on the edge of his desk. "That big buck wouldn't tell us the truth if it was written on his ass for everyone to read."

Jake wanted to argue but left it alone. "Give him a few more weeks, Commander. Then, if we don't hear anything, you can get your men together and—"

"Mount an attack. That's what we're going to do," Billings interrupted. "Scare the shit out of those savages, and let them know we mean business. That's the only way to deal with them."

"An attack would be a mistake, sir," Jake warned.

Billings studied him through narrowed lids. "Your job is to keep my men healthy, Westfield, not to second-guess my decisions."

It was foolish to argue. Jake only hoped that somehow he could keep the commander from mounting an attack against the Indians until Max returned.

Yeah, Max could talk sense into him. Something twisted in Jake's gut. But Max wasn't here.

Megan got clumsily to her feet and waddled to the window. Lexy had insisted that her sister stay with her at the clinic rather than return to the fort. Perhaps it was selfish, for they both may have been safer there, but Lexy had so much work to do she hesitated to leave. And she didn't want Megan to be alone, either.

"Thinking about Max?"

Megan half turned and issued a sad smile. "I keep hoping and praying he'll ride up any moment."

"I'm sure we'll hear something soon, Meggie." It was more of a soothing antidote to Megan's fears than a statement of fact, but it was all Lexy could offer.

Suddenly, Megan released a cry and turned from the window, her hands covering her mouth.

Lexy was immediately concerned. "What is it? Labor? Are you going into labor?"

Megan shook her head and pointed outside.

Lexy rushed to the window. Her heart dropped to her knees. There, on horseback in front of the clinic, were Eagle Eye Jim and Twisted Nose Doctor. And probably for the first time, Lexy and Megan were alone, for Lexy had sent the last of the recruits to the fort for some bedding.

Lexy tried to remain calm, for Megan's sake as well as her own. There was no Jake here to run interference for her.

"Go into the back bedroom and lie down, Megan. Draw the screen between the bed and the door."

Megan stood, her hands pressed against the wall behind her, and stared at her sister. "I can't leave you here alone with them."

Lexy turned on her. "Megan, go. I mean it, go now."

Megan opened her mouth to argue, then closed it and waddled toward the back of the clinic, her hands clasped under her belly.

Lexy strode to the door, but before she could open it, Twisted Nose Doctor shoved it open and sauntered in. Eagle Eye Jim followed.

The medicine man stopped in the center of the room and moved his gaze from side to side, a sneer on his face. "No medicine here."

Lexy's heart thumped hard, and she clenched her hands into fists so he wouldn't see them shake with fear. Perhaps, she thought, if she ignored the two of them, they would simply go away. *Not likely.*

Eagle Eye crossed to the kitchen, and Lexy hurried after him. He went to a cupboard, opened it, and stared inside, frowning. He swung to look at her. "Food."

She swallowed. "Th-those are supplies."

Giving her a look of disgust, he swept all the rolled bandages from the shelf. "Food," he repeated, his voice more threatening.

All of her clean, wrapped bandages tumbled to the floor. Anger bubbled up through her fear. "Those were clean," she accused, her hands on her hips.

Eagle Eye brushed by her, shoving her to the side. "No food," he murmured, stepping to another cupboard on the other side of the room.

Lexy cringed, for inside were her precious bottles of salve and soap and medicated powder. "No!" She rushed at him, grabbing his shirttail and pulling him away.

He swung, catching her on the jaw with the edge of his fist. Lexy stumbled, briefly seeing stars. She righted herself and watched him rifle through the cupboard, searching for something to eat.

"Here." She raced to the pantry, fighting dizziness. "Here's food." She opened the door and motioned inside, hoping to draw him away from her priceless supplies.

He loped past her and stepped into the dark pantry. Pulling out a sack of flour, he ordered, "You make fry bread."

"F-fry bread?" What in the devil was fry bread?

He flung the sack at her, catching her off guard. She tumbled to the floor, hitting her head on the edge of the table. Pain pierced her skull, and she nearly blacked out.

Drawing in some deep breaths as she fought the pain, she briefly pressed her forehead to her knees.

Something nudged her side. She blinked and looked up, finding the medicine man glaring down at her.

"Get up."

In no mood to argue, Lexy slowly rolled to her side and rose to her feet, using the table to support her wobbly legs.

"We see what you have in other rooms," he announced.

Rubbing her head, she glanced around her. Eagle Eye was gone. At that moment, she heard Megan's cry.

"Oh, God," Lexy whispered, her throat tight with fear and her own pain forgotten. She lifted her skirt, ready to run to the back of the house, but the medicine man grabbed her and held her.

She looked into his face, one that was menacing and filled with an evil glee. "Eagle Eye Jim . . . get lucky," he said.

"No!" Lexy wrenched free and raced to the bedroom. The screen had been tossed aside. Eagle Eye Jim stood over Megan, who cowered in the corner on the floor, her eyes squeezed shut and her face pinched with fear.

"Leave her alone!" Lexy grabbed the man's arm and yanked him away.

Jim raised his hand toward Lexy, but from the doorway, the medicine man spoke words she didn't understand, and Jim stopped, mid-strike. He spewed vile sounds and gestured angrily toward Megan and

Lexy, but the medicine man repeated his words, and Jim backed down.

Lexy hadn't realized she'd been holding her breath until Jim slouched toward the door, the muscles in his burly arms flexed tight with anger.

Twisted Nose Doctor continued to study them from the doorway, his thoughts inscrutable behind his dead eyes. "You." He jammed a finger at Lexy.

Again, she felt the jab of his finger. She stood tall in front of the cowering Megan. "What do you want?"

"Don't practice your weak medicine on my people."

Indignant rage welled up inside her, and all the years she'd had to take dirt from other men threatened to deprive her of her senses. She should have demurred, if only to get him out of her clinic, but she was past any possibility of deference.

"I will deal with whoever comes to me for treatment, sir."

His dark gaze narrowed ominously. "You use your medicine on my people, you will be sorry."

Braver now, Lexy asked, "Is that a threat?"

A slow, humorless smile crept over his thin lips. "No. It is what you white people call a promise."

In spite of herself, Lexy felt a shiver steal through her spine. "Please leave my clinic."

"We leave. For now." He continued to smile as he turned in the doorway and disappeared.

Lexy waited until she heard them ride away, then she helped a faint-looking Megan to the bed. "Are you all right, Meggie?"

Megan shook all over. "Oh, God, if this doesn't bring on contractions, I don't know what will."

Alarmed, Lexy asked, "Have they started?"

Megan shook her head. "No, but I can't imagine why not."

They sat quietly for a moment, Lexy trying to calm the racing of her heart. Then Megan giggled.

"What was that for?"

Megan continued to smile, though her expression was anxious. "Do you know what I was thinking when that . . . that savage had me backed into a corner?"

When Lexy shook her head, Megan continued, "I was thinking how sorry I was that I claimed that dry sink as mine when I knew full well it was yours, and I promised myself if I lived, I'd admit it."

Lexy uttered a quiet laugh. "You can have it."

Megan shook her head. "I want you to have it for Krista. It's only fair."

Lexy gave her sister a quick hug. It was amazing how much Megan had changed over the past four years. There were moments of the selfish, petulant Megan, but for the most part, she'd become almost docile. And pleasant. Thank the good Lord for Maxwell York, for Lexy couldn't imagine anything or anyone else bringing about such a change.

All of a sudden, a noise came from the front of the house. Feeling the blood drain from her face, Lexy pressed a finger to her lips. Megan nodded, her eyes huge and her lips white.

Lexy scanned the room for a weapon. Her frantic gaze found the wobbly spires on the headboard. She grabbed one, easily able to pull it loose, and crept to the door, flattening herself against the wall beside it.

Stealthy footsteps came closer, and Lexy held her breath. Out of the corner of her eye, she saw the shape enter the room, and she swung, catching the intruder in the head.

He yelped and went down on his knees, rocking and swearing as he nursed his wound.

Megan let out a cry. "Oh, my God, Lexy, it's Jake!"

Lexy dropped the club and stared at the back of Jake's head. "Jake?"

He swore again. "What in the hell was that for?"

Filled with remorse, she helped him to his feet. "We thought you were one of the Indians."

He groaned and winced as he stood, weaving slightly from the blow.

From the bed, Megan expelled a strangled giggle. The sound was contagious. Nervous relief caused Lexy to join in her sister's release, and she laughed, too.

Jake glowered at them, an egg beginning to form on his forehead. "Well, laugh your guts out, ladies. I'm sure there's a reason you think it's funnier than hell."

Lexy and Megan exploded into relieved laughter. Lexy held her stomach and joined Megan on the bed.

"Oh, Jake," she said around strangled laughter. "I'm so s-sorry. We didn't mean—"

Megan let out a belly laugh, causing Lexy to do the same.

"P-poor Jake," Megan sputtered, pointing to his head. "You have a lump—"

"I know I have a lump," he mumbled, touching it gingerly with his fingers. "What in the hell were you thinking?"

When she caught her breath, Lexy tried to examine Jake's wound, but he wouldn't let her near him.

"Oh, come on, Jake, it was an accident," she explained around a smile. "We'd just had a couple of nasty visitors, and we thought they were returning, that's all."

Jake brought out a handkerchief and dabbed at his egg. "Who was here?"

"The medicine man and the other one, Eagle Eye Jim."

His sore forehead forgotten, Jake's expression became one of concern. His gaze went from Lexy to Megan. "Are you all right?"

On a nervous chortle, Megan answered, "Oh, I'm fine." She tossed Lexy a look of relief. "Now."

She was fine, too, Lexy thought, but never mind that. It was only sensible that Jake would worry about Megan, considering her condition.

Jake turned and studied Lexy. "What's that on your jaw?"

Frowning, Lexy touched the flesh between her chin

and nose and winced. "I don't know, I—" Then she remembered that Eagle Eye Jim had backhanded her in the kitchen. "It's nothing."

Jake grabbed her shoulders and examined the wound. "That son of a bitch," he hissed.

"It's nothing, Jake, I just—"

"Eagle Eye Jim hit you, didn't he?"

She was about to deny it. Her hesitance was Jake's answer. He swore again.

"How did you know?"

With one gentle finger, he traced the bruise. She closed her eyes against the feeling of his fingers on her skin.

"He wears a special ring with a deeply etched eagle, and there's an imprint of a tiny eagle on your jaw."

Lexy's hand went to her wound. Jake's fingers were still there. For a brief moment, they touched. Jake's gaze met hers, and there was something there that made Lexy shiver with anticipation.

Quickly glancing away, he shoved his hands into his back pockets. "You shouldn't have brought Megan here. She should be at the fort, especially now. At least there someone can be on the lookout for trouble."

The hurt returned, but she knew he was right.

"But I'm fine, Jake. Lexy's the one who got hurt, not me."

Megan had been so quiet Lexy had almost forgotten she was there.

"That doesn't mean that next time it won't be you," he answered, his voice harsh with emotion.

Lexy turned away and escaped to the kitchen, her jaw and her head throbbing. She peered into the mirror that hung over the wash basin and examined her wound. It had begun to swell and turn blue. She gingerly touched the spot on her head where she hit the table and realized that, too, had begun to swell.

She poured water into the basin and prepared a

cold pack, folding it into a square and pressing it against the lump on her skull.

"What's wrong with your head?"

She jumped, unaware that Jake had stepped into the room. "I fell and hit it on the edge of the table."

"Fell, my ass. You were pushed. Why didn't you tell me?" He strode to her, pulled the compress away, and scrutinized her head.

"I can take care of my own wounds." Her words sounded churlish, and she was angry that she couldn't sound dispassionate.

"Yeah, that's you, all right," he mumbled. "You've never needed anyone, have you?"

After a poignant moment, she answered, "That's not true."

Jake cursed. "Well, you couldn't prove it by me. From where I stand, you don't need anyone or anything. You're too damned independent."

She bristled. "For a woman, you mean?"

"For a woman, for a man, for a horse." He poured fresh water onto the compress, squeezed the moisture from it, and let Lexy hold it to her head again.

"Have you ever wondered why men flock to Megan? Have you?" Without waiting for an answer, he continued, "She always appears needy. Men like that, you know. Women who need them. Men like to feel like men. Masculine. Protective. Megan makes men feel that way."

"And I don't," she managed, a sinking feeling in the pit of her stomach.

"Hell, no, you don't. You work damned hard at making a man feel worthless around you."

She caught a breath, hearing the tears that snagged in her throat. "Just where would I be if I had Megan's attitude? I . . . I could never have survived medical school if I'd been like her."

"That may be," Jake answered. "But there's a happy medium, Lexy. If I were you, I'd look for it."

Suddenly angry, she replied, "What makes you think I want to find it?"

His gaze lingered on her, causing her stomach to twist and her heart to ache.

"Because I've seen it in your eyes, Alexis Tate. I've seen it in your eyes."

He left her in the kitchen, and she turned to the mirror once again, stunned that he'd even bothered to study her that deeply. Her eyes were huge . . . and sad. The skin beneath them was slightly mauve in color. Her cheekbones, always prominent, seemed almost skeletal now. Her jaw was purple and swollen, and her hair was matted to her head over her bruise.

She bit back the urge to cry, but a tangle of emotional sounds escaped anyway. God, but she was a mess. Never before had she cared that she wasn't pretty, like Megan. She'd always been proud that she was different. Independent. Scholarly. But being a little pretty wouldn't have been hard to live with; she knew that now.

She briefly fussed with her hair, then, realizing it was a hopeless cause, rolled her eyes and left the mirror. Enough self-pity, she thought. She was what she was, and there wasn't anything she could do about it. Be like Megan? Not a chance. Unfortunately, it probably meant she would never have Jake, for he appeared to be smitten with Megan yet. But what else was new? She would never have him, anyway.

# Chapter 7

THE FOLLOWING DAY, JAKE RECEIVED A LETTER FROM HIS mentor at Stanford. With eager anticipation, Jake read:

*Dear Jacob,*
*Your observation about the fatty material in the blood vessels is very interesting, and although unproven at this point, very convincing. I urge you to continue with your writing; the possibility for publication becomes more impressive all the time. You spoke of your work with the Chinese. I can lend credence to your theory, for it is a well-known fact that as long as they maintain their native diets, they live long and fruitful lives. I believe diet has a great deal to do with the inner workings of our bodies, therefore I want you to keep your spirits up and continue your research. I have enclosed the most recent journals for your perusal.*

*Regards,*
*Henry B. Teller, M.D.*

Jake thumbed through the two newest *Journal of the American Medical Association* issues, scanning the indexes. Nothing caught his eye. He set them aside, folded Dr. Teller's letter, and tapped it against his chin. Continue the research. Yeah, he'd like to do that, but without performing another autopsy, he had no more material to do his research on.

Except himself, of course. And his Spartan diet had done little in the way of making him feel better, although he had noticed that his jeans hung looser on his hips than they had before. He had to be patient. That was a joke. Patience was one quality he'd never had.

He was at the window, staring bleakly out into the compound when a small convoy entered the fort, one of the horses hauling a wagon. Curious, he went outside.

Commander Billings came out of his office, his expression grim. He waved Jake over.

Jake glanced into the back of the wagon and felt a rush of relief and fear. "Max?"

Maxwell York lay cushioned on blankets and pillows, his face pale and gaunt, his eyes sunken. "Hello, Jake." His voice was a mere whisper.

Jake tried to steady his breathing, to keep himself detached and calm. Years of memories stormed through him. Max wasn't supposed to get hurt. He'd always thought Max was invincible. *He* was the one who was not.

"Wh-what happened?" He turned to the recruit who stood beside him. "What in the hell happened?"

Commander Billings pulled Jake aside. "I was given this wire just moments before they brought him in."

Jake took it, read it, and stared at the wagon in disbelief. Max had been missing for three days. He'd been found by a rancher. He had a badly broken leg. Compound fracture of the tibia and fibula. Gangrene had already set in.

Jake sucked in a breath and rubbed his hand over his face. At least Max was alive. He tried to concentrate on that, for above all, that was most important. But his fears continued to thwart his professionalism, for if gangrene had already set in, Max was in danger of losing not only his leg but his life.

"And they just found him now? How in the hell can something like this happen?" He returned to the wagon and lifted the blanket over Max's leg. The smell was putrid.

Max gripped Jake's arm. "Can you save it?"

Jake wanted to reassure his friend. He wanted to tell him everything would be fine. Great. Fantastic. He merely gripped Max's shoulder and squeezed. "I'll do what I can, Max, you know that."

"Megan?"

Jake forced a smile. "Still no baby. I think she's waiting for you."

Max's eyes filled with tears, and he shook his head. "If I lose my leg, Jake, I'll lose her."

Jake wanted to reassure him again, but Megan was often a superficial woman. He wanted to believe she wouldn't leave Max if he was less than perfect, but he didn't know her anymore. He couldn't be sure she wouldn't.

The York cabin door swung open, and Megan stepped onto the porch. "What is it, Jake? What's happened?" She carefully came down the steps and walked toward him.

And promptly fainted into his arms when she saw her husband in the bed of the wagon.

Little Pete had been sent to fetch Lexy immediately. When she arrived at the fort, Jake had briefed her on Max's condition and suggested she tend to Megan.

Pressing a cold compress to Megan's forehead, Lexy asked, "How do you feel?"

Tears dribbled from the corners of Megan's eyes. "Who cares? Shouldn't you be concerned about Max? Oh, poor, poor Max," she continued, sniffling.

She grabbed Lexy's arm. "Did you see him? He looked awful, Lexy. Just awful. So . . . so thin and tired."

Megan had not yet been told of his gangrenous leg. When the time came, it would fall to Lexy to tell her. But there were things to be said that could prepare her.

"He had an accident, Meggie. He wasn't found for a few days, so naturally he's dehydrated."

"But if he—"

Lexy pressed a finger over Megan's lips. "Shhh. You need to get some rest." She couldn't imagine why Megan hadn't already gone into labor after experiencing two traumatic incidents within two days, but her labor would begin soon. Lexy was sure of it.

Megan rose up briefly, then slumped against the pillow. "I want to see him, Lexy."

"Yes. As soon as it's possible."

Lexy rose to leave. "If I abandon you briefly, do I have your promise you won't try to get out of bed?"

"If you promise to come right back and tell me what's happening," Megan answered.

Nodding, Lexy forced a smile and left the room.

She found Jake and Max in Jake's office, in the room where they had kept Joseph. The moment Lexy entered, she could smell the stench of dead flesh. She fought back the panicky urge to gag.

Max's eyes, so filled with emotional and physical pain, touched her deeply. They would haunt her for the rest of her life.

Her gag reflex under control, she reached out and clasped her hand in Max's. "Megan's fine," she assured him. "It was a shock, that's all."

"The baby?" Max's voice was a raspy whisper.

"Not yet, but I think that baby will demand to make an appearance soon." She squeezed his hand.

Her gaze snagged Jake's. His face was drawn and pale.

"I gave him some laudanum," he admitted. "I want him to sleep awhile."

Lexy nodded. "He's almost beyond pain, isn't he?"

Jake led her from the room and closed the door. "Yes. That's why that leg has to come off. Now."

She hadn't had a chance to look at it, but the smell alone had warned her of its fate. "Where's the wound site?"

"About halfway between the knee and the ankle. Both bones are protruding." He dug the heels of his palms into his eyes. "It looks like Max, or someone, tried to push them back in, but all it did was make things worse. No doubt, he passed out from the effort."

Lexy paced the room, her fingers over her mouth. "The sooner we get rid of it, the better, Jake."

"I had to wait for you."

Surprised, she turned and studied him.

Before she could speak, he said, "I need an assistant. I can't do this alone."

Jake took up walking the floor, too, his fingers driving through his rumpled hair. "You want to know what my first thoughts were after the shock of seeing him wore off?"

"What?"

Jake laughed, a sharp, humorless sound. "That Megan would leave him."

"Oh, Jake, that's—" She was going to say, *That's not fair,* but truth to tell, she wasn't all that certain, either. "She seems changed. Less selfish and self-absorbed. I don't know, maybe she's grown up, maybe it's just because she's pregnant. I can only hope you're wrong."

Jake's Adam's apple bobbed with emotion. "I hope I'm wrong, too. It would kill Max if she left him because he had only one leg."

"Are you set up for the surgery?" she asked.

He released a harsh breath. "Everything's ready. The ether drip has to be prepared. The . . . the saw—" He swallowed repeatedly and blinked. "I sterilized the saw as soon as I knew what had to be done."

Lexy rested her hand on his arm. "Jake, are you sure you can do this? I mean, considering that you and Max are—"

"That's precisely why I know I must do this. Because Max is my best friend. Because I want him to live, damn it, even if it *is* with just one leg. I only hope Megan—"

He couldn't finish. Lexy knew why. "I know, I know. She's changed a lot, Jake. She's mellowed, she's . . . she truly loves Max. I believe that." She had to believe it.

"I hope you're right." He led Lexy to the wash basin, and they scrubbed, neither voicing the fear that assailed them both, that even with the amputation of Max's leg, it was possible they could lose him.

Max pulled through the surgery, but he wasn't out of the woods by any stretch of the imagination. Jake and Lexy knew that until Max began to heal, there was always the possibility that the gangrene had spread beyond the point at which it could be stopped. It could poison his blood. And they'd had to take the leg six inches above the knee, which left Max with a stump. A mere stump.

They had kept vigil together at the bedside. It was nearly midnight when Commander Billings's wife relieved them, scolding them for not calling her sooner, for she'd sat with many patients in her career as the wife of a fort commander.

They stumbled outside into the fresh night air. Lexy dragged the sweetness of it into her lungs, feeling drained. Exhausted. Elated. "I think he'll make it, Jake."

"He's got to." Jake's voice was rough with weariness.

They walked in the direction of the river. Lexy's love for Jake had grown during the surgery, if that was possible. He'd been meticulous, precise, and although she had seen his hands shake, he had immediately brought himself under control.

Would this feeling of love and longing for him ever disappear? She couldn't imagine it. There were times when she wished it would.

She gazed at his profile, barely finding it in the darkness. "What are you thinking?"

He snorted a laugh. "That life is a bad joke."

Without even thinking, she took his hand and squeezed it. He briefly allowed the contact, then pulled his hand away. She felt bereft. "Life's not always fair, Jake. Haven't we discussed this before?"

He swore. "If you're going to be so damned reasonable and pragmatic, you might as well leave."

She clenched her hand and was quiet for a moment, then asked, "Is that what you want? For me to leave? Do you mean here, now, Jake, or do you mean leave California?"

They had reached the river; the sound of water tumbled over rocks. A light breeze ruffled the treetops. An owl hooted. A bullfrog croaked for a mate.

Jake swore again. "There you go, analyzing every damned word I say."

"Well? Which is it?" She tried to hide the pain in her voice. Perhaps he wouldn't hear it. It was a good thing he couldn't see the pain she knew was mounted in her eyes.

He expelled a tired breath of air. "Do you know how easy it would be to hurt you right now? Do you?"

Her gaze wandering off into the darkness, she said, her voice hushed, "What makes you think you haven't already?"

He barked a sharp laugh. "Then my mission is complete."

She blinked back tears of anger. Frustration. Hurt. "Why is it necessary, Jake?"

Another sharp laugh. "You know why."

"No. No, I don't. Not for sure. Is it . . . is it because of Megan?"

His body turned toward hers. "Megan?"

"Because of what happened four years ago?"

Another long, tired exhalation. "I tried to tell you then that I hadn't meant it, Lexy. I apologized. If there's one thing, one damned thing I'd like to change about that night it's that I, for whatever foolish-ass reason, called out Megan's name instead of yours."

Lexy swallowed the tangle of emotion in her throat. "I thought it was because you still loved her."

He was quiet a moment, then answered, "I never loved her. Not the way—"

He paused, and Lexy stiffened with anticipation.

"Not the way a man should love a woman," he finally finished.

Through her angst, Lexy found the humor. Had she really expected him to say, *Not the way I love you?*

"I want you gone, Lexy, because . . . because to encourage you in any way would only hurt both of us."

"I don't see how you're to be the judge of my future, Jake. I came west for a reason, and I'm not leaving just because you don't want me here. And . . . and what makes you think anything you say or do makes a damned bit of difference to me?"

She strode to the water's edge, her spine stiff with anger and humiliation. "I may have had a crush on you years ago, Jake Westfield, but I'm no fool. I admit I allowed your seduction then, because I was too young to know any better. But I don't believe there's anything you can do now that will make me fall for that old trick again."

He was behind her; every nerve vibrated. "Really?"

Swinging around, she shoved at him. "Yes, really. Go to hell, Jake Westfield. Just . . . just go to hell."

His gaze snagged hers in the moonlight. "I'm already there."

Her shoulders sagged. Why? Why did he have to remind her of his date with doom? "Oh, Jake, I'm sorry—"

"Stop it," he hissed, grabbing her arm. "I neither need nor want your damned pity."

"Then why do you keep bringing the subject up?"

He didn't answer her but released her arm and moved away, lowering himself to the grass onto his back.

"I've been doing some research," he began, studying the night sky.

Curious, she crossed to where he rested. "What kind?"

"Into the eating habits of the carnivorous American male," he answered, his voice snide.

She sat beside him. The grass was cool against her ankles. "And what have you discovered?"

"That if I were Chinese, or Jasper Hansen, I'd probably outlive everyone."

Lexy chuckled softly. "I've seen the Hansens' garden. It's quite impressive."

"I'm attempting to write a paper for publication on how diet interferes with or enhances longevity. The Chinese eat no red meat. They don't drink liquor. Their diets consist of rice, vegetables, and occasional fish. They're lean and healthy well into old age."

Lexy thought about this. "But aren't there whites who eat red meat and drink and still live long lives?"

"In some cases, I think it has to do with heredity," he explained, absently taking her hand in his.

His thumb gently probed her palm, then grazed it, sending shivers through her. "That . . ." She swallowed. "That sounds logical."

His other hand found the soft skin above her elbow, on the underside of her arm. "If that's the case, and I can prove it, it seals my fate, Lexy."

"Oh, Jake, no. Don't say that." She flung her arm across his chest; he caught it and held it there.

Lexy crawled into the crook of his arm and rested

her head on his shoulder. Neither spoke. It was happening again; she was soothing him just as she had four years before. She also wondered if she would do anything to stop it.

His fingers found her face, and they moved over it, tracing her features. When they reached her mouth, she opened and drew one inside, biting down gently.

He pulled her across him and kissed her, stealing the breath from her lungs as he plundered. Again, as before, his kisses weakened her, softened her . . . moistened her.

She touched his cheek, finding the roughness of his whiskers where they met the toughened skin of his face.

He drew one of her legs across his stomach and went under her gown, moving his hand slowly toward her thigh. Again, as before, he grazed her with his thumb, and she jerked, drowning in sensations she'd both longed to feel and hoped to forget.

Heat, deep and willful, urgent and greedy, began to fan outward in slow, itching circles, taking over. She relinquished control.

His fingers became more insistent. "Take off your gown."

*Take off your gown.* The exact words he'd spoken to her four years before.

Passion drained slower this time. She panted against him, fighting the fire that had begun inside her. With all her strength, she rolled away from him and got to her knees, pressing her fists into her stomach, rocking to rid herself of her desire.

"Lexy?"

She couldn't let it happen again. She had no protection against him, except avoidance. But how many times was she supposed to fight it? *As many times as it takes,* whispered the little voice inside her.

Slowly, she got to her feet and brushed off her gown. "Good night, Jake."

She knew he watched as she strode away. She hoped

that in the darkness she appeared stronger than she felt. She knew he wondered at her abrupt actions. She knew she'd done the right thing by breaking off before they'd gone too far.

But undressing for bed moments later, as she drew off her drawers, her hand accidentally grazed her mound, and the swollen, moist center of her reminded her that nothing about Jake Westfield would be easy to dismiss.

Jake sat up, continuing to stare after her even when she had disappeared. What in the hell was wrong with him?

He mumbled a curse. He knew, all right. Whether he wanted to believe it or not, one touch from Lexy Tate, and he was a goner. She felt it, too. She wasn't immune.

But it was up to him not to let this happen again. Hell, maybe she wouldn't let it happen, but if she did, he had to put a stop to it.

He stiffened behind his fly, and he cursed the thing, swearing it had a mind of its own. And a memory.

Passion was hell. Love was hell. Sex was hell. Hell, life was hell.

He rose and made his way to the fort to relieve Mrs. Billings of her bedside vigil.

Stepping into the room, his gaze automatically went to the cot where Max slept. Mrs. Billings smiled at him and stood, stretching her back.

"How's he been?"

"Asleep. Hasn't so much as moved a muscle," she answered, crossing to the door.

"Thanks for spelling us, ma'am."

"Call me if you need me again." She tossed him a little wave and was gone.

Jake dragged the chair closer to the cot. Before getting comfortable, he checked the thick bandage around Max's stump, relieved to find it dry.

He studied his handsome friend, noting that he was

still gaunt and nearly skeletal. He took Max's hand in his.

"Hey, there, old friend."

No response.

"Do you know what I was thinking about today? The time we had our first smoke. Remember?"

No response.

"Hell, you inhaled first, I recall, and turned the shade of green apples." Jake chuckled, remembering. "You shamed me into doing it, too. I swear, I thought we were both going to die, we got so damned sick."

No response.

Jake pumped his friend's limp hand. "Of course, things didn't get better, did they? I think we were twelve or thirteen when we sneaked our first drink. Or bottle." Again, Jake's memory did not fail him, and he smiled warmly to himself. "Tasted like skunk piss, we thought, even though neither of us had even had a whiff of skunk piss. Guess we decided that if a skunk pissed anywhere near as awful as he smelled, it was pretty bad." Jake shook his head at the memory.

"Remember how hung over you were? Oh, I was, too, but I remember your words. 'Ohgod, ohgod, ohgod, I think I'm gonna die. Please let me die.'"

Max's fingers pressed slightly against Jake's palm, and Jake felt a rush of hope. Jake returned the pressure.

"Remember the cat house?"

Another squeeze, harder this time. A flicker of a smile.

"Our initiation into manhood." Jake laughed again, harder this time. "Hell, we were so full of ourselves after that, we thought we'd died and gone to heaven."

Max opened his eyes; recognition was there. He whispered something Jake couldn't hear.

Jake bent close. "I didn't hear you."

"My pecker was bigger than yours." Max spoke barely above a whisper.

Jake tossed his head back and howled with laughter.

"Like hell. If I remember right, we all called yours Little Buddy, didn't we?"

Max grinned, his lips dry and cracked over his perfect teeth. He motioned Jake close again. "Nope. That was yours."

Jake chortled softly. "Hell, your mind's gone soft. Mine was called the Big Mac."

Max laughed, shaking slightly on the cot. "Oh, no. *Mine* was called Big Max. Now, give me some whiskey, damn it. This leg is killing me."

Jake's smile wavered, but he rose and poured Max a healthy shot of his best whiskey. Tomorrow would be soon enough for him to learn that he had phantom leg pain, for he had no leg.

"I want to see Jake," Megan insisted, her jaw set.

"He's still asleep." It was true. Lexy had stopped at Jake's office before she looked in on her sister. "We had to do some surgery on his leg yesterday, and—"

"What was wrong with his leg? How did he hurt it? And why didn't you tell me about this before now?"

Lexy hardly knew which question to respond to first. It was this brief hesitation that brought on Megan's next reaction.

"There's something wrong, isn't there?"

Lexy tried not to show her concern. "Megan, he's going to be fine. We're doing everything we can."

Megan studied Lexy, her face white. "There's something you're not telling me."

Lexy briefly closed her eyes, wondering where to begin. "He has some . . . infection that we're concerned about."

Megan was breathing hard. "Where? Where's the infection?"

"It's in his leg."

"What happened to his leg, Lexy?"

"It was broken. Both bones were broken. It was a very serious break. We call it a compound fracture, because the bones break through the skin."

Megan sat straighter, leaning closer to Lexy, her expression hopeful. "But . . . but you can stop the infection from spreading, can't you?"

At Lexy's moment of indecision, Megan pressed her hand to her mouth to muffle a moan. "He's going to die, isn't he?"

"He's not going to die. As long as we can stop the infection from spreading further, he'll be . . . almost as good as new."

"Almost." She covered her face with her hands. "Oh, Lexy, I don't care if he has a limp for the rest of his life. I don't care if he has a scar. I just want him to live. Please, when can I see him?"

Lexy braced herself. "I think there's something you should know before you do."

The news about Max's amputation sent Megan into labor.

"Oh, it hurts, Lexy, make it stop!"

Even though she sounded like a child, Lexy felt a rush of sympathy for her sister. "Take some deep breaths. Come on, don't fight this."

Megan had a death grip on the rungs of the headboard. "I can't," she whimpered, her contraction subsiding.

"You have to try, Meggie," Lexy soothed, checking her sister's progress.

Megan stiffened as another contraction threatened. "Oh, I didn't think it would h-hurt so m-much," she stammered.

Lexy palpated Megan's stomach and frowned.

"You're scowling. Why are you scowling?" She shrieked as her contraction peaked, stiffening like a board.

Lexy couldn't feel the baby's head. She feared the baby was breech. "Megan, please try to breathe when you feel the contraction coming. Believe me, it will make the pain a bit more bearable."

Megan tried to comply. In the end, she screamed

anyway. "Oh, God, why didn't you tell me this would be like squeezing a watermelon out of a hole the size of a lemon?"

Smiling absently, Lexy noted that her sister was nearly fully dilated. If the baby was indeed breech, Lexy wouldn't be able simply to reach in and turn it, as she had done with the calf. She would have to cut Megan, or she would tear during the difficult delivery.

Suddenly, Jake was beside her. Relieved, she said under her breath, "The baby's breech."

Nodding, Jake retrieved her scissors. At her look of concern, he said, "I washed up before I came in here." With that, he stepped to the head of the bed.

"Well, Megan. How are we doing?"

She was panting again, anticipating another contraction. *"We* are not doing well at all, thank you very much," she whimpered. "Get it *out!*"

From the foot of the bed, Lexy finished snipping Megan just as the baby's right buttock was presenting. Moments later, the baby's head began to rotate, for the buttock moved into a more uncompromising position. Relieved, Lexy announced, "It will be over soon, Meggie. You're doing fine."

Another contraction, and Megan howled. "Now! I want it out now!"

Lexy dipped to catch the baby, and moments later, after she had suctioned out the nose and mouth, there was a lusty cry. Lexy beamed at her sister. "It's a boy!"

"Did you hear that, Megan?" Jake took Megan's hand and kissed it. "You and Max have a son!"

Megan turned her head to one side and squeezed her eyes shut. "Thank God it's over," she murmured, her voice filled with tears.

Lexy cut the cord, then handed the baby to Jake, who wrapped it in a blanket and brought it to the head of the bed.

"Here, Megan," he said. "Have a look. He's a handsome boy."

With red-rimmed eyes, Megan turned and glanced at her baby. Tears leaked, and her mouth quivered. She broke into heavy, heaving sobs.

Lexy caught Jake's gaze and wondered if he was thinking what she was, that Megan might have a new baby, but she had a husband who would never be able to run and race with him.

"Do you want to clean him up?" Lexy asked. "I'll take care of the afterbirth."

After Jake had gone, Lexy finished her duties, all the while wondering how Jake would have reacted at Krista's birth.

# Chapter 8

THE FOLLOWING DAY, LEXY RETURNED TO THE CLINIC. With her hair wrapped in a scarf, she finished scrubbing the rooms, vowing to paint them when she had time. Mrs. Billings had promised to patch the holes in the red settee. Lexy couldn't simply throw it out. She would use it in her waiting room.

She had two bedrooms ready, although she rather hoped she could keep Krista with her for a while. In Providence, she and Krista had often slept in the same bed, for they had precious little time together, considering Lexy's schedule.

Ben's theory was that a child should be forced to sleep alone. Get used to it. Not be pampered. Lexy couldn't do that with Krista. If she didn't spend time with her at night, she would rarely have seen her. And how she loved lying there, watching her precious daughter sleep.

Krista needed that time with her as well; otherwise, she might have become confused about who actually was her mother, for Ivy spent all day with her.

Oh, perhaps Lexy was merely justifying her actions,

but she knew that a bond had been forged between her and her daughter, and it was partly because they had drawn close at night.

Lexy stopped working briefly, knowing she was punishing herself by thinking about Krista every waking minute, but she worried about her daughter's welfare. It didn't matter that she was in the best of hands. They weren't Lexy's, and she missed her little girl intensely. Keeping busy was the only thing that saved her.

But was bringing Krista here the best solution? After hearing Jake's ominous words about the safety of the settlers and Lexy's own experience with the medicine man and Eagle Eye Jim, she wondered at the wisdom of it.

She was making herself a cup of tea when the farmer, Mr. Frazer, stepped into the room.

"Why, Mr. Frazer. How nice to see you. How are my patients?"

He doffed his hat and grinned. "Doin' great, thanks to you, Doc." He studied the room, nodding with appreciation. "I hear you're going to use this as a hospital of sorts."

She gave him a wry grin. "Of sorts? Do you mean, will I have a place for animals as well as people?"

He grinned again. "No. But I brought you a little gift on account of I can't afford to pay you for what you done for Millie."

Lexy swallowed a groan and gave him a generous smile. "Oh, now, you don't have to do that." Really, he didn't.

"I wouldn't be able to sleep nights if I didn't do the best I could by you."

Lexy imagined another crate of chickens. That would give her plenty of eggs. The thought wasn't unpleasant. Not really. Maybe she'd have a little side business going. "Well, then, who am I to stop you?"

He nodded toward the door. "It's in my wagon."

Hiding her cautious curiosity, she followed him outside. He groped around in the bed of the wagon, and hauled out—

"A . . . a piglet?" Lexy's hand flew to her mouth. "Why, Mr. Frazer. I couldn't take one of your precious pigs." And what in the name of heaven would she do with it?

He unceremoniously handed it to her, and it began squealing something awful.

Lexy swallowed her panic. "Is . . . is something wrong?"

Mr. Frazer chuckled. "No, ma'am. Pigs squeal all the time. It don't matter none if they're happy or sad."

"So," she answered, staring at the wiggly creature, "they have feelings, do they?"

"Oh, yes, ma'am. Pigs is smart. Smarter'n dogs."

The piglet squealed again and squirmed, and Lexy's first urge was to drop the thing, for it felt . . . repulsive. She shuddered, forcing herself not to do just that. Somehow, it had been a lot cuter when it was in the pen with the others, not lying in her arms like some woman's ugly baby.

"It'll make a fine load of roasts one day," Mr. Frazer bragged. "Loins, chops, bacon."

She swallowed hard. She lifted her wrapper and enclosed the pig in it so she wouldn't have to touch it directly. "I don't know what to say." *Help!*

The farmer grinned and hoisted himself onto the wagon seat. "I knew it'd be a nice surprise."

No, she thought, a nice surprise was finding lost money on the street, or walking in on a party planned in your honor, or getting an inheritance from a long-lost relative. A nice surprise wasn't acquiring a pig.

With a wan smile, she returned his good-bye wave, juggling the piglet in her free arm. When he was out of sight, she looked once more at her gift and made a face. "Hello."

It squealed.

With a heavy sigh, she walked through the weeds. "What am I supposed to feed you?"

It squealed again. And snorted.

"You're no help." She looked at it and couldn't stop the giggle that escaped. "And you're sure a funny-looking little thing." And ugly. And, she was sorry to say, repulsive. But she didn't dare express those sentiments out loud. After all, Mr. Frazer was convinced pigs were smart. Who was Lexy to argue?

One of the young soldiers who had been working with her ambled up to her, his face split into a wide, toothy grin. "What ya got there, Doc?"

"A gift from a satisfied customer," she answered wryly. "What am I supposed to do with it?"

"Well, he didn't leave no mash?"

"He didn't leave me anything."

"Shucks," the recruit said. "I'll get you some mash from one of the other farmers. I think they eat slop, too."

She wrinkled her nose. "Slop?"

"Stuff we throw out from the table. Scraps and such. You know," the recruit added, studying the pig, "where I grew up, the pigs were herded down Main Street every day, just to clean up the garbage."

The picture was not a pretty one. She tried to envision pigs on her street in Providence, but the concept wouldn't materialize.

"If I put it on the ground, it's liable to run away." She brightened. Now, there was an idea.

"Don't worry. I'll make a pen for her."

Hmmm. Always someone around with a solution. "Her? How do you know?"

The young man colored. "Well, er, she ain't got no, you know, a . . . a thing," he added, gesturing toward the pig's tail.

She glanced quickly at the lower end of the pig's underbelly. He was right. There was no male genitalia. Now, why hadn't she thought to look?

He cleared his throat. "The pen. Won't take me but a few minutes."

"Thank you." Her chickens squawked from their newly built pen on the side of the house. They had not yet become pets. She found them extremely short on attention span, with very little personality.

She looked into the funny little piglet's face. Well, here was yet another gift that she would not, under any circumstances, eat.

She automatically rocked it like a baby, noting that it was asleep. What a gem of a gift, she thought with dry sarcasm. Yes, a real gem. The gem needed a name. If she could get used to her chickens having names, what difference did it make if the pig had one?

She decided to name it Pearlann, after a fat primary school classmate who bullied everyone, even the boys.

When the pen was finished, Lexy found a moth-eaten blanket and placed the baby in a wind-free corner. It snorted softly and went back to sleep.

Later that afternoon, Lexy returned to the fort to see Megan and Max.

Jake met her outside Megan's cabin. Her body tingled, and her heart raced. She wondered if this would always happen when she saw him. She recalled vividly how well they had worked together the night before, when Megan had delivered the baby. There was only one man on this earth she knew she could work with, and it was Jake. Briefly, she wondered what it would be like to share a practice . . .

He looked drawn and tired. She wanted to cradle him in her arms, feel his body against hers, taste him. Instead, she drew herself tall.

"How is she this morning?" Her voice was dispassionate. Unlike her body.

"She refuses to discuss Max's condition."

"And the baby?"

Jake shrugged. "She should attempt to nurse. So far, she hasn't wanted to try."

Anger welled. "Well, she can't be pampered, Jake. She has to nurse that baby, or he will die."

"We could always get a wet nurse for him," he suggested.

"We will do no such thing. Darn it, Jake, why is it that everyone coddles her? She's stronger than any of you think, believe me."

"Then you deal with her." He took the steps to the grass. "Max is awake."

"How is he this morning?"

"Good. At least . . . physically. It looks like we stopped the infection." Jake turned and looked at her. "He had phantom pain last night."

Lexy felt a rush of sympathy. "And this morning?"

With a weary shrug, Jake answered, "He still has it. Can't quite believe his leg is gone."

Lexy's sympathy expanded. "Is he upset that we had to remove it?"

"Of course, he's upset," Jake snapped. "Wouldn't you be?"

Undoubtedly. How foolish of her even to ask the question. She couldn't imagine how she would feel, having to amputate her best friend's leg. Even though he hadn't shown any more emotion than a little shaking throughout the surgery or after, it had to have been hell. "I'm so sorry, Jake. This must be awful for you."

"Not as awful as it is for him." He turned and walked away.

Lexy followed him with her gaze for a moment, then drew in a breath and entered the cabin to face her sister.

Megan glared at her the moment she stepped into the room. "It's about time you showed up."

Lexy noticed the uneaten breakfast on the bedside table. "Good morning to you, too. Why didn't you eat?"

"Because I'm not hungry."

"The baby will need you to keep up your strength, Meggie."

Megan turned toward the window and said nothing.

"I'll fetch him for you."

"I won't feed him."

Lexy counted to ten to keep her temper. "And why won't you feed him?"

"Because I don't want to."

"You want him to die, is that it?"

Megan swung to face her. "Of course, I don't want him to die. Can't we get a wet nurse?"

"Is there something wrong with *your* milk?"

Megan squirmed. "I'm uncomfortable. My . . . breasts are hard as rocks."

"Then the solution is simple," Lexy said. "Nurse the baby, and your breast discomfort will disappear."

Megan put her hand over her mouth, and her eyes welled with tears. "How can I nurse the baby when . . . when . . . Max—" She drew in a sharp, quaking breath and started to cry.

Softening, Lexy sat on the bed and took her sister's other hand. "Let's talk about it, Meggie."

"Oh, God, Lexy, I don't know if I can."

"You can tell me anything, you know that."

"But I don't know how I feel."

"About Max having only one leg?"

Nodding, Megan sniffed. "I . . . I still love him, Lexy, but how can I look at it? How will I handle it? He's going to know how I feel just by looking at me, and it will make him feel worse than he already does."

"Then you'd better learn to be honest with him. It would be far worse for you to pretend everything is all right when it isn't. He'll notice that far quicker, believe me."

Megan's gaze probed. "Is it . . . very ugly-looking?"

Lexy dropped her gaze. "I won't lie to you. Right now, it looks pretty bad."

Megan broke into quiet sobs. "I try not to think about myself, Lexy, I truly try. This is much worse for him than it is for me, but I can't help wondering what's going to happen to us now."

Lexy brushed her sister's hair away from her forehead and wiped her face. "You're going to get on with your lives. You're going to raise your son, probably have a half dozen more, and, believe it or not, finally get out of this place. Now," she finished, patting her sister's cheek, "doesn't that sound promising?"

Megan sniffed again, then squirmed. "That part does sound good. I'll bet Max can get a job in Washington, D.C., now. Oh, I know he won't like it at first, he's always enjoyed being out in the field, but . . . he'll have no choice." Her eyes were shiny with newfound spirit. "You know, I was always anxious to return east, but I didn't want it to be this way, Lexy."

"I know that."

"But we'll both have adjustments to make. I know I can make them far easier back east than I could ever make them here. Does that sound selfish of me?"

Lexy was relieved to know Megan was willing to deal with the problems that would surely arise in her and Max's future. "A little. But not in a bad way."

"Well, I can't change overnight, can I?"

"You're doing fine, Meggie."

Megan inhaled and sat up straight. "Bring me my son, Lexy."

As if on cue, the baby let out a quivering wail from his cradle at the end of the bed. Lexy hugged her sister and went to retrieve her new little nephew.

After teaching Megan to coax her son to nurse, Lexy left them and crossed the compound to Jake's office. He was sitting at Max's bedside when she entered but left as soon as she stepped near the bed.

Lexy took Max's hand in hers. She bent to kiss him and smelled the whiskey. She raised her eyebrows, showing her displeasure. "Jake's keeping you well sedated, I see."

Max's smile was weak. "Better than laudanum, wouldn't you say?" He slurred his words, probably from the alcohol, or the fact that he was still woozy from the surgery. Perhaps a little bit of both.

"Yes, I'd say so." She lifted the blanket to look at his bandage.

He inhaled sharply.

Concerned, she asked, "Does it hurt that much?"

His eyes were shiny with tears. "I can't stand to look at it. How can you?" He paused, catching his breath. "How will she?"

Lexy's own eyes filled. "She might surprise you, Max."

A strangled laugh. "If she can live with a cripple, she'll surprise me."

Lexy bent and kissed him. "Give her the benefit of the doubt." She raised her gaze and found Jake standing in the doorway glowering at her.

After bidding Max good-bye, she joined Jake in the other room, closing the door behind her.

"You're giving him false hopes," he accused.

"What do you mean?"

"You know damned good and well what I mean."

"And you aren't giving Megan a fair chance," she shot back.

"I suppose she's resigned herself to her fate."

Lexy laughed, a dry sound, brittle. "Well, isn't this a switch? I'm defending Megan to you."

"She'll be repulsed," he warned.

"Yes. She will. She already knows that because I told her the wound wasn't pretty. But if she *is* sickened by the sight of Max's stump, I'm betting she'll beg him to help her through it."

"How in the hell can he do that when he can't stand the sight of it himself?"

They stood nose to nose. Battle stance.

"They had better learn to deal with their situation, Jake. If they ask for help, we should give it. Otherwise, we should stay out of their lives."

Jake snorted. "She'll divorce him within a year."

All of a sudden, something strange dawned on Lexy. "You know, all my life, I've listened to you defend Megan. Now, when she could really use your support, you've turned your back on her."

He gave her a studied look. "Let's wait and see who's right, shall we?"

Lexy swished passed him and went to the door. "Gladly. I can't wait to prove you wrong."

From his office window, Jake had watched Lexy leave. He continued to stand there long after she had gone, going over in his mind their arguments.

Yes, their opinions about Megan had changed. Jake wondered why Lexy had so much faith in her sister all of a sudden. Perhaps it was just that. They were sisters.

There was no question in his mind that Megan did not have the integrity to stay with a husband who would require the care that Max would. Maybe it was cruel of him to think so, but he believed it with all his heart. Max deserved the best, and as long as Jake was around to give it to him, he would.

His door opened, and Little Pete poked his head in. "Got a minute, Doc?"

Jake turned, giving him his full attention.

"A bunch of Injuns just ransacked Will Hollister's place. They rounded up some of his cattle and stole the horses. Stole flour, too. Scared the missus near to death. I think you'd better get out there and take a look at her." Jake grabbed his medical bag and followed Pete outside, worry churning in his gut. Will Hollister's place wasn't all that far from Lexy's clinic.

\* \* \*

To take her mind off Jake, Max, and Megan, Lexy began to clean. With her hair wrapped turban-style, she went into the parlor, scrubbed every corner, and washed the windows. She unpacked her trunk and put her books on a shelf, arranging them alphabetically.

She had been putting off one chore. She crossed to the window and peered outside at the pens that held her "gifts." The pig pen needed mucking out. One of the young recruits had offered to do it for her, but she bravely said she could do it. How dumb. And how did a person ever deal with the smell?

She blew a sputter of air and slipped into a pair of oversized rubber lumberman's boots, drew the back of her skirt between her legs, and fastened it at her waist, creating a pair of makeshift trousers. On her way out the door she grabbed a shovel.

Pearlann squealed and romped when she saw Lexy approach.

"Sure," Lexy answered. "It's all fun and games to you, isn't it?"

Pearlann snorted and snuffled.

As dubious as Lexy found the entire situation, she also found the pig amusing. But that in no way meant she would ever get used to having her around. Even now, every time the pig came toward her, Lexy feared she would attack or something.

The muck was slick. Pigs seemed to have a talent for making perfectly acceptable dry ground a muddy, mucky playpen.

Lexy jabbed at the sloppy earth, wondering just what she was supposed to get rid of. Everything sort of stuck together, as if the pig had used her slobber to erase the lines between manure, dirt, and slop.

Lexy did the best she could. It was her first try, after all. She patted the pig on the head, remembering the size of the mother, Hermione, and shuddering at the thought of this little piglet ever getting that big. The question of what to do with her then kept creeping into her thoughts. Fortunately, she didn't have to make that decision yet.

Just as she was finishing, a rig lumbered up the road. She shaded her eyes, recognizing Little Pete on the front seat, handling the team. As she studied his passengers, she let out a whoop that so startled her little menagerie the chickens and the piglet came to life behind her.

She tore across the grass in her cumbersome boots, waving frantically. "I don't believe it," she shouted, her eyes welling with tears. "Oh, my God, I just don't believe it."

The rig stopped beside her, and she pressed her fingers to her lips. "Why didn't you let me know you were coming?"

Ben Stillwater gazed down at her from the wagon seat, his eyes filled with warm humor and an emotion Lexy tried to ignore. "We wanted to surprise you." His smile grew wide as his humorous gaze wandered over her. "And by the looks of it, we have."

Glancing down at herself, she snorted a laugh and plucked her skirt from her waist, allowing it to fall and hide her hideous-looking, manure-coated boots.

Her frantic gaze went to the backseat, where her daughter sat with Ivy Stillwater. A shuddering sigh of delight and relief rinsed over her. A thousand pounds of worry fell from her shoulders. "Well, Benjamin, you certainly succeeded."

"Anyway," Ben continued, "we couldn't stay away any longer. Krista missed you mightily."

Krista's face was turned away, pressing hard at Ivy's ample chest. Her thumb was in her mouth, and her soft, pink "kiki," her precious blanket, was clutched to her chest. Ivy tried to coax the child to look at her mother, but she shook her head, her shiny cinnamon curls bobbing.

Once again, Lexy's heart was at risk. Her sweet, loving daughter refused to look at her. She swiped at her tears.

"Krista? Darling? Can you come to Mama?"

Slowly, Krista turned her head, exposing dark, gypsylike eyes. Eyes that always made Lexy weak. Suddenly, a smile lit up her face. "Mama!"

Lexy bit her lip and held out her arms. Krista happily tumbled into them.

"Oh, but I've missed you." She hugged her daughter close, stroking her hair, touching her limbs, feeling her weight. "Why, I do believe you've grown," she said, barely able to speak through her tear-clenched throat.

"That child talked of nothing but her mother from the day you left," Ivy announced from the rig. "I was afraid she'd get sick just worrying after you."

Lexy laughed and sniffed. "Oh, Ivy, I'm so glad you came."

"Hey, what about me?" Ben sounded indignant, but Lexy knew he was not.

"I knew you'd come. I wasn't certain you could talk Ivy into it."

"He didn't," Ivy said, sitting stiffly on the seat. "That little one did. I couldn't have let her go alone with just a man to look after her."

Ben hopped down from the rig, his gaze never leaving Lexy. "I'm not just any man, I'm Poppy."

Ivy clucked and tried to straighten the plume on her hat, which had wilted and frizzed in the heat. She gave Little Pete a sidelong glance, then whispered to Lexy, "I'm not at all sure this place is civilized enough for any of us."

"Well, then, we'll set about civilizing it, won't we?" She was so giddy, she would have promised Ivy the moon.

Krista turned in her mother's arms and held one hand toward Ben, which she clasped and unclasped eagerly. "Poppy."

With an exaggerated sigh, Ben drew a lollipop from his vest pocket, unwrapped it, and gave it to Krista. "For the rest of my life, I shall be called a sucker. A

sucker for a beautiful face, no matter what the age."
He winked at Krista and gave her a peck on the nose.

Lexy knew how Ben felt about Krista, as if she were
his own. Again, the decision to reject his many
proposals came to mind, but she felt no different now.
She'd made the right decision. At least for herself.
And, she hoped, for Krista.

The little voice in her head reminded her of the
perils of their new home, but Lexy bravely shoved
them aside. Time enough to worry about them later.
And she knew she would certainly worry.

"Let's get all of you to the house." She lifted Krista
into a more comfortable position and began walking.
"I had no idea you would be here so soon. Nothing is
ready, but at least I have beds for Ivy and Krista. Ben,
you'll have to bunk with the soldiers, I'm afraid." She
didn't think he knew that Jake was here. At least, he
hadn't mentioned it. And she wasn't about to open
that can of worms. Not yet. "Little Pete, is there
room?"

"Commander Billings has already said he can stay
with him and his wife, Doc. He could also stay with
Doc Westfield, but I ain't had a chance to ask him."

"Jake?" Ben's response was one of disbelief.

Lexy forced a calm. "Yes. If that wasn't a surprise,"
she hurried on. "He even finished medical school.
Can you believe it?"

"Jake is here." Ben's words were more of a statement than a question. He studied Lexy hard. "Does
he know . . . anything?"

Lexy shook her head, but her stomach fluttered.
"No. Nothing."

Little Pete loped beside her, hauling much of the
luggage. He seemed oddly uncomfortable. His gaze
kept moving to Ivy, who strode beside him, her spine
stiff as a broom handle.

Ivy's face had a flush to it. It was no secret to Lexy
that Ivy wore at least a dozen layers of clothing plus
her corset. She had to be sweltering, for the afternoon

sun was so hot Lexy could have fried an egg in a skillet without a fire.

"Little Pete, bring Krista and Ivy's things into the house. Ivy, I know exactly what you need. A nice cup of tea."

They trooped toward the house, Lexy exhilarated. "Oh, Krista, I have something to show you, darling."

"You go right ahead," Ivy ordered. "Just point me in the direction of the kitchen, and leave the tea making to me. Come along, Benjamin, help Mr. Byron with the luggage."

Little Pete cleared his throat as he hoisted a trunk onto his wide shoulders. "You can call me Little Pete, ma'am."

Ivy gave him a look that would have withered a rose. "I will do no such thing. This may be the wild, uncivilized West, sir, but that doesn't mean good manners are left by the wayside."

Pete cleared his throat again. "Yes, ma'am."

Lexy laughed, feeling light and gay and wonderful as she carried her daughter around the side of the building. She squatted, letting Krista down.

"Do you want to see Mama's surprise?"

Krista nodded around her lollipop, her curls bouncing.

Together, they crept toward the pens, Lexy pressing a playful finger to her lips. She watched Krista's face as Pearlann squealed and ran toward them.

Krista flung the lollipop onto the grass. "Piggy!" She clapped her little hands.

Lexy sat on the ground beside her daughter, so happy she wanted to dance and run and leap into the air. "Her name is Pearlann. Can you say that?"

"Her name is Perowann," Krista lisped.

No one had ever talked baby talk to Krista; Ivy wouldn't stand for it. Now, Lexy was glad. Her daughter had spoken in complete sentences from the time she was two years old. Well, sometimes they were complete, she amended. But she was bright and beautiful, and maybe it was Lexy's imagination, but she even appeared healthier.

She hugged her daughter again, barely able to keep her hands off her. "Oh, what a life we're going to have, you and I." Again, she shoved aside her fears.

Krista pulled away briefly and played with a lock of Lexy's hair that had escaped her turban. "Where's Poppy, Mama?"

"He's in the house with Auntie Ivy."

Krista gazed over her mother's shoulder, her interest suddenly drawn from the piglet. "Who are you?"

Lexy heard the footfalls through the grass, and thinking it was one of the recruits, she stood with Krista in her arms, turned, and smiled.

The smile died on her lips. Her heart stuttered in her chest as her startled gaze locked with Jake's. The blood drained from her face, leaving her dizzy. In a gesture of protection, she drew Krista close, hugging her tightly.

"Who are you?" Krista repeated.

Jake stared. He looked surprised. Shocked. He didn't speak. He studied Krista through eyes that darkened with emotion. His stance was taut. Finally, he answered, "I'm Jake. Who are you?"

"I'm Krista." She put her arms around Lexy's neck. "This is my mama. Poppy and Ivy and me came on the train."

Slowly, Jake's haunted gaze slid to Lexy. "Poppy?"

Lexy stood, unmoving. She gripped Krista so tightly the child squirmed in her arms until she loosened them. Nothing had prepared her for this. Not for any of it. She couldn't have been prepared even if she'd memorized a speech, for her breath was gone, zapped from her lungs by Jake's speedy and unexpected arrival.

Jake's smile widened but did not reach his eyes. "And how old are you, Krista?"

She held up three fingers. "Next time I have a

birthday, I'll be this many," she explained, awkwardly releasing another finger.

Hidden in the depths of his eyes was something Lexy couldn't put a name to.

"And you have a poppy?" His words were carefully spoken as if he'd had to use considerable restraint merely to say them.

Just as Krista nodded, Ben's laughter erupted from inside the clinic. Her eyes lit up. "Poppy!" She wiggled from Lexy's grip, jumping to the ground. "I hear Poppy!" She disappeared around the corner of the house.

Lexy slowly lifted her gaze to Jake, who was as pale as a pitcher of milk. A muscle in his jaw clenched. His nostrils flared. A pulse throbbed at his temple.

"Ben Stillwater is her *poppy?*" The word came out on a hiss of breath.

Unprepared. She was completely unprepared for this. "She . . . she calls him Poppy, but—"

Jake swore and swung away, then turned back toward her again. His eyes glistened, but when he spoke, he was in control. "Is she Ben's?"

She stared at him, stunned that he would think so. It made her angry. Resentful. She felt abused. "What do you think?"

He offered her his profile; his jaw muscle clenched hard. Again. Again. When he turned to her, he was breathing hard. "I think she's mine." His voice was husky and raw.

Pent-up indignation bubbled from somewhere inside her, hidden beneath years of repressed passions. "No. She's mine."

His gaze was so violent it was almost as if he'd shoved her.

"You can deny that I'm her father?" He felt a rage that tore at his heart, leaving him bare, wounded, betrayed.

She stood tall, her chin thrust forward. "It's easy to

plant the seed, Jake. The hard part is sticking around to tend it."

He was still breathing hard, almost hyperventilating. He wanted to plant his fist in Ben Stillwater's face, that's what he wanted to plant. He wanted to ask her how he could know if no one told him, but he was filled with such violence he knew it was better to say nothing.

She brushed off her skirt and cut a wide path around him as she strode to the front of the house, acting as if he had some sort of disease she wanted to avoid.

He was glad she was gone. His insides were going haywire, as if his nerve endings were getting the wrong messages from his brain.

He had a daughter. She was beautiful. There was a stinging behind his eyes, and his throat felt thick. The sense of betrayal returned, stronger than before. He had a daughter, but she called Ben Stillwater "Poppy."

# Chapter 9

BEFORE LEXY ENTERED THE HOUSE, SHE PAUSED AND closed her eyes, dragging in a deep breath to calm herself. At least, the initial encounter was over, such as it was. Thank God that didn't have to be repeated. Imagine, she thought, still stunned, he'd thought that Krista was Ben's.

She opened her eyes and found Jake watching her from the yard.

"She's mine."

His words sounded like a threat. Lexy grabbed the door handle.

"Lexy." Her name sounded sharp, like an order.

She turned.

"The Indians have roughed up one of your neighbors. Stay indoors."

Nodding, she turned to go inside.

"Lexy."

Sharper this time, tinged with anger. She stopped but refused to look at him again.

"You couldn't have brought her to a more dangerous place. If you did this on purpose, I can only hope you can live with the consequences."

Shuddering from the impact of his words, she hurried inside, relieved to be out of his sight. But his words haunted her, were burned into her brain, and she knew he was right. Perhaps that was the worst of it.

Little Pete entertained Krista by doing little tricks with her nose, pretending to take it, then producing his thumb. Krista giggled sweetly, her tiny hands pressed over her mouth.

Lexy had to hide her feelings. Her emotions were atumble, and her nerves were raw. Jake's words spun in her brain. Her own experiences with Twisted Nose Doctor and Eagle Eye Jim made her fear for all of them. But now, Jake *knew* he had a daughter. This worried her almost as much as her daughter's safety.

Ben stood up from the table when she entered the kitchen. "Is something wrong?"

Covering her feelings quickly, she responded, "With the excitement of your arrival, I had temporarily forgotten the news about Max York. And . . . and my sister." She took his arm and steered him from the kitchen.

"What is it?" His hand came over hers, protectively.

They stepped outside; Lexy glanced around quickly, relieved that Jake was gone but remembering his news about the Indians. She told Ben of Max's accident and his need for an amputation, and of Megan's delivery.

They wandered down the porch steps and across the grass, Lexy more alert than she'd even been—or felt she needed to be.

"So. Jake Westfield finally finished medical school," Ben said, his tone dry.

Ben's feelings toward Jake hadn't changed over the years. He still believed Jake was the reason behind all of her ills, in spite of his adoration of Krista.

"I was just as shocked as you to find Jake here, Ben." She suddenly remembered her surprise when Jake had assumed she had married Ben. "Oh, and for some strange reason, he thought you and I were married."

"He did, did he?"

She nodded. "I suppose it was a natural assumption, but I have to tell you I was surprised." She didn't bother to tell Ben that Jake had first thought Krista was his.

"Did he . . . tell you how he came to such a conclusion?"

"No. He quickly changed the subject. Probably embarrassed that he was wrong." She continued to feel the sting of the brief conversation that followed after she'd set him straight. He hadn't acted the same way toward her since. Before that, he had at least been tolerable. Since, he had taken every opportunity to make dry, sarcastic remarks clearly meant to hurt.

Ben nodded toward the road. "I think we saw only two or three farms from—Burning Tree, isn't it?"

He clearly wanted to change the subject. Lexy couldn't blame him. "There aren't many. There are more going the other direction."

"I'd like to go for a walk. Want to join me?"

She withdrew her arm. "I don't think it's a good idea to go off alone, Ben. Jake came by to warn me that the Indians are causing some trouble, and we've already wandered farther from the clinic than we should."

"Indians, you say?" Ben looked around. "I'll be careful."

"Ben, I don't think—"

"Don't mollycoddle me. I said I'll be fine, and I will."

She probably shouldn't have mentioned Jake's name, for she had a feeling Ben would have agreed to return to the clinic if she hadn't.

"I wish you wouldn't, Ben. It could be dangerous."

"Nonsense." He waved at her as he strode down the dusty road, tall, straight, and handsome.

Lexy stared after him, worrying her lower lip with her teeth. She was tempted to go after him. Plead with him to return to the clinic with her. Just then, Krista's clear voice called her from the porch.

"Mama!"

With Jake's ominous warning ringing in her ears, Lexy lifted her skirt and raced to the clinic for fear her daughter would venture into danger.

Ben studied the landscape as he walked, disturbed by the unwelcoming harshness. He didn't trust it. It was wild and uncivilized. From the moment he left the train, he had missed the interesting layering of Providence society.

Yet Lexy appeared completely at home with it. He didn't understand that. He would never comprehend how she could prefer to eke out her own living here, in the wilderness, rather than take the life he had offered her, time and time again. For both her and Krista, it would have been a good life. More than that, it would have been a happy one.

He still loved Lexy, but because her feelings for him had never changed, he forced his love for her to change. He was no fool. He knew that unrequited love was a fruitless emotion, even if she didn't.

And now, with Jake Westfield here, Ben knew a final truth. If he'd had any remnants of hope left that Lexy might change her mind, they were gone now, shredded into rags. Disintegrated into dust.

Over the years, he had often wondered why he hadn't written Jake with the truth. Probably because he had hoped Lexy would change her mind about marrying him. And probably because there was the possibility that Jake Westfield just might return and do the right thing by Lexy. Not that she would have accepted him. Her anger and humiliation had run too deep for that. But feelings change, too. He sensed

Lexy's would—eventually, especially if Jake were there to wear her down.

Hoof beats sounded behind him. Turning, he caught the dark visage of the rider.

*Speak of the devil.* With trepidation, Ben had wondered how long it would be before their first confrontation. Obviously, it would not be as long as he'd hoped.

Jake's anger was barely leashed. Hoping to give Ben Stillwater a well-deserved scare, he pulled the mount to a stop hardly inches from Ben's feet. To Stillwater's credit, he held his ground.

Jake leaped from the saddle, his fists clenched. "You son of a bitch."

Ben didn't flinch but crossed his arms over his chest. "Nice to see you, too."

"Why didn't you tell me I had a daughter?" Jake's throat clogged when he thought about her.

Ben's stare was hard. "What makes you think she's yours?"

"She's mine, all right. Why didn't you tell me?"

"Would it have mattered?"

Jake paused. "I don't know, but I don't think it was your place to decide, you pompous ass."

Ben continued to stare. "I did what I thought was best for Lexy, under the circumstances."

"So that's to be your excuse, is it? You always wanted her for yourself, everyone knew that." He sounded like a fool. He knew that, too.

Ben's smile was cold. "A lot of good it did me, didn't it?"

"You purposely led me to believe you and Lexy had married," Jake volleyed. "And now," he added, barely able to speak, "*my* daughter calls you Papa."

Ben's expression changed from anger to surprise. Suddenly, he laughed. He *laughed.*

"Stay the hell away from her," Jake growled.

Ben's expression was incredulous. "Stay away? I

couldn't if I wanted to. She depends on me. They both do."

"I don't want you poisoning her against me."

"The only way I could do that would be to tell her who you are." Ben smirked. "And that's the last thing I want to do, believe me. Not for your sake but for hers." He turned his back on Jake.

Bile rose into Jake's throat, his vision distorted by his fury. "Don't walk away from me, you bastard." He grabbed Ben's arm and swung him around to face him.

Ben yanked his arm free. "Keep your hands off me. Both of them were better off without you. At least, I can give myself credit for that much."

Jake saw red. He swung his fist, connecting with Ben Stillwater's jaw, relishing the crunching sound as bone met bone.

Ben stumbled back, falling to the ground. Rubbing his jaw, he rose, his eyes filled with disgust. "That's your way, isn't it? You've never dealt directly with your problems, you pathetic excuse for a man." He kept his distance. "You haven't changed, have you?"

Jake tried to hide his surprise but failed.

"Yes, I know all about your family history, Jake. I also know that's why, when your gut ached and you started feeling sorry for yourself, you merely pulled another prank. I heard about the wife of the anatomy professor, Jake, how you nearly frightened her to death by hiding a skull in her bed. Or how you dressed the lab skeleton in some poor girl's underwear and perched it on the dean's lawn, astride his wife's plaster-of-paris reindeer."

Jake frowned, distaste filling his mouth at the memory of his foolish college antics. His past behavior shamed him.

"You were just lucky, you know," Ben continued. "In spite of your innate stupidity, your brilliant mind is all that kept you from being kicked out on your ass long before you left."

"You always were a cocky SOB," Jake interjected. "I see that hasn't changed."

With a disbelieving laugh, Ben mused, "You know, in some small, idiotic way, I admired you. Oh, not your mind, although it was quite awesome. No, I admired your genius at giving the world the middle finger. Not that I would have wanted to have that ability," he amended, "but I admired you in some perverse way, anyway."

They studied each other quietly for a moment, Ben appearing calm, Jake seething inside. "You had no right to make Lexy's decisions for her."

Ben moved his jaw and winced. Swelling had begun along with some discoloration along his jaw line. "And you have no idea what she went through because of you." His eyes filled with hate.

Jake said nothing, but his gut churned.

Ben sneered. "You don't particularly want to know what she went through, do you?"

Jake had the grace to glance away. Maybe he didn't, but it wasn't for the reason Ben assumed. He had known that what he'd done had caused Lexy pain, but to learn the extent of it further deepened his remorse.

"She went through hell at your expense, Westfield."

Again, Jake made no response. With the discovery of his daughter, he was beginning to understand the depth of Lexy's humiliation.

"Can you comprehend what it's been like for her? Can you? Pregnancy is something that even married women don't like to talk about among themselves. Can you imagine how she felt, being the brunt of talk when it became obvious that she was carrying a child and had no husband?" He swore violently, then winced as he touched his jaw.

"I had a right to know."

"Why? This way, you can be all blustery and indignant, claiming you would have done the right thing and married her. Had you actually known," Ben continued, "you might have had to make a real decision. And knowing you, I'm not at all sure it would have been the honorable one."

Jake was uncomfortable because Ben was making too damned much sense. "You have no idea what my response would have been."

"No, I don't. But after what you did to her, I'm not sure she would have wanted your pitiful attentions. In fact, Lexy is a proud woman. I doubt that she would have tumbled into your arms even if you had offered her marriage."

Jake couldn't understand why he even bothered to listen to him. Maybe he just needed to punish himself, he thought dryly.

"For some reason I can't understand, she continued to care for you. I do believe she got over you, but even though she professed to hate you for years, I sensed her other feelings."

"And no doubt played upon her weakness," Jake added.

"She needed a friend, more than you can ever know."

Those words, if none others, hit home. Everything that had happened that night came back at him like a whirlwind. His agony at losing his patients. The storm. How pure and innocent yet provocatively seductive Lexy looked in her white nightgown, with her wild hair streaming across her shoulders.

How innocent she had been in her concern for him, her touch, her innate sweetness. The self-loathing he'd felt when he left her that night came back to haunt him, and he hated Ben Stillwater for making him remember it with such blinding clarity.

He swung himself into the saddle, continuing to feel a mixture of pain, anger, and betrayal.

Ben Stillwater glared up at him, undoubtedly wishing to castrate him. And when he had freely, without guile, admitted that Krista was his, Lexy had treated him like a leper.

The only person who didn't despise him at this

moment was his daughter, because she didn't know who he was. He even despised himself.

And deep in his wounded soul, he knew that Lexy had every reason to hate him. Not only had he taken advantage of her that night, he had betrayed her and hurt her. And taken her innocence.

Lexy had been up since dawn, relieved to find two recruits guarding the clinic. More watchful after Jake's warning, she kept her eye on Krista constantly.

From the porch, she saw Joseph and Krista disappear around the side of the house, toward the pig pen. She automatically stiffened when they were out of her sight, but one of the recruits waved at her and followed them.

She was about to return inside when a wagon lumbered up the road toward the clinic. Recognizing Mrs. Billings, the commander's wife, she waved and left the porch.

"Good morning," Mrs. Billings called. "I hope you have a minute to see me."

The wagon came to a stop, and Lexy waited as the woman debarked. "What's wrong?"

Althea Billings fussed with the hair at her nape. "Oh, I've been having these . . . pains and uncomfortable flutterings everywhere, and I know it isn't my rheumatism."

Lexy took her arm. "Come in, and we'll talk some more."

"I hear you have some company," Althea commented.

They entered the clinic, and Lexy introduced her to Ivy, who prepared them tea.

Lexy motioned Althea toward the makeshift exam table and did some necessary checking of her blood pressure and her pulse. She listened to her lungs.

"What kind of symptoms are you having?"

"Oh, I perspire something awful, and sometimes I get so nervous I think I'm going to fly apart. One minute I'm happy as a lark, the next I'm cranky as a bear. My poor husband has taken the brunt of it."

"Do you mind telling me your age?"

"I'm forty-seven, next month."

Lexy gave her a warm smile. "Sounds to me like the change of life, Mrs. Billings."

The woman gave her an exaggerated look of surprise. "Really? That's all?"

Lexy was certain she'd known it all along. "Come," she said. "Let's go into the kitchen for some tea."

On the way, Lexy gave her a tour of the clinic. Once they sat at the table, Althea Billings took Lexy's hands in hers. "I can't tell you how nice it is to talk with someone."

"I'm glad you stopped by. I hope we can see each other more often," Lexy suggested.

The woman teared up. "Unless you've lived out here, you can't know the loneliness." She offered a watery smile. "My friends back east simply don't understand what it's like to go for days and days without mail. Without band concerts, lectures, shopping, books I haven't already read twice or even three times. And . . . and oh how I miss the market near our home in Baltimore." She had a faraway look in her eyes, a sadness. A wistful longing for things she had left behind to follow a husband who would simply not understand.

Ivy had joined them, having put Krista down for a nap. "I tried to tell her that very thing before she left Providence, Mrs. Billings."

Many times, Lexy recalled. "But surely there are pleasures out here that can't be found anywhere else," she suggested.

"Like what, some form of rustic entertainment?" At Lexy's nod, Mrs. Billings said, "Oh, there's entertainment, all right, but we *are* the entertainment. For the Indians, anyway."

Lexy was not about to share her own Indian horror

stories. Ivy would have had a stroke where she sat. She felt Ivy's probing gaze.

"And here she is, setting up a medical practice in the middle of nowhere, in an abandoned brothel, with wild savages skulking about, ready to relieve her of her scalp." Ivy dabbed at her eyes. "And what of Krista? Have you thought of that, Lexy? What sort of place is this for a sweet, frail child like her?"

Krista called from her room, giving Lexy the perfect opportunity to escape. "Excuse me, ladies, I'd better see what she wants."

She left the room, her guilt and insecurity about her decision to come west growing by leaps and bounds. The finer things that Providence had to offer—concerts, lectures, shopping, gossiping with neighbors—she could live without. She had already decided those things were not essential in her life. But what about the safety of her daughter? Had she been selfish about her own needs at the expense of Krista's?

Inside herself, where she rarely ventured, she felt a secret quaking, a frightened realization that she may have made the biggest mistake of her life. She could handle the stresses of life on the frontier alone, she had already managed that, but exposing Krista to them was another matter altogether.

Later that afternoon, Joseph stopped by after his lessons at the reservation school.

"You don't have to haul wood today, Joseph," she said as he neatly stacked an armful onto the porch. "I doubt we'll need it for many months."

The boy had made a remarkable recovery, but she didn't want him to overdo. Jake had removed the stitches a few days before.

"I will gather the eggs, then. Do you mind if Krista helps?"

Krista had found Joseph immediately and had followed him around like a puppy. Lexy thought perhaps it was because she was fascinated with the color of his skin.

"Do you think she'll be much help?" Personally, Lexy hated the job. She'd tried and tried to do it herself, but the damned scrawny things kept pecking at her hands, and she felt herself shudder all over.

"Come watch," he suggested.

Lexy followed them to the little area where she kept the hens. Her hands started to hurt, probably in self-defense.

Krista walked right up to the biggest chicken and reached under her.

Lexy gasped. "Krista, wait—"

Before she could finish, Krista had pulled out an egg and placed it gently in the basket Joseph held. The hen just sat there, placid as a cow.

Joseph turned to Lexy and grinned.

Lexy merely shook her head. Her daughter, the city-bred child with the country personality. *She's mine.* Jake's voice entered her thoughts as clearly as if he'd spoken next to her ear. She shook her head and pressed two fingers between her eyes.

She had no idea what she was going to do. Not a clue. She sensed that the future would involve Jake in some way, but she couldn't imagine what.

During the night, she had awakened and watched Krista sleep, tiny snores coming from her slightly open mouth. Lexy's heart had constricted, and she'd fought the urge to draw Krista into her arms and hold her there.

*She's mine.* Again, Jake's words returned to haunt her, and she was puzzled by them. How much easier it would have been for him to deny that Krista was his. That was what she had expected, after all. She dreaded their next confrontation, for she didn't know what to expect from him.

The door squeaked open behind her, and Ivy joined her on the porch. She looked crisp and tidy, her blond hair swept on top of her head. As Lexy had come to know Ivy, she saw the beauty that Ivy hid so successfully from the world. Lexy often wondered what it was that Ivy feared, for she took pains to make herself unattractive, when, indeed, she was not. At thirty-five, Ivy was truly a spinster. But Lexy knew that in years past, Ivy had spurned a number of suitors.

When she saw Ben's infatuation with Lexy, even after her pregnancy with Krista began to show, Ivy had not warmed toward her. She had always protected Ben. It was when Lexy refused Ben's proposal that Ivy started to see Lexy in a new and more favorable light, for it had been obvious that she thought Lexy would latch on to her brother merely to save herself from the gossips. After that, it hadn't taken them long to become friends.

Ivy clucked her tongue. "Did Krista go cavorting after that Indian boy?"

"Joseph," Lexy corrected. "And he seems captivated with her."

"Do you really think it's safe?" There was obvious fear in her tone.

"Why wouldn't it be?"

"He's hardly a completely civilized child, Lexy."

"He's very civilized. He's the only Indian child I know who is obsessed with learning everything there is to know about the people who have so totally disrupted his life." She didn't add that she hadn't met any other Indian children, although she knew there were dozens on the reservation.

A superior snort. "Well, at least he has some sense in that regard. Disruption or not, their lives will certainly be better now that we are here. And they should thank us."

Raising a skeptical brow, Lexy thought it perhaps not wise to inform Ivy that few of the Indians would thank the whites for what they had done to them.

"I treated Joseph shortly after I arrived. He's still recovering, regaining strength, but he insists on helping me here, and I find his company delightful." She wondered how Ivy would react if Dooley suddenly appeared on the doorstep. She almost wished he would, she thought with a smile. *That* would be a sight worth savoring.

"Well," Ivy replied on a sigh, "I suppose you have to get your help where you can find it."

Little Pete galloped toward them, brought his mount to a halt, and swung from the saddle. His expression was serious.

"'Afternoon, Pete. Is something wrong?"

Pete removed his hat and nodded toward Ivy, his gaze lingering a moment on her hair, which, Lexy realized, gleamed in the sunshine. "Yeah, Doc. I've just come from the reservation, and there's a passel of sick kids up there."

Lexy drew him into the house and nodded toward the bench at the kitchen table. "Ivy, pour Pete some coffee, would you? Now, just what seems to be wrong?"

Ivy silently and stoically did as she was asked while Lexy sat across from Pete at the table.

"Well, I have to admit, I went to Doc Westfield first, but he wasn't there, so I come right over to you."

Lexy nodded, so accustomed to being second fiddle she hardly took notice. Suddenly remembering the medicine man, she asked, "What about Twisted Nose Doctor?"

Pete's expression became guarded. "I don't know nothin' about that, Doc. I just know that Dooley's worried, and I think either you or Doc Jake should see him."

She shouldn't hesitate.

"'Course, Dooley blames it on bad flour. Says Deke Slater gave 'em wormy stuff at the mercantile in town. The Army ain't had their load in yet, either, so we don't have the rations for the reservation."

While Pete talked, Lexy rose and began preparing supplies. Her reluctance did not stem from her disinterest in the children, it came from her fear of their shaman. She crammed as much as she could into her leather medical bag and braced herself for the trip, praying they would not come upon the medicine man.

Ivy stood by the door with a hat, cape, and gloves and shoved them at Lexy as she rushed past her.

"It's too warm for all that, Ivy," Lexy announced as she shrugged out of her wrapper and hung it on a hook.

"But it isn't proper—"

"Ivy, I love you dearly, but this isn't Providence, and I'm not on my way to a tea. Get Krista inside soon, and make her rest."

"I know what my responsibilities are to that child, Alexis. You don't need to remind me."

Her offended tone made Lexy stop. She hugged Ivy tightly and apologized. "I'm sorry, dear. You know better than I what to do with her. I'll be back as quickly as I can. Pete, get the wagon ready. We'd better be prepared to bring some of those children back here if we have to."

Little Pete took the porch steps in one leap, then ran toward the rickety lean-to where she kept the horse and wagon she had inherited from the recruits at the fort.

She waited on the porch; Ivy joined her.

"That man is barely civilized himself," she muttered.

"He's a career soldier, Ivy. He's a blacksmith and a translator. I dare say that in his youth, he spent about as much time with the Indians as he did with his own people. He speaks their language beautifully."

"Well," she huffed, "certainly no woman could live with a man like that."

On a wry smile, Lexy answered, "You might be right there, but Pete is aware of his shortcomings. At least, what he believes to be shortcomings. I, on the other hand, happen to think he'd make some woman a fine husband. He's big and strong yet gentle as a lamb."

Ivy sniffed, lifted her skirt, and made her way gingerly down the porch steps. "Strong as an ox with the manners to match, if you ask me." She reached the grass and pulled herself straight and tall.

"I'm going to rescue Krista from that . . . that *boy*. And where is Benjamin? He lit out of here so early this morning, I didn't have a chance to talk with him at all. And did you see that bruise on his jaw?" She harumphed. "Ran into a doorway at the Billingses' cottage, my Aunt Fannie. He got punched, and you know as well as I who did it."

Reflexively, Lexy touched her own jaw, which hurt only marginally. She wouldn't have been a bit surprised if Ben and Jake hadn't had a confrontation, but why Jake would have socked him in the jaw was a mystery.

# Chapter 10

PROPPED UP ON PILLOWS, MAX LOOKED HEALTHIER AND more alert than he had the night before.

"You're looking pretty good," Jake commented as he studied the stump wound.

"For half a man, you mean."

Jake understood, yet he refused to fuel Max's self-pity. "You're alive, aren't you?"

"When will Megan have to see me?"

"*Have* to? Isn't that kind of pessimistic?"

"You don't know how I'm dreading it, Jake. How will I deal with this?" His fear was evident in his eyes.

"You, who have dealt with petulant settlers, conniving Indians, and unruly recruits, are afraid of your wife?"

Max glanced away. "You know what I mean."

"Don't create problems where there are none," Jake suggested. *Yet,* he thought. He wanted to be proven wrong about Megan.

"After I change your bandage, I'm going to go over and check on her and the baby. By the way," he continued, "what are you going to name the little guy?"

"We had thought we'd name him Benjamin."

Jake's head shot up, and he tossed Max a look of wide-eyed surprise.

Max chuckled. "Gotcha."

Jake mouthed a colorful curse in Max's direction, then continued dressing his wound.

"By the way, how are you and Lexy getting along?"

Jake wrapped the bandage snugly. "I have a daughter." He didn't have to wait long for Max's surprised response.

"The hell you say."

"Yeah. She arrived yesterday on the train with Ben and Ivy Stillwater." His fist tingled as he remembered the contact with Ben's jaw.

Max whistled. "Now, ain't that a kick in the balls?"

"You've got that right. But that's not the worst of it," Jake said ominously. "She calls Ben Stillwater 'Poppy.'"

Max expelled a breathy curse. "Lexy admitted that the child thinks Ben is her father?"

"Hell, I don't know," Jake muttered. "I didn't get around to asking her that."

Max's gaze probed. "Don't you think you should have?"

Impatient with the conversation, Jake growled, "When you and Megan get your respective acts together and behave like adults, I'll do the same."

Max brought his hands up in defeat. "Something to work toward, I guess."

Jake went to the door and gave Max a friendly obscene gesture before he left him alone.

As they rode through the reservation, Lexy was appalled. The cabins were little more than shacks. She leaned into Pete's shoulder and said, her voice low, "These are hovels."

He slowed the team. "Don't be too quick to make a judgment, Doc. They ain't as bad as they look."

Lexy doubted that very much but held her tongue. The wagon stopped in front of one of the larger cabins, and she recognized Dooley's wife standing on the wooden stoop. She disappeared inside, and shortly Dooley stepped out to greet them. His expression was grave.

Lexy hopped from the wagon and hurried toward him. "What seems to be the matter, Dooley?"

"Where's Doc Jake?"

Exasperated, Lexy shot back, "I'm here, he isn't. Now, tell me what's wrong, Dooley. We're wasting time."

Her sharp tone made the proper impression. Dooley led her into his cabin and motioned her to a figure on the bed.

Lexy put her medical bag on the floor and leaned over the bed. Lying there was a little girl, younger than Joseph. She was coughing and sniffling. Lexy smiled down at her and touched her forehead with the back of her hand. "What's her name?"

"She Sarafina," Dooley answered.

"Well, Sarafina is running a fever." Lexy squinted close, but it was too dark in the cabin to see the girl clearly. "Dooley, would you bring me a lantern, please?"

A moment later, Dooley was beside her with the light. With gentle fingers, Lexy probed the glands at Sarafina's neck, finding them swollen. Her eyes were red and the rims inflamed. Lexy gave the girl a reassuring smile and drew the blanket away from her chest. Sarafina's arms were thin and bare, and she wore a ragged shift, which Lexy attempted to raise. The girl gave her head a violent shake and held the shift in place with her arms.

Lexy smiled at her again. "I understand. Dooley, will you please tell her I merely want to look at her chest? I won't hurt her."

Dooley translated, and the girl reluctantly moved her arms away so Lexy could look at the skin on her torso. It was unmarked. She moved her stethoscope over the child's lungs, hearing mild congestion.

As she brought the blanket to the girl's chin, she said, "Ask her if I can look in her mouth."

Again, Dooley translated, and the child slowly opened for Lexy. The light was bad; it wasn't possible to tell anything for sure.

"Bad flour," Dooley muttered beside her.

Lexy didn't think so but said nothing. The symptoms were more widespread, involving the eyes, the chest, and possibly even the ears.

Pete stepped to her side. "What is it, Doc?"

She glanced up at him. "I'm not sure. It could be anything. Maybe just a cold. But with the fever, I'd guess measles, chicken pox, even scarlet fever. Have you had any of them, Pete?"

Pete scratched his whisker-stubbled chin. "Might've. Don't rightly remember."

"Until more symptoms show up, I can't be sure." She took a deep breath and stretched her back as they went outside.

"What're the other symptoms, Doc?"

"It depends on the disease," she answered. She reined in her alarm. All of the three she mentioned were contagious, which meant that those who had come in contact with them would get whatever it was eventually.

Pete was quiet for a moment, then observed. "All three of 'em are diseases a body can't rightly avoid, ain't they?"

"So it seems. There's an incubation period, but I don't know that anyone has pinpointed the exact number of days or weeks a person is contagious."

Lexy watched Dooley emerge from the cabin. "Dooley, I'd like to see some of the other children before I decide what to do."

In all, she saw six children with symptoms similar

to the first little girl's. None of them had yet to show further signs. But caution was Lexy's battle cry. Caution and cleanliness.

"I'd like to take them to my clinic. We can make room for them there, and I can keep an eye on them."

Pete cleared his throat. "What about their medicine man, Doc?"

Twisted Nose Doctor. The thought of him made her quake. "Surely, he'll agree they must be treated."

Pete slid his cap off and scratched his head. "I dunno. He's likely to put up a real fuss if you take the young'uns from the reservation."

"Then he can deal with me." Ha. Words. Brave words.

"And what about your little gal, Krista?"

Lexy faltered. "Oh." She rubbed her hands over her face, pressing her fingers against her eyes. How could she purposely expose Krista to something that was potentially serious to a child in her condition?

"Well, I s'pose it ain't such a bad thing for a li'l one to get somethin', leastwise it won't happen again, ain't that right?"

"Yes, in theory that's right." But the thought of it went against every grain of maternal love she had.

"Didn't I see Joseph there this mornin'?"

Lexy's stomach dropped. "Yes, you did." He hadn't complained of anything, and Lexy hadn't noticed any coldlike symptoms, but then, she hadn't exactly been looking for them then, either. The thought struck her that with Krista following Joseph around all morning, she was exposed already, even if Joseph's symptoms were not yet obvious.

Maybe she could ask Ivy to take Krista away for a while, somewhere that was safe. She couldn't risk Krista's health on purpose, even if, in the long run, it might be prudent. To expose a child with no health problems was one thing; to expose a child with weak lungs was entirely another.

"Dooley, will these mothers let me take their children to my hospital?"

Dooley appeared uncomfortable. "Them want to wait for Twisted Nose Doctor."

On a tired breath, she said, "That means the children probably won't be allowed to come with me."

"That what it means," Dooley agreed.

"Well, I want them brought to the wagon with a blanket anyway, just in case." As much as she wanted to, she wouldn't take the children against the wishes of their parents. Confrontation with the medicine man was not something she looked forward to. In the end, she knew she would lose.

They had most of the children in the wagon when Jake rode into the reservation. He watched as Pete lifted in the last child. "What's going on here?"

Lexy quickly justified her actions. "All of these children have early symptoms of what might be measles, chicken pox, or scarlet fever, Jake. I'm preparing to take them to the clinic." She didn't mention that she probably wouldn't get them that far.

"What?" He sounded incredulous.

"Yes," she shot back. "They . . . their eyes are red and teary, they have coughs and sniffles, and, most of all, each has a high fever."

Jake dismounted and crossed to the wagon, his hand moving gently to one of the younger children's jaw. "What about the symptoms in the mouth?"

She almost hoped he'd find what he was looking for, because that would vindicate her. "I'm not certain. Those I examined more thoroughly didn't have any."

Jake peered into the child's mouth and with his handkerchief pulled the boy's cheek to one side. "This one does."

Relief mixed with her alarm.

"What? Let me see." She peered into the boy's mouth, seeing the tiny saltlike grains surrounded by red rings. "Measles," she murmured, her alarm mounting.

Jake stood back and studied her, his expression guarded. "What about Krista? Has she had the measles?"

Lexy glanced away, feeling fretful. "No. She hasn't."

"Then you're purposely exposing her to—"

"You don't have to remind me," she interrupted sharply. "Joseph has been there all morning, and Krista has followed him around like a puppy." She blinked back tears of frustration. "She's probably already been exposed."

He swore. "Bringing her out here was a careless decision, Lexy."

She fought the urge to pummel him with her fists. The presence of the children was the only thing that stopped her. "Why, you . . . you arrogant snake. As if you have any right to advise or judge me."

He glanced around, appearing uncomfortable with her tirade. "This isn't the place to discuss it."

"This is exactly the place," she objected. "Pete, get moving. I'll be along shortly."

Little Pete took off his hat and scratched his head. "But how'll you get home, Doc?"

"I'll walk. I'll run. Just . . . just take the children and go."

"But what about the shaman?"

"Blast the shaman," she snapped, feeling reckless. "Get moving."

He moved out slowly, and out of the corner of her eye, she saw him stop ahead, near the entrance.

Once they were alone, she faced Jake again, waiting for him to speak.

"Why wasn't I told about her?" His voice was raw.

"I didn't know where you were." And she wouldn't have told him if she had.

"Ben knew."

She failed to hide her surprise. "Ben? Ben knew?"

She was beginning to understand. "Is that why you socked him in the jaw?"

"He should have told me," Jake mumbled. "I wrote him. Before I . . . before I left Providence. He knew how to find me."

She narrowed her gaze. "Oh, let me guess. You asked that Ben look after poor little me, now that you'd so successfully broken my pitiful heart."

A ragged sigh escaped, and he dove his fingers through his hair. "Well, when you put it like that . . ."

"Exactly. God," she whispered, exasperated. "Men are such horses' asses."

"Your language has slid into the gutter, Lexy," he accused.

"Oh, it's gotten worse than that. Name calling has become quite a passion with me. Take my word for it. I've learned more new names and phrases for a woman like me than you'd ever believe. Bitch. Whore. Slut. Brazen hussy. Loose woman. Now," she said, unable to keep from emitting a dry laugh, "that one has always been one of my favorites. The only thing different between half the women in Rhode Island and me is that I was left either to destroy the child or marry, just to give the child a name." She swallowed convulsively, hoping he didn't notice her emotion. "I couldn't do either."

His face showed no expression. "Then why didn't you stop things before they went too far?"

Astonished and disgusted, she said, "Me? I had a mad, stupid, foolish crush on you, Jake Westfield. I would have done anything for you." She lowered her voice. "I gave you the one thing a woman can give a man that she can't take back. And you treated it like . . . like it wasn't important to you at all."

"That's not true. And if you'd listened, you would have known how terrible I felt." He paused a moment. "I apologized, Lexy. I apologized, and I truly meant it. I never wanted to hurt you."

She remembered the night all too vividly. Remembered his apology, but even now it sounded like mere lip service. "Too late for that." She jabbed her forefinger at his chest. "I was innocent. I was infatuated. And you took it all and hightailed it to safety. Am I supposed to forgive that?"

"If I was so repugnant to you, why didn't you abort? You'd had enough training to know how," he snarled.

She shook with anger, remembering the pain. The agony. "Don't think I didn't try. The vinegar douche didn't work."

He looked as if she'd struck him. All she would have to do was tell him how grateful she'd been when it hadn't. But she wouldn't. He didn't deserve it.

She lifted her skirt and ran toward the wagon. What nerve he had. How dare he suggest that she would do something that wasn't in Krista's best interest. Bringing her out here had been the best decision of her life. Krista would thrive in this climate. She would!

And Lexy would make sure that Krista was always safe. From everything and everyone.

But before they got out of the reservation yard, Twisted Nose Doctor and Eagle Eye Jim rode in, a severe reminder of the obstacles to Lexy's dreams and plans.

The medicine man stopped his mount next to the wagon. "The children stay," he ordered.

Jake was beside him immediately. "They have the measles. They need treatment."

Twisted Nose pointed to himself. "I treat the children," he growled. "If they sick, *I* treat them." He swung and pointed at Lexy. "I warn her once. She not listen."

Lexy forced herself not to shrink from the accusation. "These children must be quarantined."

The medicine man looked at Jake. "What she say?"

"The children have an illness that is very contagious. It can spread easily from one person to another. They should be kept apart from the others."

The medicine man shook his head. "No. I treat children of my people."

Jake caught Lexy's gaze. "It does no good to argue."

"But . . . but they could die," she argued.

"If they die," the medicine man threatened, "I blame *you.*"

"If they die," she responded, throwing her careful caution to the wind, "it will be because you didn't know how to treat them."

Twisted Nose Doctor's chest expanded, his nostrils flared, and his eyes were hot with hatred. He spat words at the children in the wagon, and all but Dooley's daughter slowly got out and crept toward the cabins, tossing anxious backward glances at their medicine man.

"You are responsible for their lives," Lexy charged.

"And you," he growled, pointing an ominous finger at Sarafina, who cowered alone in the wagon, "are responsible for hers."

He swung his mount away, shouted at the children, causing them to scatter like leaves in the wind as he galloped into the reservation.

As Pete and Lexy rode away with Jake bringing up the rear, Eagle Eye Jim tossed Lexy an insulting grin.

# Chapter 11

JAKE HAD RIDDEN BEHIND THE WAGON ALL THE WAY TO her hospital. Lexy had ignored him until they rode into the clinic yard.

"We shouldn't have left those children there."

"What would you have me do?"

"You could have shown some courage and taken them anyway," she answered, sensing the foolishness of her words.

"You've already reaped the medicine man's wrath. I thought it was wise for at least one of us to stay on his good side."

"But at the expense of those children?"

Jake took a deep breath and rubbed his neck. "Twisted Nose isn't as ignorant as you want to believe, Lexy. He lived through a smallpox epidemic. He knows what can happen to people who don't have treatment. I believe he has the sense to treat them. If this was cholera or diphtheria, I'd be more concerned."

"But what if there are complications?"

"Let's hope there aren't."

She didn't dare express aloud her deepest concern. Krista. Even though she had seen Joseph earlier, there was no doubt in Lexy's mind that he probably had the same symptoms that Sarafina had. And that meant that Krista had already been exposed. There was no way to undo what had already been done, but that didn't appease her. Krista would have to be monitored very carefully.

As angry as Lexy was with Jake, and as certain as she was that he wasn't going to go easy on her, she was grateful he was here. Krista would need all the help she could get.

Joseph came around the corner from the pens, looking tired. He perked up only slightly when he saw his sister in the wagon. "Why is Sarafina here?"

"She has the measles." Lexy examined the boy, noting his listless appearance. "Joseph? Are you feeling all right?"

"Yes, ma'am. I'm fine." He drew his shirt sleeve across his face. "Just got a runny nose is all," he said around a cough.

"Here, sit on the porch for a minute, and let me take a look at you."

Joseph slumped into a chair. His eyes looked feverish, and he felt warm. "Open your mouth for me," Lexy ordered softly.

She examined his mucous membranes, discovering the faint beginnings of white bumps.

Taking a step back, she looked down at him. "I'm afraid I have some bad news, Joseph."

"I'm sick, too, ain't I?"

Lexy nodded. "I'm afraid you'll have to stay here with Sarafina. I'm awfully sorry I made you work so hard this morning."

"I didn't mind," he answered. "I hope Krista is all right. We shared a lollipop."

Lexy fought back a cringe. "I hope so, too." She ruffled his hair and went inside.

Ivy stepped out from the kitchen, her eyes wide and

her fingers fidgeting nervously with the top button of her blouse.

"Ivy, make up a couple of those cots we got from the fort. Joseph and his sister will be spending some time with us."

Ivy didn't ask questions or argue but went to do as she asked. Lexy poked her head out the door. "Pete, take the pails from the back stoop, go to the pump, and fill them with water. We've got to get their fevers down somehow. Fill the reservoir on the stove, too. We'll need warmed water as well. And the tub. Don't forget to fill the tub."

Jake carried Sarafina into the room. "Pete? When you've finished, get to the fort and explain to Commander Billings what's happened here. I'll get back as soon as I can to check on Captain York and his wife, but in the meantime, find Ben Stillwater and ask him to look in on both of them."

With a nod, Pete was gone.

Ivy stood beside Lexy, clucking her tongue. "Dumb as a post."

Lexy gave her a disapproving look. "Smart in ways neither you nor I will ever be, Ivy."

Lexy hurried to the bedroom and gazed down at her sleeping child. Something painful and anxious twisted inside her, and she tentatively touched Krista's forehead. No fever. Lexy's relief was brief, for there had not yet been enough time for her to have symptoms.

But Krista slept soundly, and her breathing was even. Lexy crept from the room and was confronted by Jake.

"How is Krista?"

Lexy couldn't look at him. She didn't want him to see the fear in her eyes. "She . . . fine. She's napping."

"She shouldn't even be here."

He was right, of course, but what could she say? That she'd made a terrible mistake by bringing her west? Never. Her stomach was in knots, and she felt nauseated. It was bad enough that he thought she'd made a mistake bringing Krista here, but when he learned of his daughter's weak lungs, he would surely reinforce his feelings about her decision to spirit her away from the safety of the civilized East. And probably his own sentiments about her abilities as a parent.

Over the rim of her teacup, Lexy shot Jake an impatient glance. "You don't have to be here. I can take care of this. You should be with Max."

"Ben is capable enough to see that Max's bandage gets changed."

"I'm sure he is. I'm just surprised you think so."

Jake's eyes held no emotion. "My personal feelings toward him have nothing to do with his ability to practice medicine."

Ivy appeared in the doorway, Krista in her arms.

Lexy tossed Jake a quick glance, noting the brief look of longing on his face before he masked it. She tried to remain immune, but her heart constricted of its own accord.

Ivy's face was pinched with concern. "She . . . she seems all right, for now."

Krista rubbed her eyes with her fist.

Lexy quickly washed her hands, then held her arms out for her daughter, who tumbled into them. "Did you have a good nap, darling?"

Krista's gaze went to the front parlor, where Joseph and his sister were. "Joseph!" she lisped. She tried to wiggle from her mother's hold. "We go see Perowann, all right?"

"No, Krista. Joseph can't go outside for a while."

She pouted. "I wanna see Perowann."

"It's getting dark—"

Krista's cranky wail broke in. "Perowann," she cried, her face pinched dramatically.

"All right." Lexy gave in. "We'll go see Pearlann."

"Why don't I take her?"

Jake's offer stopped Lexy. "That's generous of you, but—"

"And while we're outside, maybe she'd like to go with me while I give Beauty some feed."

Krista studied him shyly from beneath her lavish lashes. "Who are you?"

Lexy held her breath, waiting for his answer.

"I'm Jake, remember? I have a beautiful horse. Would you like to see her?"

Krista's eyes lit up. "You have a horsie of your very own?"

Jake stepped closer. "I sure do. She's going to have a baby, and I think the two of you would make great friends."

Lexy caught Jake's gaze, silently pleading with him not to divulge more information. His expression shamed her for thinking he'd even try to explain who he really was.

"Mama had a baby once," Krista informed him. "It was me."

"That's what I've heard."

Before he turned away, Lexy caught the anguish in his eyes.

"Does your horsie's baby grow in her tummy?"

He faced them again, composed. "Sure. I'll let you touch her tummy. Would you like that?"

"Oh, yes," came her eager lisp. "Can I go, Mama?"

With a resigned sigh, Lexy handed Krista to Jake, then bit her lip hard as she watched them disappear outside.

She heard Ivy's disapproving snuffle. "Don't say it, Ivy."

"Well, I suppose you couldn't keep them apart forever. Do you think he suspects?"

Lexy turned to the sink. "He knows she's his. Not at first, maybe, but it didn't take him long to figure it out."

Ivy's hand went to her chest. "Oh, my. You don't suppose he'll . . ."

"Tell her he's her father? No, he may be angry, possibly even hurt, but he's certainly not stupid."

"Well, he has no rights at all, Alexis. None. Going off and leaving you like he did . . ." She clucked her tongue and cleared off the table. "He's a man who shirks his responsibilities."

Lexy hadn't the strength to disagree, nor the inclination. Her own insides were tumbling around like dust in the wind. He wasn't needed here; she hoped he wouldn't stay. But she had a sinking feeling that because of Krista, he would spend more time at her clinic than at his own.

She was checking Sarafina when Pete hurried inside. "Missus Billings wants you to know that if there's anything else she can do to just let her know. Says she's bringin' a pot of soup over tomorrow."

"That would be good, Pete. Thank you for making the trip. Did you happen to see Dr. Stillwater?"

"Yep, he's gonna keep an eye on the Yorks for Doc Jake." He dug into his pocket. "He gave me these, for the li'l gal."

Lexy took the lollipops and put them out of sight, in the cupboard. "Thank you, Pete."

"And, Doc?"

"Yes?"

"Is Jake around?"

"He's . . . he's outside, probably with his horse. Krista is with him." She noted Pete's look of concern. "Is something wrong?"

"Oh, nothin' much. I . . . ah . . . just gotta give him a message from the commander." He loped outside.

Lexy was giving the children sweetened warm tea when Jake returned, his visage stormy.

"Mama, he has a big horsie. We went for a ride, an' I got to sit on her. I even patted her tummy where the baby is."

Lexy smiled in spite of her rolling stomach. "And I'll bet you weren't even afraid, were you?"

Krista's cinnamon curls bounced as she shook her head.

Jake strode to Ivy and handed Krista into her arms, then pulled Lexy outside.

"Stop it," she argued, trying to yank her arm away. "Is it true?"

"Is what true?" she countered, angry.

"That our daughter has a congenital weakness in her lungs?"

Lexy forced a laugh to cover her agitation. "Oh, is that what our three-year-old daughter said? That she 'has a congenital weakness in her lungs'?"

"Don't make light of this, damn it. Is it true?"

Lexy dreaded this moment, this moment of truth that would surely, in Jake's eyes, portray her as a careless mother, more concerned with her own career than her daughter's welfare.

It wasn't true, of course, because no matter where they lived, whether in an opulent mansion in Providence provided by Ben Stillwater or a converted brothel in California that Lexy had found herself, Krista would come in contact with disease. With the harsh realities of life. And it had been Lexy's hope that Krista would not grow up pampered and catered to because of her health. She wanted her strong, independent, happy.

But would Jake understand that? She couldn't lie to him. "Yes, it's true."

Jake's eyes filled with anger and disgust, daring Lexy to maintain eye contact. She forced herself to do so.

Whatever he felt didn't concern her. He had no rights, no vested interest, and no cause for indignation. She didn't care how often he referred to Krista as "our daughter" or "my daughter," in the end, she would remain Lexy's daughter and Lexy's alone. She had no doubts that this interest in Krista was a fleeting thing. Men thrived on ownership.

He was breathing hard; he was angry. "I'm too damned mad to talk about this now, Lexy, but this conversation isn't over."

He disappeared inside, and through the window she could see him moving from Jacob to his sister, checking them.

Taking a deep breath, she trudged up the steps and went inside as well but stepped into the kitchen. She didn't want to be in the same room with him. Not right now. She checked the reservoir, finding it full of warm water, then took the empty pails and went outside to fill them at the pump. When she returned to the kitchen, Ivy was sitting at the table, alone.

Lexy glanced into the parlor. Jake was gone, although she knew he wouldn't be far away.

"I put Krista to bed," she announced. Her gaze didn't leave Lexy.

"Thank you, Ivy."

"Will he make trouble?"

Lexy fussed with the hem of her wrapper. "He already has."

"But . . . but he has no rights, certainly."

"He has the right to see her whenever he wants, I presume." She lifted a pail of water onto the table and dipped some into the cups she'd found for the children.

"The children need plenty of fluids, Ivy. They should have a cup of water before they go to sleep."

Ivy clucked. "Fluids. Water. What makes you think that will help them?"

"Because they have fevers. Fever makes a person thirsty."

"How can you be so calm about . . . *him?* What if he should tell Krista who he is?"

Lexy carried two cups into the parlor. "You already asked me that, Ivy, and I don't think he will."

Ivy took one of the cups and handed it to Sarafina. "How can you be so sure?"

"I can't. But there's no point in worrying about it.

With these children here, we have more than enough to keep us busy without thinking about what *might* happen."

After the children were bedded down, Lexy went outside for some fresh air. It was anything but fresh. The heat of the day still hung heavily in the air, and Lexy was afraid that with the absence of a breeze, it could be an uncomfortably warm night. Her clothes stuck to her skin, and she felt sticky with sweat.

She squatted beside Pearlann's pen and fed her mash plus some scraps from dinner. The piglet was growing. She was still kind of cute, in an ugly sort of way, but that would change soon enough. Then what would she do with it?

Lexy rubbed the top of Pearlann's snout, the prickly sensation of the pig's hairs causing her to shudder. "What am I going to do with you?"

"It's hard to believe you've adopted a pig."

Jake's voice sent shards of electricity through her. "Yes. Well, I could hardly tell Mr. Frazer I didn't want it."

He came closer, and all the sensitive nerves along her neck quivered.

"Let me guess. He told you it would make fine chops and bacon."

"When this pig sprouts wings and flies, I'll think about eating her," she retorted, purposely hardening her tone.

"A sow can get pretty big, Lexy."

With a resigned sigh, she stood to face him. "Is that why you're here? To inform me that my pig is going to grow?" When he didn't answer, she grilled him. "What do you want, anyway? For me to apologize for taking Krista away from the safety of Providence? Well, I won't. I can't." Even if, considering the circumstances, she should.

"Where's the nearest hospital, Lexy?" His tone was ominous.

"Right here," she shot back, pointing to the clinic.

"One with specialists, the most modern conveniences, testing equipment, laboratories."

She felt drained, and she couldn't afford it. Not now. Not ever. "Why are you doing this?"

He grabbed her shoulders hard. "Because I want you to *think* about what you've done. In whose best interest was this foolish move all the way across the country? Krista's"—he paused dramatically—"or yours?"

Years of anger bubbled up like lava, ready to erupt. She wrenched herself free, drew back, and slapped him. For a brief, poignant moment, they stared at each other.

"You arrogant son of a snake," Lexy finally said. "How dare you stand there and preach at me? How dare you! You know nothing of my life, or Krista's."

He rubbed his cheek. "To move this far merely to get away from hurtful wagging tongues doesn't sound like you, Lexy."

Her jaw dropped. "Is that what you think? That I left everything familiar to me because my *feelings* were hurt?" She uttered a disbelieving laugh. "If that had been the case, I'd have left Providence years ago, believe me. I certainly wouldn't have waited until my daughter was three years old."

"Then why did you leave, Lexy?"

"Because . . . because I wanted a warmer, dryer climate for her. This dry heat will be good for her." She prayed he wouldn't bring up the dangers.

"And you couldn't practice medicine in Providence without Ben Stillwater's help."

She blinked nervously. "Yes. That, too." She waited for his disapproval. Surprisingly, it didn't come.

"Just how serious is her condition?"

Lexy wanted more than anything to tell him it wasn't any of his business, but she realized he had a right to know. "It . . . it could be serious. I've worried about tuberculosis from the time she was a baby. And pneumonia, of course."

He was quiet for a moment. "Does she cough much?"

"Yes. At least, she did, in the winter. I'm hoping that this climate will make her stronger."

"The summers are hot and dry, that's true, but the winters can be cold and damp."

"I know," she admitted. "Ben kept reminding me of that. But there's never going to be the perfect place, don't you see?"

She hoped to convince him, to deflect his objections with her sane reasoning. She hadn't been prepared for his next words.

"She calls Ben 'Poppy.' Has she been led to believe he's her father?"

The anguished, accusatory tone startled her. "No. Of course not."

"Then why?"

"She calls him 'Poppy,' Jake, not 'Papa.' Ever since he gave her first lollipop, he's been Poppy."

"Oh. I see."

They shared an anguish only parents can know. That the child they conceived was only human and vulnerable, and in the blink of an eye or the beat of a heart, that child's life could change. Or end. But in spite of that, in spite of all that they now shared, she continued to wonder what he wanted.

"What do you want from us, Jake? Why do you even care?"

He sighed, a heavy sound, one that could have been filled with regret if Lexy chose to believe it.

"Would it surprise you to hear that I want what every other man takes for granted?"

"No, it wouldn't," she answered. She was angry with him, upset that he'd discovered her secret, disgusted with her own feelings for him, but she did understand him.

On a husky sigh, he said, "You're a good mother, Lexy. You could be nothing less. I don't mean to imply that you're not. It's just that . . . all of this is such a damned shock to me."

"None of this would have been a shock if you hadn't left, Jake."

A tormented sigh. "That can't be changed, no matter how many times you bring it up."

And why did she continue to bring it up? To add to his guilt? To add to his pain? She didn't know . . . she truly didn't know.

"You can't imagine what I felt when I first saw her." His voice held a ragged edge.

She didn't want to hear about his weakness for Krista, but she could hardly walk away. "What did you feel?"

"That I'd received a gift. A gift I didn't deserve, and one I couldn't accept."

"Because you believe you're going to die," she finished for him.

He didn't respond. Suddenly, he straightened and turned away. "I have to meet with Commander Billings. I'll arrange for a couple of the men to stay the night and stand guard. I don't want to frighten you, but since your run-in with the medicine man today, we could be in for trouble."

She sank to the ground, her legs weak. What had she gotten herself into, anyway? And she'd done it to herself; she couldn't even pretend to blame him. Or anyone else.

She followed his shadowy figure until she could no longer see him, then remembered that he hadn't responded to her statement that he feared he would die. He believed he was living on borrowed time. And even if he weren't, what were his choices? To do the "proper" thing and marry her to give Krista his name? Lexy didn't want that. If she had, she would have tried to get in touch with him years ago.

Things were piling up, threatening to bury her. The threat from the Indians. Joseph and Sarafina's measles. Krista, and the very solid possibility that she would come down with symptoms in a week's time. Max's amputation. Megan's response to it. Their future with their new son. And, of course, Jake. Jake. Jake.

Lexy kept the windows open, hoping to catch any perceptible breeze. The two recruits Jake had promised were somewhere, she surmised, but she hadn't seen them in hours. Pete was snoring in the stable, and Ivy had gone to bed with Krista. Joseph and Sarafina went to sleep with little fuss.

Lexy entered the kitchen, retrieved an empty pail, and left the house to get some water. She returned, stopping on the back stoop where the previous owner had left an old washstand.

The house was dark; a single kerosene lamp flickered on the kitchen table. The moon cast a faint glow outside, and there was a hint of a breeze, making it much more appealing than the stuffy room where she usually slept. The only sounds she heard were from crickets and frogs. She relished the time alone; it would not happen often during the next few weeks.

She peeled off her soiled wrapper, unbuttoned her blouse, and shrugged out of it. Her chemise stuck to her skin, but she didn't really care, for at least she had quit lacing herself into a corset.

She drew her handkerchief from the pocket of her skirt and dipped it into the pail. The water was cool; she immersed her entire arm, bending it at the elbow to get the most of her enjoyment.

After cooling her other arm, she dabbed her face, neck, and chest, shivering with pleasure as rivulets of water ran down between her breasts. Oh, how she yearned for a bath. Yes, she would admit to missing a few of the luxuries she had enjoyed in Providence. Of course, there was a tub in the room between the back bedrooms, but they would use it to sponge off the children if their fevers went up. And now wasn't the time for self-indulgence, anyway. That could come later.

The night air cooled her skin, drawing her into a seduction she had no will to deny. She slid her arms from her chemise, baring her torso, sucking in a breath as the air pebbled her nipples.

She squeezed water over her breasts, sighing at the pleasurable sensation. She dragged the handkerchief over her nipples, remembering how sensitive they had been when she'd first started nursing Krista. And unable to forget how they had responded to Jake's touch.

Seldom had she allowed herself such indulgence. Truth to tell, she had worked hard for years to suppress the feelings she had so openly shared with Jake the night Krista was conceived.

But once in a while, she would dream of Jake. She resented the dreams, for she had no control over them. Especially when she would relive that first burst of arousal. That hungry, itchy need that burned hot between her legs.

She would always wake up before the shattering climax, her breathing deep and her body quivering with anticipation. And frustration. If she could will herself not to dream at all, she would.

Bringing the damp handkerchief to her throat, she pressed it there, over the notch in her clavicle, where the pulse so often throbbed when she thought of Jake, which, unfortunately, was often. He was a hard man to ignore, and his current concerns puzzled and angered her.

She had to wonder if he had motives for his actions regarding Krista, or if he was simply being a man, wanting to take control of a situation even though he had no right to.

After pulling up her damp chemise to cover her breasts once again, she slumped into the old wooden rocking chair that sat next to the washstand. She rested her head against the high scrolled back. Maybe she could catch a few minutes of sleep before one of the children woke.

Jake led Beauty into the rickety stable, Little Pete's raucous snores coming from the other side of the room.

As he brushed down his mount, he recalled Commander Billings's news that the fort would close before the end of the year. The man wanted to wipe out the Indian threat before that happened and had begun to reinforce his troops. No amount of argument or pleading would change his mind.

Jake had stopped in to see Max before returning to Lexy's clinic and told him of the commander's latest impending fiasco. Max promised to speak to his superior but warned Jake that once Billings had an idea, he ran with it no matter how much criticism he took from everyone else.

Jake left the stable, unsure of where he would sleep. He could have returned to his office, and maybe he would in a day or two, but with Ben there, he felt comfortable leaving. He needed to be at Lexy's clinic, if for no other reason than that he didn't trust any of the recruits to keep a sharp eye out for trouble. When he'd ridden up, he found the two he'd sent earlier asleep under a tree, smelling vaguely of whiskey.

He approached the back of the clinic, noting the outline of someone sitting in the rocker. As he got closer, he realized it was Lexy, not so much because he could recognize her but because she smelled like fresh lilacs after a rain, and the gentle scent was carried to him on the night breeze.

Trying to study her in the moonlight, he slowed his steps, stopping at the base of the stoop. She hadn't heard him approach; he sensed she was asleep.

Her head lolled to one side, and her breathing was

even. The moonlight gleamed off her shoulders; they were bare. All there was between him and her breasts was her chemise.

She sighed and shifted in the chair.

There was a catch in his throat as he gazed at her. In the moonlight, her breasts quivered slightly with the rise and fall of her chest as she breathed.

She looked so innocent. Vulnerable. Like a sweet child when she slept. The peace that stole over her camouflaged the fire, the independence, and the complexity that made up Lexy Tate.

She was peaches and lemons. Pillows and bed slats. Apples and onions. Complicated. Contrary. Diverse. A man could live with her a lifetime and never know the whole of her. But he'd have a hell of a good time trying.

A longing began somewhere inside him, and he felt vulnerable himself. He'd be wise to leave before she woke and discovered this sappy side of him.

His boot crunched gravel.

She cleared her throat.

Their gazes met in the moonlight, and Lexy hastened to protect herself with her arms.

"It's too late for that," he advised, covering his feelings with sarcasm.

Her mouth moved, and she cupped her hands over her breasts. She was like a young virgin bathed in moonlight. Chiseled from marble and put on a pedestal. Close enough to touch but untouchable.

She began to rock, the rhythmic sound of the rockers smacking the wooden stoop echoing in the night.

"How long did you nurse Krista?"

His words caught her off guard. "I . . . I . . ." She bit her lip, confused by her sudden feelings of shyness. "A year, maybe longer."

He didn't respond, simply studied her in the gloaming. "If it's any of your business," she was able to say.

"I think it is my business." His voice was soft. Harsh. Like whiskey mixed with sweetened tea.

She wanted to fold up and press herself into a corner. Disappear. "It isn't. You don't have the right to ask those questions, Jake. You lost the right four years ago."

"It's still my right. She's my daughter."

A strangled laugh. "I told you before that she's mine. You might have planted the seed, but I'm the one who was there to tend her and watch her grow."

"Only because I didn't know, Lexy. Only because I didn't know."

She shook her head. No. She couldn't allow this. Couldn't allow herself to weaken. Soften. "Let's not dredge up all the old excuses, Jake." Besides, she didn't like remembering the whispers and snickers from the staff when she would disappear into the lounge to nurse her baby.

His expression was pained as he continued to stare at her. "I should have been there."

"Why?" Braver now, she asked, "So you could ogle me?"

"That's not fair, Lexy," he answered, his voice husky.

It wasn't, that was true. She felt a bite of remorse but waited for him to speak.

He stepped closer, drawing in a lingering breath and expelling it slowly. "Your scent reached me before I was even certain it was you. Lilac, isn't it?"

She nodded, but she wanted to tell him to stop talking about scents and smells. One of the memories hardest for her to shake was the smell of his skin. She especially had enjoyed standing near him when he'd returned from riding his mare, for he smelled of wind and woods and earth.

"What do you want?"

A mirthless laugh. A step closer. "To turn back the clock."

Her breath came quickly. "Step away, Jake."

He moved closer and drew her hands from her breasts, brushing her nipples with the backs of his knuckles as he did so. She gasped as the night air found her breasts and drew them tight.

"Do you ever wonder what would have happened to us if I hadn't . . . broken the spell that night?" he asked.

Yes. Dozens of times. Millions. Zillions. More often than she wanted to admit, she wondered what her life would have been like if he'd called out her name instead of Megan's. "No," she lied. "I was much too busy trying to put the pieces of my life back together."

"How can I ever repair that damage, Lexy?" He reached out and touched one nipple with his thumb, and she closed her eyes, willing herself not to respond.

She swallowed hard. "You . . . you can't." *Be strong. Oh, God, help me to be strong.*

He continued to examine her. "They're no longer the nipples of a sweet, young virgin." He found the fullness of her breast and, with gentle fingertips, moved over the surface.

Lexy swallowed repeatedly and choked back a sob. She wanted to push his hand away, shove him to the ground, knee him in the groin. At least, part of her wanted to. At least, that's what her head told her she wanted. Another part of her, the part that held her heart, feared all of her defenses would fall away if she responded at all.

His fingers dipped to the front of her skirt, and she could almost feel him through the thickness of her clothes.

He put his arms around her waist and pressed his face into her stomach, inhaling deeply. "A woman who has had a child is exquisitely beautiful," he murmured against her.

She stared down at the top of his head, willing

herself not to touch his hair, hair that had once curled itself around her fingers.

She didn't feel very beautiful. For three years, she had refused to look at herself in the mirror because of the thready marks left behind by her pregnancy. She didn't resent Krista for them, she no longer hated Jake for being the cause, but she didn't feel beautiful.

Jake had awakened in her a multitude of sensations and feelings that she had successfully repressed the night he left her room. Beauty, sensuality, desire, these were things she had put out of her mind. Until now.

She tried to push him away, her fingers twining in his hair. She suddenly remembered the texture, part coarse, part fine. "Jake, don't—"

"I missed so much . . . so much . . ."

Oh, how easy it would be to succumb to him, she thought. How willingly she could abandon herself to loving him again. Her desire for him went beyond the physical, although that was surely there, pulsing inside her. He was the mate of her soul.

"Jake, please don't," she pleaded, trying to force him away from her.

He gazed up at her, his eyes shining in the moonlight. "I missed lying beside you. Comforting you. Encouraging you."

Too many images assailed her. "What do you want from me?" was her anguished cry. She needed to know, for her own sanity. Had he claimed to have found a prevention for his own early demise, she might have understood. Had he come to terms with it, knowing he might not live to see his child grow up but willing to take the chance, she would have comprehended. Had he admitted his love for her, she would have drawn him into her embrace.

He slumped onto the stoop. "I don't know. I don't know," he repeated, his head in his hands.

There was a slight noise behind her.

"Mama?"

With difficulty, Lexy composed herself. "Krista, darling. Why are you awake?"

Krista pushed open the screen door and toddled onto the stoop, her nightdress white in the moonlight. She climbed onto Lexy's lap and stared at Jake.

"Why did he have his face in your lap, Mama?"

Abruptly, Jake stood. "I'll go inside and check on the children."

Lexy cuddled Krista close, but she squirmed and watched Jake enter the house. "Hello, Mr. Jake," she lisped. "Are you sad?"

Jake stopped and glanced at her and, after a moment, smiled. "Seeing you makes me happy, Krista."

"But if you're sad," she continued, "you can put your head on Mama's chest like this." She demonstrated by resting her cheek on the pillow of Lexy's breast. "Can't he, Mama?"

Jake stood before them, his smile suddenly so wide Lexy could see his teeth, white in the moonlight. "Is that a promise?"

"Go see to the children, Jake," Lexy admonished, hiding a smile.

"Out of the mouths of babes," he answered, disappearing into the house.

# Chapter 12

THE FOLLOWING MORNING, LEXY HAD AWAKENED BEFORE dawn, trying to make sense of Jake's behavior the night before. She had tried to understand his frustration, his anger, but it wasn't easy, for she had her own feelings to deal with.

For a brief, poignant moment, she had imagined how things might have been between them had circumstances been different. It was a painful vision, and she should have known better than to dwell on it, for she'd spent the better part of the past four years trying to erase it from her mind.

She had slid from bed, relishing the cool early-morning air, sensing it would not last once the sun came up. The room where the children slept was not well lighted, for the windows faced north. But that meant it was cooler there, and she was able to draw the curtains across the windows during the brightest part of the day, for the children complained of the light bothering their eyes.

She was examining Joseph when Ivy hurried into

the room, her eyes the size of blue crystal saucers. Alarmed, Lexy asked, "What is it? What's wrong?"

Ivy appeared to have difficulty speaking, for she swallowed repeatedly before answering, "A . . . a . . ." She raised her arm high, indicating something tall. "A savage . . ." She pointed toward the door.

Attempting to hide her own fear, Lexy asked, "There's an Indian outside to see me?"

Finally collecting herself, Ivy said, her voice hovering somewhere between fear and indignation, "The size of a railroad box car."

Lexy crossed to the window and peeked outside, half expecting to see the medicine man. Turning, she grinned at Joseph. "It's your father."

"Why in the world are you smiling?" Ivy asked.

"Because Joseph's father is a friend of mine, and he's also the biggest man I've ever met. He's even bigger than Little Pete, isn't he, Ivy?"

"Not by much," Ivy responded. "But I swear he crept up on me just to frighten the daylights out of me."

Lexy winked at Joseph. "I'd better see what he wants."

"Can I see him?"

"I'll let him come to the window." She slicked down his cowlick with her palm. She hurried toward the front door, passing a nervous Ivy, who stood in the shadows.

At the bottom of the porch steps, Dooley stood beside a cow, clutching a rope in his hand that was fashioned into a sort of leash. She was almost afraid to ask. She did, anyway. "Good morning, Dooley. What do you have there?"

He looked puzzled. "A cow."

Trying not to smile, Lexy said, "I know it's a cow, but why did you bring it here?"

He held out the rope to her. "For the children."

Momentarily speechless, Lexy took hold of the rope

and stared into the animal's big brown eyes. "For the children," she repeated.

"Sick children need milk," he announced.

"Oh," she said on a sigh. "Milk." Of course. "Why, Dooley, how thoughtful of you."

"How are Joseph and Sarafina?"

"They're both doing well. I wish I could let you see them, Dooley, but—"

"Dooley understand." With that, he strode to the window and peered in. There was a shriek and a clatter, and Lexy cringed. Laughter erupted from inside, and Lexy knew that Ivy would not be amused by the children's glee at her expense.

Dooley turned. "Who that woman?"

"She's a friend of mine," Lexy answered.

He grinned. "I like scaring her."

Lexy wagged a finger at him. "Shame on you." Remembering the other children the medicine man wouldn't let her treat, she asked, "How are the others?"

He didn't look at her. "They fine."

"They are? You're sure?"

Dooley scowled. "If I say they fine, they fine."

Lexy dropped the matter, but his attitude left her suspicious.

He glanced through the window again, waved at his children, then loped down the road toward the reservation.

The cow bawled, startling Lexy. Gathering her composure, she looked into the deep, dark eyes. "Well, at least you, like the chickens, serve a function that will save you from some knife-happy cook."

She didn't know how to milk a cow, and she didn't want to be the one to try, but if worse came to worse, she could do it. She wouldn't enjoy it much, she realized, making a face, but she'd be damned if she'd let anyone know that.

She tugged on the rope. The cow bawled. "Come

on," she urged, pulling on the rope again. This time, the cow complied, and they ambled toward the shed.

Jake appeared from inside, smiling at her. He caught her gaze and winked. As always, her fragile heart pitter-pattered at the sight of him, and again she wondered if that would ever change. He hadn't yet shaved; his beard was a dark shadow over his cheeks.

"We're ready for her."

Puzzled, she asked, "Ready for her?"

"Pete and I have fashioned a stall for her inside, away from the horses."

"So you knew she was coming?"

He nodded. "Dooley wanted to do something, and this was the one thing we all agreed on."

Again, she felt insulted because a decision was made without her knowledge, but she held her tongue. "So who's going to milk her?"

"Oh, we thought you'd like that pleasure."

She snorted a laugh. "You're hilarious, you know that?"

He raised his head, his eyes twinkling. "Just thought we'd give you first chance."

In response, she merely rolled her eyes, although she loved this playful side to him. A side she'd sorely missed, she had to admit. "So, how will we keep her from wandering away during the day when she's eating?"

"Grazing," he corrected.

"Grazing," she answered, accentuating the word.

"Pete and a couple of the recruits are putting up a fence behind the stable now. Until it's ready, we'll just tie her around back. There's plenty of grass for her there."

Lexy released the rope. "She's all yours." She turned to leave.

"Lexy?"

Glancing over her shoulder, she noted Jake's earnest expression. "Yes?"

"Aren't you going to name her?"

She had thought he was going to bring up their little meeting the night before, say something poignant or tender, or apologize for embarrassing her.

She narrowed her gaze. "You are a laugh a minute, you are."

From their perch behind the house, the chickens squawked. Pearlann wasn't making any noise, but Lexy envisioned her rolling around in her muddy pen. Now she had a cow. She tried to imagine what other critter she could possibly obtain from well-meaning farmers and Indians, but she hadn't a notion. Not one.

By the end of the first week, both of the children had developed the final symptom, a full-body rash. They were doing well. Lexy was pleased with their progress. Pleased enough that she felt she could send them home to the reservation.

She and Ivy had just finished feeding them lunch. The dishes were stacked on the table in the kitchen, and the leftovers were heaped in a pot, ready to go out to Pearlann later in the afternoon.

Lexy discovered that the pig had begun to recognize her and waddled to the edge of her pen the moment she heard Lexy's voice. Pearlann wasn't really cute anymore. She was growing into a real pig, and truth be told, it wasn't a pretty sight. At least, not to Lexy. But Pearlann had more personality than a lot of people Lexy knew, and that made up for her lack of beauty.

Jake stepped into the front parlor, looking tired. They had taken turns sitting up with the children, who had become fretful being house-bound for so long. She had sung them songs she learned as a child; Jake told them outlandish stories. The children found him far more amusing, but she was glad. Some of the old Jake had returned, and with it the charm that had drawn her to him in the first place.

"The wagon is ready," Jake announced.

Joseph and Sarafina left, excited about returning home. Pete and Jake accompanied them.

When they were gone, Lexy stripped the bedding from the cots, anxious to get it clean and put away.

Ivy came from the back of the house and helped her. "I put Krista down for a nap, but she wasn't the least bit happy about it."

Krista had yet to come down with a single symptom. Lexy didn't know if she should feel relief or dread, for she couldn't imagine it not happening sooner or later. "She's going to miss all the commotion."

"Well," Ivy responded, "I, for one, will not. I will admit they were charming children, but I'm relieved they're gone. I still don't know what there was about me that amused them so."

"If they hadn't seen your corset on the clothesline, flapping in the breeze, they probably wouldn't have been so fascinated."

"I declare," she muttered. "I would feel absolutely scandalous without it. I don't know how you were able merely to discard it."

"The heat had something to do with it," Lexy answered dryly.

They worked in comfortable silence for a while, until they heard a noise from the kitchen. Lexy was almost ready to investigate when Krista toddled through the kitchen door. She looked as though she'd been caught in a dirt storm, for her little cotton shift was smeared with something dark, and her hair was filthy.

"Oh, my God," Lexy whispered, gazing at her child. "You were supposed to be taking a nap, young lady. Where have you been? Rolling around in the garbage?"

Ivy turned and gasped. "Lord in heaven, what happened to her?" She hurried to Krista and lifted her in her arms, turning her face away and expelling a disgusted sigh. "She smells like she's been rolling around with that silly pig of yours."

"Perowann is hungry," Krista responded.

Curious, Lexy asked, "Were you outside, Krista?"

Krista pointed to the kitchen. "Perowann is hungry."

Ivy and Lexy glanced at each other. Ivy's expression was one of horror. "You don't think—"

"No," Lexy interrupted. "She probably just—"

There was a crashing of dishware from the kitchen, and Lexy ran to the door, stopping short.

The back door was wide open, and Pearlann was on the table, slurping up her slop from the pot.

"Ivy, don't come in."

Ivy's exasperated scream ripped through the air. "Dear heaven!"

Lexy took a deep breath, stepped to the table, and pulled the pot away from the pig.

Pearlann grunted and squealed, clattering down from the table amid pots and broken dishes, and followed Lexy outside. When they reached the pen, Lexy discovered that the little door in the fence was open.

She coaxed the pig inside, dumped the remaining scraps on the ground, and left the pen, closing the gate behind her.

She hurried into the house and whisked Krista from a stunned Ivy. "Don't worry, Ivy, I'll clean her up."

"But I don't mind, dear."

Lexy nodded and gave her a quick smile. "I know, but I haven't spent enough time with her this past week. I'll be happy to do it. If you want to do something, why not get the water started for the bedding?"

Ivy went to do as she was told.

Lexy expelled a mouthful of air and held her nose as she looked down at her child. "That's not just mud in your hair and on your shift, is it?" She didn't expect an answer, but one whiff of Krista's head was answer enough.

Jake stopped back at the clinic before returning to his office. As he rode up, he saw Ivy outside, filling the wash tub. Without disturbing her, he went inside to look for Lexy. He heard her talking to someone in the back of the house.

As he got closer, he heard water splashing. Between two of the bedrooms there was a room that they had been using as a washroom. There was a tub in there as well, where they had sponged off the children when their fevers rose.

He found Lexy there, kneeling beside the tub in her underwear, bathing Krista. Her back was to the door, and her rump moved suggestively as she dipped into the tub and washed Krista off.

She had a beautiful back, her spine barely visible beneath the surface of her flawless skin. As she worked, moving from side to side, her breasts, loose beneath her chemise, swayed seductively. She had whisked her hair up, and spiraling tendrils draped her neck.

"You were in Pearlann's pen, weren't you, sweetie?" She wiped something brown from Krista's hair, poured some water over it, and began to lather it up.

"Perowann plays in mud," Krista announced.

"Hmmmm," Lexy responded. "That and much more, I'm afraid."

Jake detected the incandescent odor of pig manure. He bit back a grin.

"Perowann likes me."

"Yes," Lexy answered, sounding preoccupied as she scrubbed their child. "No doubt, she gets lonesome out there all by herself. But you shouldn't have opened the gate, sweetie. Pearlann might wander away and get lost."

Under the soapy lather, Krista shook her head.

"Joseph say Perowann follow him around like a puppy. I want Perowann to follow me like a puppy."

Lexy's laugh pierced Jake's heart, leaving him weak.

"Then maybe we should just get you a puppy instead. Poor Auntie Ivy nearly fainted when she saw a pig on the kitchen table."

Jake watched the two of them. His thoughts, once scabs covering his dangerous, wounded emotions, began to crack and bleed. What he was feeling could not be more painful if it were a physical lesion, open to a sandstorm. He wanted to be part of this. He wanted permanence. He wanted to raise his child, this one and many more.

"Mama?"

"Yes, sweetie?"

Krista splashed at the water beside her. "Come in."

On a sigh, Lexy answered, "Normally, I would, Krista, but . . . I'm afraid the water is a bit grimy for me."

He could envision her in a bath. He had no trouble imagining it. Her wild hair would be knotted on top of her head, as it was now, her cheeks pink from the steamy water, and her healthy body gleaming.

Krista sneezed and rubbed her chubby fist under her nose.

"Oh, I hope you're not coming down with something," Lexy murmured. She squeezed water from a cloth over Krista's little chest.

Krista glanced over Lexy's shoulder, her face splitting into a wide grin. "It's Mr. Jake!"

With a quick yank, Jake pulled up his facade to cover his pain.

Lexy gasped and turned, her gaze locking with his. "How long have you been standing there?"

He shoved himself away from the door jamb and sauntered toward her. Her composure was threatened. He stood beside her at the tub, grinning down at his daughter. And he winked at her. His shirt was open at the throat, revealing the taut cords of his neck. Hair, thick and dark, threatened to shove through the open V, and the fabric was pulled tight over his chest. His shirtsleeves were rolled to his elbows, and his forearms, tan and hair-dusted, displayed the hardened veins of a man comfortable with hard work. And he needed a shave. He was beautiful.

"Long enough to know Krista was playing in the pig pen and Pearlann was in the kitchen."

Lexy turned, trying to hide—from him and from her feelings. Krista's splashing had gotten her chemise wet, and her breasts were boldly outlined beneath the gauzy material.

"You look like hell, by the way," she murmured.

"You don't," he countered, sending sweet pleasure coursing through her.

"Don't you know it's not gentlemanly to enter a lady's bath?" she scolded, loudly enough for Krista to hear.

"There's no room for you in the tub," Krista informed him.

He knelt beside Krista and studied her, then raised his gaze to Lexy.

"She has a fever."

With a quick shake of her head, Lexy dropped to her knees beside him. "No. She's just warm from the bath."

"I can tell by her eyes," he insisted.

Krista sneezed again, and Lexy felt a rush of guilt. He couldn't be right. She didn't want him to be right. "Close your eyes, sweetie, so I can rinse the rest of the soap from your hair."

Finishing the job, she lifted Krista from the tub and allowed Jake to enfold her in a large towel. She gently rubbed Krista's hair with a smaller towel. "Do you feel all right?"

Krista didn't answer, for she was busy studying Jake. "Can I see your horsie again?"

"Yes. Very soon, I promise."

Lexy held out her arms. "Give her to me."

He handed Krista into Lexy's arms, but, as he left them, his eyes warned her to watch their daughter carefully.

She clutched Krista to her. "She'll be fine." *Oh, God, let it be so,* she prayed. She would keep a close, vigilant eye on her. Lexy knew that if Krista got the measles, she would not ever get them again, but she also knew that Krista was at risk, for with her weakened lungs, pneumonia could set in, and that would be dangerous. Even life-threatening. She refused to let herself think beyond that.

She got Krista to sleep, then shampooed her own hair and sponged herself off, dressing in clean clothing. She found Ivy outside, boiling the bedding. "I'd like to go see Megan," she began. "There's so much to do around here, I feel guilty leaving, but—"

"Go," Ivy ordered. "She's probably at her wits' end, over there with just Ben to look after her. The sooner she can cross the compound to see her husband, the better."

Lexy took the rig. It was the first time she had managed it by herself, and she was more skittish than the poor horse that pulled it.

She had barely gone a quarter of a mile when the hair on the back of her neck stood up, signaling alarm. She stifled the urge to prod the horse into going faster. Instead, her gaze shifted from one side of the road to the other, but she saw nothing.

Suddenly, without warning, Eagle Eye Jim and Twisted Nose Doctor were in front of her, blocking the road. Her horse whinnied at her clumsy attempt to pull it to a halt but stopped of its own accord, mere feet from the frightening men.

Lexy's heart pounded. They were dour, unsmiling, unsavory, and decidedly savage-looking. Worse than usual.

"What do you want?" God, her voice squeaked.

They did not respond but simply stared at her.

Gathering her courage, she said, "Please let me pass."

They continued to study her, threatening her with their leers and their glares, but said nothing. Suddenly, they let her pass.

Her heart was in her throat as she rode into the fort. She vowed to put the encounter behind her, but she couldn't help but wonder why they had stopped her. She should have inquired about the other children. She would have if she hadn't been quivering with fear.

With trepidation of a different kind, Lexy entered Megan's cottage. Mrs. Billings waved at her from the kitchen.

"How is she?" Lexy asked as the woman came toward her.

"She's fine. Just fine. I'm so glad you're here. I have to leave for a while, and I hate to leave her alone."

"Where's Dr. Stillwater?"

"He's looking in on her husband." Mrs. Billings clucked her tongue. "He's been more of a messenger than a doctor, seems to me." She stepped close, confidential. "Truth to tell, I would have thought *she* would be the one who would have the biggest problem with her husband's . . . disability. But from what I can gather, it's him."

Lexy knew there would be problems; she wasn't surprised. "Thank you for staying, Althea. Why don't you take a break?"

When the woman had gone, Lexy stepped into the bedroom. Megan was asleep. The baby was sleeping as well, and by the looks of him, he had fallen asleep satisfied, for Megan's breast was still exposed and the baby's tiny mouth mere inches from it.

At the sight of the child, Lexy felt a catch in her throat, and bittersweet memories of Krista's birth washed over her in waves.

She reached down and rescued the baby, drawing the blanket up over Megan's exposed breast. The baby sucked instinctively, and Lexy left the bedroom, studying him.

She crossed to the window, checking his color. He was a handsome boy, that was for sure. But then, why shouldn't he be? Both Megan and Max were gorgeous.

He woke and looked up at her, his big, dark eyes serious. "You're a handsome lad," she murmured. "I wonder if your mama has given you a name."

He squirmed, appearing ready to squall, so Lexy put him on her shoulder, and he graced her with a healthy burp. After that, she laid him on the sofa and unwrapped him. His legs were drawn up, rather like a frog's, a common feature after a breech birth. She would have to show Megan how to exercise them to draw them down.

"Ben? Ben!"

Megan's voice was a command.

Lexy returned to the bedroom and gave her sister a questioning look. "Ben? Not 'Ben, you old bore'? Not 'Ben, you donkey dressed in fine clothing'?"

Megan expelled an exasperated sigh. "Well, it's about time you got here." She had closed her gown.

"I do apologize, Meggie, but I didn't want to risk passing the measles on to the baby."

Megan's expression was petulantly thoughtful. "I suppose it was for my own good, but I missed your company. Lord knows it's quiet around here with no one to talk to." She reached for the baby. Lexy delivered him into her arms. "When can I get up?"

"How about tomorrow?"

Megan shrugged, her expression changing. "Fine, I guess." After a thoughtful moment, she added, her voice trembling, "Max doesn't want to see me."

"I'm sure he'll get over that," Lexy assured her.

Megan hugged the baby close, her eyes filled with tears. "And what if he doesn't?"

Lexy did have to admit that she was a bit surprised at Max's attitude. "You'll simply have to be patient with him, Meggie."

"I know." Her voice was small, childlike. "He hasn't even asked to see the baby."

There was a shuffling behind them, and Lexy turned, finding Jake in the doorway. He looked like hell. He still hadn't shaved, and his face appeared haggard. He was beautiful.

"Jake!" Megan squealed from the bed.

He responded with a tired smile. "Thought I should stop in to see if you've settled on a name for the little guy yet."

Megan's radiance at seeing Jake dimmed. "It's something Max and I have to decide together." Tears welled again. "But if he won't see me, we can hardly discuss it."

"Don't let him call the shots, Megan. I've got an old wheelchair somewhere in my office, and I think you should pay him a visit."

Megan's gaze flew to Lexy. "Today? I can go today?"

It was easy for Lexy to allow it. She wanted her sister and brother-in-law to resolve their problems, and the sooner they started, the better. "You'd best make yourself pretty," she suggested with a warm smile.

While Megan fussed with her hair, Jake and Lexy stepped into the other room.

"You look awful," Lexy told him.

"I feel awful."

Frowning, she asked, "Have you had the measles?"

"Yeah, I've had them. I'm tired, that's all."

Lexy sniffed and frowned. He smelled like whiskey. His eyes were red-rimmed from lack of sleep, and his face was flushed. He had looked bad enough hours ago when he found her bathing Krista. Now he looked like walking death.

A stab of fear made her tremble. "Jake, please get some rest. Please. I'm worried about you." On impulse, she reached up and probed the side of his neck. His skin was hot.

"Your glands are swollen," she said, drawing in her panic. "And you have a fever."

He brushed her hand away. "I need a little sleep, that's all."

She stared at him, worried and concerned. "If you hadn't just told me you'd had the measles, I'd think you were getting them now."

"Trust me, Lexy, I've had them." He went to the door. "I'm going to get the wheelchair. Have her ready when I return."

As she helped Megan prepare for her meeting with Max, Lexy continued to worry about Jake. Perhaps he wasn't coming down with the measles, but there was very definitely something wrong with him.

# Chapter 13

MEGAN'S MEETING WITH MAX HAD NOT GONE WELL. LEXY and Jake had left them alone with their new son, but it wasn't long before Megan called for Lexy and tearfully demanded to be taken back to the cabin.

"He doesn't seem to care that he's hurting me." Megan's words were choked with sobs.

"He's hurting, too, Meggie."

Megan blew her nose. "I didn't believe Max was capable of self-pity. H-he wouldn't even look at the baby and said I could name him whatever I wanted. He d-didn't care."

"I'm sure he cares." Every time she was with her sister, Lexy had to reassure her that Max eventually would come around.

Megan sniffed and blew her nose again. "He was always so strong. And . . . and even though he was handsome, he seemed surprised when someone mentioned it to him. He was so unaffected by it." She wiped her eyes. "I didn't think he'd be vain, Lexy."

Lexy took the baby and laid him in the cradle. "I doubt that it's vanity, Megan. He's repulsed by his

*214*

own deformity. He can't imagine that you aren't, too."

"I hope Jake can knock some sense into him," Megan mused as she slowly made her way to the bed.

"If anyone can, Jake can," Lexy assured her. It was going to take time. But between the pending closure of the fort and the skirmishes with the Indians, how much time did they have?

Lexy's fears and concerns took a turn for the worse when she returned to her clinic.

Ivy paced the parlor floor, Krista in her arms. Krista's dry cough and sniffly nose brought panic—raw, liquid, and cold—to Lexy's stomach.

"She woke up from her nap coughing," Ivy explained, a hint of panic in her voice as well.

Lexy motioned her to sit, and she sat down beside her. Krista's head lolled against Ivy's shoulder. Lexy examined her daughter, finding swollen glands and fever. She lifted her onto her lap and stroked her hair.

"Measles?"

Closing her eyes, Lexy nodded. "I'm afraid so. I suppose it could be just a cold, but I don't think so."

Ivy was quiet for a moment, then said, "I don't imagine there was any way to avoid it, dear."

Lexy fought the urge to cry. "It could have been avoided if I hadn't insisted on coming west."

"Nonsense. She could just as well have contracted them in Providence."

Yes, Lexy thought, but Jake's words came back to haunt her. The closest hospital was probably in Sacramento, which was three hundred miles away. San Francisco would be better, but it was another hundred miles or so beyond that.

"I've put water in the tub. I was just waiting for you to return."

With a nod, Lexy stood, clutching Krista close. "We're going to give you another little bath, sweetie."

Krista was listless until they placed her in the tub.

The tepid water against her hot flesh made her howl, and Lexy cried as well, silent inward sobs, as she gently scooped water over her daughter's fevered skin.

> *30 August—Correlation between diet and health too strong to ignore. I continue to use myself as a guinea pig, relying on a strict diet of vegetables and rice and fish. So far I feel no different, although am currently feverish. Probably the grippe, but my new concern is, can illness such as this affect the heart? Learning of my daughter has given me impetus to live, but in what way can I become involved in her life?*

Jake coughed and reached for the bottle of whiskey, then drew his hand back. No more of that stuff.

He massaged his neck muscles, trying to relieve the tension that had given him such a headache. Christ, he couldn't remember when he'd felt so awful.

Krista slept fitfully. Lexy sat on the bed and watched every movement. Took note of every breath. Measles. She knew it was passed through the air from one victim to another, but no one knew whether or not a person who had already had the measles could spread them to someone else merely because he had been in contact with someone contagious.

Krista whimpered and began to cry.

Ivy poked her head in. "I'll fill the tub."

Lexy couldn't contain her panic. The skin on her neck and behind her ears began to prickle and sweat. Krista's eyes were glazed and shiny, and she was burning up with fever. Again.

They sponged her off for nearly an hour. As she had before, Lexy wept with her daughter. Ivy had wept so hard, Lexy told her to leave and heat some broth.

After trying to feed her, Lexy sponged her face and neck again, and under her arms, dressed her in a clean cotton nightgown, and put her to bed. She had to monitor Krista closely, especially for signs of pneumonia. Should they appear, Lexy had to be prepared with a moisture tent.

She was ready to collapse into bed herself when Little Pete came to the door.

"Ready for some bad news?"

*Now what?* Lexy thought, hiding her exhaustion.

Pete nodded toward the wagon. "In there. I'll need some help."

Too tired to argue, Lexy followed him outside and peered over the side of the wagon. "Jake!" She swung her gaze to Pete. "What happened?"

Pete scratched his chin through his beard. "I went in to see if there was anything he wanted me to do for him and found him facedown, on the floor."

Lexy crawled into the wagon, bent over, and examined him. "He still has a fever." She probed his neck under his ears. "His glands are swollen, too. I told him earlier that he was sick, but he wouldn't listen to me."

"Think we can get him in the house, the two of us?"

"Maybe, with Ivy's help." She called, and Ivy appeared on the porch. The three of them somehow got Jake into the house. They put him in one of the beds in the back room.

"I figured," Pete said, "that with Doc Stillwater tendin' both the Yorks, I'd best try to bring Jake here, to you."

"Yes. Well, with Krista sick, too, I might as well take care of both of them. Pete, if you would fill the tub, we can get Jake in there to bring down his fever. Ivy," she added, "would you heat up a quick bowl of stew for Pete? I'm sure he missed his supper at the camp."

They left the room, and Lexy sat on the bed next to Jake and removed his boots. She unbuttoned his shirt, then attempted to turn him on his side so she could remove it, but he was dead weight.

"Jake." Her voice was firm. "Jake, wake up. I have to get your clothes off."

His eyes fluttered open. They were glazed and shiny, like Krista's. "What'd you say?"

"We have to cool you off."

He shook his head. "That's not what you said the first time. You wanna undress me," he slurred.

She tossed him a dry look. "Just like a man. You only hear what you want to hear."

He struggled to sit and pulled his shirt from his jeans.

"We're going to put you in the tub to get your fever down, Jake."

He coughed, a deep, dry sound. "You gonna join me?"

She softened. Smiled. Even in this state, he could tease. "Don't be stupid."

She hung his shirt over a chair. When she turned to face him again, he had collapsed against the pillows, his arms flung to his sides. Although he was at rest, his biceps bulged beneath his skin. Veins, hard as granite, stood out against his flesh, forming a ridge down each arm.

His beard was thicker now, covering the area under his chin. The hair on his chest curled against his hot skin, and Lexy wondered how any man could be so beautiful. It was a foolish time to notice his brawn, but for a fleeting moment, she admired it.

"Are you awake?" She purposely made her voice stern.

"Only because you keep talking at me," he mumbled.

"Come on, Jake, help me get your jeans off." She unbuttoned his fly, forcing a return of her professionalism.

He opened his eyes and grinned. "I'm really not in the mood to play, Lex."

Butterflies attacked her stomach. "Nor am I," she assured him, repressing a smile of her own. "But if we don't get you cooled off, that clever brain of yours may fry, and you'll never practice medicine again."

"Will I play the violin?"

She chuckled in spite of herself. "Not unless you played it before."

He lifted his hips so she could tug off his jeans. She folded them and put them on the chair beside the bed, her gaze snaking to his bare legs. She'd never seen them before. Even though they were generously covered with dark hair, the muscles of his thighs and calves were well defined beneath.

He wore a pair of drawers that had been cut off indecently above the knee.

"I wonder why you bother to wear underwear at all," she murmured, mostly to herself.

His grin was lazy, almost sleepy. "If I'd known you were going to undress me, I wouldn't have."

The old, familiar warmth trickled into her blood, softening her further. This was the old Jake. The Jake she'd fallen so madly in love with. The Jake who could melt the coldest heart.

"Can you make it to the tub?"

He swung his legs over the side of the bed and sat, unsteadily at first, then he seemed to gather strength.

"I'll call Pete."

"No," he interrupted. "With your help, I can manage. Leave Pete and Miss Ivy alone. They need some time together."

She stared at him, her mouth agape. "What?"

He grinned again. His teeth were white against his tanned, flushed skin. "You mean you haven't noticed?"

"Noticed what?"

He stood, shaky at first, and draped his arm around her shoulder. She put hers around his waist. His skin was hot. His body hard.

"That Pete can't take his eyes off her?"

They began a slow promenade to the bathroom.

"Pete is interested in Ivy?" Lexy was stunned.

"You aren't very observant, are you?"

"I just didn't think—"

"Too wrapped up in your own little world to notice anyone else's, is that it?"

"No. That's not it at all." But . . . Little Pete and Ivy? Ivy had done nothing but belittle the man since she arrived. Surely, poor Pete was beating a dead horse.

They arrived at the tub, which was half full, and Jake tested it with his foot. "God, that's cold."

"It's lukewarm," she argued. "Now, get in."

He started to skim his drawers over his hips. She stopped him. He tossed her a questioning look.

"Keep them on," she suggested, her heart skipping dangerously.

There was a twinkle in his feverish eyes, a quick wink, then he stepped into the tub, sinking into the water with a cringe and a groan. "This is hell."

Lexy got to her knees and began pouring the water over his shoulders with a small pot from the kitchen. He rested his arms on the sides of the tub, his head against the rim, his eyes closed.

They were quiet for a spell, Jake lying against the tub with his eyes closed and Lexy scooping water over him.

Her gaze started at the top of his head, where his dark hair curled like a boy's around his ears and over his brow. His eyelashes drew her gaze. So like Krista's, thick, dark, and curled at the tips. His bottom lip was fuller than the top, and his chin was squared off, strong and stubborn.

Her gaze skimmed his wet, curly chest hair, then stopped at the juncture of his thighs. Through the fabric of his drawers, she could see the dark hair and the outline of his genitals.

"No fair peeking."

With a gasp, she straightened and looked away, feeling the blush spread up her cheeks.

"Anyway, it isn't fair to me, either."

Cryptic response. She should let it go. She didn't. "Why is that?"

"Because there's always shrinkage in cold water," he answered, appearing serious. "I want you to remember that I'm bigger than that."

With a nonchalance she didn't feel, she poured a pail of water over his head.

He sputtered but laughed. "I knew I'd get to you sooner or later."

She made a face at him. "It was far easier bathing Krista than it is you."

Suddenly, he was serious again. "Krista?"

She was reluctant to admit he'd been right. "She did have a fever. In fact, I'm . . . certain she's coming down with the measles."

His feverish gaze was hard as it pierced hers. "I probably shouldn't say I told you so. But God, Lexy, I told you so." He cupped water in his hands and splashed his face. "What are you doing for her?"

"I'm doing what anyone would do for a child who has the measles," she answered, feeling defensive. Guilty.

He continued to scoop water over himself with his hands. "Have you thought of a moisture tent?"

"Of course. We have everything here if we need to construct one." She handed him the pail.

He took it and poured water over his head numerous times, and under his arms. "You know how serious this is, don't you?"

Had his words been arrows, her skin would have been tinged with blood. She was at fault here. Bringing Krista west was Lexy's crime, and if something happened, she would bear the responsibility for the rest of her life.

Instead of lashing out at him because he was right and she was wrong, she merely nodded. "Yes. I know how serious this is."

She picked a towel off the shelf, helped him from the tub, then stood back as he wiped himself. Her thoughts were filled with their daughter and the kind of care she would need to pull through this trauma. This nightmare. This living hell.

Lexy stood at the kitchen door and looked at the morning. Her eyes felt gritty from lack of sleep. For a brief moment, she forced her thoughts away from her daughter, who had had them all night long and well into the dawn.

What amazed Lexy the most out here was that every day was just like the one before. Each morning, the temperature would climb, reaching a peak toward four or five in the afternoon that was so hot it was difficult to draw a breath.

The landscape didn't change, either. The earth appeared garbed in yellow, from the scrubby grass that grew over the meadows and foothills to the wheat that billowed in the fields.

By evening, when the sun sank behind the hills, cool air would inevitably bathe the land. By morning, the air was refreshed, waiting to accept another sweltering day of sunshine. Rarely did a cloud meander through the sky. No ridges of thunderheads slicing the sky in half. No rain spattering the scorched and dusty roads.

But she didn't miss it, and she wouldn't complain.

Unable to stifle a yawn, she rubbed her hands over her face and returned to the table for her coffee. Both Jake and Krista had slept fitfully, and Lexy had found herself hopping from one to the other all night long, sponging, forcing fluids, soothing.

Well, Krista got soothed, anyway, Lexy thought with a dry lift of her mouth. Jake had spent his waking moments grumbling like a big, overgrown baby. It was true that doctors made the worst patients.

Ivy had spelled her at Krista's bedside early in the morning. Now, needing to keep herself busy so she wouldn't fall asleep, Lexy grabbed a clean cloth from her stack in the kitchen and headed outside. Joseph met her near the porch.

"Joseph, how good to see you. But are you sure you should be up and around?"

"I feel good," he answered. "What do you want me to do today?"

"It's too soon for you to resume your duties," she answered. "But I'm going to see Pearlann. Join me?" She enjoyed his company. He was a bright boy, enthusiastic and very clever. She wondered if there was any place for him to go beyond the reservation.

"Is Krista sick?"

Lexy nodded, memories of her fitful night with her daughter making her stomach hurt. "And Dr. Jake, too."

"I'm sorry," he answered, remorse in his voice. "Krista prob'ly got her sick from me."

"Don't feel bad, Joseph. There was no way of knowing this would happen."

They arrived at the pig pen. Pearlann squealed as she hurried toward them.

"What're you gonna do to her?"

Lexy wrapped the cloth around her fingers. "She needs her ears cleaned." She squatted, and the pig came to her. However, the moment she tried to hold her in any way, Pearlann squealed. Loudly.

"Well, for heaven's sake." The pig ran away from her, continuing to sound as though she were being slaughtered.

Joseph ran after her, tackled her, and held her down.

Lexy almost covered her ears. "You'd think we were murdering her."

When Joseph had a good grip on her and rolled her to her side, Lexy gingerly wiped out the pig's dirty ears. Pearlann continued her noise.

"Pigs are very . . . um," Joseph said, trying to think of the word.

"Theatrical? Dramatic?" Lexy raised an eyebrow at him.

He grinned and nodded.

Above the porcine din, Lexy mumbled, "I suppose that's why actors are called hams."

Joseph got the joke and laughed. It was music to Lexy's ears.

After Lexy cleaned Pearlann's ears, she couldn't get rid of her. She followed Lexy everywhere. Finally, after gathering the eggs and watching Joseph milk the cow, Lexy simply sat on a clean patch of ground near the pig pen and let Pearlann crawl into her lap.

"This has got to stop," she warned. Pearlann squealed.

The back of her neck prickled, and Lexy turned to the window. Jake stood there, staring out at her.

She quickly dropped Pearlann into her pen and hurried into the house. Jake met her at the bedroom door.

"Get back into bed," she ordered, her gaze skimming his wide, naked chest.

"I'm bored."

Dragging her gaze from his half-dressed body, she scolded, "You shouldn't be up."

"And you shouldn't treat that pig like a pet. Before you know it, she'll weigh three hundred pounds and want to sit in your lap."

He winced and massaged his neck, drawing her gaze to the sharp line under his arm where muscle overlapped ribs. She felt a dizzy excitement when his underarm was exposed.

She was also alarmed at the pain on his face. "Are you all right?"

He continued to rub his neck. "Just a headache."

"Stay away from the window," she scolded again, forcing a firmness into her voice that she didn't feel. "And go lie down."

He did as he was told.

"Are you hungry?"

He made a face. "Not for another egg. I've noticed what you're trying to do, Lexy. You're using as many eggs as you can, trying to convince yourself those chickens are more useful to you alive than dead on a plate."

"Oh, Jake," she answered, disgusted. "Don't even mention it. And I think having so many eggs is wonderful."

He shuddered. "I can't stand another big, yellow eye looking up at me." He paused, stabbing her with a glare. "You know what eggs are, don't you?"

She snorted a laugh. "Of course, I know what eggs are." She thought for a moment, then said, "I simply don't like to think about it."

"You mean it doesn't bother you that you're eating baby chicks that haven't been fertilized by a rooster?"

Her stomach rolled, and she swallowed. "Oh, Lord." With a painful sigh, she thought about one of her main sources of food. "Well, thank you so very much," she mumbled. "You didn't have to remind me of that, Jake. Now what will I do? I can't kill the chickens, and you've successfully turned me against the eggs."

"Sell them in town. Or stop thinking of the chickens as people. They spend their lives pecking around in the dirt. Think about it, Lex."

"Well, if I can't give you eggs, what do you want?"

"I wouldn't mind some broth, I guess. And some rice. I know Ivy has some, because she made that rice pudding. Are there any of those steamed vegetables left over from last night?"

Lexy made a face. "You want steamed vegetables for breakfast?"

He shrugged. "I wouldn't mind."

She crossed her arms over her chest and stared at him. "What kind of diet is this, Jake?"

"One I'm trying on myself. I don't expect anyone else to eat what I eat," he assured her.

She continued to study him. "For your heart research?" When he nodded, she glanced away briefly. But her gaze returned to him automatically. Even lying on the bed, he was too close, his half-naked body too overwhelming. She turned and looked outside, focusing on a butterfly as it fluttered in the air, allowing the wind to gentle it onto a flower.

"What do you see out there?"

His breath whispered against her ear, causing her to jump away. In her haste, she stepped on his foot.

"Oh, I'm sorry, I—"

He steadied her, his touch fiery against her skin. She raised her gaze slowly to meet his, and deep in his eyes she saw more than his fever glinting there.

He drew her close; she felt the hitch in her throat, and although she had soundly told herself she would not let him do this to her, she didn't fight him.

The kiss was gentle, exploratory, like examining a mental wound, one that no longer hurt but would not heal. There was pain. Pleasure. Memories of the taste of him. The smell. The texture of his stubbly skin against her mouth. His tongue seeking entrance. And gaining it. Scrubbing against hers. The warnings sent to the other parts of her body.

"Jake," she began, forcing a firmness into her voice.

"Entertain me," he murmured, rubbing his thumb against the palm of her hand.

She wanted to fight him. She had no strength. "I'm not here for your amusement."

"Odd," he whispered against her cheek. "I thought you were."

In spite of herself, she smiled. "Why do I want to hate you?"

"Because I'm prettier'n you?"

She chuckled. "That's always been the case," she answered honestly.

His fingers gripped her chin, and he looked straight into her eyes. "I was kidding."

She rested against him, feeling a curious sort of peace. "I wasn't. I've always thought you were the most handsome man I'd known. Handsome and beautiful. Only Megan could rival you in physical beauty, Jake."

He crushed her to him. "You have more beauty in your little finger than any woman I know."

Her answering smile was sincere. "Thank you for saying so." She touched his forehead again. His tender words were probably the result of delirium, she thought wryly. "Your fever is up."

"Oh, good. Another bath. Join me this time, all right?"

She regarded him sagely, allowing a small smile to touch her lips. It was the old Jake again, teasing, taunting, and drawing her into his confidence. She should have been ecstatic. But too much had changed. Nothing would ever be the way it was before. She was saddened at the loss.

"It doesn't work anymore, Jake." And she was truly sorry.

"What do you mean?"

"Your boyish charm," she explained.

It was his turn to study her. "You think that just because I have a fever, I'm out of my head, is that it?"

She moved from his embrace and, with brisk, professional movements, straightened the bedding. "Something like that."

He expelled a sigh. "I'm perfectly lucid, Lexy. Hell, I want you and know I can't have you. How much more rational can I be than that?"

She held his gaze, shoving into the recesses of her mind the smell of him, the feelings he inspired within her, the love she had for him and probably always would have. "If you were truly rational, you'd realize that you have something to live for."

He swung away. "Let's not get into that."

"Oh, right. Let's not think about reality. Let's just wallow in self-pity."

"I said, let's not get into it." Another level of pain entered his voice.

Ivy stepped into the room with Krista. She looked at Lexy, then at Jake, appearing to sense the tension, but the question she probably had on her tongue remained unasked as Jake left the room.

Lexy cleared her throat and forced a smile in her daughter's direction. "Did you get another bath, sweetie?"

Krista nodded around the thumb in her mouth.

"She's ready for a nap, I think." Ivy's voice was carefully couched.

Lexy stepped to her daughter and touched her. "How are you, sweetie?"

Krista rested her head against Ivy's shoulder and blinked. "I wanna see Perowann."

Lexy couldn't stop her dry smile. "Well, if that pig had her way, she'd be on the bed with you." She kissed her, then smoothed her unruly curls. "When you're feeling better, we'll step to the window and see Pearlann."

She put Krista to bed and sat beside her, continuing to smooth her curls. "One day, you'll be well enough to ride Mr. Jake's horse," she promised her.

Krista nodded and coughed, deep and dry.

The pain in Lexy's chest could have been no worse had it been physical. "Do you want me to tell you a story, Krista?"

Krista nodded again. " 'Billy Goats Gruff.' "

"You know that one by heart. You should tell it to me," Lexy said, a wedge of tears tightening her throat.

Suddenly, Krista looked at her. "Mama?"

"Yes, dear?" she answered expectantly.

"Is Poppy my papa?"

Lexy's stomach sank like a stone. How would she answer such a question from a child not yet four years old?

"Well, is he?"

"Poppy is Poppy. He's not your papa, Krista."

"Why?"

Lexy closed her eyes briefly, praying for some sort

of intelligent spirit to enter her body and give her child an answer she could live with. And understand.

"Because Poppy is a good friend, that's all."

Krista turned on her side and brought her knees to her chest. "But can't a papa be a good friend?"

Oh, her daughter would have an analytical mind. Lexy was grateful, of course, but this once, just this once, she wished Krista were merely a pretty child who contemplated pretty, shallow things.

"Yes, a papa can be a good friend. Don't you want that story now, sweetie?"

Krista seemed to weigh the question.

Lexy crossed her fingers.

"I don't have a papa, do I, Mama?"

Another wedge of tears threatened Lexy's careful, calm composure.

At that moment, Jake poked his head in the door. "Hey, what's going on in here?"

"Hi, Mr. Jake," Krista said, her eyes lighting up.

"Hi, yourself. I thought you were supposed to nap, little girl. How can you visit Beauty if you don't get your beauty sleep yourself?"

On the promise of seeing his horse again, Krista grabbed the edge of her blanket, planted her thumb in her mouth, and closed her eyes. "I'm going to sleep, Mama."

Lexy swallowed convulsively and tossed Jake a grateful look. She stepped into the hallway, her heart hammering. He couldn't have interrupted at a more opportune time.

"I heard what she asked you."

Lexy's gaze flew to him. "I was at a loss for words."

A grim smile. "I sensed that." He disappeared into his own room.

In the kitchen, Lexy poured herself a strong cup of coffee. Ivy studied her.

"How does she seem to you?"

Lexy expelled a sigh. "Well, there's certainly nothing wrong with her thought processes."

Ivy frowned, perplexed. "Her what?"

Lexy slumped into a chair and hung her head to release the tight muscles in her neck. "We had a conversation about Poppy, and if Poppy wasn't her papa, did it mean she didn't have one?"

Ivy inhaled sharply. "Oh, my."

"Jake apparently heard the conversation and interrupted at a most convenient time."

They were silent for a spell.

"Intellectually, I knew the time would come when I'd have to deal with this problem, but I never figured it would be so soon."

# Chapter 14

ON THE THIRD DAY OF KRISTA'S QUARANTINE, JAKE decided it was time to become better acquainted with her. After overhearing her questions to Lexy, he knew that sooner or later, Krista would insist on knowing who her father was, and Jake wanted to make sure he was in her favor. His own fever was gone, and the only remnants of his illness were a few aching joints.

After checking on Beauty, he washed up and mentally prepared himself for the visit—only to find Ben Stillwater in her room. An odd jealousy touched him deep inside, and he stood outside the door and listened.

"Trip, trap, trip, trap," Ben said, his voice low and dramatic. "'Who's that tripping over my bridge?' the ugly old troll roared."

"It's the littlest Billy Goat Gruff," Krista lisped.

The sweetness of her voice weakened Jake and he leaned against the wall.

"That's right," Ben answered. "And where was the little billy goat going?"

"To the meadow to make hisself fat," she said.

"And what was the troll's answer to that?"

" 'No, you're not, for I'm gonna gobble you up.' "

The sound of Krista's tiny voice pitched an octave lower gave Jake a knot in his throat. Could he ever match the love that was obvious between Krista and his adversary? Deep down, he knew he had to, mainly *because* Ben was his adversary. Jake didn't like to lose.

"And did the troll gobble up the little billy goat?"

"Huh-uh," Krista answered. "He say he's too little and that he should wait 'til the second Billy Goat Gruff comes, 'cause he's much bigger."

Jake closed his eyes. He must be a masochist to stand here and listen to Ben Stillwater entertain *his* daughter. Yet he didn't leave. He couldn't.

"And did the troll eat the second billy goat?"

"Huh-uh. Him said he's too small, too."

"So," Ben continued, "what happened when the third Billy Goat Gruff came to cross the bridge?"

"Twip, twap, twip, twap," she growled. " 'Eat me if you can, ugly troll.' "

"And did he?"

"No," she answered, her voice earnest. "The third billy goat is too big."

"So, what happened next?"

"The big billy goat pushed the ugly troll in the river."

"And he went in after the troll for a swim," Ben teased.

"No!" Krista giggled. "He went to eat in the meadow with his brothers, and they all got fat."

Jake couldn't stand it. He thought of all the years that Ben Stillwater had acted as a father to *his* daughter. Had filled the gap when her mother had worked. Had tucked her in. Told her stories.

A crushing pain gripped Jake's chest, and he gritted his teeth until it passed.

He shoved himself away from the wall. It was a foolish waste of energy, this angst, this purposeless jealousy, for in the end, Jake Westfield would never be a father to his child. He merely wished it had been another man, and not Ben Stillwater, who had the privilege of acting as one.

But as he walked away, he knew that was a lie. Jake didn't want any man but himself to be a father to his daughter.

He stepped into the clinic, where Lexy was examining a young, very unhappy patient.

"It h-hurts," the child complained.

"I know it does, Leona, but it will feel better after we clean it, I promise."

The child had an open wound on her arm. Lexy was washing it with soapy water, and even Jake cringed, for he knew how such a wound would sting.

He crossed the room, picked up the jar of salve, and went to the exam table. Lexy nodded her thanks. She smeared salve on the sore, then bound it tightly with a bandage.

"Jake, this is Leona. She was running away from her big brother and scraped her arm on the barbed wire fence. Leona, this is Dr. Jake."

Leona sniffed and studied Jake with serious eyes. "The lady doctor delivered my calf," she said. "Can you deliver a calf?"

Jake slid onto the table next to the child. "I've been known to."

"Whose did you deliver?" she demanded.

Jake rubbed his chin. "Do you know Billy Barstow?"

Leona's eyes darkened. "He's a bully."

"Well, I delivered a calf at his placc."

Leona was unimpressed. She swung her gaze to Lexy. "Will I get to see you again?"

"I'd like to see how things are in a few days, Leona. Maybe I can come to you instead. Would that be better?"

Leona nodded. "Ma likes you to come. She says that you're a better doctor than a man because you understand things." She shot Jake a suspicious glance. "She says men doctors tell you you're fine even when you're not, because they don't think women have real problems."

Lexy raised her gaze to Jake. "She told you this?"

Leona shook her head and hopped down from the table. "I heard her talking to her friend, Mrs. Billings. They gossip about lots of things. Did you know that Commander Billings snores so loud he wakes the dead?"

Lexy hid a smile, and Jake coughed.

"Leona, I really don't think—"

"And sometimes he breaks wind so loud the windows rattle? That makes both Ma and Mrs. Billings laugh and laugh."

Mr. Frazer poked his head into the room. "Everything all right now?"

"I'm fine, Pa. How's the pig? Is the lady doctor taking good care of her?"

"Pearlann is doin' right well, honey. The doc's takin' good care of her."

Leona beamed up at Lexy. "She's gonna come out and see us in a couple of days. Can she see the calf, Pa? Can she?"

Lexy walked Leona to the door. "I'd love to see your calf. Now, be careful when you wash, Leona. Try not to get the bandage wet."

When they had gone, Lexy cleaned up her office.

Jake examined her bookcase. "So. It seems you're developing a clientele of your own."

"I'm sure you're disappointed," she countered.

"And why would I be disappointed?"

"Because now I have a reason to stay. I have patients."

Jake studied her. "The fort will close soon. You won't be safe out here."

A brief bite of fear lit her eyes, then was gone. "I can't believe I won't be safe, Jake."

"At the very least, you should move your practice to town." He paused for effect. "If not for you, then for Krista."

She swept up bits and pieces of gauze from the floor. "I'll definitely give it some thought." She stopped and leaned on the broom handle. "For Krista's sake. And not because you suggested it. I would have done that anyway."

Jake was reluctant to leave, so he put away her salve and straightened the cupboard. Her supply of bandages appeared low. "I have extra supplies at my office, Lexy. I'd be happy to share them with you."

"Thank you. I'm going to see Megan today, and I'll stop in to see Max, too. How was he this morning?"

Jake was reluctant to tell her there was no change in Max's attitude, but he knew she'd discover it for herself, anyway. "He's the same. I'm worried. His body is healing all right, but I can't say the same for his spirit."

"Well, Megan can get up and around now. Maybe that will help."

"I hope you're right." But he wasn't certain at all.

"What about you, Jake? What will you do when the fort closes?"

"I'm in the Army. I imagine I'll get another post." It's what he'd always thought he wanted. But he didn't know anymore. Since Lexy's arrival, he'd questioned the path his life was taking. Since learning of Krista, he began to wonder. To hope. He found himself thinking in terms of the future. But a future without his daughter was unthinkable. Unfortunately, a future *with* his daughter was unthinkable as well.

Lexy wished that Jake would leave. He always seemed to bring up subjects she didn't want to deal with. Yes, when the fort closed, she would have to think about moving, but it pained her to think that she'd have to start all over again.

Besides, whether she wanted to admit it or not, she did not want to see the last of Jake Westfield, no matter how much he annoyed her.

"Ho! Here she is, your majesty."

Ben entered the room with Krista on his shoulders. "Mama, Poppy says I'm better. Am I better, Mama?"

Lexy grinned up at her daughter. "You certainly seem to be, way up there."

"I'm a princess, Mama. Poppy said so."

Ben lifted her off his shoulders and handed her to Lexy, who automatically felt her forehead. It was cool. "You're becoming spoiled, that's what you are."

"No, I'm not spoiled. Am I spoiled, Mr. Jake?"

Lexy had almost forgotten he was there. Almost. The look he gave his daughter caught Lexy off guard. It was warm and tender, gentle and deep. It nearly made her cry.

He smiled. It softened his often harsh features. "No, your majesty. If you were spoiled, you'd smell like Pearlann."

Krista studied Jake, then giggled. "I like you, Mr. Jake. Can I see your horsie?"

Lexy intervened. "It's nap time, Krista. Time for that later."

"I don't want a nap," Krista whined, rubbing her eyes.

"I'll put her down," Ben offered, taking Krista into his arms. "I think I have another story in me. What do you say, princess?"

Reluctantly, Krista nodded, then yawned.

Lexy glanced at Jake and saw the tenderness there. The sadness. The anguish in his gypsylike depths.

She retreated to the kitchen, leaving him standing there alone. She was pouring herself coffee when Little Pete came through the back door.

"Came by to get Doc Westfield," he announced. "We got a meetin' with the commander." He poured himself coffee and was about to sit when Ivy stepped into the room. His appreciative gaze flew to her. "'Afternoon, Miz Ivy."

She gave him an imperious nod, crossed to the stove, and poured herself a cup of the tea she always had brewing.

"You're lookin' mighty fine today, ma'am."

Lexy watched the unfolding of the moment. Yes, Pete was definitely smitten. Poor Pete.

"Thank you, Mr. Byron." Ivy's voice was not as sharp as Lexy had imagined it would be.

"Might I say, ma'am, that I ain't seen nothin' quite like your hair, the way it shines and shimmers when the sun lights on it."

Lexy watched the exchange, her head moving from one to the other, waiting for Ivy to chase him from the kitchen with a broom.

"Thank you again, Mr. Byron. And I appreciate your carrying the water in this morning. It was very thoughtful of you."

Little Pete blushed red. "Happy to oblige, ma'am." He stood abruptly, his hat in his hand, and strode to the door. "Well, guess I'll find Doc Jake. I, er, milked that there cow and picked the eggs. Does the hog need sloppin', Doc?"

Lexy made a face. *Hog* and *sloppin'* were two words that she would never have thought she would hear directed at her in her lifetime. "Probably. Thank you, Pete."

With a gentlemanly nod in Ivy's direction, he was gone.

Lexy stared at Ivy, who obviously felt her scrutiny, for her face and neck were a bright pink, although she didn't respond.

"Well?"

Ivy fiddled with the handle of her cup. "Well what?"

"I thought you'd chase him from the room."

Ivy's color deepened. "I ought to. It's like having a bull in the kitchen."

"But a handy one to have around, is that it?"

Ivy looked her straight in the eye. "Yes. That's it. And," she added thoughtfully, "I . . . I rather enjoy having someone around who admires me, even if he is a big, clumsy lout."

Lexy laughed. "Why, Ivy Stillwater. I do believe you're thawing."

Ivy continued to blush. "Oh, you know nothing will come of it."

Lexy wasn't so certain. Even though it didn't seem at all plausible to her, she supposed something could come of it. And the notion wasn't unpleasant at all, because it would mean that Ivy wouldn't return to Rhode Island. That thought warmed her.

"I'd like to peek in on Megan again, Ivy. Do you mind if I leave?"

"Of course not."

Lexy bathed, washed her hair, and changed into clean clothing. Once again, she hitched up the rig and rode toward the fort.

There she found Megan and the baby visiting Max in the separate room off Jake's office. Max had more color to his cheeks than she'd noticed before, and Megan was actually beaming.

"We've decided to name the baby Maxwell Jacob," she announced.

Lexy smiled at both of them. "I think that's a fine name."

After visiting a few minutes, she excused herself and went into Jake's office. Megan followed her.

"I think everything's going to be all right," she said, hope in her voice.

Lexy hugged her sister. "I knew it would. We had to give him some time, that's all."

Megan sniffed and wiped her eyes. "He thought I wouldn't love him anymore."

"And only you could convince him he was wrong, Meggie."

"This morning, I watched Jake change the bandage," Megan said. "I didn't even feel faint, Lexy. I was so intent on learning what to do, I didn't think about it."

"I'm proud of you, Megan. I truly am."

They hugged again, and Megan disappeared into Max's room once again.

Lexy mentally noted Jake's medical books, which were neatly lined on a shelf beside the window. Behind a glass-covered case were bottles of medicine, tinctures, elixirs, and even some herbal remedies.

On his shaving stand were his Kropp razor and his soap. Lexy lifted it to her nose and inhaled, remembering the smell. Savoring it.

Scolding herself, she returned to the glass case and removed a bottle of tincture of iodine and some salve. Some papers lay on his desk, and she scanned them, noting that they were part of his article on health and diet.

She dropped into his chair and paged through them. Underneath, she saw his leather journal. This was where his research was. She wanted to read it but knew it would be snooping.

There was a commotion outside, distracting her. In her haste, she inadvertently shoved the journal into her black bag with the supplies and left the office, anxious to return to the clinic.

Jake leaned against the window facing and stared outside at the men milling about in the compound. "You mean no one saw her leave?"

"Megan was in here, with me. We didn't know what was going on, Jake, or we wouldn't have let her go." Max's voice was filled with the frustration of one who is temporarily useless.

The men outside were soldiers, settlers, and townsfolk. And they were angry. A herd of Martin Sterling's cattle had been stolen by the Indians. It gave the militia the ammunition needed to fuel the rest of the settlers into a frenzy.

Impatient, the commander had sent a small contingent of men out to confront the Indians. There had been a skirmish, and three of the soldiers were injured. Jake had patched them up.

Things were getting out of hand. The Indians had fled into the lava beds, where they could regroup. And Lexy had left the fort but had not returned to the clinic.

His conversation with a frantic Ivy seared his brain.

"You didn't give her a moment's thought all those years ago," Ivy had scolded.

He'd been surprised at the contempt in her tone. "You've only heard her side of the story, Ivy."

"I can't imagine anything you say would change my mind. I've wanted to tell you what I thought of you for years, Jake Westfield. If it hadn't been for you, maybe Lexy would have married my brother, who, by the way, has adored her for years. And if it weren't for you, perhaps Krista would have a home that is more than a hovel. A converted brothel, no less! If it hadn't been for you, none of this would have happened."

"And if it hadn't been for me," he had answered, softening his tone, "Krista wouldn't even exist."

That had halted the conversation. He had left the clinic, retracing his steps, hoping to come across some clue to Lexy's whereabouts. He had found nothing.

# Chapter 15

THEY HAD CROSSED A FORBIDDING PLATEAU, ONE THAT conjured up thoughts of ancient lakes and long-dead creatures, when Lexy first saw the lava rocks. Black rock and pumice stone spires dotted the harsh landscape. The sounds of the horses echoed off the rocks around her. It was haunting. As if they had been thrown back in time.

From beneath the veil of her lashes, Lexy watched the two Indian men ahead of her and the two who rode beside her. She felt some relief that she recognized none of them.

They had approached her with silence and stealth. She had not thought to argue with them, although she probably should have. But at the time, fear had stolen her voice, and if she'd had to, she couldn't even have screamed. The shaman and his friend, Jim, had conditioned her for that response.

They had abandoned her rig an hour ago, and she was forced to ride the old swayback mare that had so patiently drawn the small carriage. Oddly enough, she'd been so frightened of the Indians she hadn't had time to be afraid of the horse.

One of the braves toted her medical bag.

When her fear had ebbed and her voice returned, she had tried to ask them what they wanted from her, but they either didn't understand or chose not to. She thought she had done remarkably well at hiding her fears, but now and then, the braves would talk among themselves, look at her, and laugh. Once, one of them had even lunged at her, shouting "Boo!" They all had a good chuckle over that one, because it had startled her so that she squeaked a scream and jumped.

After that, she had relaxed somewhat, sensing somehow that they weren't going to harm her. Or at least hoping that was the case. It would do no good to show any more of her fears, anyway, so she held her chin high and put on a stalwart facade.

Up ahead, she saw a series of caves made from the tumblings of rock formations. There were dwellings there, too, set into shallow excavations, appearing to be made from willow poles and tule matting. They looked to Lexy like inverted birds' nests.

From a larger, more sturdy building came a spiral of smoke. It was to this building that she was directed.

She slid from the horse and was prodded at gunpoint into the dark, hot, smoke-filled subterranean room.

"Aw, Doc, I should be the one to go, not you," Little Pete argued.

Jake had returned to the clinic. Lexy had not. He and Pete had scoured the countryside, checking the farms where she might have gone to see a patient, but had found nothing. Not a trace. "It'll do no good to argue, Pete. I'm going after her."

"But, Doc, I know them Indians better'n anybody. I know where they hide up in them lava beds. You don't."

"You're needed here, Pete. You and Ben must stay

here at all times. There will also be a couple of soldiers guarding the place. I don't want either of you to leave Ivy and Krista alone. Don't let them out of the house. Not for anything. Not for anyone."

Jake had to go after Lexy, not only because he wanted to but because in spite of Pete's knowledge of the lava beds, he had no knowledge of medicine. If Lexy was hurt, or if she'd been taken because someone else was hurt, Jake wanted to be there. It was also possible that she'd been taken as leverage. Blackmail.

"Do you think the Indians have her?" Ivy's question was tight with restraint.

Not wishing to frighten her more than she already was, Jake answered, "It's possible. Anything's possible, Miss Ivy. Maybe one of them is hurt. You know Lexy, she'd go anywhere to help."

Ivy went pale. "Somehow, I don't think you're telling me everything."

Pete went to her side and helped her to a chair. He solicitously took her hands in his and hunkered beside her. "Now, don't you go gettin' fretful, Miz Ivy."

"But if she's all right, why hasn't she sent word?" Ivy's voice was weak, puzzled.

Pete's meaty hand gentled Ivy's slender shoulder. "Now, Miz Ivy, Doc Lexy is a mighty clever woman, but I'll just betcha she's so busy fixin' somebody up, she ain't had time to even give us a thought. Don't you think that's so, Doc?"

Jake nodded. "Keep an eye on things here, both of you. Ben should return with the soldiers shortly."

Pete continued to argue with him all the way to the stable. "I don't like it."

"Promise me, Pete."

"Aw, Doc, you ain't even a real scout."

"Promise me."

Pete didn't answer him, but his expression spoke volumes. He didn't want Jake to go alone. Hell, he didn't want Jake to go at all.

And Jake hadn't gone far before he was set upon by Indians, who swiftly knocked him unconscious.

The inside of the sweat lodge was stifling. Lexy had gone so far beyond hot and sticky that she barely noticed the discomfort. She was too tired. She tried to remember when she'd had a full night's sleep. Probably the night Krista had arrived from Providence.

A twinge knifed Lexy's stomach, slicing an anguished path to her heart. Krista. She prayed her daughter would continue to get better despite the fact that Lexy wasn't there. She prayed there would be no signs of pneumonia in Krista's lungs. She prayed, she prayed, she prayed.

Lexy scrubbed her palms across her face and stifled another yawn as she peered into the dim light. The fire, constantly fed, cut through the smoky haze as it drifted up through the opening in the roof.

Twisted Nose Doctor slept fitfully, away from the fire. Fighting her weariness, she struggled to her feet and went to check on him.

He'd been shot, the bullet entering beneath his heart and exiting to the left of his spine, nicking either a large vessel or an organ on its way out. She prayed it was an organ, for if by some chance it was an artery, the shaman would surely bleed to death, no matter what she tried to do for him. Her fate would be sealed if he died, for she would be blamed, no matter what she had done to try to save him.

When she had arrived, he'd already lost a lot of blood. Grateful to have fresh supplies with her, she had cleaned the bullet hole and packed it, even using some whiskey mixed with the iodine tincture she'd taken from Jake's office. After that, she tightly wound strips of cloth around his abdomen to stem the bleeding. He had not awakened.

She'd had no idea what to expect when she stepped into this building. Dozens of thoughts had gone through her mind, the foremost being that she'd been kidnapped for some nefarious reason and that if anyone wanted her back, they would pay dearly for her. Blackmail.

Never in her wildest thoughts had she imagined that the braves had simply needed a doctor—for their doctor.

She glanced down at her skirt, remembering that she'd had to tear off strips of her petticoat to use as washcloths to clean the shaman's wound. Much of the rest of it went into bandages to bind the wound.

At first, the conditions of the sweat lodge had appalled her. Everything was sooty. There was not a whit of fresh air, and she'd almost felt claustrophobic. But as the hours dragged on, she saw the value in it, especially when she learned, through one of the men who deigned to speak to her, that after a session in the sweat lodge, they took a swim in the river. Which was cold and refreshing, she was sure.

She had just settled into her corner when she heard a commotion outside. Two men entered, carrying someone on a makeshift stretcher. Before the men in the lodge had circled the stretcher entirely, Lexy noticed the shirt the unconscious man was wearing, and she felt a jolt of recognition.

"Jake!"

Startled by her explosion of speech, the Indians spoke quickly among themselves and stared at her.

She elbowed her way through the men and gazed into Jake's face, which was void of expression. "Oh, God," she murmured, forcing back her fear.

The men laid the stretcher near the fire, where there was light. Lexy pushed them away and fell to her knees beside him.

"What happened? Can anyone tell me what happened?"

After a moment, one of the braves stepped forward. "We found him. He had fallen from his mount."

With swift, nervous fingers, she examined him. Incensed, she said, "He has a lump the size of a fist on the back of his head. He was hit." She tossed them an angry look. "Why did you hit him?"

They backed away from her and said nothing.

She pulled off his boots, then his stockings. Behind her, she heard the buzz of conversation. One of the Indians appeared at her side. He briefly touched her arm. She turned, giving him what she hoped wasn't an impatient look.

"You want help?"

She shook her head. "Just more water. And . . . and some food."

They didn't leave the sweat lodge. There was more mumbling among them. The one who spoke English stepped forward again. "We take Twisted Nose Doctor to our camp now."

As much as she wanted the medicine man gone, she couldn't simply let them take him. "He shouldn't be moved yet. He's still bleeding."

"We take him," the brave announced.

"I won't be responsible for what happens if you move him," she threatened. "If you want him to live, you'll leave him here."

"We take him," he repeated.

If the medicine man died, Lexy would fear for her own life. Even if some of the more placid Indians released her, Eagle Eye Jim would hunt her down. Somehow, she knew this. She knew it would be terrible. She had not the energy to think in terms of details.

With a weary shrug, she returned to Jake. Why had they hit him? She had avoided the commotion at the fort when she left earlier, anxious to return to the clinic. She had thought it strange that so many of the settlers were riding toward the fort as she rode away from it, but she had kept to a side road and hadn't been seen, therefore hadn't asked any questions.

With deft fingers, she tore off another piece of her petticoat and dipped it into the water bucket. She pulled him toward her and dabbed his head, leaving the cloth there as she laid him down on his back again. She touched his forehead lightly, etching with her finger the barely visible remainder of the bruise she'd given him when she'd clubbed him in the head with the piece from the headboard.

Had he come looking for her? She wasn't even certain he was completely well, for although she hadn't voiced her fears, she had worried that his bout with fever could have triggered something that would affect his heart. Before Jake had spoken of his concerns, she would never have put the two thoughts together.

She felt a crushing frustration at how little the medical profession knew about the heart. She couldn't help but wonder if illness of any kind wouldn't weaken it.

Her shoulders slumped, and she thought about Krista. Further worry stirred in her stomach.

Near the fire were three buckets of water and what she assumed was food. She crossed to the fire and discovered two bowls of rice along with some smoked fish. She ate some of each but found it hard to swallow, although she should be hungry.

Returning to Jake, she sank to the floor. He hadn't moved, hadn't even twitched an eyebrow. There was little to do for him but wait. Inside the sweat lodge, the heat from the fire intensified, and she continued to sweat profusely.

She sat cross-legged on the floor beside him and allowed herself the luxury of studying him. In his handsome features, she saw her daughter, discovering the miracle of genetics, how a strong, square chin on a man becomes a sweet, stubborn chin on a child.

Eyelashes, thick and dark, that rim a man's eyes and give the appearance of gypsylike danger became coquettish on his daughter.

She ran a gentle finger over his full lower lip, recalling how Krista's generous lower lip would stick out when she pouted.

She allowed herself a bittersweet smile. They were alike in so many ways. How many times had she convinced herself that she needed no one else in her life but her daughter? How often had she scoffed at Ben when he had insisted that every child needed a father?

She had slowly begun to understand. Perhaps she had been a bit militant about raising Krista, considering the circumstances of her conception and her birth. It had all seemed quite easy and reasonable, inasmuch as she had Ben and Ivy to help her, both of whom Krista adored.

Now there was Jake, who had enticed her with promises to ride his horse. It would not be easy to begin anew, just she and Krista, after everything that had already happened in Krista's life. And in her own.

But they would. Lexy tore another length from her petticoat and dabbed at Jake's forehead. Over his cheeks, he had days of stubble, so thick and dark he'd look menacing—if he hadn't been helpless as a babe.

She ran the tips of her fingers over it, discovering the different directions it grew, wondering how much it would soften as it got longer. Trying to imagine what he would look like in a full beard.

Not wishing to hurry through any task that involved Jake, she slowly moved a wet cloth over his neck. She unbuttoned his shirt and marveled at the hair that grew over his nipples. Briefly tossing the cloth aside, she allowed herself the extravagance of touching him. Beneath her palm, the hairs on his chest teased her. She spread her fingers, feeling the fur between them, luxuriating in the texture.

With a swift shake of her head, she moved away, her hand discovering Jake's journal. She rescued it from the floor, returned to the firelight, and, with a minimum amount of guilt, opened it.

She read with interest his observations on the arteries and was fascinated at his findings.

Time lost meaning as she read deeper and deeper

into the journal, discovering the extent of Jake's passion to learn his history and her own elation at the intensity with which he wanted to live.

She reached the end and discovered a letter. To her. Barely able to breathe, she read on.

*What is in my heart you will never know. I can't forgive myself for hurting you. I was saddened and disappointed that Ben couldn't persuade you to meet with me before I left Providence, but in many ways, I understood.*

Puzzled, she rested a moment. Certainly, if Ben had brought a message from Jake, she would have remembered. She wondered how she would have felt, knowing that he wanted to see her. Oh, certainly, she would have been angry, and, if she was honest with herself, she might have refused. But . . . Ben had mentioned no such meeting.

*Seeing you again after all these years was painful for me, because I discovered that you truly had erased me from your mind and your heart. I saw it in your eyes that day I came after you outside my office.*

She closed her eyes, remembering how difficult it had been that day to pretend he meant nothing when her heart was so full of him. She read on.

*But I could never forget the countless things about you that made me fall in love with you.*

She pressed the journal to her breast, the sting of tears tangling in her throat.

*I saw the suspicion in your eyes when I told you I hadn't requested this fort, but I would be lying if I told you I hadn't been pleased to get it. Not because of Megan, but because of my friendship with Max . . .*

Lexy briefly closed her eyes and knew again Jake's pain at having to amputate his best friend's leg.

*Megan has meant little to me since I discovered the wonder of you, but that's not important now since Ben wrote me of your marriage . . .*

She raised her eyes and studied the author, an excitement inside her that nearly overwhelmed her. So their lives had taken this turn because of Ben. Sweet, well-meaning Ben Stillwater. She should be angry with him. And perhaps she would be when she saw him again, but right now, what was important was that Jake loved her. He actually loved *her*.

*Asking Ben to watch out for you was like asking the proverbial fox to guard the hen house. I should have known the end result. It's unfair of me to hate the man who has your love, but the world is an unfair place, and no one knows this better than I. But I dream of loving you, of learning every inch of you, of watching your passion, for I know you have so much of it. I have discovered how much I want to live. I only hope I live long enough to find a way to save myself. I want what every man wants, Lexy, I want a life. And although I am undeserving after what I've put you through, I would prefer one with you. But that's a fairy tale, and we both know it. There is no way I can save myself. I'd like to believe that I'll discover a cure and that we'll all live happily ever after, but it won't happen, Lexy, and I can't let you waste your life waiting for it. I won't.*

She closed the book and held it against her heart. Poor Jake. Her gaze went to him again, and the love she felt swelled inside her like water in a sponge, soaking every available pod of air.

He stirred, and she touched him. Feeling sleepy, she curled up against him, resting her leg over his and flinging her arm across his chest. The questions she had were too numerous to count, but for now, she didn't want any answers. She just wanted to lie with him and listen to the beating of his heart. And know that he loved her.

# Chapter 16

JAKE CAME AWAKE WITH A START, WINCING AT THE ACHE in his head. He opened his eyes, unfamiliar with the surroundings. A fire burned nearby, but he wasn't outside. He looked to one side, his chin skimming the top of someone's head. Inhaling deeply, he produced a sleepy smile. Lexy. Too tired and weak to move, he simply curved his arm around her and brought her closer to his chest. Holding her felt as natural as breathing.

The tips of his fingers moved across the soft surface of her arm as it lay across his chest. Her breasts were pressed against his side. Her breath, warm and moist against his skin, was deep and even.

He managed another grin. She had a sweet, feminine snore.

He took stock of himself. The last thing he remembered was leaving the clinic.

Once again, he looked around him. They were in a dwelling with earthen walls. A fire burned in the center of the room, and the smoke wafted up, disappearing through a hole in the ceiling. A sweat lodge.

He squeezed Lexy's waist. She was safe. He frowned. Or was she? Was *he?*

She coughed and rose onto her elbow, awake now, and perplexed. Recognition was instantaneous. "Jake."

With his forefinger, he hooked a curl of her hair and draped it behind her ear. She looked damned desirable, all sleepy and succulent and disheveled.

Her brow furrowed with concern, and she touched the back of his head. He winced.

"How are you?"

He drew her to him and kissed her, surprising her. Her mouth was warm and wet, and she opened for him. In spite of his weakened condition and his current confusion, there was a stirring in his groin.

She drew away. "Oh, Jake . . ." She ended with a reluctant sigh.

"All right. If you don't want to kiss me, then tell me where we are."

Her glance fluttered away, and he chose to believe she did want to kiss him after all.

He gazed around the lodge. "Why did they bring you here, anyway?"

She sat and stretched her lower back. "Because the medicine man had been shot."

He told her of the theft of the cattle and of the militia stirring up trouble, hoping to engage in some kind of skirmish with the Indians.

"Krista?"

The fear in her voice was evident. "I've posted soldiers at the clinic, and Pete and Ben are there."

She bit her lip. "Oh, God, Jake. What if—"

He pressed a finger over her lips. Her hair was wild around her shoulders, and sweat gleamed on her face and neck. Smudges of soot were evident along the line of her jaw and her forehead, and her gown was a wrinkled mess. He didn't think he'd ever see her looking more beautiful.

Her gaze became guarded. "What's wrong?"

"I know you'll worry anyway, but we have to believe things at the clinic will be all right."

She shifted nervously. "But my baby . . ."

He drew her to him and held her. "I know. I know."

They sat quietly. Jake knew her thoughts were with their daughter. Suddenly, she pulled away.

"Jake, I read your journal."

A knot formed in his stomach. "The whole thing?"

After a nod, she apologized. "I'm sorry. I know it wasn't any of my business, but . . . after you told me you'd started to study the heart and the arteries surrounding it, I . . . I guess I couldn't resist."

After a brief bite of alarm, he answered, "Then you know all of my secrets."

She frowned, concentrating. "Probably."

"You read the letter?"

She didn't look at him. She merely nodded.

The knot in his stomach grew. He hadn't imagined how he would feel if she actually knew his thoughts. "I, ah, well, I didn't ever expect you to read it."

"Then why did you write it?"

Her gaze, so sweet and earnest, tugged at him. "A moment of weakness, I guess, when I thought I'd lost you forever."

Her sweet expression was replaced by a wry one. "And now that you know I'm not married, you've changed your mind, is that it?"

He swore. "I'll never change my mind about what I feel, Lexy, just whether or not it's wise to pursue those feelings."

She studied her hands in her lap, which twisted at the fabric of her skirt. "All of life is a gamble, Jake. There's no certainty in anything."

He cursed again, wishing she weren't quite so logical. "It scares me to think of my future, Lex. You know that."

With a shuddery sigh, she answered, "I know."

He touched her thigh, feeling her stiffen beneath his

fingers. The knot twisted inside him like a knife. "I've destroyed everything, haven't I?"

She cocked her head. "What?"

"With one word four years ago, I destroyed your feelings for me."

She grew angry. "Why does it matter? No matter what happens, you'll hide behind your fears about the future."

He cursed. "I'm not sure I even have a future."

She laughed, a miraculously refreshing sound. "Oh, Jake, you're such a fool."

Feeling anything but playful, he attempted a light-hearted grab in her direction. "Oh, I'm a fool, huh?"

"You're such a fool," she repeated, her smile reaching her eyes.

"Tell me why I'm such a fool," he urged, feeling the faint stirrings of hope.

"You tried to get in touch with me before you left Providence."

"Of course I did. I couldn't leave things the way they were."

"But Ben never gave me your message."

He snorted a soft laugh. "Ben. That doesn't surprise me. He's been a pain in the ass since the day I met him."

She stroked Jake's chest; he closed his eyes and sighed.

"He only did what he thought was best for me."

"And why was it up to him to take on that responsibility?"

"Because he loved me, and I knew it. He'd asked me to marry him at dinner the night you showed up at my apartment. It wasn't the first time, and it wouldn't be the last."

The reality that she would have accepted had she been any other kind of woman frightened him. "He could have given you everything."

With a soft smile, she answered, "He could have

given me many things, that's true. He could even have given me love. The trouble was, I couldn't return it. It wasn't fair to him."

"Do you ever wonder what would have happened if we had met again, after that night?"

"Sometimes. Do you?"

"Yes. I often wonder if I had learned about Krista early on, would I have been noble enough to do the right thing?"

Her stroking became tentative. "And would you?"

"To be perfectly honest, I don't know. I wasn't in a very good frame of mind back then, you know."

"And what frame of mind are you in now?"

He detected an attempt at lightness in her tone, but underlying it, he heard the stress. "I've grown up. At least, I'd like to think I have. I could still keel over and die tomorrow, Lexy, but—"

"So could I," she interrupted.

He knew her meaning. Life was a gamble.

She snuggled against him once again. "Were you in love with Megan that night?"

"I don't know. Truthfully, she had absorbed my thoughts for so many years, I don't know when I began to realize she was so wrapped up in herself she had no time for anyone else."

"But you thought she was beautiful."

"Yes," he admitted. "I still do."

Lexy rose up and gave him a hurt look.

He shrugged. "So what? She has a beautiful face. Beyond that, she has nothing that interests me. The more time I spent with you, the more I realized how much more there was to you. And," he added, tweaking her nose, "you weren't exactly a troll."

"Thanks a lot."

"But you did hate me, didn't you?"

She pressed her forehead against his chin. "I thought I did. At the time, maybe I truly did."

He was quiet for a moment, remembering. Hurting. "You gave yourself a vinegar douche after that night."

Her hand stopped at his navel. "Yes."

An ache developed in his chest, and he had difficulty swallowing. "It was the sensible thing to do."

"Yes," she answered softly. "It was."

He drew a breath. "Just how disappointed were you that it didn't work?"

She rose up again and snagged his gaze. "Honestly?"

"Of course, honestly," he answered, unsure that he wanted to know.

"By the time I knew I was truly pregnant, I was so relieved the douche hadn't done its job that I wept."

He continued to struggle for breath. "But . . . you must have known how difficult it was going to be for you."

"Intellectually, I knew." She paused, expelling a ragged breath. "Not until I was unable to hide my condition did I realize I would be fighting an uphill battle for the rest of my life."

"And did you regret it?"

She gave him a beautiful smile. "Not for a minute."

A swelling, a surging of life and strength, poured through him. He glanced toward the darkened doorway. "Do you suppose anyone will come and check on us?"

A cautious look. "Why?"

"Because I've been waiting for years to see you naked."

She laughed, embarrassed. "What makes you think I want you to see me that way?"

"I'm hoping my instincts are right." He ached to touch her, to love her the way she deserved to be loved.

She put her fists on her hips. "Just like that? No sweet, loving words of desire, no coaxing, no . . . no romance?"

He grinned, his gaze on her breasts. "When you sit that way, I can see your nipples."

She laughed and swatted him. How long had she

waited for this? How many times in her secret dreams had she imagined what it might be like to be this way with him? To have him want her?

"Now I'm wondering what's on your mind," he mused.

With a sly smile, she answered, "Do you really want to know?"

"I do."

"It might shock you."

He lay back, folding his arms behind his head. She had the raw urge to nuzzle his bare underarms.

"I'm strong enough."

There was a pulsing between her thighs. "Sometimes," she began, feeling brave, "when I daydream, I think about what it would be like to tell you exactly how I feel. I get . . ." She inhaled sharply, remembering.

"You get what?" His words were like caresses, fanning her desire.

She swallowed as the pulsing between her thighs thickened. "I get . . . amorous. Aroused. And you have no idea what I'm feeling. I'm cool and calm and aloof on the outside. I hide it well, you see."

His eyes darkened. "I see. Go on."

"Well," she continued, warming to the game, "I imagine your concern, because, after all, I've summoned you, and you're certain there must be something drastically wrong."

"And is there?" His fingers teased the area above her breasts, and her nipples tightened.

She shook her head. "Only that I've dreamed about you and was rudely awakened just about the time something sweet and rough and exciting was about to happen." That part was so very true.

His fingers found her breast, and he rubbed his palm over her nipple. "Something like this?"

With a shuddery sigh, she answered, "Oh, more than that."

"Are you telling me that when you dream about me, you get excited?"

She swallowed repeatedly as his hand forged a path down her rib cage. "Yes."

"And you wake up hot and disappointed, is that it?" His hand snaked beneath her skirt.

"You have no idea," she murmured.

"Tell me how it feels," he insisted.

"Like . . . like I'm on the verge of exploding." The sensation was beginning.

Firelight glanced off his gypsy eyes. "I'd like to watch that explosion sometime."

"What do you think you'd see?" she asked bravely.

He briefly closed his eyes. "You're sitting in a big chair, your—"

"Me?" Her pulse jumped, forcing a path to her pelvis.

He waved her away. "Now it's my fantasy, Lexy. You're sitting in a big chair, one leg thrown over the arm, the other bent at the knee. I can see by your expression that although you're aroused, you aren't certain you should do what you're about to do."

"How . . . how can you tell I'm aroused?"

"A lot of ways."

"Tell me," she urged, wondering how she could sound so sensible when she throbbed all over.

"Well, for one thing, your eyes are closed, and there's this incredibly provocative anticipation on your face."

"What else?"

"Even from across the room, I can see how wet you are."

She fought the urge to squeeze her legs together. "Anything else?"

"To heighten your arousal, you play with your breasts, pinching and pulling on your nipples like you imagine your lover doing if he were there."

"That much is—"

"No more interruptions," he demanded.

"Sorry."

"Your fingers continue to touch your breasts," he continued, his fingers finding her through the fabric of her gown, "and you discover that your nipples are sensitive. Itchy. You pinch them again, gently, of course, tugging on them, imagining that they are between your lover's teeth and that he's nibbling on them."

Lexy swallowed, waves of desire weakening her as he fondled her breasts.

"Then, with tentative fingers, you cup your breasts, remembering the stretch marks that were made during your pregnancy and after, when they filled with milk. You briefly wonder if your lover would find them repulsive."

"And . . . and would he?" She held her breath.

"He's already told you he wouldn't, but you can't fully believe it. You go a step further and wonder what it would feel like to have him nurse at your breast like Krista did."

She gasped, the idea shocking. And naughty. And exciting. "Jake!"

He ignored her outburst. "That's another thing men dream about. Sucking milk from a woman's breast."

"They don't," she argued, not quite believing her own disbelief.

"Trust me. They do."

"And . . . and do you?"

His fingers deftly unbuttoned the top of her gown. He insinuated his fingers inside, beneath her camisole, and she bit down on her lip to keep from crying out.

"I would have given anything to take your nipple into my mouth and drink from your breast."

She became weak and hot and aroused. "Oh, Jake, damn you, don't say it."

He pinched her nipple, just enough to make her gasp. "You asked, sweetheart."

She drew his hand from her breast and rested it firmly on his chest. "We're getting off the subject here. What happens next?"

He muttered a put-upon sound, then continued. "You slowly make your way down your torso, past your navel, remembering the hair that surrounds your lover's navel, and wishing you'd had the nerve to touch him there with your tongue."

"My . . . my tongue?"

"Yeah. You know how much your lover likes it when you lick him with your tongue."

She swallowed. Hard. "I do?" At his nod, she asked, "Then what?"

"Then, your anticipating mounting, you touch the top of your furry mound, threading your fingers through the hair, teasing yourself by barely touching the place that screams to be touched."

Jake's fingers were on her inner thigh, stroking the sensitive surface of her skin.

"And and how does a woman go about touching herself there?"

"She begins by lightly drawing her finger over it, feeling her entire body quiver in expectation."

He hadn't touched her there. She wanted him to, oh, God, she wanted it.

"Then, in slow, lush degrees, she circles it, now and then teasing the spot, then drawing away."

Why wasn't he showing her? Why wouldn't he touch her?

"You want me to touch you, don't you?"

She frowned, frustrated. "Are you a mind reader?"

"No. But this is my fantasy. You'll have to touch yourself."

She gave her head a quick shake. "I can't. I just can't, Jake."

With a sigh, he continued. "All right. Soon, probably all too suddenly, she feels it begin, that deep, uncontrollable spasm that starts somewhere inside her and screams to be relieved. Her head lolls to one side, her face becomes a beautiful mask of passion and desire, and she rubs herself, shuddering and making sweet, throaty noises as her climax overwhelms her."

Feeling drowsy with desire, she asked, "How is it that you know so much about it?"

"It's just a fantasy," he answered.

She wasn't convinced. "And you fantasize about watching a woman pleasure herself?"

"Not just any woman, Lexy. You."

She expelled a nervous laugh. "Sorry I can't accommodate you."

"Don't be too sure."

She glanced away, nervous, excited. "You can't force me to touch myself."

His fingers moved higher. "Oh, I could. And even if you profess to hate me forever, you'll delight in the feeling of making love to yourself."

"I don't believe that," she argued.

"And why not?"

She took a deep breath. "Because . . . I think that a woman would much prefer to be touched by the man she loves. Men might think they know women, Jake, but what excites a woman isn't always the same thing that excites a man." Through her logical monologue, his fingers drove her insane.

"Jake, stop doing that. Someone could come in."

"Thrilling, isn't it?"

She made a half-hearted attempt to push him away. "No. It's nerve-racking."

He continued to rub her thigh, avoiding that place that wanted his touch the most. "Undress for me."

"Jake!" Her gaze nervously scanned the dim room. "I can't do that."

"Yes, you can." The seductive sound of his voice was like a caress.

"But what if—"

"If *ifs* and *buts* were candy and nuts, we'd all have a wonderful Christmas," he teased.

Despite her nervousness, she laughed, because she loved this side of him. The old Jake. The one who teased and prodded and drove her crazy. "You are incorrigible."

"I'm also very horny."

She glanced at the tenting of his underdrawers. "But you've been sick. You had a fever, and you shouldn't be . . ." Her voice faded.

"All that naughty talk made me well," he announced. "I'd undress for you first, but as you can see," he said, indicating his erection, "I couldn't be any more naked than I already am."

"Oh, yes you could," she answered around a sly grin, amazed at her boldness.

Their gazes locked, and suddenly he whipped his drawers down his legs, kicking them off.

She knew her mouth was open. She knew she stared. She knew she had to touch him. Swallowing the tangle of arousal that climbed her throat, she pressed two fingers to the tip, gasping in awe as his juices oozed very slightly.

"Be careful." His voice was strangled. "I have a whole closet full of fantasies."

With gentle fingers, she gripped him, sliding the skin slowly up and down, delighting in his swift intake of breath. "Tell me." She'd often wondered what he would feel like, all engorged and aroused. She thought perhaps if she hadn't wanted him inside her so badly, she could have touched and stroked him for hours.

He swallowed, unable to stifle a groan. "You keep doing that, and it'll be over before we start, sweetheart."

She moved her fingers to his thick thatch of dark hair. "Tell me," she repeated.

"Every man's fantasy," he began, his voice sounding strangled, "is to have a woman make love to him with her mouth."

Somehow that didn't surprise her. It didn't even really shock her. It did excite her. "And is that your fantasy?"

"Oh, yeah."

She bent over him, but he stopped her. At her questioning look, he gave her a sexy lopsided smile. "Just not at this moment."

"Why not?"

"Because first I want you to undress for me."

Reluctantly, she moved away from him and stood. Their gazes continued to lock as she finished unbuttoning her dress, shrugged it from her shoulders, and removed her arms from the sleeves. When it hit the floor, she stepped out of it and kicked it away.

Slowly, she pulled the tie at the waist of her camisole, then unbuttoned it, allowing it to hang open just over her nipples. They throbbed, burning a path to her groin.

She unbuttoned her torn petticoat and stepped out of it, kicking it on top of her gown. She was just about to untie the string that held her drawers up when he shook his head.

"Come here," he ordered.

Through her heavy, almost thunderous arousal, she forced a feeling of lightness. "You didn't say please."

He grinned and sat up. "Please."

She stepped to him.

He brought his hands to her hips and drew her close, pressing his face low on her belly. Her knees buckled.

"Men have another fantasy," he murmured against her. His hot breath penetrated the cotton of her drawers and singed her skin.

"Do I dare ask?" Her heart was drumming.

"It doesn't matter. I'm going to tell you anyway."

She felt his mouth open over her. He brought his arms around her and held her.

"Those of us who are honest with ourselves admit

we want to make love to a woman with our tongues." His words were muffled.

She whimpered and slumped to the floor. "Oh, God, Jake."

He moved away and regarded her through heavy lids. "Now you can finish undressing."

With a shake of her head, she admitted, "I don't think I have the strength."

"Then let me." He drew her arms from the camisole, letting his thumbs nudge her nipples. In the light of the fire, he examined her, finding the stretch marks on her breasts with the tip of his tongue.

She had no strength. Her entire body was thick with arousal.

He pulled her drawers down her legs, bending to place one kiss on her fur. She gasped and rose up off the floor, the stirrings of excitement clamoring for completion.

His fingers traced the stretch marks on her stomach. "Silvery lines of beauty. Honor. God, but I love them." He bent and kissed each one.

All she could do was stare, amazed, at the top of his head.

He stopped and moved up beside her. Their mouths met in a kiss, deep, wet, with tongues darting and rubbing. She threw her arms around his shoulders, drawing him close, needing him there.

Before he moved on top of her, he touched her, as if testing her readiness. He groaned. "You're wet."

"Yes," she said with a whimper.

His fingers moved to the insides of her thighs. "It's running down your legs."

"Yes." Gasping at the sensation, she spread her legs and took him inside, squeezing hard, as if to keep him there. She met his thrusts, wrapping her legs around him and clinging to him, for if she hadn't she would surely have fallen off the edge of the world.

# Chapter 17

Later, much later, she woke and found him watching her. She touched his stubble, remembering how it felt on the sensitive areas of her own flesh.

She snuggled against him, tangling her limbs with his, and drew her arm around him as he held her and stroked her back.

"I love this part," she murmured.

He gave her a grand hug. "What part is that?"

"This part. This . . . snuggling. It's like I can't get close enough to you." She threw one leg over his and snagged it, pulling it to her. "Sometimes I think I want to be absorbed into your skin."

He murmured a satisfied sound. "Years ago, I learned something about women."

She closed her eyes, smiling sleepily. "Want to share it?"

"A very wise man once told me that after making love to a woman, one should always hold her."

She rose up briefly. "You mean it's not automatic?"

He shook his head. "Unfortunately not. Our first instinct is to roll away and go to sleep."

She snuggled again and kissed him. "I love that wise man."

He returned her kiss. "We had company earlier."

She inhaled sharply and attempted to cover her nakedness.

"Don't worry," he soothed. "I covered you with my body when I heard them coming."

A laugh bubbled up from somewhere inside her. She felt happy. Warm. Contented. Loved. "Why am I still exposed to the world, then?"

"Because I love to watch you."

She drew in a breath, rolled to her side, and nuzzled her face into his rib cage. She let her fingers wander over him, finding the hairy nooks and crannies of his body. "But you won't make a commitment to me and Krista, will you?" She dared a brave look at him as she spoke.

His eyes darkened and became remote. "I can't. You know that."

She wanted to rehash all the old arguments, about Krista needing a father, about them being a family, about loving and living whatever time they had together. She knew it would do no good. Still, she had to try.

"Krista needs a father, Jake."

He hissed a curse and rolled away from her into a sitting position, his back a hard, impenetrable wall against her. "That's not fair."

"Life isn't fair, Jake. You were the one to assure me of that." She was being relentless, maybe even cruel. She didn't care.

Suddenly, he turned to her, his eyes hard and shiny with emotion. "Don't you think I want to? God in heaven, Lexy, I haven't thought about much else since the moment I saw her. I want to watch her grow into a young woman. I want to be there when the young men begin to flock around, because, by God, they will come in droves, believe me."

She watched his throat work, and the pain that was

in his eyes pierced her heart. But she had feelings of her own. "Then don't be selfish, Jake."

"Selfish? You think I'm being selfish?" Disbelief showed on his face.

"Yes," she shot back. "Only a man who thinks about himself would turn his back on his child."

He laughed, a hard, sharp bark. "Yeah, that's me, all right. A selfish bastard if there ever was one."

"You are, Jake. You would deprive your child of however many years you have left, preferring to live them alone, pitying yourself, rather than sharing them with those who love you."

Tears tangled in her throat, but she stood bravely and dressed, refusing to look at him for fear he would see that her harsh words merely covered her shattered heart.

His gaze was on her, but he didn't speak until she was completely dressed and at the door. "Where do you think you're going?"

"To get some air. It's suddenly become very stagnant in here."

"Lexy, don't go outside. It's dangerous."

She heard him curse and knew he was looking for his own clothes, but she ignored him and stepped out into the sunlight. Blinking against the brightness, she dragged fresh air into her lungs, releasing it slowly.

Startled by a footfall, she turned. Eagle Eye Jim stood near the opening to the lodge. He held a rifle. He wore a lascivious smirk.

After her heart banged against her rib cage, she touched the healing wound on her jaw.

"Come," he ordered, jabbing at her with the rifle butt.

Had it been anyone but Jim, she would have called for Jake. And because it was Jim, she should have. But she feared him. He was irrational.

She was marched to another upside-down bird's nest and hustled inside. Twisted Nose Doctor rested on a bed of furs. He motioned her closer.

Glancing to either side, looking for a quick retreat, she took tentative steps toward him.

He pointed to his bandaged abdomen. "You do this to me."

"I did." She forced herself not to glance away, but held his gaze despite her fear.

"Why you not let me die?"

"Because I took an oath," she explained.

He frowned. "Oath?"

"I promised that as a physician, I would treat anyone to the best of my abilities." She paused, feeling braver. "Even you."

A hint of an appreciative smile touched his hard mouth. "The soldiers are fighting my people. There will be deaths."

There was scuffling behind her. She turned just as Jake stepped into the room.

"Are you all right?"

She nodded, grateful he was with her.

"You." Twisted Nose Doctor pointed at Jake. "Why do soldiers fight us here? They don't know the lava beds. They will die."

"You know why. They want you on the reservation, Twisted Nose."

The shaman spat a curse. "The reservation land is useless. There is no hunting on that land. It is like the lava beds. Dead."

"Can't we talk about it?"

"Talk." Twisted Nose spat again. "All we do is talk. Your government does not keep promises even after talk."

But Jake had to try. He knew that if an all-out war exploded, the Army would lose hundreds of men, for even though the Indians were outnumbered, they knew every cave and cranny in the lava beds and could ambush the soldiers at any number of places.

"Let me try one more time, Twisted Nose. Let me talk to our chief, Commander Billings, and warn him of what you say. Let me bring him here to you. To smoke. To talk."

The medicine man appeared thoughtful, then pointed at Lexy. "Because she save my life, I will listen one more time." An almost impish smile touched his mouth. "I would not have saved hers."

Jake and Lexy were led outside and given a horse. Checking the placement of the sun, they headed south, across the lava beds toward the trees.

Lexy's arms came around Jake, and he thought about her words. She'd called him selfish, but he wasn't. No, selfish would be to marry her, have her begin to rely on him, have Krista so embedded into his soul that he would curse whatever God there was for his destiny. As it was, things were bad enough. Krista was already embedded into his soul, and Lexy would be a part of him until the day he died. Maybe even after that.

In his mind, it was far more selfish to marry the woman he loved, who bore his child, and give them so little time. It was far more generous to force them to make lives of their own, lives that had not been touched by his any more than they already were.

And who was to say that he would even live beyond the summer? Even revising his lifestyle couldn't promise that. He would be no better than the fool who married his sweetheart before he went off to war, then died before they could have a life together, preventing her from making a new life for herself. That was selfish.

Little Pete gazed at Miss Ivy's stricken expression, his heart melting like a puddle in his chest. He gripped her tiny hand in his paw, careful not to squeeze it too hard. She was so delicate. So fragile. Like . . . like the wartberry fairybell, the prettiest danged wildflower he'd ever seen in his life.

"Now, now, Miss Ivy," he soothed. "Doc Jake's not gonna let anything happen to Doc Lexy."

Miss Ivy hiccoughed and sniffed. "Oh, how do you know that? You're simply trying to patronize me, you big oaf."

"Now, don't you go callin' me such names, Miss Ivy, I might get the feelin' that you're sweet on me," he teased, surprising himself at his boldness.

It paid off. She smiled, expanding his heart.

But the worried look returned, and she dabbed at her eyes with a white lacy handkerchief that was so tiny he didn't see how it could handle even one snoutful.

"Why haven't they sent word? Surely, they would let us know they're all right, especially because of Krista."

"Yeah," Pete considered. "He's sure sweet on the little gal."

"Well, he should be," Miss Ivy huffed. "He's her father."

Pete knew his mouth hung open. His expression obviously surprised her.

"You didn't know?"

Struck dumb, he merely shook his head.

Her forehead wrinkled, causing a dimple between her eyes. "Why, I thought surely someone would have let the cat out of the bag by now, especially since Jake has known since he first set eyes on Krista that he was her father."

"But that would mean . . .." He felt the blush start at his neck and work clear through to his eyebrows.

Miss Ivy actually smiled. "Why, Mr. Byron. You're blushing."

On a nod, he answered, "Yes, ma'am."

Her smile widened, and he saw her teeth, prettier than pearls hanging from a string. He felt as if someone had blown sunshine up his underwear.

"That's very . . . sweet."

Little Pete hardly knew what to do with himself. He cleared his throat, ran his rough fingers through his hair, and turned away. Sweet? She actually thought he was sweet? Why, that was better than thinking he was a clumsy ox or an uncivilized savage. But he could think of no proper response. Hell, how did one respond to such a thing?

"Yes, ma'am," was all he could say. He felt as if he were sitting in butter and the warmth had spread into his privates.

Her expression changed, and she was pensive and frightened again. "Oh, I do so wish they would show up this minute and surprise Krista when she wakes from her nap."

"Yes, ma'am." All he could think about was how beautiful Miss Ivy was and how much he wanted to reach out and touch her hair. Maybe smell it. Hell, if she knew what he was thinking, she'd no doubt drive him from the house with the handle of her broom.

"I never did approve of that Jake Westfield," she was saying.

"No, ma'am. I mean, he ain't so bad. I mean, he's a real nice fella and one heck of a doctor, Miss Ivy."

She fussed with the frilly bow at her neck, and his gaze was drawn to the clean line of her jaw. She was finer made than a racing filly.

"Well," she answered with a deep sigh, "I just hope he doesn't muck up Lexy's life as well as Krista's."

Little Pete didn't know how to answer, but he kept batting around the news that Krista was Jake's daughter in his mind and knew that meant Doc Jake and Doc Lexy had to have . . .

He pushed a lungful of air through his mouth, unwilling to let his imagination work further. "Well, if you'd like, I'll go lookin' for them again, Miss Ivy."

"Oh, Mr. Byron, would you do that?" She put her fine, fragile fingers on his arm, and he burned clean down to the holes in his wool socks.

"Yes, ma'am." He hated to leave, for she hadn't removed her hand. He glanced at her, finding an odd expression on her face. "Somethin' wrong, Miss Ivy?"

Flustered, she quickly took her hand away and

smoothed her palms over her hips. "No. N-no. Of course not. Get along with you, then."

Puzzled, he merely frowned, shook his head, and left the room. But even when he was outside, he had the feeling she was standing at the window watching him. Now, why would she do such a dadburned thing?

He stole a quick glance before he entered the shed to saddle his mount, and his heart expanded like plumped-up sausage. She was still standing there, watching him.

Before he'd ridden out of the yard, she ran from the house. "Parnell!"

Startled at the sound of his God-given name, he brought his mount to a quick stop and watched her run across the grass toward him. The very tops of her bosom jiggled beneath her clothing, and he thought for sure he'd come undone right then and there.

"Yes, Miss Ivy?" His mouth was dry as an August riverbed.

She was breathing hard when she reached him, her cheeks flushed, her eyes shiny. "It's Krista. She just woke up, and she's got a terrible cough. And . . . and her fever's back up. Oh, Parnell, I'm so afraid she's coming down with pneumonia. Please, please, you must hurry!"

Little Pete felt as if a buffalo had crushed his chest. He kicked his mount into a run, wishing he could fly.

Lexy and Jake had ridden in silence, each deep in thought. Suddenly, Jake chuckled.

"I can't imagine what's funny about this situation, Jacob."

"I wasn't thinking about this. I forced myself to think about more pleasant things."

"Like what?"

"I remember when you were six."

"I don't think I can remember that far back." She rested her head against him.

"I was chasing you with a frog, remember?"

She almost caught her smile. "And you ran into a tree. That's how you got that bump on your nose."

"Yeah, yeah," he said impatiently. "But don't you recall what happened after that?"

She frowned. "Megan probably went in and tattled on me for something I didn't even do."

"Oh, you did something, all right."

She rested her chin between his shoulder blades. "What did I do?"

His chest shook again. "You planted the most delicious wet kiss on my mouth."

She gasped, suddenly remembering. "Oh, Lord. I did, didn't I?"

"Oh, yes, you did."

"I can't believe I did that. I was probably missing my two front teeth."

"That's what made it so memorable."

She reached around and tried to find enough flesh to pinch. He was hard as an oak everywhere. "You're crazier than an outhouse rat," she muttered.

"That's a shithouse rat, honey."

She could tell by the sound of his voice that he was laughing at her. "The word isn't in my vocabulary," she argued. "Anyway, I was a mere six. I didn't know what I was doing."

He squeezed her thigh. "It's something I'll never forget, sweetheart."

She physically had to prevent herself from wrapping her arms around him and hugging him. She never got enough of him. Never. She'd been in love with him her whole life.

"But, Jake, you were twelve years old. You must have laughed yourself silly."

He reached around and gave her another squeeze. "Not at all. It's one of my fondest memories."

"Look at me when you say that," she dared, hoping he wasn't laughing at her. She tried to peer around him to catch his expression but didn't dare move too much for fear of falling off the horse. Surely, he was joking. He had to be. Didn't he?

They had ridden in silence for a few moments when a brave appeared in front of them. Jake drew his mount to a stop.

"What is it, Kono?"

With a nod, he indicated a direction into the trees. "Come, please."

Lexy gripped Jake's waist.

He touched her knee, as if reassuring her. "What's wrong?" he asked the brave.

Kono's expression was one of concern. "Please, just come."

Jake nudged the mount into a trot, following the Indian into a dense brush. There, in a clearing, was another upside-down bird's nest structure.

Kono was off his mount and waiting for them at the door. Lexy slid from the horse and followed Jake inside. Sunshine dappled the interior through the reeds and twigs used to construct the building.

On the floor was a child, one of those she had not been allowed to treat for measles. Feeling a jolt of alarm, she rushed to him and sank to the floor beside him. His eyes were closed; he was unresponsive. She felt for a pulse and found a thready one. But he wasn't breathing. "Oh, Jake," she whispered, catching his gaze as he knelt beside her. "He's stopped breathing."

Frowning, Jake nudged her aside. "Let me try something."

*Anything,* she thought, afraid.

She scooted out of Jake's way and hugged her knees, watching him. He pressed his ear to the Indian boy's chest, caught Lexy's eager gaze, and nodded.

Then he did something she'd never seen before. He bent over the Indian, put one hand under the boy's neck, and blew into his mouth.

Kono, who had been on the other side of the boy, murmured a frightened sound and stepped away.

Every few seconds, Jake blew air into the Indian's mouth, and suddenly, the boy struggled beneath him, sputtering, coughing. Jake brought him to a sitting position and rubbed his back as he continued to cough.

Lexy bit her lip and pressed a hand to her mouth.

Kono was on his knees beside the child, his expression one of awe as he gazed at Jake. "You bring him from the dead."

Jake shook his head. "He wasn't dead, Kono."

"But he not speak. He not breathe."

Lexy followed Jake outside, her heart pounding, her pulse racing. "You did save him, Jake."

"His tongue had just closed off his esophagus."

"Don't be so modest."

"You'd have discovered the same thing," he argued.

"I'm not so sure. I was so certain he had died from some complication of the measles, I didn't think beyond that to something as simple as his tongue." And it was true.

Kono approached them, leading his pony. He handed Jake the reins. "For you."

Lexy stifled a gasp but was certain Jake wouldn't accept such a precious gift.

Jake took the reins, then shook Kono's hand. "Your gift is generous, Kono. Thank you."

"Jake, you—"

"Hush," he insisted as he mounted his horse and drew her up behind him again.

The pony in tow, they rode away from the small camp, and Lexy could hold her tongue no longer. "How could you take such a precious thing from him? It's probably the only thing he has in the world."

"Yes. And if I hadn't taken his gift, I would have insulted him beyond reason."

"Sort of . . . sort of like refusing a crate of chickens or a newborn piglet or a cow," she answered, remembering her menagerie.

"Exactly."

With a sigh, she rested her cheek against Jake's strong, broad back. It was certainly an odd way to practice medicine, she mused quietly.

They hadn't ridden far when they saw Little Pete heading toward them, waving his hat.

Delight turned to fear when Lexy saw Pete's expression. Fear turned to terror when she heard his words.

"Come on. We gotta hurry back," he urged. "It's the little gal. She's got a cough somethin' awful, and her fever's back up."

# Chapter 18

LEXY SLID FROM THE MOUNT AND TORE INTO THE HOUSE. "Ivy!" She ran from room to room, continuing to call Ivy's name.

From the back of the house, she heard her answer. Lexy hurried into the room that held the tub. Her heart squeezed in her chest. Her daughter was whimpering. Ivy was sponging her off.

Lexy fell to her knees and grabbed Krista, holding her to her, stroking her hair, her back, her neck. "Oh, God, I was afraid of this . . ."

Ivy wrung her hands beside her. "I didn't know what else to do. She isn't responding this time, dear. I've not been able to get her fever down."

Lexy swallowed her terror. "We'll have to use a moisture tent."

Suddenly, Jake was behind her. "I'll get it ready."

She heard the clutching fear in his voice and bit her lip to keep from wailing. Pressing her face against Krista's limp body, she failed to choke back her sobs.

* * *

The tent was set up in the bathroom around the tub. Pete kept heated water in the tub, which filled the tent with moisture. Lexy kept warm compresses on Krista's chest, hoping to loosen the mucus she knew clogged the air sacs in her daughter's weakened lungs.

After two days, Lexy hadn't left the room. Finally, Jake forced her to let Ivy relieve her. She had no strength to argue. He led her from the room.

"You're going to make yourself ill," he scolded, his words gentle.

Her lips quivered, and tears rolled down her cheeks. She hadn't believed she had that many tears inside her. "You know," she began, not really caring whom she spoke to, "when your parents die, you're an orphan. And . . ." She sniffed and wiped her face. "And when your husband or your wife dies, you're a widow or a widower. But . . ." She gasped a breath, then pinched her lips together so hard she tasted blood. "But when you lose a child, there's no word strong enough to define the agony you feel."

He held her, and she went into his arms. "You've got to rest."

She shoved him away. "No. I can nap in there, Jake. I can't leave her, I just can't." She glared at him. "I don't know how you can."

His expression became remote. "One martyr in the family is enough."

His words stung. "If I could sacrifice myself for Krista's life, I would. If it was possible to assure her a long, happy life, I'd have done it years ago."

"And you don't think I would?"

She barked a raw laugh. "I hardly think so. After all, you aren't even willing to share with her a few years of your precious life, are you?"

His gaze hardened. "You have no idea what I would do for my daughter."

Rage burned through her. "No, but I know what you won't do for her."

Ivy poked her head out the door. "I can hear you

two arguing from inside the tent. Stop it right now, do you hear me? I'm no doctor, but it seems to me that even if someone doesn't appear to hear what's going on around them, they just might anyway. Now, wouldn't you hate for Krista to hear you two hammering away at each other?"

Lexy pressed her hands against her face, took a deep breath, and prayed for strength. "You're right. I'm fine, Ivy. You can go and fix the men some lunch. I'll sit with Krista again."

"I'll take my turn after lunch," Jake announced.

Lexy pierced him with a narrow gaze. "Don't let it interfere with your other plans."

Ivy grabbed her arm. "Stop it," she hissed, dragging Lexy into the bathroom. "Now, get down there and change that compress."

Lexy resumed caring for her daughter. Time became meaningless. Krista's coughs stabbed at her heart, and her own chest ached. She lay beside her, whispering to her, hoping that somewhere, deep in that precious sleeping brain, Krista knew her mother was there and wouldn't leave her.

She willed her daughter to gain strength, to fight the infection, to live. Her little body, moist from the cooling tent, still felt feverish. Lexy dozed, awakening with a start, scolding herself for having the audacity to sleep in front of her child.

But she often did. She lifted her heavy head from the pillow beside Krista and found Jake sitting opposite, his hand dwarfing their daughter's. Too tired to respond, Lexy merely watched through hooded lids.

Great tears rolled down Jake's cheeks. He was talking softly, whispering, really, for she couldn't hear the words. Somewhere in the other part of the house, Ivy sang softly.

"'Amazing grace, how sweet the sound . . .'"

Lexy pressed her face into her arm to smother a sob.

"'. . . That saved a wretch like me.'"

She gently took Krista's other hand, automatically feeling for a pulse at her wrist. So relieved was she to find one, her sobs nearly choked her.

"'. . . I once was lost but now am found . . .'"

She bravely glanced at Jake, whose face was crumpled with pain. She reached across Krista and took his free hand in hers, gripping it tightly. He returned the pressure.

"'. . . Was blind but now I see.'"

They didn't speak; they simply sat, one on either side of their child, holding hands.

She looked at him, hoping he saw that she hadn't meant to be cruel. His gaze spoke volumes. They both knew, without speaking, that the only thing that mattered now was the life of their daughter.

Jake tore himself away from the moisture tent. He stumbled outside, dragging in the cooling night air. Tears snagged in his throat, and he swallowed repeatedly.

He looked into the sky, feeling a rage spread through him like fire. If someone had to die, he thought, it should be him. He was expecting it. He was prepared . . .

He spewed a curse and flung himself off the porch. . . . *Was blind but now I see.* He had begun to see things differently since returning to find his precious, beautiful daughter struggling to cling to life.

She had to live. She *had* to. He would trade places with her in a heartbeat, just as Lexy would. Again, he had difficulty swallowing. He'd make a pact with the devil to keep his daughter alive.

But he knew now that what he wanted most in his life was to be a part of hers, for as long as he was allowed.

The porch door squeaked open. "Jake?"

He swung to face the door. Ivy stood there, her expression unreadable. Beyond, from the back of the house, came Lexy's sobs.

Without stopping to acknowledge Ivy, he tore past her and raced to the moisture tent, his heart in his throat, his pain filling every empty space inside him.

He whipped back the tent opening and crawled inside. Lexy had flung herself across Krista and was sobbing uncontrollably.

"Don't cry, Mama," Krista crooned, stroking her mother's hair.

Jake sagged to the floor beside them, drawing them both into his arms. They stayed there, the three of them, until they fell asleep.

Lexy woke with a start and immediately felt for Krista, who was snuggled against Jake's chest. Lexy touched her forehead, expelling a sigh of relief to find it cool.

"I'm better now, Mama."

Her voice was croaky, which made Lexy smile, although she wanted to cry. "It sounds like you have a little frog stuck in your throat this morning," she said, to deflect her emotions.

Krista coughed, the sound loose. Lexy quickly dug for her handkerchief and held it for Krista to expectorate into. "Always remember that, sweetie. Don't swallow what you cough up. All right?" At Krista's nod, Lexy glanced at Jake.

Something low in her belly dropped, and she repressed a pleasant shudder. "I'm sorry I was so cruel, Jake. I didn't mean what I said."

He took her hand, brought it to his lips, and kissed it. Repeatedly. "Yes, you did. At the time."

She gazed at their hands, his so big and dark, hers so small and white. "Yes, maybe I did. At the time."

"I deserved it."

Krista reached up and stroked her father's stubble. "Mr. Jake, you need to shave."

He caught her tiny hand and pressed it to his cheek, his eyes welling, but he blinked the tears away before they escaped. "I'll do that," he answered, his voice thick. "Just for you, princess."

With a giggle, she closed her eyes and snuggled deeper into his embrace. "It's nice here, Mama. I like it."

Lexy held her tongue but was thinking that her daughter hadn't better get accustomed to the luxury of Jake Westfield's embrace. She knew firsthand the kind of withdrawals a person could get when that embrace was no longer there.

"Where's Poppy?" Krista asked, startling both Lexy and Jake.

"Why, I don't know, exactly, sweetie." Come to think of it, she hadn't even thought about Ben. Not for days.

Jake answered her. "He's at the fort, treating . . . the wounded soldiers. And keeping an eye on Megan and Max."

Krista slept again, but neither Jake nor Lexy left her.

"What's happening at the fort, Jake?"

"Pete says that the commander is willing to talk with the medicine man but feels it will be a useless conference."

Lexy absently stroked Jake's arm. "With that attitude, how can they resolve anything?"

"There's going to be trouble, Lexy. Maybe even a war. Not a big one, but a war nevertheless."

"And we won't be safe here."

"No."

Lexy's gaze went to Krista, who slept innocently and soundly beside them. "I had no idea there would be real danger out here, Jake. Maybe I was being naïve, but I simply didn't think about Indians and wars. All I thought about was starting over, in a place where Krista could grow up strong and independent."

"And she will," Jake assured her. "Now," he said, getting to his feet, "I'm going to my office to get cleaned up. While I'm there, I'll check to see how things are going between Commander Billings and the Indians."

"Is there any way you can find out about the sick children who had to stay at the reservation?"

"I'll stop there on my way," he answered.

"And Jake? Look in on Megan and Max, will you?"

"Of course."

"And Jake?" she said again. He turned, waiting for her to continue. "Be careful."

While he shaved, Jake thought about the children who had been left at the reservation. Dooley was truly upset when he had to tell Jake that two of the children had died. Jake wasn't looking forward to informing Lexy.

He changed his clothes and met with Commander Billings. He took Max along in a wheelchair.

"I don't like it," the commander groused. "We'll be leaving here soon, the fort will close, and the damned savages will continue to wreak havoc on the settlers."

"But if we don't at least try, Commander, we'll never know if they're willing to give a little." Max was the commander's devil's advocate.

Commander Billings snorted a laugh. "With that Twisted Nose Doctor and the buck with the bulging eye calling the shots, there will be no giving in, believe me."

"Perhaps not," Max agreed. "But to rush headlong into a war is imprudent, especially when we have so many civilians to think about."

"The settlers are gearing up with their own band of volunteers."

"I don't mean the settlers, Commander. I mean our families. Yours and . . . and mine."

"And mine," Jake added, reminding them that Lexy had a clinic right in the path between the fort and the lava beds.

The commander stood, fumbled for his cigar, then

made his way to the window. "Even if we wait, we can't trust the volunteers to do the same. Some of those men are so eager to kill Indians they don't need an ounce of encouragement."

"Then we'll have to rely on those who are more cautious. If we were to take a vote, the cautious ones would outnumber the others."

As always, Jake admired Max's ability to look at a problem from all sides.

Billings turned from the window. "All right. We'll try it your way, York. Are you up to a powwow with that medicine man?"

Max shot Jake a questioning glance. "I'm up to it if my doctor says it's all right."

Jake grinned. "Want me to come along?"

"Only if you want to," was Max's answer.

"Westfield," Commander Billings said, "I'd rather you organized getting our families out of here. Do you mind?"

A bit disappointed, Jake merely nodded. "If that's what you want, sir."

After returning Max to his room in Jake's office, Jake strode across the compound to look in on Megan.

She beamed at him when he entered the cabin. "How's my husband today? I haven't seen him yet."

"He's doing very well." He studied her. "I'm proud of you, Meggie. I have to admit I didn't think you had it in you."

She expelled a shaky sigh. "I didn't, either. But when I thought about my life without Max, it was an endless gray tunnel with no sunshine." She smiled and shrugged. "I guess I've changed. Why, I even kept a secret about Lexy's daughter. You know by now that she has a daughter, don't you?"

"Yes," he answered. "I know she has a daughter."

"I almost told you about her one day, but Lexy made me promise not to say anything to anyone. I haven't seen the child yet, but I'm very anxious to."

"She's my daughter, too, Megan."

Megan's expression was one of stunned surprise. "Yours? Did you know about her?"

With a shake of his head, he said, "Not until Ben and Ivy Stillwater brought her out here."

She frowned, puzzled. "But . . . why . . . what—"

"I'll let Lexy explain everything to you later, Megan. Right now, I have to get back to the clinic. Krista's been a very sick little girl, and I hate to be away from her."

"Will you help me cross to your office to see Max before you leave?"

"It will be my pleasure." Best not to tell her that Max was preparing to travel to the lava beds to confer with the shaman about peace. It was time the two of them started discussing things between them without using Jake as an intermediary.

# Chapter 19

LEXY STEPPED FROM THE TUB, WOUND A TOWEL AROUND her hair and one around her body just as Jake stepped into the room. Her tummy took that little dip it always did when she saw him.

"I just had a bath," she announced inanely.

He gave her a private look. His eyes darkened. The pulse at the hollow of his throat pumped. "So I see."

Suddenly, she felt nervous. Awkward. "How are things at the fort?"

His gaze wandered the length of her. "The commander is willing to sit down with the medicine man and talk."

Lexy twisted the towel nervously. "That's a good sign, isn't it?"

He ran the tips of his fingers over her shoulder, down across her clavicle to her breasts that plumped out above the towel. "Max is going with him."

"Max? He's up to it?" She shuddered as he pressed a kiss on her bare shoulder.

"He is. Even so, it's my duty to get the families to safety." He kissed her neck.

"Meaning us, too?"

His gaze was on the tops of her breasts. So were the tips of his fingers. "Of course."

Lexy gripped Jake's shoulders as the towel she wore fell to the floor. "Wh-when?" She wrapped one leg around his hip, and he held it there.

"Soon." His other hand stroked her back, her buttocks. "You have a dimple here," he murmured, pressing his thumb into the base of her spine.

Again, she nearly collapsed against him. "Jake, be serious. Wh-when do we have to leave? Krista is still—"

"We should be out of here by the end of the week. After that, we can't promise anyone safety."

He kissed her, his mouth open, his tongue caressing hers. "By the way, I told Megan that Krista is my daughter."

Lexy pulled away. "You did?"

"I did."

She paused, bit her lower lip, then raised her gaze to his. "What else did you tell her?"

"Only that. I told her you'd explain everything else to her."

She threw herself at him, wanting to devour him, to crawl inside his skin. Be absorbed by him. "Oh, Jake, we need to talk."

His fingers traveled to the juncture of her thighs, and he stroked her. "You're wet."

She punched him and laughed to diffuse her arousal. "Of course, I'm wet. What did you expect?"

He continued stroking her. "Since you're naked, now would be a good time for me to have a taste."

She bit back an embarrassed laugh, but the prospect wasn't unpleasant. "And how would that look if our daughter walked in?"

He nuzzled her ear. "She'd probably say, 'Mr. Jake, what are you doing down there between my mama's legs?'"

Soft laughter bubbled into her throat, and she hid

her face against his neck. "And what would you answer?"

"I'd say, 'I'm looking for the little man in the boat.'"

She forced herself to pull away, but she continued to laugh. "Get out of here, you naughty man, and let me dress before Ivy comes looking for me."

He pulled an exaggerated frown. "Now, that's reason enough to go."

"But we do have to talk," she reminded him. "Oh, Jake," she said, remembering. "What about the children at the reservation?"

His eyes clouded. "Two of them died, Lexy."

She bit down on her lip to keep from crying out. "Oh, I feel responsible."

"There was nothing you could do, Lex. Stop chastising yourself."

She pressed her fingers to her lips, her anguish eating at her heart. "Oh, dear. Those poor parents . . ."

His expression was one of sympathy, but he said nothing. He merely hugged her briefly, then left the room.

She went into the bedroom and dressed. Yes, this was medicine in the uncivilized West. She would have to get used to it, for it would be slow to change. But how did one become callous enough to ignore the deaths of children?

Ivy stepped into the room, her expression mutinous. "Was that man in the bathroom with you?"

Lexy rolled her eyes. "That man was, Ivy, I can't deny it."

"That is not at all proper, Alexis."

"Probably not," she said on a sigh.

Ivy shook her head as she studied her. "What's going to happen between the two of you?"

Lexy dried her hair with a towel. "I wish I knew."

"Is Krista ever going to know who her father is?"

That question clutched at Lexy's heart. "I wish I knew that, too."

Krista wandered into the room, looking pale. She crawled onto the bed and watched Lexy draw a comb through her hair. Lexy blew her a kiss, which Krista caught and brought to her mouth. A game they had played for years.

"I saw Mr. Jake," she announced.

"Do you like him, Krista?"

She shrugged. "He has a horsie." She gave Lexy a studied look. "Why was he crying when I was sick, Mama?"

Lexy stopped combing the snarls from her hair and touched her daughter's chin. "Because he's a nice man, and he was very, very worried about you."

"Were you worried about me, Mama?"

Lexy pulled Krista onto her lap and pressed her lips to her forehead. "More than I can ever tell you."

"The angel wasn't worried," Krista said.

"The angel?"

Nodding, Krista added, "The angel who told me it wasn't time for me to come and play with her."

Reflexes, born of fear and relief, made Lexy squeeze Krista tight. She couldn't speak.

"Ouch, Mama, you're hurting me."

Lexy released her. "I-I'm sorry, sweetheart."

Krista squirmed from her mother's lap and played with her doll.

Lexy looked at Ivy, and her gaze, which mirrored her own, was fraught with the kind of pain that cannot be expressed in words.

Jake met Ben outside on the clinic's porch. They had not spoken other than to discuss medical treatment since that day Jake punched Ben in the jaw.

"I'm glad Krista's going to be all right," Ben said.

Jake had trouble swallowing. "We almost lost her."

"But you didn't."

Jake shoved his hands into his pockets and studied the warped wooden boards that made up the porch steps. "God, but I envy you."

Ben barked a surprised laugh. "Me?"

"I wish I had the kind of rapport you have with my daughter."

Recognition flared in Ben's eyes. "Oh, you mean the Billy Goats Gruff story?" When Jake nodded, Ben said, "Remember, she's known me as long as she's known her own mother."

As hard as it was to say, Jake had to say it. "She thinks of you as her father."

"But she knows I'm not," he explained.

"I want her to know that I am, but . . . I don't know how to go about it."

Ben's smile was sincere. "Take your time. You've got plenty of that now."

"Let me ask you something."

"What is it?"

Jake studied Ben, trying to find the right words. "Why didn't you ever give Lexy my message four years ago?"

Ben glanced away. "Because at the time, I thought if she never heard from you again, she might give in and marry me."

"I guess I'll always wonder what would have happened if you had told her I wanted to see her, and if she'd agreed."

"Maybe the truth would have scared you," Ben suggested.

"It could have. I guess I'll never know, will I?"

"I apologize for my arrogance."

"It's moot now. Anyway, you were there for her, and for that I thank you."

Ben snorted a laugh. "Those are words I never thought I'd hear from you."

Jake didn't laugh. "I mean it, Ben. Through all of this, you've been her best friend. And you've been to my daughter what I may never be. I'm envious."

Ben was suddenly serious as well. "Yes, I've had Lexy's friendship. But I never had her love." He paused and looked Jake square in the eye. "You always had that. And as for being a father figure to Krista, well, I guess I'd always wanted more, but ultimately I was grateful for what I had. It shouldn't be that hard for you to be the father you rightfully are."

Jake pondered the statement. Digested it. Hoped Ben was right. "What will you do now?"

Ben inhaled sharply. "Get back to Providence and resume my practice." He made a face. "This place isn't for me. I knew it the moment I stepped off the train. Oh, that reminds me." He drew out a letter from his waistcoat and handed it to Jake. "This came for you yesterday morning."

Jake opened it and read the contents. Excitement tinged with dread coursed through him. It was from his mentor at Stanford.

Lexy was trying, without much success, to get Ivy to finish the ironing so she could get things packed up in the kitchen. The mere fact that Lexy had to string those particular words together in her mind regarding Ivy was absurd, because Ivy had never needed prodding from anyone to do her work. In fact, Ivy was the Queen of Prodders herself.

But today, her gaze kept wandering to the window. She also made several unnecessary trips past the window. Lexy would watch as she peered outside, her gaze undoubtedly lingering on Little Pete, who was stripped to the waist, clearing brush from the rear yard of the clinic.

Even though they were leaving, Jake had promised Lexy that when things were safe, they could return, if that's what she wanted. He reminded her, though, that without the fort, she might have no business at all. He suggested that they look into Doc Hasley's office in town, for word was that his nephew had decided against practicing in the West.

Even so, Pete, who needed to be busy, was cleaning up the yard.

Lexy would like to have been a fly on the wall during that period when she and Jake were at the camp and Ivy and Pete were here together, alone with only Krista as a chaperone.

Ivy placed the iron on the stand and walked to the window again, apparently oblivious to Lexy's presence.

Lexy quietly stepped up behind her and followed the path of Ivy's gaze. Pete was drinking from the water bucket ladle, water coursing down his beard. His chest was wide and hard and covered with a mat of thick, dark hair that was peppered with generous amounts of gray.

Lexy felt a wicked streak coming on. She brushed against Ivy's shoulder. Ivy suddenly cleared her throat and pretended to straighten the curtain.

"Why, Ivy Stillwater, I do believe you're drooling."

Ivy gasped and colored, swatting at Lexy ineffectively. "I was merely thinking how uncivilized it is for any man to work without a shirt when there are ladies around."

Lexy made a sound of agreement in her throat. "Yes. Why, there's just nothing more disgusting than a big man at work, sweat streaking his chest, cords the size of ropes flexing and relaxing as he lifts tree trunks from the earth with his bare hands—"

"Now, you stop that," Ivy scolded, her face a brighter pink than Lexy had ever seen before.

Lexy hugged her shoulders. "There's nothing wrong with admiring the way a man is made, Ivy."

"Well, a body shouldn't go about dripping spittle over it, either."

Lexy laughed. "Is it so hard for you to admit you're soft on the man?"

On a snort, Ivy answered, "I've gone soft in the head, if that's what you mean."

Lexy studied Pete's movements as he returned to his task. Huge muscles bunched and relaxed as he worked, and she could see his appeal.

"He's certainly finely made, wouldn't you agree?"

Ivy's gaze was on Pete, and Lexy saw the pulse at her throat flutter against her skin.

"He's a barbarian," was Ivy's soft response.

Lexy frowned and gave her an exaggerated nod. "Yes. Yes, he's truly crude. I can see why he's never married. Why, who'd have the likes of him, anyway?" She clucked and shook her head. "He even told me once that he doesn't have two nickels to rub together. What good is he? And he can't dance. He said that to me, too." Lexy made a disapproving sound in her throat. "And he knows nothing but the Army. Probably can't leave the West, or he'll dissolve into a puddle."

Out of the corner of her eye, she saw Ivy's look of disgust. And it wasn't at Lexy's description of Pete, it was at her.

Lexy laughed, continuing her charade. "Can you imagine the likes of Little Pete in Providence? At a reception where they use china teacups?" She tittered dramatically. "He'd undoubtedly bumble around, breaking things right and left. Someone would have to escort him out on his ear, poor man."

Ivy's gaze was hot. "I know what you're trying to do, Alexis."

Lexy gave her an innocent look. "Me? Do?"

Suddenly, Ivy smiled and leaned casually against the window sill. "I'll freely admit that when I first saw the man, I feared for all our lives. Yes, he's unpolished. Yes, he's far too big to be comfortable at a tea in Providence. But he is the kindest, most wonderful man . . ."

Lexy bit back a smile and went to the ironing board to finish the task that Ivy apparently couldn't concentrate on.

She was touching up the last of Krista's dresses when Ivy swung from the window. "Ben is here."

He stepped into the room, and, after hugging his

sister, he opened his arms for Lexy. She went into them, allowing the embrace.

"I hear you're leaving."

"I want to get back to civilization, Lexy."

She looked into his face. "I know. Before you go, though, I want to ask you something."

"Anything. You name it."

"Why did you never tell me that Jake wanted to talk to me four years ago?"

His expression became sheepish. "I thought I knew what was best for you."

She wasn't angry; she understood Ben so very well. "You thought I might weaken and forgive him." She paused, then added, "And then I wouldn't be able to marry you."

Contrite, he said, "That's true. But honestly, I had your best interest at heart, Lexy. And when Krista was born, I merely wanted both of you to be a part of my life."

Lexy stretched and kissed his cheek. Recriminations were unnecessary. And fruitless. "I wish you well, Benjamin. I'll always love you. Please keep in touch."

He smiled. "I will. I can't let Krista forget her Poppy. That said," he added, "I think I'll go find her and say good-bye."

Not long after Ben left, Ivy, who continued to sniffle at the absence of her brother, turned from the window again. "Jake just rode in."

Now it was Lexy's turn to quake inside. The sound of his name did one thing to her, but the sight of him, each time she saw him, sent her stomach pitching and tossing.

And indeed that's what happened when he stepped into the room. Their eyes met, he gave her a quiet wink, and her stomach did somersaults.

"I just received a letter from Dr. Teller, my mentor at Stanford." He hesitated briefly. "He has a proposition for me."

"A proposition?"

"He wants me to come to Stanford and continue my work on the heart vessel research."

Lexy swallowed the lump in her throat. Her stomach pitched downward. "Well. That . . . that's very exciting." She forced a wide smile. He didn't return it. "You *are* excited, aren't you?"

Jake glanced around the room, his gaze landing on Ivy. "Let's take a walk, Lexy."

He took her arm and led her outside. Neither spoke as they turned the corner to the animal pens.

"Oh, that darned pig," Lexy murmured. "She's never in her pen anymore." Pearlann had an agenda every day, so it seemed, and there had been no way to keep her penned up.

"I don't want to talk about the pig, Lexy."

She was anxious for this meeting, yet she feared it.

"Ben is taking the next train back to Providence," Jake reported.

Lexy said, "I'll miss him."

"You could go with him," Jake suggested.

"I could not," she argued, getting angry.

"He can give you everything, Lexy. And Krista, too."

Lexy felt sick to her stomach. "Is that what you want, Jake, to have Ben Stillwater become Krista's father?"

His response wasn't explosive as she'd expected it to be. "No. I merely wanted to make sure it wasn't what you wanted."

He gripped her fingers; she returned the pressure but didn't dare speak.

He did. "My entire adult life, I've merely lived to fulfill my family's sense of doom. As I got older, I came to expect it over every hill. Around every corner. Even finishing medical school didn't help. It merely frustrated me further, because I knew so certainly that there was nothing I could do to save myself. If I was going to die, I would die."

Still unable to speak, Lexy continued to squeeze his hand.

"Then I began studying the vessels surrounding the heart, discovering that substance that clogged some veins and not others."

"It had the consistency of chicken fat, you said."

He nodded. "But how could it be that simple? I mean, if I took five boys and followed them through manhood, fed them the same food, ordered the same amount of exercise, monitored their alcohol and tobacco intake, could I get five men who were exactly the same inside?"

"Probably not," she assured him. "Heredity is too strong, I think."

"Then what chance do I have to survive, Lexy?"

"You're not just your father's son, you know. You're your mother's. And what of her father? Her uncles? Did they die young as well?"

Jake was quiet for a moment, but she could feel an excitement coming from him. "No. As a matter of fact, they lived to be quite elderly."

"See? Average it out, Jake. Surely, some of your mother's genes have offset your father's."

They sat beneath a tree. He was quiet for a while, studying her. It always made her uncomfortable, this intense scrutiny.

"I wish you wouldn't do that," she said.

"Do what?"

"Stare at me like that."

"I like to look at you."

She suddenly felt foolishly shy. "I wonder what you see."

"I see a woman of beauty and strength, of honor and virtue. Of power."

She attempted a nonchalant shrug. "My. Such qualities. How can I possibly be human?"

"I've wondered that myself."

She choked back an angry sob. "What are we doing, Jake? What kind of music are we dancing to? You know what I want. I've made that perfectly clear. If nothing else, I would think you'd want to try your hand at becoming Krista's father."

"I want that more than anything," he responded fiercely.

"Then what's stopping you?"

He gazed at the hills, appearing to follow the course of an eagle in flight. "You know that song Ivy was singing when Krista was so sick?"

"'Amazing Grace,'" she answered with a nod.

He laughed, a soft, disbelieving sound. "It could have been written for me. The words hit me like they *had* been written for me."

"'Amazing grace, how sweet the sound that saved a wretch like me,'" Lexy spoke. "'I once was lost but now am found. Was blind but now I see.'" She sniffed and wiped at a damp eye. "That song always makes me cry."

"That song is me, Lex." He shifted beside her, stretching his long legs out in front of him and resting on his elbows. "I was blind to everything but my own doom. Or what I thought to be my doom. Intellectually, I knew the odds were there that I could outlive my father. But the reality was that I probably wouldn't. And I let that eat at me. Drive me. Nearly destroy me."

He brought Lexy's hand to his mouth and kissed her palm. "When Krista lay near death and I heard Ivy singing that song, I knew I'd been a lost soul. A blind wretch. Nothing really mattered except Krista's life, and at that moment, if I could have traded places with her, I'd have done so gladly.

"But I did know that life is too precious to let it escape without a fight, and love is too exceptional to ignore." He kissed her fingers one by one.

Lexy could barely keep her heart out of her throat. "Are you saying what I think you are?"

He gazed into her eyes. Earnest. Intense. "I want to make a home with you and Krista. I want you to be my wife. I want her to know I'm her father. She wouldn't understand it now, but one day, I hope we can tell her and she won't be sore at us for keeping the truth from her.

"Just remember," he continued, "we'll never be rich."

"And . . . and we'll go with you to Stanford?"

He shook his head. "No."

Bereft, she merely looked at him. "But . . ."

"I think we should go there briefly, as long as there's trouble here, but as soon as it's safe, we're coming back. We'll reopen the practice."

"But what about your research?"

"I'll continue it. I have to. I want to. But it won't be a priority in my life, sweetheart. You and Krista are my priorities. And I don't want to waste any more time. I want us to start now, because I could have a year, five years, or, we can hope, fifty."

"Oh, Jake," she said around a smile. "Those are all such wonderfully lofty words, and I'm happy you feel the way you do. But," she said, tracing his mouth with her finger, "I'd have married you on the basis of your kisses alone."

She shoved him to the ground and lay on top of him, kissing him with abandon. When she came up for air, she said, "You've got to be the best kisser in the entire world."

His grin was lazy and hot. "It takes one to know one, honey."

They lay entangled, Lexy's head on Jake's chest, where she could hear his strong, bounding heartbeat. She would savor the sound for the rest of her life.

"Mama?"

She turned, finding Krista watching them. "Yes, sweetie?"

"What's wrong with Mr. Jake?"

Jake's laughter rumbled in his chest. "I'm fine, little princess."

"Why is Mama on top of you? Are you fighting?"

Lexy rolled off Jake and sat, motioning Krista to join them. Their daughter toddled to them and flopped onto Jake's chest.

"We're not fighting, sweetie. Mr. Jake just asked me to marry him."

Krista digested this news, then smiled. "Does that mean Mr. Jake's gonna be my daddy?"

"How does that sound to you, Krista?" Jake asked.

Her smile widened. "I think I'd like Mr. Jake to be my daddy," she enthused, "because he has a horsie."

"At least I'm good for something." Jake scooped her up into his arms and held her high. "Well, that settles it, then."

Lexy's heart did that little dance again, for when Jake and Krista were together, there wasn't a soul alive who couldn't see the resemblance. They laughed together now, gypsy eyes sparkling, smiles so similar it made Lexy ache.

"What's all this commotion out here?" Ivy rounded the corner.

"Mr. Jake is going to marry us," Krista explained.

Ivy cleared her throat and fiddled with the collar of her blouse. "Well, I hope you have room for me in your busy lives." She sounded put out. Petulant. Unlike Ivy.

Lexy sat up. "You're not going back to Providence with Ben?"

She cleared her throat nervously. "Mr. Byron has asked me to stay."

Lexy's jaw dropped. "And you would? You'd stay?" Oh, what could be more perfect?

Ivy's complexion was nearly purple. She was truly stressed. "Well, now, I . . . I suppose I should really accompany Ben back to Providence."

"Not on your life," Lexy said. "We want you to stay, don't we, Krista?" At Krista's eager nod, Lexy continued, "But what about the fort? It will close soon, and won't Pete have to go somewhere else?"

"It appears he's put in a good twenty years and can

retire." Ivy laughed. "And when he discovered I had a bit of money, he almost changed his mind about asking me to stay. Men are so funny about a woman's money, don't you think? Well, I convinced him that my money was only a pleasure to me if I could share it, and I wanted to share it with him."

She smoothed her hair and shook out the wrinkles in her skirt. "I do have my work cut out for me, though, believe me."

She hauled Krista into her arms. "Beginning with this little tartlet," she murmured, nuzzling Krista with her nose. "Too much excitement for one day, by far. After all, I understand there will be a wedding to prepare for, and we have to pack up the whole clinic." She clucked. "I'll hardly have time to think about my life with Parnell."

She took Krista into the house, leaving Jake and Lexy alone.

She looked at him, found him watching, and felt her heart skip a beat when he winked at her. "Well," she managed, feeling skittish and new, "now what, Dr. Westfield?"

He drew her into his arms and graced her with one of his deepest, wettest, most intimate kisses. "I think we ought to find a place to start making a new little brother or sister for Krista," he whispered against her ear.

She remembered their night in the sweat lodge and felt a warm glow all over. "I wouldn't be surprised if we already have," she answered.

He drew back, a frown creasing his brow. "I have another fantasy I have to run by you—don't spoil it."

"In that case, I wouldn't dream of it." They wandered off toward the tree-studded hills. Life could sometimes be a dream. This time and for always, life for Krista, Jake, and Lexy would be the same dream.

# Epilogue

THEY STOOD LIKE STEPS ON A STOOL, WAITING FOR THE photographer to take their picture. Jake marveled at his daughters, beauties all. Krista, fifteen, was all grown up and on the verge of a sophistication her mother had. She already planned to attend Stanford, then medical school, following in her mother's footsteps. At this moment, for their photograph, she held the baby in her arms like a professional.

Karna, eleven, was a studious girl, poring over any book she could get her hands on. Secretly, Jake had learned his second daughter adored romances, having one day discovered worn copies of *Little Women* and *Jane Eyre* beneath her schoolbooks.

Nine-year-old Keeley was their tomboy. She rode roughshod over all the boys in town, and they were all smitten.

Kerry was seven and was just emerging into her own. Having three older sisters was not an easy act to follow.

Then there was Kathleen. She was four. And looked

so much like Krista had at that age that Jake's throat clutched when he looked at her.

His daughters squirmed, impatient to be done. The photographer, a man with the patience of a saint, moved among them, posing them, gently scolding them when they laughed or talked. It was an impossible task, keeping five giggly girls and a new baby still long enough to photograph them. Jake didn't envy the man.

"Papa, Kathleen won't stand still," Karna shouted.

"Papa," Kathleen wailed, "something's sticking me."

Jake meandered down the steps, motioning his four-year-old to him. She squirmed in front of him, her big puppy-dog eyes gazing at him seriously.

"It sticks me here," she explained, motioning to her neck.

Jake examined the neck of her frock. "Oh-ho, what do we have here?" He pulled out a pin. "Looks like Miss Ivy forgot one."

Kathleen took it and thrust it toward her sisters. "See? There *was* something pokin' me."

Jake gave her a light swat on the rump. "Now, get over there and get that picture taken, sugar plum."

The door opened, and his wife stepped beside him. Something inside him quivered; she always affected him that way.

She put her arm around his waist. "How's the baby doing?"

Jake squeezed Lexy to him. "He's the only one who's not complaining."

He'd been elated to have a son, although he wouldn't have cared if their sixth child had been another girl. Matthew Jacob Westfield had come into the world two months earlier. Jake had delivered him, as he had all of their children after Krista. Lexy had wept with joy that she had finally given him a son. He prayed that the boy would live to a ripe old age.

Lexy stood on tiptoes for a kiss. Jake complied. She

wrapped both arms around his waist and snuggled against him. "It's time for him to be fed."

Through her clothing and his, Jake felt the hardness of her breast. "Lucky boy."

Lexy chuckled. "You've had your share." She gave him a quick hug, then left the porch and sauntered toward her children, waiting for the photographer to finish. He never tired of watching her. Even after six children, she was shapely and beautiful. Still stubborn and independent, but he loved her that way.

Jake settled into his chair and picked up the most recent issue of the *Journal of the American Medical Association*. He hadn't been surprised to have his article turned down again. He wouldn't give up, though. One day, someone was bound to find his research valuable.

As it was, no doctor on the board of the *Journal* would consider publishing his outrageous theory: that too much fat in a diet clogged arteries. They all believed that fat was the antidote to tuberculosis, the wasting disease. That fat was healthy in any man's diet.

He'd been called a charlatan. A fraud. A quacksalver. The terms bothered Lexy far more than they bothered him. He was convinced he was right. He also knew there were people for whom diet could not control the condition of their arteries. The research was frustrating.

He ate little fat himself, continuing to feel good. Healthy. Full of energy. He had passed his forty-fifth year without a heart attack, and for that he was grateful. Each day was a blessing.

Their medical practice was booming. Doc Hasley had passed his practice on to Jake and Lexy together, giving them his blessing. They had built a house in Burning Tree, adding on an office because Jake was not convinced that the old clinic was safe, even though the Indians had settled down and caused few problems.

There had indeed been a war. Five battles and several skirmishes had been fought, Indians against whites. Deaths had been many. In the end, it was not so much that the Indians had lost but that they had lost faith in their shaman, Twisted Nose Doctor.

Later, both Twisted Nose Doctor and Eagle Eye Jim had died mysteriously in a fire. The law in Burning Tree chalked it up to an accident, but everyone sensed it had been set on purpose by the militia.

For Dooley's part in trying to maintain peace, he had been allowed to live where he chose. Jake and Lexy offered the old clinic to him and his family. They continued to live there, planting their garden year after year, keeping the place looking comfortable and lived in.

Of course, Lexy allowed the chickens, the cow and the pig to stay, and while they were at Stanford, all but the cow mysteriously disappeared. They all knew what had happened, but in deference to Lexy, no one brought it up.

Pete had married Ivy—a romance for the record books, Jake always believed. If opposites truly attracted, he thought, their marriage would last into eternity. Pete worked as Jake's carpenter, plumber, woodcutter, and overseer. And friend.

When Ivy wasn't fussing over Pete, she sewed dresses for the girls and gushed over Matthew. Or expounded on Ben's new young wife, who was a beauty, to be sure, but not much of a housekeeper. Little did it matter to Ivy that Ben could afford a house full of servants. Jake secretly wondered if, in Ivy's eyes, any woman, except perhaps Lexy, was good enough for her baby brother.

Lexy walked toward Jake, their son in her arms. "Max and Megan will be here the end of the week," she reminded him.

Max had been reasonably happy to get his desk job with the government in Washington, D.C. Jake sensed it was because Megan was elated to be back among the civilized.

"And their brood, I imagine," he said, actually looking forward to a house filled with screaming, active children.

"They only have three, dear," Lexy reminded him. "If there's noise in the house, it's mostly from our own."

"Yes," he said, grinning at her. "And I love every boisterous minute of it."

She sat in the rocking chair beside him, unfastened her gown, and put their son to her breast. "I heard at the mercantile this morning that Joseph is returning from his first year at Stanford sometime this week."

On a wary smile, Jake said, "Does Krista know?"

Lexy shook her head. "I haven't told her yet. She wouldn't have been able to stand still for this photograph any better than Kathleen if she knew."

Jake shook his head and sighed. Although he wanted his children to be happy, he wasn't certain what kind of happiness Krista could find with an Indian boy, despite how much they cared for each other. Times were hard enough as it was. Loving an Indian could make his daughter a pariah, and he didn't want that for her.

Lexy touched his shoulder. "Don't ruminate on it, darling. She's only fifteen. Many things can change."

His wife knew him so well. He didn't have to speak; she read his mind.

"I merely want Krista's happiness."

"As do I," she assured him.

Jake leaned over and watched his son nurse. Something tugged at him, something that he rarely put a name to yet had drawn him from the first moment he had learned, so many years ago, that he was a father.

It was his heart. It was full. And when he looked at his children, it overflowed with a tumbling of emotions including pride, disbelief, relief, joy, and love. And gratitude.

He knew it had taken his eldest daughter's brush with death to make him see how he was messing up his life.

The girls scrambled up the steps; the photographer was done.

"Change your dresses, girls," their mother called.

They all went into the house except Krista. She stood before him, hands on hips, her eyes a tad angry.

"Papa?"

It didn't matter that for some reason or other, she was upset with him; his heart expanded anyway. She'd called him Papa from the time she entered school, realizing that's what the man who married her mama was called. Four years ago, when Kathleen was born, Krista was told that Jake was indeed her real father. She had taken it very well, asking why they hadn't explained it all to her sooner.

"Yes, princess?"

"I heard that Joseph is coming home this week. Why didn't you tell me?"

He uttered a dry chuckle. "I just learned about it from your mother. If you're going to scold someone, scold her."

Krista swung to Lexy, who had Matthew on her shoulder, trying to elicit a burp. "Is that true? You knew and didn't tell me?"

"Only because I didn't think you could stand still for the photographer if you knew, Krista."

Krista's eyes lit up. "Oh, I have so much to do before he comes. So many things to tell him." She expelled a healthy breath of air, then followed her sisters into the house.

Later, around the dinner table, Jake listened to the chatter, loving it. Living for it. Knowing that if he lived another thirty years or died tomorrow, he would have had a full, rich, and blessed life.

# Jane Bonander

Jane Bonander creates characters that will "surely touch your heart."
—Gail Collins, <u>Romantic Times</u>

## *Wild Heart*
❑ 52983-8/$5.99

## *Winter Heart*
❑ 52982-x/$5.99

## *Dancing on Snowflakes*
❑ 50110-0/$5.50

## *Warrior Heart*
❑ 52981-1/$5.99

## *Scent of Lilacs*
❑ 00916-8/$6.50

## Available from Pocket Books

**Simon & Schuster Mail Order**
**200 Old Tappan Rd., Old Tappan, N.J. 07675**
Please send me the books I have checked above. I am enclosing $_____ (please add
$0.75 to cover the postage and handling for each order. Please add appropriate sales
tax). Send check or money order–no cash or C.O.D.'s please. Allow up to six weeks
for delivery. For purchase over $10.00 you may use VISA: card number, expiration
date and customer signature must be included.

POCKET
B O O K S

Name _____

Address _____

City _____ State/Zip _____

VISA Card # _____ Exp.Date _____

Signature _____ 1153-03

# LINDA LAEL MILLER

☐ CORBIN'S FANCY                    73767-8/$5.99
☐ ANGELFIRE                         73765-1/$5.99
☐ MOONFIRE                          73770-8/$5.99
☐ WANTON ANGEL                      73772-4/$5.99
☐ FLETCHER'S WOMEN                  73768-6/$5.99
☐ MY DARLING MELISSA                73771-6/$6.99
☐ WILLOW                            73773-2/$5.99
☐ DESIRE AND DESTINY                70635-7/$6.99
☐ BANNER O'BRIEN                    73766-x/$6.99
☐ MEMORY'S EMBRACE                  73769-4/$6.99
☐ LAURALEE                          70634-9/$5.99
☐ DANIEL'S BRIDE                    73166-1/$6.99
☐ YANKEE WIFE                       73755-4/$6.99
☐ TAMING CHARLOTTE                  73754-6/$5.99
☐ THE LEGACY                        79792-1/$6.99
☐ PRINCESS ANNIE                    79793-X/$5.99
☐ EMMA AND THE OUTLAW               67637-7/$6.99
☐ LILY AND THE MAJOR                67636-9/$6.99
☐ CAROLINE AND THE RAIDER           67638-5/$6.99
☐ PIRATES                           87316-4/$6.50
☐ KNIGHTS                           87317-2/$6.99
☐ MY OUTLAW                         87318-0/$6.99
☐ EVERLASTING LOVE: A collection of romances by Linda
   Lael Miller, Jayne Ann Krentz, Linda Howard, and Carla Neggers
                                    52150-0/$5.99
☐ THE VOW                           00399-2/$6.99

## All available from Pocket Books

- - - - - - - - - - - - - - - - - - - - - - - - - - - - - -

**Simon & Schuster Mail Order**
**200 Old Tappan Rd., Old Tappan, N.J. 07675**
Please send me the books I have checked above. I am enclosing $_____ (please add
$0.75 to cover the postage and handling for each order. Please add appropriate sales
tax). Send check or money order–no cash or C.O.D.'s please. Allow up to six weeks
for delivery. For purchase over $10.00 you may use VISA: card number, expiration
date and customer signature must be included.

**POCKET**
**B O O K S**

Name _____

Address _____

City _____ State/Zip _____

VISA Card # _____ Exp.Date _____

Signature _____

                                                    779-16

Printed in the United States
By Bookmasters